HUNTERS

of the

DARK SEA

TOR BOOKS BY MEL ODOM

HUNTERS OF THE DARK SEA

THE ROVER

HUNTERS

of the

DARK SEA

—————•—————

MEL ODOM

A TOM DOHERTY ASSOCIATES BOOK
NEW YORK

HUNTERS OF THE DARK SEA

Edited by Brian Thomsen

This book is printed on acid-free paper.

A Tor Book
Published by Tom Doherty Associates, LLC
175 Fifth Avenue
New York, NY 10010

www.tor.com

Tor® is a registered trademark of Tom Doherty Associates, LLC.

Library of Congress Cataloging-in-Publication Data

Odom, Mel.
    Hunters of the dark sea / Mel Odom.—1st. ed.
        p. cm.
    A "Tom Doherty Associates book."
    ISBN: 0-765-30480-5 (acid-free paper)
    1. Human-alien encounters—Fiction. 2. Whalers (Persons)—Fiction. 3. Whaling ships—Fiction. 4. Whaling—Fiction. I. Title.

PS3565.D53H865 2003
813'.54—dc21

                                                                        2003042616

First Edition: July 2003

Printed in the United States of America

0   9   8   7   6   5   4   3   2   1

HIS FRIENDS CALLED him Eddie, and the kids on the Tar Heels team called him Coach.

To know Eddie was to love Eddie. He looked like nine miles of bad road, the last man in the world to pick a fight with. But the boys he coached knew him by his heart: He was one of them, a believer and a dreamer, someone who more than anything in the world just wanted to play baseball—not win or lose, just play and be the best that he could possibly be at that given moment.

I coached with Eddie, and he taught me to understand and to love the game of baseball. He taught my son, Shiloh, how to bat, how to field, how to throw, and how to dig down deep when he needed a little more. He taught Shiloh how to steal a good lead off base, how to use his glove to block the sun from his eyes in the outfield so he could snag a long fly ball, and how to spit sunflower seeds with attitude and bravado.

Eddie could take the hill and throw batting practice all day. He could throw a long, flat ball all the way from the outfield, and I'd never have to move the catcher's glove behind the plate. He threw right but batted left so he could be one step closer to first base. And when the boys needed a boost during practice, he'd swing on one of our good five-dollar balls and plant it on top of the manufacturing plant behind the center-field fence.

Eddie left us at the young age of thirty-four during the summer of 2002. He was in the middle of a softball game, doing what he loved doing most. Eddie left behind a wife, Jenifer, two children, Bobby and Sasha, and a legacy at the Moore Youth Baseball League at Buck Thomas Park in Moore, Oklahoma, that will live for years.

God called Eddie up to the Bigs, to play on fields that are always level and green, to a game where no one keeps score, to a place where the boys of summer never have to call it a season.

I love you. I miss you. And I will never forget you.

ACKNOWLEDGMENTS

Hunters of the Dark Sea would not exist without the help of the finest ship's crew to ever board a sailing vessel:

Tom Doherty, publisher of Tor Books, and one of the finest gentlemen I've ever had the pleasure of meeting. You can feel the Irish in him, and you know that his blood carries the salt of the sea and memory of ancestors who found their futures there. Thanks again for the lunch in Austin, for believing in me, and for the football discussion with my son, Shiloh. (Leather helmets! Hehheh.)

Brian Thomsen, editor and friend and quartermaster—and you can put those in any order you like and I'll stand to it—whose belief in this tale of the darkest heart of the sea came in the early stages. Thank God you and I share similar tastes in fiction, buddy, and you understood the story early enough to put your hand on the tiller as well. Of course, those tastes in fiction would probably get us thrown out of all the classy places.

Jim Minz, who is an entertaining and supportive person. I can't imagine a voyage without him, but I would never put him in charge of the grog barrels.

Natasha Panza, who stepped into the breach and took on this whale of a tale without batting an eye.

Laura Pereira, of the New Bedford Whaling Museum in New Bedford, Massachusetts (www.whalingmuseum.org), for all her kind help in rounding out the facts of the manuscript relating to whaling and whalers. The mistakes, of course, are all mine.

And props for my ship's crew: my son, Shiloh (who insists on the second mate's position), and his friend Dewey Webster (the third mate wannabe), who read through the manuscript and kept a sharp lookout for troubled waters and hidden reefs.

HISTORICAL NOTE

In June of 1812, the fledgling United States of America again went to war with its onetime parent country, Great Britain. Since the shortest distance by sea between the two countries was the Atlantic Ocean, a number of battles and military actions took place on those waves.

The great whaling ventures of the time were among the first to be attacked by the British, and those fleets were decimated before the war's end. However, many naval battles also took place on the Great Lakes, and there was action in the Pacific Ocean. Britain, at that time, was considered to be the ruling master of sea warfare. Lord Admiral Horatio Nelson had died at the Battle of Trafalgar in 1805, but he left behind the mightiest navy in the world.

In addition to military vessels that sailed the seas seizing ships and impressing men, privateers were granted letters of marque, permission to hunt and plunder merchant and military vessels of opposing countries. Sir Francis Drake, considered to be a naval hero in the defeat of the Spanish Armada in 1588, started out as a privateer in the service of Queen Elizabeth of England.

Not all privateers were heroes. Many were cutthroats and thieves given special dispensation by host countries, granted a license to steal as long as they didn't prey on ships that flew the flag of the host country. Privateers apprehended by hostile nations were charged with piracy. After a swift but "fair" trial, the sailors were hanged, not exactly a hero's death.

Not all pirates were villains. A number of those pirates were men who had no luck at legitimate trade and often practiced smuggling (slipping into and out of ports without paying taxes on the goods they carried). Those pirates also preyed on merchants of all nations, stealing cargoes but never killing crews or passengers. Stories of Blackbeard and Captain Kidd, however, dominate the tales and legends that grew up around pirates and piracy.

By 1813, a sailing man took his life in his hands by plying his trade. Pirates and privateers ran rampant over the seven seas, and both left murdered victims and ships burned down to the waterline in their wake.

But sailing men knew that the pirates and privateers, the storms and treacherous waters, weren't the only things to be feared out on the salt. There have always been, even to this day, stories and legends of unknown things that dwell in the sea.

The sea is a harsh mistress, and she hides her secrets well. But every now and again, one of those secrets comes to light . . .

PROLOGUE

Nantucket Island 41° 17' Lat.—70° 05' Long.

YOUNG ETHAN SWAIN waded out into the shallows of Children's Beach and threw his line into the slate gray sea. The tide was going out from the land, and the receding waves carried the cork bobber farther out. With luck, he might land a striped bass, flounder, blue, or a scup for dinner so his mother would forgive his abandoning the chores she'd given him. And failing that, there was still time to go crabbing along the beach.

He heard the voices of the sailors at the North Wharf loading the merchant ships and whaleships. All of them were getting ready to go on what Ethan believed to be great voyages. He was ten, and going on such a voyage himself was surely no more than three or four years away. At thirteen or fourteen, he'd be able to sign on as a greenhand. Maybe sooner because he was already showing his father's tall, wide-shouldered build.

He brushed stray locks of sun-streaked fair hair from his eyes and kept the pole and the line steady. To his right, Brant Point Lighthouse stood tall and imposing. Mr. Higgins, the lighthouse keeper, sat outside with his customary pipe and a piece of scrimshaw he was carving.

Only a few minutes later, Ethan spotted the tangled mass that floated just under the surface of the retreating sea. At first he thought the mass was seaweed, then a bit of torn yellowed canvas rolled to the top of a wave.

Ethan guessed that the canvas was a scrap abandoned by a ship, but when the next wave rolled over the top, more canvas showed. The section of material was too large to be a scrap.

A small boat then? Ethan knew that some of the older boys liked to rig their fishing boats with miniature sails to learn the ways of the wind and get the feel of a boat out on the ocean. The experience wasn't the same, but pretending was great fun for a time.

He watched the next wave roll over the spot. If one of the town boys had lost his boat, everyone on Nantucket Island would have known about it. Especially if the boy aboard the small craft had gone missing as well.

Ethan's scalp prickled. Drownings occurred even in the whaling town, where most folks respected and feared the sea.

Drawn by his curiosity, Ethan took up his line. He checked the hook and discovered something had taken his bait. He threw the line back toward the beach, then waded out more deeply into the tide. Only a few steps later, he had to swim, but took to the effort naturally. His father had taught him to swim, telling him that a man who lived on the sea had no reason not to learn to swim. Most sailors who worked the ships that came to the harbor didn't feel that way. A sailor's job, they told Ethan, didn't involve leaving the ship while at sea.

A few strokes later, Ethan closed on the pool of canvas floating below the sea's surface. He raised his head from the water, salt stinging his eyes, and saw that rigging and broken wood was wrapped in the canvas. The sail had tangled on one of the rocks that jutted up from the sea. This part of the island hadn't been cleared for use as a harbor.

Ethan treaded water. The rigging clinging to the canvas posed a real danger. If he became tangled in the rope and the sea chose that moment to rip the sail free of the rock, he knew he could be dragged out by the tide.

His heart thudded. By rights, he should return to town and let others know about the tangled mess. But he couldn't. His curiosity, that sharp-toothed need to know that got him into trouble now and again, wouldn't be properly slaked by alerting others. The choice of the men might be to leave the tangle alone, and he would never know if the canvas was from a ship or a boat, or was just a discarded remnant. They would also keep him from finding out.

He wouldn't go back then.

Taking a deep breath, Ethan dived into the cold brine. Submerged, he felt the strong pull of the sea, and only then thought of the undertow his father had often warned him about. With the water all around him, he felt the chill soaking bone deep into him.

Ethan swam forward, feeling his body rise and fall with the warring currents. He had to fight his own natural buoyancy to stay submerged. The murky water limited his vision, but the stinging salt was more annoying than painful.

The sail wrapped the rocky outcrop thrusting up from the sandy ocean bottom. Fish gathered around the tangled knot of canvas, rigging, and broken wood. For a frozen moment, the thought that the fish swarmed the canvas like they were drawn to a fisherman's bait filled Ethan's head.

He kicked and swam closer. Some of the rigging fanned the area, moved by the current. For an instant, panic welled within him as he imagined that the tangles of rigging were the tentacles of a giant squid wrapped around the rock and waiting on fresh prey.

Then, caught by the rays of the sun already beginning the slide into the sea on the mainland side of Nantucket Island, the glint of gold caught Ethan's full attention. Thoughts of pirate treasure cascaded through his head.

Newfound excitement overcame Ethan's fear, tipping the balance but not eradicating his wariness. Gold meant his father could open his shipwright shop sooner. Gold meant that his mother wouldn't be spending all her free hours sewing quilts and hoping to interest ships' crews in trade.

Gold changed everything.

Kicking again, Ethan swam to where the golden glint had caught his eye. Crabs scuttled lazily across the canvas surface, withdrawing into the folds. A vague shape pressed against the material.

A sickening certainty of what he was about to find crawled through Ethan's mind. The canvas had swaddled the figure in the ripped yellow folds. Before he could stop himself, he reached forward, caught at the folds, and pulled them back.

Freed from the precarious hold of the torn canvas, the corpse tumbled free into the sea. The current gave the dead man a twisted semblance of life as the arms and legs spread wide. Two gold front teeth caught the light and flashed even in the murky water.

Mottled flesh clung to the dead man's face. Fish had been at the corpse, ripping and tearing away small strips. Evidently the rigging and canvas wrapped around the dead man had prevented the sharks that roamed the seas around Nantucket from tearing him to pieces. Guessing his age was impossible.

All that Ethan knew was that the man had been in his middle years and wore a beard that only clung to his face in patches now that so much flesh had been torn away. Paralyzed with fear, Ethan couldn't move. The ocean currents caught the dead man and turned him in a lazy sprawl.

Swim! Ethan screamed inside his mind. *Swim!*

But he couldn't. He hung there in the water as the dead man swept toward him. Unbelievably, the corpse's left eye leapt from the socket and swam away. Ethan only had a moment to identify the hermit crab that had been coiled up inside the dead man's empty eye and feeding at its leisure. Then the dead man was on him, wrapping its grisly arms and legs around him.

Weighted by the corpse, paralyzed by fear, bubbles exploding from his mouth as he tried to scream, Ethan sank toward the waiting ocean floor.

THE FUNERAL PROCESSION wended through the town and out to Old North Burial Ground. Several shopkeepers, townspeople, and sailors stood with their hats off and heads bowed as the coffin bearing the dead man passed.

All of them, Ethan knew, realized that the dead man could very well be any one of them under different circumstances. The sea played no favorites and ultimately proved both harsh and demanding. The sea could never be truly known and continued to keep secrets. Daniel Swain said that often.

The Old North Burial Ground consisted of a plot of rocky ground covered with dying grass. Despite the nearness of the sea, freshwater wasn't in such abundant supply that things grew easily on Nantucket Island. Vegetable gardens took considerable effort and God's grace. A white picket fence surrounded the burial ground. The paint was peeling, but the fence was in good repair, so no one had been assigned to whitewash the slats again yet.

Elder Gardner opened the gate and let the pallbearers through.

"Obediah Pollack," the Widow Macy called out. The church elders had put her in charge of the children during ceremonies and gatherings. Dressed in severe black and hardened by the sun and the sea as well as a life devoid of much happiness, the woman looked like the wrath of God Himself. She wore her gray hair pulled back.

"Yes, ma'am." Obie stood at Ethan's side as he had for years. Obie was short and fat, although he insisted that he was just preparing to shoot up straight and tall. Ethan didn't think that was going to happen since both of Obie's parents were short and fat, and they could afford to stay so. Wind-whipped blond hair framed Obie's freckled face with a pug nose set squarely in the center of his sour features. He put on an air of sweetness and goodness.

The act was something he was accomplished at, but most adults saw through it. However, the Widow Macy had not quite been able to do that yet. Or perhaps she chose to believe that at least one of her charges could appear to like and respect her.

"Hurry up there, lad," the Widow Macy instructed. "Take over the gate for Elder Gardner."

"Yes, ma'am." Obie scurried forward and clamped onto the gate. Elder Gardner thanked him and strode after the pallbearers. Obie had on a beatific smile as Ethan passed, but his whisper held only contempt and venom. "Old sow."

Ethan followed the line till they reached a fresh-dug hole in the southeast corner of the burial ground. Hiram Owings and his oldest two sons stood in the shade of a nearby oak tree. The three men wore leather gloves and leaned on their shovels. Elder Gardner had given them the job of covering the dead man over.

The pallbearers placed the coffin on the ground near the open grave.

Elder Gardner stood at the top of the hole and opened his battered Bible. As the passages were read, Ethan looked out over the burial ground. None of the stones were set neatly in straight rows. They were just thrown in where they needed to be.

Some of the stones, Ethan noted, didn't have names, only the dates of the deaths. They didn't even have that for the dead man he'd found. All they knew was the day the body had been found.

The quiet of the burial ground lent weight to Elder Gardner's words as he read the passages. Looking around, Ethan was only a little surprised to see that several sailors had followed them up the hill from the docks and the stores. When a man died an untimely death in the sea, as the dead man no doubt had, other sailors often felt beholden to attend the services if they were able.

When Ethan had asked, his father hadn't been able to give a proper reason why sailors felt compelled to do so. They'd been at a sailor's funeral that day. The man had been brought in wrapped in shrouds on a whaleship, stinking to high heavens. The dead man had been buried in the sail because the captain and sailors hadn't wanted the canvas back in case the dead man's luck stuck with the material.

"It's the sea," Daniel Swain had said, his hands firmly on his son's shoulders. "The sea makes brothers of all men. No matter what their nationality, religion, or station in life, the sea humbles them all and teaches them the true meaning of fear. When one of them falls, no man likes to see such a brother go unmourned."

Elder Gardner spoke in a strong, clear voice. He'd spoken over several graves during his time at the church. Ethan stood there feeling restless and sorrowful at the same time. He hadn't wanted to leave the dead man in the hands of the church elders after having found him, but he hadn't known the service would take so long. If he behaved properly, he might be able to talk his mother into letting him go back down to the docks.

A gasp shot through the crowd.

Startled, Ethan looked around and saw the crowd starting to look skyward. Shading his eyes, he gazed upward. A white streak stretched through the blue skies, like a needle pulling thread through material.

"What is that?" a man asked.

"That there is a fallin' star," a sailor answered. "Usually ye see them at night when the sky is black an' their tails have got more color."

"For us to see a fallin' star in broad daylight like it is," another sailor said, "it's got to be big."

"Will it fall on us?" one of the women asked in a tremulous voice. She took the hand of her small child.

"No, ma'am," the sailor said. "Why, if'n that fallin' star was to fall on us, we'd never see it until it was right on top of us."

"Like as not," one of the older men said, "it will burn up before it ever reaches the ground."

"I heard tell of a fallin' star that smashed a city in France," a third sailor said. "Took down all them fancy buildin's they got, includin' one of Napoleon's castles, an' took 'em straight down into a hole what let to Hell itself."

Mr. Mordecai, owner of a barbershop in town, raised his voice. "I'll remind you that you are a gentleman, sir," Mr. Mordecai said, "and thank you not to talk so roughly around my wife."

The sailor looked contrite. "Beggin' yer pardon, sir. I taken a knock on the knob now an' agin. Sometimes I speak without ever given a thought oncet to how it's gonna come out. Or even if it should."

Mr. Mordecai looked somewhat mollified.

Ethan watched the white streak carving the blue sky. He wondered about falling stars, about how they fell and from where they fell and what made them fall. He had no answers. He glanced at the sailors again, discovering that he knew the ships that two of them belonged to. The next time he got the chance, he was determined to ask after the nature of falling stars.

"That star," one of the townsmen said, "is an omen. Here we are burying this stranger among us, on the island where we've built our homes and raised our children, and now there's an omen."

Even as the conversations started up around him in the burial ground, Ethan watched the white streak of the falling star disappear past the western horizon. Wherever the falling star was going to fall, the thing was in an all-fired hurry to get there.

And omens, Ethan knew, were bad things that could hang around for years and change the lives of everyone.

1813

CHAPTER I

Pacific Ocean 3° 28' S. Lat.—107° 12' W. Long.

"THAR SHE BLOWS!"

The call to arms, after so many weeks at sea without a single sighting, caught Ethan Swain by surprise. At first, he thought he'd imagined the lookout's bawling voice.

He'd given his attention over to the fishing net he'd been mending. Whenever his mind was too full of thinking, especially of mistakes or bad judgments he'd made in the past—and especially of the pain and guilt that was Teresa, he found working with the focused effort required to sort out the tangled skeins of a net or mend canvas helped keep his worries at bay.

These days, there'd been far too many worries and not nearly enough distraction. After almost two years at sea, *Reliant*'s holds were only half-filled with whale oil barrels. They'd been so long without taking a whale that the ship's cooper had begun saying that he didn't know if he'd even remember how to build another barrel. He'd been joking with some of the rest of the crew. Captain Folger had caught wind of that tale through the ship's spy, who still yet remained unidentified, and had set Henry Paulk to making and unmaking barrels during his watches as punishment.

Cap'n Folger, Ethan thought in disgust as he looked into the topgallant rigging of the mainmast where the lookout kept watch, *is more of a problem than not sighting whales.* But he fought to steer himself clear of such thinking. Thinking like that had gotten him into trouble just out of Boston and nearly ended his sailing career.

"Thar she blows!" Bill Fedderson cried out again.

Realizing that the call wasn't his imagination, Ethan stood and looked out at the rolling green sea that was so different than the steel blue of the Atlantic Ocean he'd grown up around.

"Where away?" Ethan shouted. Hope flared through him, and he chose to let the emotion live instead of quashing it.

Over the last seven weeks without taking a whale, there had been two other sightings. Both of those sightings had been hailed by Robert Oswalt, the greenhand they'd lately taken on under auspicious circumstances only a month before. A month, Ethan had reflected grimly, was no amount of time to train a greenhand and have him standing a lookout's watch. But Folger had ordered exactly that.

Both of those sightings had turned out false, and poor Robert had been made to feel bad. Some of the crew faulted him, saying not only had he imagined whales, but probably he'd missed them while on his watches as well. Robert was still working in the ship's galley on double shifts, serving the punishment Folger had meted out for those mistakes.

Bill Fedderson was an experienced whaling man, though, with several whaling voyages under his belt. He now pointed dead ahead. "Whale's lyin' two points off port bow, Ethan," the man called back through cupped hands.

Ethan ran for the mainmast. At twenty-six, he stood a shade over six feet tall. He was broad-shouldered like his father, but ran more to lean because he didn't have his mother's cooking these days. He wore his dark hair pulled back in a queue and usually kept his face clean-shaven, but now carried three days' growth of beard stubble. He wore a loose blouse with the sleeves hacked off and light cotton trousers to accommodate the heat. Unless he was tending official ship's business or leaving the ship, he usually went barefooted, as he did now.

The ship's crew turned from their daily cleaning chores, which were purely wasted effort but ordered by Folger all the same. Most of them felt their time would have been better spent carving scrimshaw for possible sale in port. At least that would have put a little money in their purses to be spent later on women and drink. The crew looked expectantly out to sea. Some of the men started climbing up into the rigging to look for themselves. Their exuberant and hopeful voices drowned out the sound of the waves slapping against *Reliant*'s prow and the light crack of the square-cut canvas sails filling with the constant breeze.

Reaching the mainmast, Ethan caught hold of the rigging and swarmed up to the main topgallant yardarm. He climbed like a monkey, automatically shifting his body side to side and back and forth to account for the whaleship's rocking motion over the gentle swells of the Pacific Ocean.

Bill, a short, compact man who hailed from Boston, Massachusetts, stood on the yardarm within the lookout's ring. He had one beefy hand wrapped around the mast and rested a hip against the iron ring that *Reliant* used instead of a crow's nest. He wore only a blouse and long underpants. A long kerchief wrapped round his balding head protected him from the sun's harsh rays.

"There she breaches!" he yelled.

Pausing in his climb, hooking his fingers and toes into the rigging, Ethan swung out to peer past the main topsail. Out toward the horizon, where the rolling green sea curved up to meet the sky across a field of whitecapped curlers, he spotted the gray-black back of the whale. Ethan took in the blunt, thick head and the heavily fluked tail with a trained eye before the creature disappeared underwater.

"Is it a sperm whale, Bill?" Ethan demanded as he caught hold of the yardarm and hauled himself up.

"Aye," Bill said, handing over the spyglass. "That's what I make him out to be."

Ethan silently prayed that the whale was what they believed the creature to be. Bull sperm whales were known to swim alone without the accompaniment of others of their kind, so they only had to worry about sneaking up on him. Ethan fitted the spyglass to his eye and stared at the black shape cutting neatly through the ocean. The moment of good luck was holding: The whale hadn't disappeared down into the sea for a long dive to force them to have to guess where the beast was.

Locking his legs over the yardarm and hooking his toes into the rigging, Ethan kept both eyes open as he tracked the whale. Some men hadn't ever learned the trick of properly using a spyglass with both eyes and shifting back and forth in the mind to get the broad view of the natural eye as well as the narrow field of focus afforded by the glass.

Suddenly, a thick column of water shot up from the side of the whale's head. From his vantage point trailing the whale, Ethan saw that the water blew forward. Only sperm whales blew through the top side of their heads and forward.

"Thar she blows!" Ethan yelled. Then he turned and yelled down to the decks. "C'mon, lads. That's a fine bull sperm whale out there just waiting for men that are brave enough to take him."

A ragged cheer broke from below.

Despite the cheering, Ethan knew that the men also recognized the dangers ahead if they pursued the whale successfully. Too much time off made a whaling man sloppy in his work. They'd had too much time off.

Nantucket whaling men had started out in their professions hunting what were called right whales. The Wampanoag, the native people on Nantucket Island, had hunted the whales from the shoreline for the oil as well as their bones. After that, an inhabitant of Cape Cod named Paddock had journeyed to the island and taught the English immigrants how to hunt the whales from boats. The right whales, called that because they'd been the *right* whales to catch, had since been hunted nearly to extinction. But the sperm whales had been discovered before that happened.

Although more fierce by nature and much larger than the right whales, the sperm whales turned out to be a whaling man's bounty. Oil-soaked blubber loaded their flesh. And inside the blunt-shaped head, once the skull case was cracked open, lay nearly five hundred gallons of spermaceti, the highest quality of oil that could be taken from a whale.

It was the intestinal tracts of a sperm whale that yielded liquid gold, though. Ambergris, the dark, oily substance that lined the sperm whale's intestines, was used to make perfumes and went for the highest price when a cargo was sold.

"Mr. Swain," a strong voice called up.

Hooking an arm in the main topgallant rigging, Ethan peered back and down into *Reliant*'s stern. Anger rolled in the pit of his stomach and he had to restrain himself from cursing. *Remember Boston,* he told himself. *Remember Teresa.*

Captain Simon Folger stepped onto the deck from the aft companionway. He looked calm as could be as he pulled on his officer's uniform coat. He was tall and heavy, carrying a belly on him this past year that hadn't been there when they'd left Nantucket.

"Aye, Cap'n," Ethan yelled in response.

"Is this a true sighting then, Mr. Swain?" Folger demanded. "Or are we again led astray by a false report?"

Ethan felt the tension from the captain's words seethe over the deck. Robert Oswalt might have gotten the punishment for the false alarms, but Ethan knew the ship's captain faulted him for them as well. Folger's accusation was like a slap in the face for the crew.

"The sighting's true, Cap'n," Ethan replied in a strong voice. He tried to keep the anger from his words. "I've seen the beast myself. Looks to be a sperm whale."

A greedy smile lit Folger's moon face. "Then what are we waiting for, Mr. Swain? This ship can't make the money the investors want to see returned on their trust if the crew is going to dawdle about and watch whales go by."

"Aye, Cap'n." Ethan passed the spyglass back to Bill. He leapt into the rigging, swinging down so fast that an untrained eye would have thought him plunging to his doom. Seconds later, he landed barefoot on the rolling deck, well ahead of Bill, who made his way a trifle more slowly.

The crew moved briskly, aided in their efforts by the caustic lashings of the captain's spite-laden tongue. Men loaded the aft larboard whaleboat and the waist whaleboat just ahead with tubs of harpoon line.

Ethan ran to the mainmast rack, where the harpoons and spears were kept neat and true. *Reliant* carried nearly two hundred such weapons in all, most of them belowdecks in the cargo space. The spares would be brought up as needed. He grabbed a half dozen harpoons in his arms and glanced over his shoulder.

Creel Turpin, one of the older hands aboard *Reliant,* ran behind Ethan.

"Lances, Creel," Ethan said, turning from the rack and sprinting for the waist whaleboat. "If you please."

"Aye," Creel responded. "I gots 'em for ye." He was a small bear of a man with slightly rounded shoulders and a potbelly, but there wasn't a harder-working man on the ship. He was in his late thirties, a man with a wife and children back on Nantucket. Gold earrings glinted in his ears. A knife scar marred his face, and more decorated his left arm, proving that he knew his way around tavern brawls.

"Furl the sails," Folger bawled from the ship's stern.

"Furl the sails," Ethan cried out as he dropped the harpoons into the whaleboat.

"All ahead stop," Folger ordered.

"All ahead stop." Ethan joined the crew, calling out instructions to the men swarming the rigging to draw up the sails. The windlass cranked, dropping the anchor toward the ocean floor below. They were far out from coastal waters, and Ethan knew that getting the anchor to sea bottom would take time.

"We'll take the whale by boat," Folger said. "If the brute gets a look at this ship, we may scare him off. And I don't want him scared off. Is that clear?"

"Aye, Cap'n," Ethan replied, knowing several of the men were close to ignoring Folger's orders.

"*We,* says the pompous bastard," Horace McBain growled in a low voice. "An' him a-gonna park his fat arse on board this ship an' wait all impatient-like for the men what's bravin' the sea fer that whale." He was one of the older hands, gone gray for years, but still good with rope and sail.

Thankfully, McBain's words didn't carry far. Ethan shot the man a look. "Talk like that," Ethan warned, "could cost you the hide from your back, Horace McBain. This ship has ears, you know."

Chastened, the man nodded and moved for the larboard whaleboat with his clutch of harpoons.

In less than a minute, the canvas had been cleared from the three masts, dropping it down on the same lines that were used to muscle the sheets into position. The upper masts of the ship looked as bare as oak trees in winter.

Ethan felt pride in his crew. As first mate, he'd driven them hard, rehearsed them at times almost cruelly, but he'd never pushed them so hard that he'd broken them, as Folger tried to do. Despite *Reliant*'s advanced age of nearly twenty years, they kept her neat and trim, better than Folger had any right to expect. Except that the captain's demands kept rising every time the crew managed to rise to meet them. *Reliant*'s keel measured 118 feet and supported a deck 141 feet long. She was 37 feet across her beam. All in all, she was a sizable ship with plenty of work aboard her.

Sliding back down the rigging, Ethan landed on his bare feet. Breathing hard from his exertion, his breath singing in his ears, he noticed the change in *Reliant*'s speed immediately. With her sails furled, the whaleship started to turn sluggish, more at the mercy of the ocean rather than slicing through whatever the sea brought. She was at her most vulnerable when she was still.

Robert Oswalt, still clad in a dirty apron from his duties in the ship's galley, ran across the deck toward Ethan. He carried a pair of heavy leather boots.

"Ethan," Robert gasped, coming to a halt, "I've brought your boots." He was barely five feet tall, and surely no more than fifteen or sixteen years old. He was fair-haired and fair-complexioned, carrying a bright pink tint to his skin at all times. They'd found him adrift in the ocean a little more than a month ago after he'd jumped overboard, no longer able to handle the abuse he'd been constantly treated to.

"So you have," Ethan said, taking the boots from the young man.

"Mr. Swain," Folger called from the stern quarterdeck. "I want that whale, Mr. Swain. Not your excuses about why it couldn't be brought back."

Damn your eyes, Ethan thought, noting that several other men in the whaleboat crews were visibly stung by the harsh words. But he said, "You'll have the whale, Cap'n. You've got stouthearted men working for you." He glanced up at the young man standing in front of him and lowered his voice. "Robert."

"Yes." Robert looked at him with rapt attention.

"Lose the apron."

The young man glanced down at the apron, looking as though he were see-ing the garment for the first time. He untied the apron strings and took the apron off. With the apron folded neatly in his hands, he started back toward the galley.

"Robert," Ethan called gently. When the young man turned to him, Ethan took the apron from him, then led the way to the port side of the ship. He tied the apron tight around the railing.

"Won't it blow off?" Robert asked.

"No," Ethan answered. "That apron will be here waiting on you for when you get back. But you won't be working in the galley anymore."

"I won't?"

"No." Ethan watched as his boat crew readied the waist whaleboat.

THE WHALEBOAT HUNG from a block-and-tackle assembly called the falls. The falls held the vessel over the ship's side. The boat was twenty-five feet in length and was equipped with oarlocks, gunnels, and a simple single mast that could be added for the times when the craft could be powered by the wind.

Reliant carried five whaleboats. With the way Folger insisted on using them, only two of them were in the water at any time, but the others were kept in reserve. Two of the whaleboats hung from the port side and another from the starboard side. A fourth hung from the ship's stern. The final whaleboat hung below the mainmast rigging high enough above the deck so that men wouldn't bump their heads in passing.

Moving to the stern of the boat, Ethan took up position and sat. Timothy Madison, rawboned and thin, already sporting an old man's face and him twenty years too young for it, sat in as boatsteerer in the prow of the whaleboat. He had pale green lizard's eyes, too close-set to trust.

Glancing back at the boat crew at the larboard whaleboat, Ethan said, "Lower away." He pulled at the ropes on the falls, slipping the whaleboat free. He braced himself as the whaleboat dropped and his stomach tried to turn inside out from the falling sensation.

The lines burned through the falls, shrilling like a bird caught by a cat for a moment, then the whaleboat slapped into the water with a crash that spattered foaming sea brine up into Ethan's face. Bill kept the craft on a tether from above.

Light and flat-bottomed, the whaleboat twisted and gamboled across the surface of the sea like a small fish fighting the fisherman's line. A dozen times, the whaleboat slapped against the ship, creating hollow thumps that echoed over the gentle sea swells.

Ethan grabbed one of the oars and stood in the boat's center. He used the oar to keep the small craft from thumping against the bigger vessel. In seconds, Robert Oswalt, Bill Fedderson, Creel Turpin, and Holy Jordan swung down the falls lines to join Ethan and Timothy Madison in the boat.

Looking back over his shoulder, Ethan saw that the larboard whaleboat had only then settled onto the water. His crew was ahead in the mad race to reach the whale. Even though the crew worked as one, competition remained fierce between the individual whaleboat teams. Hunting whales was what the sailors lived and died for on these voyages. As dangerous as it was, the hunt broke the tedium and despair of the long voyages, and stories of victory lasted longer still.

The men in Ethan's boat already knew their places. With the addition of young Robert to the boat crew to replace Horace McBain (at Folger's insistence that the young man earn his keep aboard *Reliant*), Ethan had worked his boat crew fiercely to bring them all back up to speed. Being quick and smart aboard the whaleboat wasn't just about the competition between boat crews. Those skills and trained instincts also kept a man and his boat mates alive.

With Timothy Madison in the boatsteerer's position at the prow of the whaleboat, Bill took his place as bow oarsman because he was the most experienced of the lot. Ethan had stationed Creel as midships oarsman because he was the strongest of them and most able to handle the heaviest oar of the five that propelled the whaleboat. Holy, one of the younger men aboard *Reliant,* took up his oar but kept the two tubs of harpoon line between his feet so he knew where they were at all times. Robert, being the slightest built of the six men in the boat, was the after oarsman and soon-to-be harpooner.

Ethan looked at his crew. All five of them sat with their faces to him and their backs to the whale over a mile away. "Give way all, lads, and may God keep us in His sight today."

"Amen," Holy Jordan said. He bowed his head quickly and made the sign of the cross.

Back on Nantucket, Ethan knew, the Quakers would have looked upon Holy's Catholic ways with disfavor, and probably would have run him off the island. But men on ships, especially whaling ships, prayed to every friendly and benevolent power whose name they knew.

Robert, as after oarsman, set the pace for the rowing, calling out the beats in a low, strong voice.

Ethan stood in the stern and looked toward the black hump of the whale on the horizon. In his years of whaling, he'd taken dozens of whales. Each one was different in some way. Ethan approached his prey with the same technique each time, but he had learned to be adaptable. His skills had earned him the first mate's job on three different whaleships since he was sixteen.

But you haven't made captain yet, have you? Ethan chided himself. That was his goal and his ambition, and that desire had very nearly been the reef that had torn the guts out of his future in Boston. He shook those thoughts away.

The whaleboat caught the gentle rolls of the Pacific Ocean. Where *Reliant* cut through the waves, the lighter whaleboat had no choice but to be tossed above them. Each time a wave passed them, the front end of the whaleboat lifted from the water, then crashed back down. Salt spray wet the backs of the rowing crew and stung Ethan's eyes.

"Larson's got his boat away," Bill advised.

Ethan nodded but didn't look back. He remained focused on the whale, hoping the huge animal didn't decide to sound. If the whale dived, the return to the surface could be in as little as ten minutes or as much as an hour.

"There hisself sits," Timothy sneered, looking back at *Reliant*. "Prancin' the ship's decks like some kind of proud popinjay. An' when we taken this whale, it's gonna be hisself that claims credit for it."

Ethan knew Timothy was talking about Captain Folger. Ethan resisted the impulse to turn and look. From past experience during the voyage, he knew the captain would be standing in the prow with his arms folded across his chest.

"He's the cap'n," Ethan replied evenly. "The credit's his."

"An' the bulk of the profits is his, too," Bill said contemptuously.

Ethan didn't argue that. A ship's captain always got the biggest lay of the profits. Sailing men without position or prestige on a voyage got small wages paid out of the profits at the end. Those wages were called lays, and they were sometimes only a fraction of a percent of the profits. On some ships, Ethan had seen men walk away with less than two hundred dollars in their pockets after a three-year voyage. Luckily, he hadn't sailed with those ships. The vessels he'd taken berths on had proven profitable for the investors, and his own stock had risen with the captains of ships.

Until Boston, he reminded himself. Boston had changed many things.

Signing on with Folger had been a mistake, but Ethan had realized that only on reflection. Until this voyage, Folger had been lucky taking whales, too.

"Ye can't just keep ignorin' the way the cap'n's treatin' ye, Ethan," Bill said.

Ethan waved Bill's comment away, trying to stay focused on the whale. Only the man wouldn't let the subject go.

"Ye're the first mate, Ethan." Bill pulled on his oar. "Ain't a man on that ship that won't foller ye should ye so choose."

Standing with surefooted ease in the whaleboat's stern, his knees bent to maintain his balance, Ethan suddenly felt as though the ocean was going to open up and swallow him. The unrest between the crew and the captain had been growing by leaps and bounds.

Ethan spoke in a low voice, just loud enough to be heard over Robert's count. "This conversation is a dangerous one, Bill."

"We're talking mutiny," Holy said.

"I don't want to push you, Ethan," Creel said calmly, "but Bill is tellin' ye true. Ye an' me both been on bad ships afore. An' this 'un's gonna be a bad 'un if'n somebody don't knock in Folger's horns."

"The situation with Folger might not come to that," Ethan said.

Creel eyed Ethan steadily, ignoring Ethan's warning glance and not backing down an inch. "Ye know it will. Ye can feel it in yer bones same as me. Ye've had yer taste of it."

For an instant, memory dusted Ethan with a gossamer wing. Images of men dying with musket balls in their chests or their stomachs laid open by a cutlass slash played against the backs of his eyes. Through the brine of the sea, he smelled the brittle iron of blood and gunpowder. The harsh cracks of pistols and muskets mixed with the rolling thunder of a full broadside of cannon.

"No," Ethan said, unsheathing the steel in his voice. "And I don't want to hear any more talk like this." The whale was little more than two hundred yards away. "I'm a man of my word, and I gave it that I'd see this ship through storm and sea, and bring back a full hold of whale oil to show for it. That's the same job you signed on to do."

"I didn't sign on to work meself to death like a dog," Bill growled.

Ethan divided his attention between the men and the whale. The whale blew again, the forward tilt of the spray more pronounced as they caught up with the massive animal.

"Ye're the first mate," Creel said. "As mate, ye're supposed to stand in for the crew agin the cap'n an' take our part should it come to that. An' the crew feels as though it has come to that."

"Ever'body's surprised you ain't felt it's come to that," Bill added.

"Not that nobody thinks ye're the cap'n's man," Timothy hastily added.

"Speak fer yer ownself, Tim," Bill said.

"Shut yer piehole, Bill," Creel growled. "If'n we thought that poorly of Ethan, we wouldn't even be talkin' to him now." He was quiet for a moment, his eyes meeting Ethan's fearlessly. "Somethin' ye need to know. There's a circle of names bein' prepared. Men who's writin' their names down sayin' as how they'd like to elect a new captain."

A cold chill passed through Ethan. As bad as things might get, he hadn't been expecting that announcement. He couldn't believe the talk had gone that far without his knowing it. Now, when the dissatisfaction all came out, he was likely to be crushed between the two forces threatening to tear the ship apart. The crew would blame him for not siding with them earlier, and the captain would fault him for not apprising him of the situation in time to prevent an uprising.

"We want ye as that new captain," Creel said. "But we want yer name on that list when we give it to the cap'n."

Captain, he thought. Just like that, and he'd be a captain. But it would be captain of a mutiny, and he knew there would be no honor in that. He imagined trying to write that in one of the letters he faithfully sent back to his family on Nantucket. There was no way.

Ethan looked at the black mountain of the whale lying in the ocean little more than fifty yards away. "Let's take the whale, lads. One thing at a time."

The five men in the whaleboat stared hard at Ethan. Only Robert and Holy didn't have accusation in their gazes.

"Aye then," Bill said in a cold voice. "Have it as ye will. But when the time comes that yer name ain't on that list, an' that time will come soon enough, the crew's gonna figure ye're agin 'em, too. Likely ye won't have a friend left on *Reliant,* an' no ready-made captaincy a-waitin' on ye either."

Ethan gave the man a hard eye. "I want that whale, Bill. Nothing else matters right now, and if you do anything to hurt my chances at taking that whale, I'm going to beat you down. You have my word on that."

Bill's face colored a deep red. "All right then. Let's take yer damned ol' whale."

"Shift the oars. Steady, now, and let's paddle in if we can. Robert, slow down the beat. Let's see if we've caught this monster sleeping."

Dropping into a kneeling position to present a lower profile in the whale-boat, Ethan watched the whale with a trained eye. Whales had a tendency to ignore small boats, although sometimes a whale was skittish of everything.

If a whale swam away, the whaleboat crews had no choice but to row after the creature and hope they could keep up. But the most fearsome possibility of all was that the whale might decide to attack the whaleboat.

The crew behaved liked the well-trained machine that it was. The oars rose and dipped, barely catching the water in slow strokes and hauling the whaleboat back. None of them turned to look over their shoulders.

"Pull two," Ethan whispered.

Bill and Holy kept their oars moving to Robert's whispered beat while the other three rowers shipped their oars.

The whaleboat came around slowly, pulling in toward the whale.

The oily black body was slightly longer than fifty feet, Ethan judged. The blunt, squared-off head marked the creature clearly as a sperm whale. No other whale resembled the huge monster floating more than half-submerged in the water. The ocean lifted and dropped the whaleboat, but Ethan felt totally in tune with the great beast.

Triumph or tragedy lay only a few feet away.

"Robert," Ethan called softly. "Stand, lad, and pick up that harpoon."

With some obvious reluctance, Robert shipped his oar and took up one of the harpoons from the center of the whaleboat. The harpoon was eight feet of polished hardwood that had been fired to make the wood stouter. The iron head at the end of the harpoon was cruelly barbed, designed to rip into a whale's flesh and hang. The back end of the harpoon had been drilled through so the heavy-test whale line could be tied there.

"Holy," Ethan said, "are those tubs ready?"

"Aye," Holy replied, glancing at the line-filled tubs sitting between his feet.

"I don't want that line fouling," Ethan said.

"It won't."

"And I want that line kept wet so it doesn't catch fire on the loggerhead." The loggerhead was a post at the stern of the ship. As the tub oarsman paid out the line, the line whipped around the loggerhead to stay taut and provide lever-age for the crew as they took the line back in. If the line wasn't kept wet, often the hemp would catch fire from the friction and either burn in two or weaken and snap.

"The line will be wet."

The whale blew, shooting a spout of water sixty feet high. The spray blew back over the whaleboat crew. Salt stung their eyes and noses as the mist covered them in foul-smelling reek.

Bill cursed.

Standing in the prow of the whaleboat, leg locked against the thwart, Robert stared at the great brute they'd come more than a mile to kill. His hands shook, and his lower lip trembled.

"Robert," Ethan whispered. "Are you okay, lad?"

"I'm scared, Ethan. I'm just so damned scared that I'll make a mess of this."

In the next moment, the whale shifted. The flukes flicked nervously, propelling the creature forward a few feet.

"It's Larson's boat," Creel said. "Stupid bastards is comin' up on the starboard side of the fish. Whale must have caught 'em from the corner of his eye."

Gracefully, unbelievably quick for something so massive, the sperm whale started forward.

"Give it to him!" Ethan roared, knowing they couldn't lose the whale. "Give it to him now, Robert!"

CHAPTER 2

Pacific Ocean 3° 28' S. Lat.—107° 12' W. Long.

ROBERT CURSED IN a broken voice as he managed to maintain his balance. His jumble of harsh words came out wrong, like a child mimicking a language unknown to it. Then he leaned forward, putting his weight into the throw.

Anxiety rattled through Ethan when he saw the harpoon leave Robert's hand. The chance existed that the young man would miss, and they'd still end up going back to *Reliant* and Captain Folger empty-handed.

The harpoon flew true though. Sunlight caught the great barbed iron head of the weapon streaking through the intervening space. The whale line zipped behind the harpoon, whipping back and forth, uncoiling effortlessly. The humming rush of the line sounded over the noise of the sea slapping against the whaleboat.

Grimly, fear alive in his guts and burning like lye soap, Ethan watched as the whale line payed out. *Remains to be seen,* he told himself, *whether we're the ones that have the whale. Or if it's the whale that has us.* Without looking at Holy, he said, "Keep water on that line, Holy."

"The Lord is my Shepherd," Holy began praying as he always did to keep measured cadence with the work at hand. "I shall not want." He took the small leather bucket's strap from around his neck, wound the piggin's strap around his wrist, and reached over the whaleboat's side. "He maketh me to lie down in green pastures."

"Ain't no damn pastures here," Timothy said sourly.

Not paying the other man any heed, Holy lifted the brimming piggin to the tub and poured the contents over the whale line whistling from inside as the whale continued running. "He leadeth me beside the still waters."

The first tub emptied of rope and the second began.

"Ship those oars," Ethan ordered, watching the dregs of the whale line in the second tub. "Take up the slack." He leaned down and picked up the other end of the whale line. With a few practiced tosses, he wrapped the remaining slack in the rope around the loggerhead, pressed both feet against the stern, and prepared himself as best as he could.

The crew followed Ethan's example, leaning back toward the whaleboat's prow as they hung on to the line. For a moment, Ethan didn't think they'd be able to hold the huge creature. They weren't actually able to hold the whale back, only hang on to it like fleas clinging to a dog. He felt the whale line biting into his hands, chewing at the heavy calluses he'd developed from all the rough work he did in the harsh elements of the sea and the wind and the sun.

Despite the fact that the whaleboat was twenty-five feet long and burdened with the weight of six grown men, the whale yanked the craft like the wind seizing a falling leaf. Ethan and his crew had a harder time holding on to the line than the whale had in hauling the craft.

Pulled by the forty-five-ton whale—and Ethan was now certain the beast weighed that much—the whaleboat bounced across the ocean surface like a flat rock skipping a pond. They hit a wave and went airborne as a blanket of spray crashed back down over them.

Salt stung Ethan's eyes and nasal passages as seawater flooded them. Pain gnawed at his mind, but he shut the agony away and concentrated on the whale.

Incredibly, the line went slack.

Ethan's hands banged into his thighs. His left hand brushed against the ivory hilt of the broad-bladed sailor's knife he carried sheathed there. "Take up slack!" he roared. He sat up and reached for the limp whale line, ignoring the new pain that flared as he opened and closed his cramping hands to haul in the line.

"Larson's comin' about," Bill said. "Lookit that whoreson. A-tryin' to horn in on our kill that way. He's just a-wantin' some of the glory fer himself. We get back to *Reliant* an' I'm liable to wallop him for his troubles, I am."

The whale came around in a circle with a sudden explosion of movement.

" 'Ware the line," Ethan warned. The rope was woven to hold several hundred pounds. Strained taut between the loggerhead and the whale, the rope could cut into a man or break his bones if he was trapped against the side of the whaleboat and couldn't give ground.

The whale didn't come around far enough for the line to be a threat. Another spout of water blew above the whale's head as he settled in to look back at the hunters. Larson's crew aboard the second whaleboat had their oars dug in deep, hauling for all they were worth.

Ethan pulled on the line more tightly, yanking the whaleboat into motion and sliding himself and the vessel closer to their prey.

The harpoon wiggled in the whale's side, but the barbed head held. Sometimes, when the whale got too active, the harpoon shaft would snap off and leave the iron head embedded in the thick blubber. Even heavily injured whales had escaped at that point.

Just hold steady, Ethan prayed as he continued pulling on the line. Under present circumstances, the flat-bottomed whaleboat worked for them. Without any kind of draw, the whaleboat glided across the sea surface whether being dragged by the whale or propelled by the oars. Caught by the waves, men and boat were lifted into the air for a moment, then tumbled back down the foreside of the approaching wave with a bone-shaking crash.

Larson's craft moved quickly across the sea. Ethan heard Larson calling out rowing commands to his team, urging them closer. He stood on his hands and knees in the whaleboat's stern.

"There," Creel said, his eyes focused over Ethan's shoulder. He pointed. "Larson's havin' his go at the whale."

Ethan turned and watched. Mixed feelings danced within him. He wanted the whale for himself; every whaling man worth his salt wanted to be able to claim the victory. But he also wanted a safe return for his boat and his crew.

"Damn fool," Timothy snarled. "Whale's comin' around, an' he's gonna be takin' the monster on head-to-head."

Ethan cupped his hands to his mouth as the slack aboard their own whaleboat continued to pay out. "Larson! Shove off! Shove off!"

The whale bore down on Larson's whaleboat. The second mate kept his crew steady till the creature was fifty yards out and closing fast.

"Give way all!" Larson shouted. "Give way all!"

The oars dipped into the water and pulled at the same time. Powered by the strength and fear of the sailors, the whaleboat leapt from the whale's path. Larson drew back his harpoon and let fly as the whale shot past.

The harpoon buried in the whale's body just back of the massive head. As if crying out in agony, the whale's small lower jaw opened, exposing the conical teeth that could bite an unlucky man in half.

A cheer exploded from the crew aboard Larson's whaleboat.

"Got ye, ye big bastard!" Larson screamed in victory. He remained standing in the whaleboat's prow, legs braced against the thwart as he held on with one hand and shook a fist at the passing monster. "Ye won't escape Donald Larson, by God!"

The whaleboat was only ten feet out from the huge whale, coasting up one of the gentle ocean swells. Incredibly quick for something so large, the whale threw his flukes out, catching the whaleboat squarely at the apex of the swell.

Wood shattered in an instant. Sailors and pieces of the boat went flying. Before the debris and bodies had time to return to the ocean, the slack on the whale line to Ethan's boat grew taut. He called out a warning just before the whaleboat jerked into motion again.

There was no chance to see what remained of Larson and his crew. Cutting free to return to the site only meant that another target of opportunity would be in the water for the whale to attack if the great beast so chose. And by the time they rowed back to where the second whaleboat had been shattered, the men who could save themselves already would have.

Ethan clung to the line with all his strength. He called out encouragement to his hurting crew even though the effort cost him dearly of his own resources. *Two months,* he reminded himself grimly. *Two months have passed since you've taken a whale. That's too long. It's time to break that bad luck streak, and now is the moment.*

Ethan counted to three. Together, the crew hauled in on the line, taking up maybe three feet of line to coil in Holy's first tub. Three feet was a good draw. Sometimes a crew fought for only inches.

And then the true battle began. Ethan guided his crew by voice, taking in precious inches and feet of the line as the whale tried to flee. Robert's cast had been a good one, though, and the barbed head of the harpoon had sunken deeply enough that it wasn't coming out. Luck stayed with them regarding the harpoon's wooden shaft as well, because the weapon held together and didn't snap.

Then they'd watch the slack they'd fought so hard for disappear in a twinkling before the line grew taut again and they once more had to endure the hard, bone-breaking ride across the sea. Whaling men out of Nantucket had christened the act of being yanked across the sea as a Nantucket sleigh ride.

As he worked, Ethan's back felt close to breaking. His arms felt pulled loose from their moorings, and his legs felt like they'd been driven up inside him. He hurt all over, and his body trembled with near exhaustion.

The whale continued the fight, and strength and courage and endurance were measured between the great animal and the men in the whaleboat. Ethan couldn't tell how long the give-and-take of the battle lasted, but he knew as solidly as Robert had hooked the whale that the end was only a matter of time.

Provided he and his crew could stay the course.

Sudden slack in the line sent Ethan crashing back. His legs shook powerfully from the sudden release. Hauling in the line as quickly as he could, at first fearing that the knot at the end of the harpoon had somehow come undone, he sat up and stared at the whale.

Silence rolled over the ocean for a moment, marred only by the cry of gulls that had gathered in the blue sky. With the sun shining down full upon it, the sea looked the color of jade, a shimmering sheet with only occasional rolling ripples. *Reliant* was nowhere to be seen, nor any possible survivors from Larson's boat.

The whale floated less than a hundred yards away. Both harpoons jutted from his sides. Water flew from his spout, turning to mist and fog before descending again to the waterline.

"Ye think he sees us?" Timothy whispered.

"I don't know," Ethan said. "Get the oars ready in case he does. Leave go the line." He drew in great drafts of air, trying to fill his lungs and not thinking there was ever going to be enough air again. His lips felt parched, and his mouth was dry as sand.

The crew took up their oars and waited.

The whale blew again, then he bowed and shoved his head deeply into the water.

"God Almighty!" Bill shouted in warning. "He's soundin'! He's soundin'!"

With a final wave of his flukes, the great whale disappeared, plunging into the depths. His black body vanished from sight in the depths in seconds, and the line started whistling from the tub.

"Grab hold!" Ethan shouted. Next to actually having a whale turn on them, this was the event that whaling men most feared. In the next instant, he heard Bill scream.

CHAPTER 3

Easter Island, Chile 27° 9' S. Lat.—109° 26' W. Long.

"HELP!"

When he first heard the cry for help, Professor Thaddeus J. Bullock believed the call had only been the product of an overtired mind and a willing hand on the part of his imagination. The professor had been staring out to the dark sea to the south of Easter Island. The dregs of the sun's last light died like orange coals in an untended firebox to the west, fading into more of the Pacific Ocean.

"Help!"

The second cry, though weaker than the first, couldn't be mistaken.

Alarmed, Bullock rose from the shelf of rock he'd chosen as his office of sorts during the early evening. The beach offered a natural harbor for the vessel he'd arrived on, but little in the way of comforts. His small scientific team and the ship's crew had established a base camp farther up the hill.

Automatically, he closed the journal he'd been working on. He slid the leather-bound book into an oilskin pouch with a string tie, drew the string tight, and shoved the package inside his shirt. He took up the lantern that he'd used to work by and scoured the shoreline.

"Help! God, help me!"

Bullock's first thought was of Katharine. His daughter had accompanied him on the trip. Since they'd rounded South America, memory of the falling star that had shot from the heavens and landed in the ocean in 1797 had been with him constantly. The impact of the falling star had caused the huge tidal wave that washed his wife from the deck of the ship he'd taken passage on. Meg had been gone in an instant. And when the sea had settled, there had been no sign of her or the falling star or the other men who had been lost during that voyage.

Bullock pushed the painful memories away and raised the lantern high, scrutinizing the shoreline below. Crabs scuttled across the hard rock and darted into tide pools that had been left on the beach from earlier in the day. The ship's crew had investigated the sinkholes and tide pools with great success when they'd put in to shore. Crabs and fish had gone into the chowder or been baked or roasted over the main campfire.

"Hello the camp," Bullock called. He kept searching the shoreline.

"What is it, Perfesser?" one of the men called back.

"Some poor wretch is calling for help down here." Assured that someone had heard him, Bullock started down the hillside. The moonlight rendered the way even more treacherous than the earlier climb upon their arrival. Loose rock slid out from underfoot, and cracks tripped Bullock as he went down.

"Perfesser! Wait!" The man's voice rose in consternation. "There's heathens on this here gob o' stone an' sand. Cannibals. When they ain't a-eatin' on them hapless ship's crews that end up here, why they're a-eatin' on each other. *Perfesser!*"

Swinging the lantern in front of him, Bullock surveyed the shoreline. He knew the man spoke truly. Several of the island populations in the Pacific Ocean had taken up feasting on human flesh by choice and out of necessity.

"Damn all, ye dogs!" the camp guard roared. "Gather up yer muskets an' foller me down this here hill! The perfesser says he heard somethin'! Johnson, pick three men an' secure the camp!"

Bullock reached the shoreline. His heart pounded from his exertion and the fear that filled him. For the first time, he realized that he could be walking into a trap laid by some of the natives they'd seen earlier. The man Captain Mayhew had promised would contact them concerning the creature he had come hunting had not yet arrived.

Perhaps he's been eaten since the good captain has been here, Bullock thought before he could stop himself. The skin across the back of his neck prickled, and the trade winds blowing across Easter Island suddenly felt chill instead of balmy.

Almost two hundred yards away, the ship lay at anchor a comfortable fighting distance from the island should anything untoward occur. The shore was out of musket range, dictating that any attackers would have to approach by boat. The ship carried eighteen cannon for defense, though, and all of those could reach the shoreline.

But a wolf doesn't attack a whole herd, does it? Bullock reminded himself. *A wolf chooses one sheep and takes that sheep while the others are running in fear.*

Waves crashed against the rocky land stabbing out into the sea. A salty spray lifted up into the air and drifted back over Bullock. The stray droplets that landed on the heated glass of the lantern hissed and left dusty tracks as they skidded down.

"Perfesser."

Bullock turned at the approach of the crew. The area was suddenly flooded with the light of their lanterns, but the darkness remained steadfast beyond the reach of their lights.

Perkins led the group of men. He carried a .69-caliber Springfield musket that had been in production for the last four years. The year-old war with Great Britain had generated the manufacture of thousands of such weapons. The money-eyed interests behind Bullock's expedition had equipped the ship and crew with the best weapons and equipment available. President Madison's mission to find the truth about the monster reputed to be living in the area made those weapons easy to acquire even during wartime.

Lean and rawboned, sporting the broken cheeks of a man prone to hard drink, Perkins was third mate on the ship. A lock of sandy hair threaded with silver hung across his low brow.

"Whyn't ye let us handle this, Perfesser?" Perkins coaxed. "Ye see, Cap'n Mayhew would be fit to be tied if'n he thought I's a-lettin' ye walk around out here in the dark all by yer lonesome." Captain Mayhew had assigned Perkins to keep Bullock safe during his studies ashore.

Bullock fell in behind the shorter man. He took some comfort from how quickly Perkins assumed control.

"What about my daughter?" Bullock asked.

"Never ye worry yer head about her," Perkins replied, gazing down to the foot of the hillside fronting the sea. "I got men what's with her. She'll be fine, I'll warrant ye that." He paused, looking out to sea. "Whyn't ye point that lantern ahead of us, an' let's see what's what down by the water."

Bullock shined the lantern. Together, they descended. Perkins had no difficulty passing over the rocky shoals left by the ravages of the sea.

"What was it ye thought ye heard?" Perkins asked.

"A man calling for help," Bullock answered, gazing around the beach.

"In English?" Perkins asked.

That question, Bullock realized, *reveals a very astute mind.* The crew had seen him reading books in Spanish, French, and German. They also knew he was conversant in those languages because some of them were.

"Yes," Bullock replied.

"American or British?"

"My ear is not that finely tuned, Mr. Perkins."

"Well, we have to be careful. They's Britishers in these waters, ye know. Got a British navy cap'n named Harrin'ton that's a right proper bastard from what I heerd tell. An' there's privateers what the British has signed on."

"I haven't heard of such a man." Bullock did know about privateers, though. Although given letters of marque by their parent governments and permission to attack and loot the ships of unfriendly countries, the privateers were essentially pirates bearing a license to steal. The Atlantic and Pacific oceans were both theaters of violent encounters between such men.

"Perfesser," Perkins said with a quick, cold grin, "me an' ye, we don't hang out in quite the same places. Nor do we talk much about the same things. Way I heerd tell, ol' Harrin'ton is a-huntin' whalin' ships fer ol' King George. He's supposed to take the cargoes, an' then put the ships down if'n he can't put a prize crew aboard her to send her back to England. But I've heard he's more apt to sink a ship than raid it."

"I wasn't told about Harrington," Bullock said.

Perkins nodded. "Cap'n Mayhew, he said not to be a-worryin' ye about it." He paused. "I figgered to put a bee in yer bonnet whilst we was here. Them rock statues—"

"The *moai,*" Bullock supplied, naming the huge carved statues that sat in a loose ring around the island's outer perimeter.

"The *moai,*" Perkins went on. "I know they's important to ye, but all the while we're a stayin' here, why we're exposed to the likes o' Harrin'ton an' pirates what's in these waters. Whalin's big business, an' it's fortunes that are made by them that owns them ships. The British already like to done crippled the whalin' business in the Atlantic."

"You think we should go," Bullock said.

Perkins faced him, conviction in his bloodshot gray eyes. "Aye. That I do. Havin' men on shore with ye an' yer daughter to pertect ye, why we've done split up *Brown-Eyed Sue's* crew somethin' fierce."

Bullock started to launch into the argument he'd prepared for Captain Mayhew only days ago. In return for his agreement to return to and study the Pacific Ocean breeding grounds of the sperm whale—and President Madison's assignment that he regarded with disdain because men of science did not chase monsters that were undoubtedly the products of drunken or bored sailors—the professor had been allowed special dispensation to investigate the nature of the *moai*.

A sharp cry broke Bullock's train of thought.

"Perkins!" a man cried. "Over here!"

"Come along, Perfesser," Perkins said, taking up his musket in both hands. "An' mind yer step. Ye're a big man to be a-carryin' back to camp."

At six and a half feet tall and 250 pounds, the professor was the tallest man in the expedition and one of the heaviest. He'd always been physically powerful, which had made him stand out in his usual crowd of intellectuals. His beard was the same dark red color as his hair, only now starting to streak with gray. Setting himself in pursuit, Bullock raced across the rocky shoals to the west.

Three sailors gathered around a prone form lying half-in and half-out of the water. The light from the lanterns two of the sailors carried illuminated the scene well.

The man lay on his face. Seaweed draped his body like a funereal shroud. His clothing hung in tatters. One ear appeared to be missing, then Bullock realized that a huge section of rotted flesh had collapsed the ear in on itself.

"Sweet Mary and Joseph!" one of the sailors cried out in a low voice. "Look at his face!"

For a moment, even in the steady light offered by the lanterns, Bullock believed the man's face had been severely lacerated. Then he realized that the wounds in the man's face weren't from knives, swords, or any other sharp object.

The flesh had broken open like overripe fruit under a harsh sun.

Drawn by the horror of what he was looking at, Bullock dropped down to one knee and surveyed the ruin of the man brought in by the tide. The man's mouth was a series of bloody and peeling scabs. Another patch of rotted tissue clung to his jaw, exposing yellowed and cracked bone. The professor didn't know how the man had even been talking. Through the tattered remnants of clothing, weals and cracked flesh showed evidence of further wounding.

Fever bright, the man's good right eye focused on Bullock. The iris and pupil of his left eye shone like moon-kissed ivory, more pale even than the bloodshot white.

"Help me," the man pleaded in a husky voice.

"Easy there, swab," Perkins said in a dry voice. "This here's Perfesser Bullock. He's a man o' science. Come straight here from Princeton University in New Jersey. He'll know what ails ye, an' he'll have ye fixed up right as rain in no time."

The man convulsed and passed out. When his eyes closed, the ragged and torn eyelid over the left one was unable to cover the staring white iris and pupil.

"Send for a blanket," Bullock told Perkins. "We'll make a litter and carry him up the hill to the tents."

"We don't need no blanket," one of the sailors said. He was a hulk of a man, young and still prideful of his strength. "I can carry him by meself."

Bullock tried to stop the young sailor, but reacted much too late.

The sailor gripped the wounded man's right upper arm and started to lift. The injured man's bicep and triceps tore away with a liquid ripping noise. Blood, thin as gruel fresh off the stove, splattered over the rocks. Thankfully, the blood stopped almost as soon as it began.

The sailor who had gripped the wounded man's arm yowled in panic at what he'd done. He darted back so quickly from the horror before him that he ended up falling on the flat of his back. An incoming wave swept over him, drowning out his cries. Then he grabbed the wrist of the hand that had gripped the wounded man and held the hand before him, searching it with an agonized gaze. He screamed again, but this time in pain.

"Oh God!" the man shouted. "It burns! It burns!"

Moving his lantern closer, Bullock watched in stunned fascination as the sailor's palm and fingers blistered almost immediately. Clear blains the size of seed corn knotted up on the man's flesh.

Cursing, Perkins took the sailor by the wrist and walked him farther into the sea. The man's pain was so great that the mate had to bear much of his weight. Together, they wiped the man's hand through the cool sea.

"Does the salt water help?" Bullock asked, not taking his eyes from the man lying so near death at his feet.

"No," the sailor said, voice breaking from the pain. He cursed. "Feels like I'm holdin' on to a burnin' coal. Can ye make it stop?"

"I don't know," Bullock said distractedly. Despite all the copies of letters he'd read preparatory to leaving Princeton for the voyage to the South Pacific, he truly hadn't believed the strange information he'd been given. Monsters simply didn't exist.

And yet, he was looking at the proof of those letters and wild stories. No creature that he knew of in these waters caused this kind of damage. Yet those papers had talked of bodies that had been found with the kind of damage the wounded man and the young sailor bore.

Counting whales and speculating on their breeding numbers suddenly took secondary standing to the enigma lying before Bullock. Was a new disease developing in the South Pacific that no one had heard of? Or was this an event localized to a new species that had been discovered, or even one that had somehow changed radically?

One of the men fled back up the hill.

Bullock gazed at Perkins dealing with the man out in the ocean, then turned his full attention back to the man at his feet. Only the slow, sporadic rise and fall of the man's chest offered testimony that he was still alive. The professor could only guess at the secrets the man held.

"GENTLY, GENTLEMEN," BULLOCK said as he walked beside the four sailors who carried the victim washed in from the sea. "Gently, if you please. This man has to be in excruciating pain."

The young sailor, Clarence, who had mistakenly touched the injured man, continued to agonize over his blistered hand. Several of the swellings on his hand had already burst and leaked fluid mixed with scarlet threads that had to be blood.

The unconscious man rocked in the makeshift hammock provided by the men carrying the blanket. Several of the pustules formed on his body broke open and wept infection and blood. More cracks opened in his body.

The camp established on the fairly level ground atop the long climb up the rugged shoreline consisted of a half dozen tents. The threadbare tarp used for the tents stank of the sea and fish and unwashed flesh, and carried fleas and lice. Bullock had spent an hour fumigating the tent he had arranged for his daughter before he'd let Katharine enter the temporary domicile.

The tents sat in a half circle around the bonfire that lit up the center of the camp. The half circle faced the interior lands of the island so that the bonfire remained in full view of *Brown-Eyed Sue* lying at anchor in the harbor.

Trepidation touched Bullock as he considered the dangers the island might in reality offer. When the sailors had told him of the cannibals who inhabited the island earlier, he'd thought they'd only been telling stories. The information Bullock had ferreted out from among the sources open to him had also borne those stories out, though. But the professor had disregarded those tales as well.

However, after seeing how desolate Easter Island was, looking like a chunk of rock thrusting up from the sea that even a locust would pass over, Bullock knew that the savages living on the island had limited resources. Other men, men from outside the tribal unit, might easily have been considered a source of fresh meat.

"Where do ye want him, Perfesser?" Perkins asked.

"My daughter's tent," Bullock answered. "Give me a moment to wake her—"

"Father," Katharine called, "I'm already awake." She swept aside the tarp flaps and stepped aside. She was a chestnut-haired beauty of twenty-one, no longer the little girl Bullock had dandled and doted on. She was tall like her father, but fine-boned like her mother. Her hair, normally kept up because of the wind, fell below her shoulders. She wore a long brown skirt, shoes, and a long-sleeved white blouse.

"My cot is clean," Katharine said, looking at the sailors as she held up the tent flaps. "Put him there. Put the other man in my father's chair."

Bullock gazed into his daughter's brown eyes, gleaming like copper in the bonfire light. "Did we wake you?"

"I was reading," Katharine replied. "I didn't want to sleep until you'd returned."

Perkins seated Clarence in the chair while the sailors laid the wounded man in the folding cot.

Bullock entered the tent, focusing almost entirely on the unconscious man. "Mr. Perkins, clear the men from the tent."

Perkins shooed the men back.

Bullock leaned over the cot. He slipped his glasses back on and peered at the injured man they'd recovered from the water. "You've laudanum among the stores we transported from the ship to the camp?"

"Aye," Perkins answered.

"We'll be needing it. I'll also want that bottle of rotgut whiskey Mr. McClary seems to favor. I know Captain Mayhew doesn't want Mr. McClary to have unsupervised spirits aboard the ship, but I'm also aware that Mr. McClary picked up at least three bottles at our last port of call."

"Aye. I can't say how much McClary has left, though."

"I'll take what he has," Bullock said.

Perkins hesitated. "McClary may deny the havin' of it."

"Tell him if he does, I'll go speak to the captain myself."

"Aye." Perkins left the tent.

Drawn to the mystery of the ailing man, listening to the stifled sobbing that shook Clarence, Bullock took out his journal and fumbled for a quill.

Katharine stood at his side, slightly behind him, positioned so that her presence wouldn't interfere with light from the two lanterns she'd set up inside the tent.

Opening the journal, Bullock found the next blank page. He noted the previous page number, then labeled the current page he was working on in a fine hand. He wrote the day's date and the time from the pocket watch he carried.

Sailors' voices came from outside. Their words were trapped inside the tent and echoed lowly. Only moments had passed before the whole camp had roused.

"Katharine, can you help me?" Bullock asked.

"Yes." Katharine's own curiosity regarding the unconscious man and the condition he was in was palpable.

Bullock couldn't help feeling that Katharine's interest in the sciences was entirely his fault. He'd dragged her to all the sites and meetings he'd been assigned to or had taken part in. And, worst of all, he'd trained her to do parts of the research and investigatory work he did. Still, his daughter had turned out to be the best assistant he'd ever worked with. She was precise and capable of independent thinking that sometimes led his own in new directions.

"Take up one of the fresh artist's sketchbooks," Bullock directed. "I want renderings done of this man. Of his overall appearance, then specialized detailing done of his face and hands. Also of his feet. I want the extremities recorded. The damage seems to be worst in those areas."

Katharine crossed the tent to the weathered oak trunk that had accompanied them on every journey they'd undertaken for the last dozen years. She unlatched the trunk and took out a bound sketch pad. A small onyx box contained artist's pencils and pens. After making her selection, she stood at the foot of the cot and began drawing.

"Perfesser," Clarence said in a choked voice, "is there something ye can do for the pain?"

"Not until Mr. Perkins returns with the laudanum."

"It hurts somethin' fierce." Clarence sat cradling his hand, the fingers curled slightly inward and trembling.

Noting the creeping red coloration suffusing the flesh, Bullock moved from the cot to the crewman. The blisters on Clarence's hand had multiplied, building one upon the other till they were two and three deep.

"Do you feel pressure inside the blisters?" Bullock asked.

"God, I don't know," Clarence said. He broke suddenly and took a deep, shuddering breath as tears slid down his face. "It just *hurts*. Like nothin' I've ever had before."

"Mr. Perkins will be along soon, Clarence," Bullock said softly.

Returning his attention to the unconscious man, Bullock began his inspection. Blood and pus had already stained the blanket the man lay on. The odor of decay and rot clung to the man.

My God, Bullock thought, looking at the wrack and the ruin of the man, *how has he survived this long? And in the uncaring sea, no less!*

Perkins returned to the tent with two brown bottles. "I got the laudanum and the whiskey."

"Good," Bullock said. "Please administer the laudanum to poor Clarence."

"Aye. An' how much do ye want to give him?"

"The man is in a great deal of pain. I don't want him out of his head and capable of howling at the moon. I want to be able to pour him from that chair should the need arise."

"Aye." Perkins crouched beside the younger man and began administering the laudanum in huge gulps.

For himself, Bullock preferred not to use the laudanum. But neither he nor *Brown-Eyed Sue* had anything better to take a man's mind away from his misery.

"Katharine," Bullock said, "excuse yourself from the room. I need to view this man's body."

Katharine turned and left the tent.

Bullock fetched the black bag containing his scientific apparatus from the oak chest. Using care and tongs, Bullock peeled the ragged clothing from the man's body. On more than one occasion, flesh stripped away with the tar-coated cotton material.

Blisters covered the man's body from head to toe. But the most interesting aspect was the grievous wounds in the man's right side and the back of his left thigh.

Black rot, dead meat shot through with glistening green-and-yellow pus pockets, ringed both wounds. Moving the man's left thigh only slightly revealed that the wound at the top of the thigh had gone all the way through.

"Looks like he was shot an' the ball went through."

Bullock glanced up at Perkins, who was leaning over his shoulder.

"Have you ever seen a gunshot wound that left such markings or infections behind?"

"No," the mate replied. "I can't say as I have, an' I served with Stephen

Decatur in '04 when we went ashore in Tripoli an' burned *The Philadelphia*. I've fought pirates an' privateers now an' again, too, an' I ain't seen nothing like that."

"I think this man's leg is also broken," Bullock went on. "I heard and felt bone grate when I moved it."

Perkins squinted and peered closer. "I don't think whatever passed through him hit the leg bone."

"Nor do I," Bullock agreed. "Which leads me to believe that the venom riddling this man's body was applied in some means through this wound as well, weakening the bone. The residual venom is what did for poor Clarence there."

The young seaman sat in the chair, no longer sober and mostly out of pain. He pulled the bottle of laudanum to his lips and swallowed. Drops ran down his chin.

The tent flap yanked open.

Turning, Bullock watched Captain Aaron Mayhew stride into the tent. Perkins snapped to, standing ramrod straight, eyes forward.

Anger stamped Mayhew's narrow, pinched features. He commanded himself and his ship with hard-edged authority. If the man had any other emotion at his disposal, Bullock had never seen proof.

Standing something less than six feet tall, Mayhew was nonetheless an imposing figure. He had fiery red hair and brown eyes so dark they were almost black. Despite nearly twenty years spent at sea, his skin remained fair and freckled, constantly carrying sunburn.

Mayhew raked his eyes over Clarence in the chair and the unknown man lying in the cot. Then he locked his gaze on Bullock.

"Do you realize you have recklessly endangered my crew?" Mayhew asked.

Bullock rose from his crouch beside the unconscious man and stood so that he towered over Mayhew. "And how did I do that?"

"This attempted rescue of a man probably fraught with some disease," Mayhew responded, glancing at the unconscious man. "A rescue that is obviously doomed to futility."

"We don't know that this man is diseased," Bullock argued.

"Sir," Mayhew stated, putting force into his voice, "even a man unlearned in the sciences such as myself can tell that man is in the advanced stages of some tropical disease."

Bullock scowled. "You know enough to admit your own inadequacies, Captain, yet you insist on overstepping those self-imposed boundaries."

Mayhew's eyes narrowed. He came forward a step. "I take great umbrage at your tone, Professor Bullock."

"And I insist on at least a modicum of civility when I am addressed," Bullock replied.

Mayhew's face reddened further, stained by the anger within him.

When he'd been informed as to the choice of captains, Bullock had found out what he could about Mayhew from navy men stationed around Princeton to defend American shores from British aggressors. Mayhew was a man born to command, following in his father's footsteps. Mayhew's father had been a Revolutionary War hero. But Aaron Mayhew lacked the charisma with which his father had reportedly brimmed.

Perkins stepped sideways and sidled toward the tent flaps.

"You'll remain as you were, Mr. Perkins," Mayhew ordered. "And you'll bear witness to this conversation between Professor Bullock and myself."

"Shall I also bear witness then, Captain Mayhew?" Katharine stepped back into the tent and faced the naval commander with her direct gaze.

Bullock felt slightly embarrassed by his daughter's boldness, but part of him felt proud. He took a step back and covered the unconscious man's genitals with a hasty throw of a sheet. Perhaps Katharine wouldn't have the good sense to be mortified at the sight, but Bullock knew he would have been mortified enough for both of them if Mayhew hadn't been a problem.

"I can even transcribe the conversation you wish to have with my father," Katherine offered in a flat voice. "I have trained myself to be quite good at such endeavors. My father has me transcribe presentations at the university."

Bullock studied his daughter in amazement. In one masterful stroke, Katharine had placed the ship's captain in a defensive posture. Mayhew had to acknowledge her gender due to his position and because of his Virginia upbringing, and the offer of such a transcription of the argument that was surely brewing could only be viewed as a double-edged sword. And most telling of all, she had reminded the captain who was in charge of the voyage they'd all undertaken.

"The health and welfare of my ship's crew is under my purview." Mayhew's nostrils pinched.

"And well those things should be, Captain," Katharine continued, unruffled. "I can't think of a man more capable for the responsibility of master of a ship. Just as I know that if you had been in my father's place, you would not have turned your back on this man."

"Just so, Miss Bullock," Captain Mayhew said.

Katharine's gaze remained somewhat wide-eyed and innocent. The look was one Bullock had seen his daughter use on several occasions. With the death of Meg, many university colleagues and visitors familiar with Bullock's work weren't surprised to see Katharine step forward to take care of his shepherding during social events when she was old enough. Katharine performed most admirably in that capacity.

Cold rebuke shown in Mayhew's eyes as he turned to the professor. "You don't think this man's condition is a result of disease?" the captain asked.

"No," Bullock replied. "I do not."

"I am going to hold you responsible for that judgment, sir," Mayhew said.

"As you will, Captain. Now, if there is nothing else, I need to return my attention to my patients." Bullock stood his ground.

Without another word, Mayhew clapped his hat back on, touched the brim with a forefinger, and departed. Perkins followed immediately after.

"He is not a happy man," Katharine observed.

"Yes," Bullock agreed. "And he won't be any happier when he discovers that we are going to have to find out what happened to this man."

Katharine regarded her father. "You know something about this man's condition?"

Bullock felt a little guilty. As much as he trusted his daughter, he had not told her everything about the voyage. She knew that the voyage and Captain Mayhew's services had been conscripted by the board of investors, but she did not know about the letter President James Madison had written for him, entrusting him to find out what he could of the monster that had been reported in the area where the falling star had plunged all those years ago.

"I know that this man's condition has been seen before."

"In the books that you've kept locked away?"

"Yes." Bullock wasn't surprised that she knew about those. "Our mission here has been to replicate the work regarding the sperm whale breeding grounds that I first did here sixteen years ago, but that was not the greatest reason for coming here."

"What was?"

"That man's condition. If I can, I'm supposed to discover what caused those wounds." Bullock took up his equipment bag. "Please continue your sketches while I attend Clarence."

The sailor sat drunkenly in his chair and looked up at Bullock's approach.

"Do you still have pain, Clarence?" Bullock asked.

The young sailor stared at his hand and made a valiant effort to focus. "Some'at, Perfesser. Some'at. Right now, my hand, he seems a long ways off from me."

Bullock took the man's forearm, careful not to touch the wounded area, and lifted it to the table at Clarence's side. "I'm just going to lance one of the blisters. To let the juice out and see if that alleviates some of your pain."

"Aye. 'At's fine."

Bullock reached into the bag and took out one of the precision-made German steel surgical knives he'd brought with him. He'd been very specific about the equipment he'd wanted. A scientist was only as good as his tools.

CHAPTER 4

Pacific Ocean 3° 28' S. Lat.—107° 12' W. Long.

THE SUN HAD moved on toward the west while the whale hunt had dragged out. Ethan pulled the oar that Bill was no longer able to. Bill's arm had become entangled in the line during the whale's final death throes. Ethan had cut the line in an attempt to save the sailor's life, willing to risk losing the whale, but it had been too late. Bill's arm was torn and bloody. Thankfully, the man slept now, passed out from the excruciating pain he'd endured.

The whale had died, though. Blood had filled its lungs, then blossomed from the spout when no air remained. Whalers called the huge gout of blood "chimney afire."

After making Bill as comfortable as they could, Ethan had tied the whale on to the whaleboat and they'd begun the long, arduous chore of rowing their kill back to *Reliant*. More than three hours had passed before they'd caught sight of the whaleship standing out like a dark shadow against the amber-and-rose sunset.

Lanterns flitted across *Reliant*'s deck, letting Ethan know the ship had spotted them as well. The rest of the whaleboat crew saw that relief was close at hand and pulled with greater vigor, eager to be away from the cool wisps of fog that swept across the sea. Two whaleboats set out from *Reliant* and joined them, adding their efforts to the recovery of the whale. They reached the ship in minutes.

" 'Ware below!"

Ethan Swain stood in the middle of the whaleboat and watched as Solomon Pilcher tossed a fishing net over the side. The heavy rope slapped against *Reliant*'s hull, then dropped into the water.

Captain Simon Folger peered over the side. The silvery moon made his round features look pasty. "Are you hale and hearty, Mr. Swain?"

"Aye, Cap'n," Ethan replied. "Requesting permission to come aboard."

"Granted," Folger said, then disappeared from view.

"Solomon," Ethan called up.

"Aye," the grizzled old seadog called back down. Light from the flames blazing under the tryworks just back of the foremast shined behind him and caught the gold hoops in his ears.

"We've got wounded down here," Ethan said. "I'll need a line and a blanket."

"Aye, Ethan," Solomon said. "I'll have that down to ye straightaway, I will." He disappeared.

The crews of the other two whaleboats scrambled up the fishing net. Larson, the second mate, commanded one of the boats. Only Larson and two other men had survived the whale's attack.

Three men had been lost at sea. All of them had been good ship hands, and men that Ethan had known well. Two of them, Clark and Henderson, had had wives and children in Nantucket.

Solomon returned and lowered the rope and blanket. Ethan folded the blanket lengthways twice, then wrapped it around Bill Fedderson under his arms. Bill was groggy and nearly unresponsive, but he tried to fight until Creel calmed him while Ethan knotted the rope under Bill's arms over the folded blanket. Once he was secure, Solomon ran the rope through a block and tackle and pulled Bill up. The injured man yelped and cursed the whole way.

The lines holding the dead whale were passed up as well.

During the approach, Ethan had positioned the whale on *Reliant*'s starboard. He'd also made certain the head had gone toward the stern to make the efforts at cutting in go a little easier.

The ship's crew pulled the whaleboats from the ocean on the stern falls and the two portside falls. The shrill squeaks of the block and tackles keened over the excited voices of the crew. The starboard falls remained empty, mute testimony to the loss Larson and his crew had incurred.

Almost effortlessly, Ethan gathered the crew into four groups. He called out the beats as they pulled on the lines, dragging the dead whale near *Reliant*. The whole time, the sailors whipped themselves into a frenzy, screaming and cursing, cheering and singing. They'd spent almost two unendurable months whaleless. Now they were the men they'd signed on to be.

Despite his fatigue and the fact that the crew was working by lanternlight and moonlight, Ethan found himself caught up in the excitement. The aches and pains were forgotten for a time.

In relatively short order, the whale's carcass lay chained alongside *Reliant*.

"Whale's secure, Cap'n," Ethan called out.

"Fine, Mr. Swain. Then let's be about harvesting the bounty we're going to provide our investors. Break the men into two groups. The first group will start cutting in while the second group rests belowdecks." Folger gave Ethan an icy stare. "I expect you to lead the first group, Mr. Swain."

Ethan hesitated only a moment. "Aye, Cap'n." Normally, the crew that brought in the whale rested the first turn during the harvesting.

"You cost me a whaleboat today, Mr. Swain," Folger said. "And the lives of three men."

Stunned, Ethan stared at the captain and worked hard to refrain from saying anything. The black anger that had swelled over him outside Boston was upon him again in an instant. He fought it back down with difficulty, reminding himself that he wasn't the captain.

"Oh yes," Folger went on. "Mr. Larson was quite explicit in describing how you and your crew failed to properly attack the whale. I'll be docking your pay for the replacement of the whaleboat, Mr. Swain. And for the repairs necessary for the other one you brought back. The cost of those men's lives I'll leave between you and your Maker."

A few of the sailors, including Creel and Robert, started to complain beneath their breaths. However, the cumulative backlash gathered steam and grew steadily louder.

Folger glanced at Larson. The second mate stood beside the captain. Larson wore a brace of pistols strung on a bandolier across his shoulders and carried a whip in one hand.

In a flash of movement, Larson cracked the whip over the heads of the men. "Silence, ye flea-infested mongrels!" the second mate shouted. "The next one of ye what opens yer trap to disrespect good Cap'n Folger, by God, I'll cut the face off of ye, I will!"

The crew fell silent at once. Some of the men had served with Larson on other ships. All of them had stories to tell of his inhuman cruelties and demonic skill with the whip.

Larson coiled his whip with a smirk. "I'll be expectin' a full shift's work from ye, I will. An' if'n I don't get it, why I'll have the price of a good shift's work from yer backs." He paused, glaring at Ethan.

Ethan breathed out and forced himself to look through the man as if he wasn't there. As second mate, Larson should never have stepped forward as he had with Ethan on hand.

"Now get to work," Larson said.

Gathering the men, Ethan quickly sorted them into two groups. The second group was sent to their quarters belowdecks. None of them wanted to stay topside even though the crews' quarters would be sweltering. All of them knew the deck would soon be running with blood and whale oil, and sweltering from the heat of the tryworks as the massive iron pots boiled the blubber to oil.

Ethan called for the cutting stage. Quickly, the narrow plank was brought forward, tied with ropes at either end that were attached to the block and tackles, and lowered over the side. The narrow plank wobbled and swung under his weight as he turned to survey the waiting crew and pick a man to go with him.

"I'm with ye," Creel said, stepping over the railing to the other end of the cutting stage to better balance them out. The block and tackle creaked menacingly overhead.

"You were with the second group." Ethan had put the man there as he had all his whaleboat crew, so they could get six hours' rest before working on the whale.

"I changed with Parsons." Creel glanced back up at the foredeck where Larson stood. "I thought maybe it would be best if we weren't separated much till we seen this whale through." He paused, then looked back at Ethan. "An' I thought mayhap ye might need someone to watch yer back fer ye. A lot of things can go wrong when a whale's bein' harvested."

As Creel's words drifted away, the cutting stage started dropping in stuttering steps to the whale's corpse. Ethan looked at the black water between the ship and its prey.

So which is it to be, Ethan? he asked himself. If things were different, if Boston hadn't happened, if there hadn't been all that madness with Teresa and Jonah McAfee before Boston that was waiting out there to hang him—

But he'd been all out of choices the day he'd signed articles with *Reliant*.

Easter Island, Chile 27° 9' S. Lat.—109° 26' W. Long.

"FATHER."

Blinking his eyes open, Thaddeus J. Bullock found his daughter staring at him in concern. "What is it?" he asked.

"He's awake," Katharine replied.

Bullock swiveled his head toward the pathetic figure on the cot.

The man's fearsome wounds had opened further during his slumber despite Bullock's best efforts. In the end, the professor had resorted to cloth restraints to keep the man in place and from flailing about enough to rupture more of the sores that riddled his body. More blood and pus stained the bedclothes. He was, literally, falling apart.

Bullock pushed himself up from the chair he'd taken over once young Clarence had passed out. He took his glasses from the open book lying on the table. He'd been in the middle of a discourse regarding the treatment he'd given the young sailor. Vaguely, he remembered closing his eyes just to rest them, then nothing more until Katherine called.

"What time is it?" he asked Katharine as he approached the cot.

"Three-seventeen A.M.," she replied.

The man's single eye tracked Bullock but blinked several times. The professor knew the man's vision was failing. The pupil no longer dilated in response to the lanternlight, and was now as narrow as a pinprick. During the intervening hours that he had slept, the man had lost control of his ruined white eye, which sat somewhat recessed in his head and stared straight up at the peaked tent roof.

The man gasped for his breath, and from the cracking sound of his wheezes, the professor guessed that his lungs slowly filled with fluid. If the process continued, and there was no remedy in sight, he would drown.

The man flicked his eye back to Bullock. "Am I dying?"

The question was a hard one, though not unexpected. Bullock answered as truthfully as he could. "I don't know." He paused. "What is your name?"

"Johnstone. Warren . . . Johnstone."

"You're a sailor, Mr. Johnstone?"

"Aye." Johnstone took a rattling deep breath, then his lungs whistled in a long release. His eye closed, and his face went slack for a moment. "I'm . . . cold."

"Do you still feel pain, Mr. Johnstone? I have some laudanum."

"No . . . no pain. Just feel cold. Numb."

"Can you tell me how you came to be in the water, Mr. Johnstone?" Bullock asked.

"I was . . . on watch," the ailing man wheezed. His eye focused on the tent roof above Bullock's head. "I had . . . was or . . . middle watch. Must have . . . been toward . . . the end of it." He struggled for breath. "I was . . . tired. At first . . . I didn't . . . see it."

"Didn't see what, Mr. Johnstone?"

"The whale," Johnstone said. "I turned . . . to alert the crew. *Meadowlark*, she's . . . a whaling ship . . . she is. But I was . . . caught . . . off guard. The whale . . . was a big sperm whale . . . but he had . . . burns . . . scarring . . . across his head. Like . . . he'd been . . . put up hard . . . against hot coals."

Bullock watched the man's eye close in frustration. He couldn't shake the man to wakefulness. In fact, judging from the amount of damage that had been done to poor Clarence's hand, the professor knew he dared not touch Johnstone at all.

"What happened then, Mr. Johnstone?" Katharine asked.

"I don't . . . remember. I . . . don't know . . . if I even knew. Some . . . some*thing* . . . grabbed me. I felt . . . it wrap around me."

"The whale?" Bullock asked.

Johnstone swallowed hard, gasping for breath even harder than before. "I don't . . . know. It . . . couldn't have . . . been the whale. It was . . . something else. I was pulled . . . over *Meadowlark*'s . . . side. When I went under . . . the water . . . something pierced my . . . side. There was . . . something in the sea . . . with me."

"The whale?"

"Don't know. Maybe. I just remember . . . I wasn't alone. I heard it . . . talking . . . talking to me. There was a voice . . . a voice in my head . . . that wasn't . . . wasn't my own. I was scared. I fought. God, how I fought. I don't remember . . . getting free. But I must . . . must have gotten free. Or else I . . . I wouldn't be . . . here."

Before Bullock could ask another question, Johnstone's blemished eye suddenly erupted. Liquid and matter landed on the bloodstained sheet covering the man's chest. Then the eyeball descended within the man's head, like something was pulling the eye down inside the skull.

Johnstone gagged and choked. He turned his head violently, raking off a flap of meat and skin from one cheek and revealing the bone beneath. Vomit discharged from the man's mouth and nose. Gore, fluid, and blood ejected onto the sheet, splattering widely enough to chase Bullock back in his chair.

The paroxysm shuddered through Johnstone. When the seizure ended, so did Johnstone's life. His corpse dropped back into a supine position on the cot.

"Dear God," Bullock whispered. He glanced up from the dead man to his daughter. "Katharine."

She had her hand over her mouth. Her features had blanched white. Tears of disbelief and hurt and fear tracked down her face.

Bullock went to his daughter, wrapping an arm around her shoulders and escorting her from the tent into the fresh air outside. He stood beside her, not knowing what to say as she recovered her composure.

A dozen men sat around the fire and at the openings to their tents. All of them wore bleak looks.

Perkins got up from the small keg of molasses he was using for a seat. He took his pipe from his mouth and walked through a wreath of smoke.

"Is it done then?" Perkins asked. "The poor swab is done fer?"

Bullock nodded. "His name was Warren Johnstone. He was a sailor on a ship called *Meadowlark*. God rest his soul."

"There weren't nothin' ye could do fer it," Perkins said. "I'll round a burial detail together, an' we'll see to the buryin'."

"We'll bury the man later," Bullock said. "For now, there are still questions he might be able to answer."

"But the man is dead."

"That sad fact of affairs doesn't mean that the matter ends there," Bullock replied. He gazed down toward the sea where *Brown-Eyed Sue* sat at anchor. Only a few lanterns showed aboard her. "Something lies out there in that ocean, Mr. Perkins, and part of our duty here is to find out what that thing may be."

CHAPTER 5

Pacific Ocean 3° 28' S. Lat.—107° 12' W. Long.

DESPITE HOW SMALL a whaling ship looked against the vastness of the sea, Ethan Swain had forgotten how large such a vessel could seem when every inch had to be searched. According to Captain Folger's inventory, a pistol was missing from the ship's armory and had only just been discovered to be missing. At the captain's orders, Ethan and Larson had searched throughout the night, accompanied by men the second mate had chosen who were known to be loyal to him.

The rest of the crew knew the search was going on as well, though they didn't know what was being searched for. This wasn't the first search initiated aboard *Reliant*, but nothing as heavily controlled as a firearm had ever been taken.

In fact, as guarded as the ship's armory was, Ethan couldn't believe a weapon was actually missing and believed it would be found upon a recount of the pistols. He was certain that Folger and Larson were staging a show for the men.

The second shift was in full swing now, and the cutting in and removal of the whale's blubber continued. Most of the blubber had been stripped from the whale, going faster than Ethan had expected given everything that had gone on. The men cut the blubber from the carcass in long strips, yanking the blubber from the body like orange peel sections that were winched up and lowered into the hold to be cut into foot-square sections called Bible leaves.

More than twenty-four hours had passed since Ethan had last slept. His eyes burned from the whale hunt of the day before as well as suffering from the thick, black smoke from the tryworks as the blubber boiled all night. Even now, the acrid stench burned his nose and robbed him of any scent except the burned meat stink of the oil brewing in the two great iron pots. From a distance, he was certain the ship looked as though she were burning to the waterline.

Captain Folger stood on the stern deck in full uniform. Lincoln Stroud stood at his side, a sharpshooter's musket gripped in one hand. Stroud was the ship's third mate. Three other men, similarly armed, stood in a loose circle around the captain. The sharpshooters had been assigned to the crew at Folger's insistence, and it had become obvious they were there primarily to enforce the captain's orders.

Stroud, according to the stories Ethan had heard, was never a true sailor. He was a professional fighter, a man who had worked as a bouncer in bars, taverns, gambling halls, and whorehouses. He'd left New York, hunted by a rival gang, and signed aboard *Reliant* as a hired gun to keep the crew in line. Stroud was a man of medium size and dapper in his appearance, a man who would have looked at home as a deacon in a church rather than having the reputation of a stone-cold killer.

Folger was presenting a challenge, Ethan knew, letting the crew feel the heel of his boot across the backs of their necks. The crew resented Folger, and that resentment built as they talked louder and louder among themselves and more carefully watched Larson and Ethan cross the deck.

Creel Turpin sat amidships on the port side of the ship with most of the other men from the first group of harvesters. He rested his big arms on his bent knees, leaning on his back against the railing. Blood covered him from crown to toe. A bloody knife rested at his side, reminding Ethan that all of the crew were similarly armed.

Larson led the way to the aft companionway. Since the search had begun, none of the sailors had been allowed down into steerage, where their bunks were. With no place to sleep and the search in progress, none of the men had gotten to sleep any of their allotted six hours they were off shift.

Harvesting a whale was hard even with the on-again, off-again six-hour shifts, Ethan knew. And men pushed to the point of exhaustion made mistakes—with the knife, with the ropes, and around the boiling oil in the tryworks.

Death hung in the air. Ethan felt the specter's cold breath down the back of his neck. A storm was about to break over *Reliant,* and there was nothing he could do to stop it.

Larson's men hurried down the companionway. They were big and blustering, keeping their hands on their cutlass hilts.

Ethan followed in the wake of Larson and his goons. He made no effort to help them as they tore through the small, personal chests of the sailors.

Ethan felt certain that Larson and his cronies wouldn't find the missing pistol among the crew's personal effects. Any sailor worth his salt would have stashed the weapon elsewhere on the ship. Aboard a vessel of *Reliant*'s tonnage, there were any number of hiding places.

Larson stood watch as the two men with him bashed at the small locks holding the trunks closed with hammers taken from the tool kit of the ship's cooper. Locking mechanisms, some of them clever and having nothing to do with the ornate locks upon their lids, shattered and scattered across the rolling deck.

"Larson," one of the men called, standing with a chest held in his hands. "I found the pistol."

Ethan stepped forward then, enforcing his role as first mate aboard ship for the first time since the search had begun. "Where?" he demanded.

The sailor glared at Ethan in open defiance. His name was Miller, and he was one of the few that belonged to Larson from previous ships.

"Let him see it," Larson growled.

With obvious disrespect, Miller thrust the chest out for Ethan's inspection.

The long-barreled .58 Harper's Ferry flintlock pistol appeared massive in the small chest.

Panic clawed at the back of Ethan's throat, but he seized hold of the emotion and walled it away. "You or your men planted that weapon. No sailor in his right mind would store that pistol in his own kit."

Larson nodded and scratched his whiskered chin in speculation. "Aye. Mayhap ye're right. Mayhap we're dealin' with a madman what's come aboard our ship. Mayhap we fetched up the bastard just in time before he tried to kill the cap'n."

"That's not what I said."

Larson shrugged. "Whose name is on that chest, Miller?"

"You already know the name, don't you?" Ethan accused.

Larson only smiled and stepped back. His hand rested on the hilt of his cutlass. "Give me the name, Miller."

"The name it says here on this box is Timothy Madison."

Ethan felt like he'd taken a punch in the stomach. Of all the men on board the ship, Timothy would be the most likely to steal something—in fact, he had been accused of that on more than one occasion during the voyage they were currently on. But Timothy was also the most likely to be sly about his theft.

"Why did you set Timothy up?" Ethan demanded. But he knew why. After the rebellious attitude the crew had shown the night before, Larson had chosen to break them down again, to show them how powerless they were while they were aboard *Reliant*. Timothy Madison was going to be made into an example.

"Ye're gonna try to protect that man?" Larson snarled. "Timothy Madison is a thief."

"He's part of my boat crew," Ethan said.

"Only because ye wanted the bastard there where ye could keep an eye on him."

Ethan knew the accusation was true. Since Timothy had realized that Ethan was going to be keeping a close watch over him, his light-fingered ways had disappeared. Or they had become so modest that no one noticed.

"This ship is about to split apart at the seams," Larson said. "Ye know it, an' I know it. Cap'n Folger, he ain't any too wise in the ways of handlin' situations like these. That's why he's got Stroud an' his men. If'n this gets handled badly, why there's apt to be some men a-dyin' up there in the next few minutes."

"One of those men could be you," Ethan said.

"If'n we fight," Larson said, "me an' ye, that fight will spill over from belowdecks throughout the ship." He shook his head. "I won't back down. I ain't got it in me to do." He paused, his dark eyes searching Ethan's. "But ye will, won't ye? Ye'll back down an' give up one man if'n it'll save the lives of the others, won't ye?"

In that instant, Ethan understood the trap that had been laid for him. If he stood against Folger and Larson, the crew would split, and a mutiny would ensue. But if he supported Larson's claim that Timothy had stolen the pistol, the crew would turn from him, and he'd have no choice but to side with the captain and the second mate.

"Ah," Larson growled happily, "ye see the way of it, then. I told the cap'n that I thought this might bring ye into our camp, so to speak."

Ethan stood mute, frozen silent by the cold helplessness that filled him.

Larson nodded toward the aft companionway. "So what's it to be, Ethan Swain? Are ye a-gonna force the cap'n's hand over a known thief an' get them sailors what ye call friends killed in the bargain? Or are ye a-gonna save what ye can of the crew?"

Ethan wanted to move to stop the man, but he knew that Folger would do exactly as Larson had stated. The captain had already proven he didn't know how to handle the crew. At this point, any move that might be misconstrued as mutinous would be dealt with lethally.

The pistol that Miller had "found" in Timothy Madison's gear was a grim reminder that Folger kept all the ship's weapons under lock and key.

Larson headed up the aft companionway. "Are ye a-comin' then? The cap'n might not take so kindly to ye not bein' on hand."

Clambering out onto the deck, Ethan blinked his eyes against the harsh brightness. While they'd been in the crew's quarters the sun had burned through the cloud layer. Sunlight dappled the green water of the Pacific Ocean. The rollers looked like they were crusted with diamonds.

The men continued working, cutting the blubber free, feeding the squares of meat into the tryworks, and straining out the skin cracklings to feed the flames that gathered around the two boiling pots of oil. Two men worked in leather aprons and used long-handled scoops to dip the oil from the tryworks into barrels. Later, the oil would be filtered again and properly stored in casks.

Creel and the first group still sat at the portside railing. Every man was attentive and alert, watchful of Captain Folger's chosen men and Ethan.

"Mr. Larson," Folger said. "Did you find my missing pistol?"

"Aye, Cap'n."

"Where was that weapon, Mr. Larson?" Folger asked.

"Crew's quarters, Cap'n," Larson answered. "Found that pistol in a chest that belonged to Timothy Madison."

"No, Cap'n! That's a lie! I ain't taken no weapon from the ship's armory!" Timothy stepped out away from the second group of workers. Sunlight glinted on the bloody blade he carried. He'd been helping cut up the whale strips into Bible leaves down in the hold.

"Mr. Larson," Folger said, his round face filled with dark excitement, "apprehend that man. I want fifty lashes delivered to him, and thirty days in the brig spent with only bread and water."

"Nooooo!" Timothy turned to Creel and the other sailors, seeking support.

All of the crew turned away from Timothy.

Ethan felt sick. This had been Folger and Larson's plan from the beginning. They had known that no one would stand up for Timothy Madison, that the crew barely tolerated the man because of his petty thieving ways and because no one liked his big-mouthed stories and coarse humor. In turning away from Timothy, though, they'd also be turning away from each other, creating doubt that they could work together as a team.

Larson started for Timothy.

Braying fearfully, Timothy dodged the second mate. He slipped on the blood and gore covering the deck. He almost fell into the pots of whale oil boiling on the tryworks before he recovered his balance.

Miller lunged at Timothy but slipped in the blood and the grease staining the deck and went sprawling, fetching up hard against the railing. Then Timothy was around the smoking tryworks and running toward Ethan.

Unable to turn his back on the man, Ethan stood his ground. Timothy seized a double fistful of Ethan's shirt. "Please! I'm beggin' ye, Ethan!"

Ethan gripped the man's hands, but he didn't try to force Timothy away. "There's nothing I can do, Timothy."

"Ye're the first mate!" Timothy railed, as Larson and his two cronies closed in on him. "Ye're supposed to represent the crew's interests!"

I am, Ethan forced himself to remember. *I'm preventing a mass execution.* He knew that if he stood against the captain and Larson, then that most of the crew would stand with him. But he was also aware that Stroud and the other three men surrounding Folger were armed with a brace of pistols each as well as cutlasses. The ship's swords, like the ship's small arms, were locked in the armory.

"It's only fifty lashes," Ethan told Timothy in a quiet, desperate voice.

"*Only fifty lashes!*" Timothy gasped in dismay. "Are ye a-listenin' to yerself, Ethan Swain? Larson will strip me down to bone in those fifty lashes."

"I won't let them kill you," Ethan whispered fiercely. "God as my witness, I won't let them kill you." He kept his words low so that no one else could hear him. "Get ahold of yourself, Timothy. If you don't, you're going to get other people killed."

The sailors talked among themselves, their voices growing stronger and louder.

Larson and Miller grabbed Timothy by the arms and forcibly hauled him away from Ethan. The screaming man's hands ripped Ethan's ragged shirt. Timothy fought, yelling shrilly as fear possessed him and lent him a madman's strength. Fierce as Timothy was, though, he was no match for the brutality that Larson dealt. The second mate elbowed Timothy in the face, splitting his lips and knocking a front tooth out. Larson kicked his captive in the shins in an effort to hobble him, then he stamped Timothy's bare feet.

Crimson bubbles burst from Timothy's broken mouth as he screamed in pain and fear. He choked and cursed Larson and Miller as he fought them, tangling them all up so that they slipped and slid across the blood-drenched and oil-soaked deck.

Larson fought back, striking Timothy repeatedly in the face with his fist. He head-butted the sailor once, momentarily dazing him and driving him back. But the fear that claimed Timothy's senses wouldn't be denied. He kept pushing and pulling and fighting and trying to escape till the three men were up against the starboard railing where the whale was tied up.

Unable to stand apart from the struggle anymore, Ethan started forward, not knowing what he was going to do when he reached the three men.

"Mr. Swain." Folger's voice rang out clear and strident over the ship. "Stand your ground right there, sir, or by God you'll get a reckoning yourself."

Reluctantly, Ethan stopped. He suddenly realized that Creel and some of the other sailors had gone into motion behind him. Sides were already being drawn.

"Aye, Cap'n," Ethan said.

For a moment, Larson and Miller appeared to gain the upper hand on Timothy. Then Timothy bit Miller on the hand, causing the man to step back. Too late, Ethan saw the flintlock pistol sticking out of Larson's waistband. Before Ethan could shout a warning, Timothy ripped the weapon free of Larson's pants.

Timothy cocked and leveled the pistol at Larson's head. The barrel held steady only inches from the second mate's flesh. Everyone aboard *Reliant* froze.

Slowly, Larson spread his hands away from his body. He looked at Timothy over the .58-caliber pistol's long barrel. "Put the pistol down, Timothy Madison," Larson said. "Put it down, an' I'll see to it ye live."

"You lie!" Timothy blinked rapidly. "Ye will have me killed right away after this, I know ye will!"

"No," Larson said. Miller started to step forward, but the second mate waved him back.

"Ye've been a-ridin' us hard these past few weeks, ye an' the cap'n," Timothy said. "More'n most men could bear. Now look at what ye've gone an' done!"

"Timothy," Ethan called. He didn't know if the man was even capable of hearing in his present state, but if there was any one voice aboard *Reliant* that Timothy Madison might be willing to listen to, he suspected it was his own.

"Damn me, but I've had a run of bad luck, I have, Ethan!" Timothy gasped. "Do ye see what this bastard has up an' made me do?"

"I see," Ethan said, "but it doesn't have to end like this."

"How else is this gonna end?" Timothy asked. The pistol wavered almost uncontrollably in his hand. "I'm a thief an' a coward, Ethan. Ye know that. If'n I put this pistol down, things will go hard on me. Larson an' Cap'n Folger will see to that."

"No," Ethan said, taking a step toward Timothy. If he could get close enough, he was certain he could seize the pistol and control the situation.

"Ye'd lie to me, too, Ethan," Timothy cried. "I know ye would. To save yerself an' them others. I know ye would, an' I don't hold it agin ye." He took a deep, snuffling breath, then nodded. "But mayhap I can make it better fer all of ye. Larson an' the cap'n, why they done trapped me an' did fer me, but I can make it better on ye."

Without warning, Timothy yanked the weapon up over Larson's shoulder, aiming at Folger.

"No!" Ethan shouted.

Looking down over the pistol's barrel, Timothy screamed, "Die, ye black-hearted pig, an'—"

"Stroud!" Larson thundered.

Ethan watched helplessly as Stroud brought his musket up to his shoulder and fired almost in the same motion. The puff of smoke from powder burning on the frizzen puffed out just a moment before the powder in the musket barrel exploded and sent the ball whizzing through the air.

The heavy ball caught Timothy Madison in the center of his chest before he fired the pistol and caused a bloody rose to blossom against his shirt immediately. Knocked back, Timothy lost his hold on the pistol and dropped the weapon to the deck as he fell over the ship's side.

Ethan broke into a run at once, bending down to take up the pistol, then gazing over the ship's side.

"He's dead," someone said.

"Ball took him dead center in the chest," someone else said. "I saw it with me own two eyes."

Ethan stared into the green water. Shadows from the whale's stripped carcass darkened the sea between the corpse and the whaleship. Pieces of ragged and bloody blubber floated on the sea. Seagulls strutted on the whale, tearing pieces of meat free with their sharp, cruel beaks, then crowing warnings to other birds that dared encroach on their claimed territory. On the other side of the dead whale, the triangular dorsal fins of four sharks cut the surface.

"There!" Creel shouted, pointing.

Incredibly, Ethan saw Timothy float toward the ocean's surface. The man's legs kicked feebly and only one arm seemed capable of movement. His eyes were wide, as if amazed or surprised. His mouth moved slowly, and a thin trickle of blood spun from his lips. He flailed again, then his eyes locked on Ethan.

Knowing the wounded man wasn't going to make it to the surface and that Timothy didn't know how to properly swim, Ethan kicked out of his boots. He scooped the pistol from the deck and thrust the weapon at Creel. "Hold this," he said.

Creel took the pistol.

Before Creel could ask the question that was on his lips, Ethan stepped up onto the starboard railing and dropped overboard into the shark-infested waters.

CHAPTER 6

Easter Island, Chile 27° 9' S. Lat.—109° 26' W. Long.

THE AUTOPSY ON Warren Johnstone hadn't taken long. Whatever had been injected into the man's body had almost destroyed everything within him. While Professor Bullock had watched, even bones had dissolved. Most of the skeleton had been rendered brittle, and the professor could only suspect the same foul venom that had filled the dead man had been the cause.

Perkins and some of the shore team had seen to the grave digging and the interment. For an hour, the men had labored with picks and shovels, first breaking into the stony ground, then scooping out the hole.

Captain Mayhew had reluctantly given over a small bit of secondhand canvas to serve as the dead man's shroud. In short order, the grave was a mound of rocks marked by a small wooden cross.

Katharine stood at her father's side. Quiet tears stole down her cheeks and drew the attention of the rough sailing men who made up the burial detail. Shamed by Katharine's emotion over the dead man, the sailors took their woolen hats off and bowed their heads.

Despite the willingness Mayhew had shown to undertake the burial duties, he didn't mind letting Bullock know how having to lie at anchor chafed him.

While part of the shore crew had prepared the grave, Bullock had compelled Mayhew to send search parties out across the beach and through the nearby shallows in an effort to find more bodies.

Katharine took up the journal she'd brought with her when the grave digging had commenced. After Bullock had realized that nothing more could be gained from Warren Johnstone's body, he'd sent for Perkins and made the arrangements. Katharine had asked for time of her own, and the professor had graciously granted it. When he'd been called down to the funeral, Bullock had found his daughter sketching in her journal higher up the sloping land leading to the sea.

"I was working on the drawings from the autopsy," Katharine said, "while I was sitting out here. It's never truly quiet by the sea's edge, but I felt calm out here. Then, when I saw the men opening the grave, I felt moved to turn my attentions to something else."

Bullock watched the journal pages flip by. Several partially completed sketches of the autopsy, laid out in the abbreviated manner Katharine had perfected for her drawing assignments, covered the pages. Combined with her phenomenal eye for detail and her memory, the bare bones of the sketches would be fleshed out in amazing detail when she finished.

A half dozen other pictures also caught Bullock's eye. There were three small sketches of the gravesite on the same page: one before the ground had been broken, one while Perkins and his men had dug, and one after the grave had been filled and the wooden marker placed.

"I want to finish the sketch of the gravesite completely," Katharine said. "Later, perhaps, I can render the gravesite again on a proper canvas and in color. If Warren Johnstone had a wife or a mother, then I'll send that painting to her. That way, she can more properly see this place where he rests. If she wants such a painting, of course. Some people might think a painting of a grave would be a garish and uncouth thing."

Pride and love for his daughter swelled within Bullock. "That's a fine idea, Katharine. Take as much time as you need, but make sure you never get out of sight of Perkins or one of the men from the shore party."

"I won't."

Bullock left her there and walked back up to the camp.

Clarence, the young sailor who had grabbed Warren Johnstone the night before, still lay in a laudanum-induced slumber in the tent. When he was conscious earlier that morning, he'd complained of the pain in his hand. Bullock had freely given the medication.

Squatting beside Clarence, Bullock carefully unwrapped the bandages covering the young sailor's injured hand. The foul odor from the oozing sores on the hand almost made the professor sick even though he'd thought himself prepared for the experience.

The crusty scabs broke, and bloody pus ran from the blemished areas as Bullock unveiled them. Clarence stirred fitfully, but remained deeply within the narcotic effects of the laudanum.

"Is the boy gonna keep the hand?"

Startled, Bullock glanced up to find Perkins leaning into the tent with concern written heavily on his weathered features. "Yes," Bullock replied. "He'll keep the hand, and I believe he'll be able to use it properly. Provided he works with it after it is healed."

"Fair enough." Perkins pushed his cap back with a thumb. "We've had us enough bad luck on this trip. Time to be shut of such things."

Carefully, Bullock rewrapped Clarence's injured hand. "Have you ever seen a wound like this before, Mr. Perkins?" the professor asked.

"Can't say that I have."

"Do you get spiders down in the hold?" Bullock pushed himself to his feet with effort. Staying up nearly all night and working on the autopsy starting with the dawn had nearly sapped his reserves.

"Aye," Perkins answered. "'Course we get spiders now an' again. Get more'n a few rats, too."

"Have you ever been bitten by one of those spiders?"

Perkins shrugged. "I have. They's all kind of vermin what share a sailor's bed."

"Did you ever have any reactions to the spider bites, Mr. Perkins?"

Perkins nodded. "Now an' again. Mostly they just itched somethin' fierce, but sometimes they hurt."

"Ever have any of them make boils or pustules?"

"Aye."

Bullock recalled spider bites he'd had himself and seen on other people. "What did you do with the boil?"

"Lanced it. Or cut it open with a knife."

"But the wound didn't heal very quickly, did it?"

"No. Ye can't ever completely draw the venom out of a spider bite, I've found."

"But when the wound finally healed, what happened to your flesh?"

"Got a bit of a rot spot in it," Perkins said. "Most of them spider bites, why they left holes in whatever part of ye they bit."

"That effect of the spider's venom is called necrosis," Bullock said. "The venom essentially kills part of the body's tissues. It takes time for the affected area to heal over and expunge and replace the rest of the diseased flesh. In North America, the brown recluse spider is the most plentiful of the lot, but the tarantula and the black widow spider are equally harmful."

Perkins was quiet and thoughtful for a moment. "Are ye a-thinkin' that young sailor was hauled off his ship by a spider that lives in the sea? Because if'n ye are, I'm here to tell ye I've never seen such a thing. I ain't even heard of one even in a sailor's most wildest tales."

"There are spiders that deign to live in the water, Mr. Perkins. They're called *Argyroneta aquatica,* which translates to 'with a silvery net,' and they are a genus unto themselves. They actually capture air bubbles and carry them down to their watery nests. But none of those spiders are of sufficient size to pluck a man from a ship or survive on their own in the middle of a great body of water like the Pacific Ocean. Also, they live in freshwater, as long as it's not running." Bullock reflected on his encounter with the creatures while on a biological study in New York. Flora and fauna were particular favorites of his, after the studies he enjoyed regarding past civilizations. He was still poring over the information about new animals and insects gleaned during the recent Lewis and Clark expedition to the West.

"I've seen other bites that leave holes the same way," Perkins said.

"Bites from what?"

"Jellyfish for one," the sailor answered. "An' last time I was in Boston, I talked to an old seaman that had been impressed by the British at the end of the last war while he was still a young man. During his voyages with the British, he went out to Australia." Perkins stared at Bullock. "Ye've heard of Australia, haven't ye?"

"Yes," Bullock assured the man. The professor was well aware of the newest continent to be discovered, and knew enough to be extremely curious about the species oddities in Australia.

"Well, this sailor showed me a scar on his arm," Perkins went on. "Told me he'd been bitten by a blue-ringed octopus."

"I've never heard of such a thing," Bullock said.

"Neither had I," Perkins agreed. "I thought he was tellin' a whopper, I did. But maybe not. He said ye could hold the thing in yer hand. That's one of the reasons I got to where I believed the man. Most sailors, they start in a-lyin', things just get bigger and bigger."

The idea of a venomous octopus lodged itself deep in Bullock's mind. One of the most legendary sea creatures of all was the great kraken, the giant squid that was capable of dragging a large three-masted ship under the sea.

"Do ye think whatever done fer that young sailor is still a-waitin' out there?" Perkins's voice was soft and uncertain, as if he were ashamed that he'd even be asking.

"Yes," a low vibrant voice answered from behind Bullock. "The monster waits in the deep water. It knows when men are about, and it lives to hunt them these days."

Startled by the voice, Bullock spun around to stare at the speaker.

The man was old and wizened, stoop-shouldered and narrow, little more than skin over bones. His hair was cottony gray, matching his wispy beard. His eyes were deep-set, haunted. He held a long pole in his right hand. The tattered remnants of dungarees hung about his bony hips like swaddling cloth.

Perkins moved smoothly, lifting the flintlock musket from where the weapon's butt had been resting on the top of his right foot. The musket came to his shoulder in what seemed to be a twinkling and cocked with a metallic click that filled the camp.

"Stand yer ground!" Perkins growled.

"I mean you no harm," the old man said. His left eye caught the light then, glowing a pale blue that didn't match the dark brown luster of his right eye. He made no effort to move. He fixed his good eye on Bullock. "I came to talk to you."

"Why?"

"You have an interest in the monster that killed the man you pulled from the sea."

"You know what killed that man?" Bullock asked.

"Yes." The old man looked out to sea. "It is an evil thing."

"What is it?"

The old man spoke indecipherable words.

Bullock shook his head. "I don't understand."

"Those are words of my people. They mean 'Death-in-the-Water.'"

"You have seen the creature?" Bullock asked.

"Yes."

"What is it?"

The old man shook his head. "Death-in-the-Water wears the mask of a whale. Many things wear masks to hide their true natures. Snakes are sometimes beautiful to see, but their colors hide their great fangs."

Other men in the shore party started to gather around. All of them raised their weapons as well. Several of them gazed around the hard broken terrain as if expecting cannibals to leap from hiding at any moment.

Moving slowly, offering no threat to Perkins or the old man, Bullock gripped the flintlock musket's barrel and pushed it toward the ground. "Mr. Perkins," he spoke calmly, "I don't think we have anything to worry about here."

"Those that accompanied me here left me on my own," the old man said. "For many years, the Europeans and South Americans have taken my people prisoner and sold them into slavery. I have stood on the slave blocks and served masters in New York City. I came only because of Death-in-the-Water. In the hopes that you hunted the creature." He wet his lips with his tongue, for the first time betraying nervousness. "I also came knowing that you might try again to enslave me."

"I won't let you be enslaved," Bullock responded. The mere idea was repugnant. "But I would like to know more of this creature."

"Then," the old man said, "I will tell you of it."

CHAPTER 7

Pacific Ocean 3° 28' S. Lat.—107° 12' W. Long.

ETHAN SWAIN PLUNGED into the sea feet first, toes pointing down to lessen the impact against the water. The drop wasn't much, but the waves were uncertain, and he'd seen bad things happen even on short dives. Dropping into the sea while sharks savaged the whale's corpse almost guaranteed events would turn out badly.

Light penetrated the shallows of the sea easily. Ethan peered up to get his bearings. *Reliant* remained to port and the whale to starboard. Timothy Madison—kicking weakly, silvery bubbles bursting from his mouth, crimson still leaking from his lips and the hole in his chest—hung in the water in front of him.

Swimming close, desperately aware that he was taking his own life into his hands by coming within reach of the wounded and drowning man, Ethan seized Timothy's shirt in his balled left fist. *Please let the fabric remain strong.* Then he kicked for the surface as Timothy gripped his forearm and held on for dear life.

Fear pounded inside Ethan, lending him strength and speed. Even with Timothy's near deadweight holding him back, he came head and shoulders out of the water.

"Creel!" Ethan yelled, looking up at the sailors lining *Reliant*'s starboard railing. "A rope! Quickly!"

Creel disappeared instantly.

"Ethan," Timothy croaked in a weak voice.

"I've got you," Ethan said, but in truth he was barely forestalling their return to the depths. "Just lie back and let me help you stay up."

"I don't want to die," Timothy whispered.

Ethan slid through Timothy's grip, coming around behind him to hook his forearm under the other man's chin so he could keep his face up out of the water.

"I'm not going to let you die," Ethan said.

"Shark!"

"Bastard's comin' from the starboard end, Ethan!"

"Swim, Ethan!" Holy yelled down. "Swim for your life!"

Sweeping his arm through the water, Ethan peered behind him, gazing over his shoulder. A triangular fin cut through the water in front of the whale's head, slowly and sedately, then glided into the narrow channel between the whaleship and the corpse.

"Creel!" Ethan shouted.

"Rope!" Creel shouted back.

In the next instant, the braided hemp splashed into the sea less than a yard from Ethan's head. A loop, looking suspiciously like a hangman's noose, floated on the water. Ethan grabbed the rope and tried to pull the loop over his head and one shoulder as the triangular fin sped straight for him.

"Pull!" someone yelled.

But the order was given prematurely.

The rope leapt from Ethan's fingers, burning across his neck and the side of his face, catching his ear and almost ripping the bit of flesh from his head. He hadn't had time to get the rope properly seated, but he kept his fingers wrapped tightly around the loop. Incredibly, for a moment, he held on as the combined strength of the sailors pulling on the rope lifted Timothy and him partly from the water. Pain lashed through Ethan, leading him to believe that his shoulder was coming out of its socket.

The surge of water moving ahead of the shark slapped against the backs of Ethan's calves. That was the only warning he got before he was yanked from the rope.

At first, with the way his senses were blurred from the fear and the exertion of the moment blending with the unbelievable encounter, Ethan thought the shark had gotten hold of him. Eyes wide open, he plunged beneath the water again, going deep into the sea and aware of the sinuous body of the shark heaving against him. The creature's rough skin rasped at his own and tore his shirt.

Timothy's hands gripped Ethan's arms with renewed strength. The sailor had been spun around by the impact, almost torn from Ethan's grip. His eyes were wide, venomous in the dimmer light of the sea. His mouth gaped, and bloody bubbles spat forth in a whirling rush.

Ethan saw then that the shark had bitten into one of Timothy's legs. The shark flicked its tail again, then yanked a second time. Unable to brace himself properly while being dragged toward the bottom of the sea, Ethan watched helplessly as Timothy was torn from his grip.

A shadow flicked into view from the left, racing through the sea. A second shark caught Timothy's head in its powerful jaws. An explosion of crimson clouded the sea as Timothy's head was torn from his shoulders.

Ethan swam toward the surface, kicking his feet and pulling with his hands. The rope plopped back down into the water, and the noose floated on the water.

The second shark opened its greedy jaws and swallowed Timothy's head. Smoothly as a seasoned oarsman's delicate stroke, the shark came about, twisting so that it studied Ethan with one soot black eye. Then it flicked its tail and swam straight at him like an arrow from a bow.

Knowing he would never reach the rope before the shark overtook him, Ethan let himself float in the water, drawing his legs in so he could kick out, shoving his left arm out so he could grab the water and turn himself around. He closed his right fist around the handle of his fighting knife and drew the blade free of the sheath.

A third shark came up from under the whale's bulk. Instead of coming for Ethan as he'd feared, the third hunter seemed content to wait for the attack of the other.

In that frozen moment, as the shark bore down on him, Ethan surrendered to the inevitability of the attack, certain he would not survive. But the stubbornness that had earned his mother's ire upon occasion and his father's pride at other times stayed with him.

When the shark was close enough, Ethan kicked out, putting his body into motion. Then he caught the water with his open left hand and pulled himself to the side. The shark grazed him, rasping its rough skin across his stomach.

By instinct honed in many face-to-face battles aboard ship, Ethan's right hand flashed forward. He held the fighting blade in an experienced knife fighter's grip, edge out and running parallel to his forearm, so long it stretched almost to his elbow. The razor-sharp edge bit deeply into the shark's flesh and skated half the length of the hunter's body.

Blood gushed into the ocean from the long wound in the shark's side, creating a thick dark cloud that muddied the water.

Evidently stunned by the damage that had been dealt it, the shark swam away. It didn't get far before the third shark attacked. In the blink of an eye, the third shark's jaws ripped a chunk of meat the size of a pie plate from its victim's back.

Keeping the knife in his fist, his lungs burning for air and the fear still loose inside him, Ethan kicked again and swam for the loop of rope. He surfaced, coming up with his head and one arm surging through the hemp circle.

He sucked in one quick breath and shouted, "*Pull!*"

"Pull!" Creel echoed. "Pull, God damn yer eyes if I find any of ye slackin'!"

The line whined as it whipped over the railing, reminding Ethan of the way dry line payed out behind a harpoon. The crushing grip around his chest released for a moment, and he dropped a few inches: then the men pulling him up got fresh grips and yanked him higher, hauling him from the water. He rose, desperately watching the shark hurtling at him through the water.

Without warning, closer than Ethan had dared think, the shark lunged up from the water. The carnivore rose from the ocean well past its midpoint.

Sunlight flashed on the rows of serrated teeth that filled the shark's gaping pink-and-red maw. Ethan pulled his feet up, just clearing the liquid snap of the great jaws closing. Then the shark fell back into the ocean.

Near the top of the railing, Creel caught Ethan's outstretched hand and hauled him onto the ship's deck.

"Are ye all right?" Creel asked.

Ethan nodded.

"What about Timothy?" Robert asked.

Ethan shook his head. "The sharks took him."

Holy stood there as well, a sad look in his eyes. "Then I will take special care when I pray to God tonight. That the Lord will grant mercy on his soul and that his passing was quick and painless."

It was quick, Ethan thought, but he doubted that Timothy's death was painless.

"Mr. Swain." Captain Folger's voice rang out over the ship.

Ethan turned, suddenly realizing again that not all the danger surrounding *Reliant* and her crew had passed. His voice tightened so much that he was afraid he wouldn't be able to speak.

"Aye, Cap'n," Ethan said.

Folger looked troubled. "That man didn't have to end up dead."

Merl Porter, a sailor who had come up from North Carolina, cursed virulently, talking about Folger and his mother and their mutual infatuation with diseased sheep.

"The hell ol' Timothy didn't have to come up dead like that," Merl exclaimed. "Ye an' yer pet barracuda there wouldn't a-had it any other way."

The crew suddenly formed a line, most of the men drawing up behind and to the side of Ethan. In seconds, they had chosen him as their leader.

"Steady on," Creel whispered at Ethan's side. "This has to be done. Ol' Bill was right about this. He seen it comin', an' now's the time to be done with it."

"No," Ethan said. If the crew mutinied, Folger's men would kill several of them, and Ethan's sailing career would be over. He'd be lucky to ship out as an able-bodied seaman, and he'd never know a captain's braid on his shoulders. Worse yet, more of his past might come to light. He could still yet hang at the end of a gibbet for the things he'd been forced to do and been part of.

Stroud stepped forward and cocked his musket. He pointed the long barrel in the direction of the crew, but he kept his eye fixed on Ethan.

"First one makes a move against the cap'n," Stroud roared, "I'm a-puttin' a ball through yer face, Swain. Ye got me word on that."

For a moment, Ethan almost let his anger go unchecked. All Stroud had was one shot, and then Ethan knew he could be in the middle of the man, raking the fighting knife all the way from Stroud's crotch to his windpipe.

Ethan made himself breathe out and wash the image from his mind. Those days, God help him, those bloody days were behind him.

Teresa was behind him.

But he still remembered her crimson-stained face and the maniacal child's grin she'd worn while holding up Cat's-Eyes John's severed head for inspection.

"Ye can't kill us all, Stroud," one of the crewmen shouted.

"Maybe not," Stroud replied, "but I'm bettin' that we can put no few of ye down if'n ye decide ye wanna takes yer chances. I'm gonna kill Swain fer certain, then we'll see which of ye I kills next."

Uncertainty cycled through the crew. Ethan felt the emotion shift in them, like a nervous hound facing a master who was considerate when sober and brutal when drunk. They waited, like the hound, for a clear indication of what Folger was going to do.

"Ye men stand down there!" Larson ordered. A few of his toadies still stood behind him.

"To hell with ye, Larson!" one of the sailors behind Ethan barked.

The crew's mood turned even uglier. All of them awaited Folger's next words, wanting to know which way to take the confrontation. The battle balanced precariously on the edge of a knife.

Folger hesitated, then started to speak.

Not trusting Folger to be able effectively to hold the crew under his command, Ethan stepped forward and turned to face the crew behind him. "Stand your ground!" he ordered.

Creel glared at Ethan with dark displeasure. "Ethan—"

Ethan cut the man off. He knew after he did what he felt compelled to do that Creel would probably never feel the same way about him. Nor would any other sailor who was sympathetic to his cause.

"Stand your ground!" Ethan roared again. "By God, if a man raises a hand to the cap'n, I'll take it the same as if he raised his hand to me!"

"Is that how it is with ye, then, Swain?" Merl Porter demanded. He was a hulking brute of a man, broad-shouldered and thick from long, hard years as a cargo handler before he'd signed on as a greenhand. Coarse blond hair bleached almost white from the sun stuck out in all directions. White eyebrows looked like wooly caterpillars, one of them split from a deep cut that had left a crooked scar trailing up his forehead. His nose was crooked, mute testimony to the fights he'd had in bars and saloons in the dockyards where he'd worked.

Without warning, Ethan backhanded Merl in the face hard enough to burst the man's lips and send him backward two staggering steps. Blood dribbled down over his whiskered chin as surprise and a murderous intent filled his eyes.

"Are you going to lead these men?" Ethan demanded, turning all his attention to Merl and taking a step forward in pursuit. "Do want to take a turn trying to get back there at the captain before one of Stroud's men cuts you down?"

Growling in rage, Merl heaved himself forward, never realizing that Ethan still clutched the fighting knife along his arm. Ethan swept the man's hands away with his right forearm, taking care to keep the knife turned away from his opponent. Stepping to his right, Ethan powered his left fist into Merl's chin, knocking the man backward through the crowd of seamen.

Losing the struggle to stay on his feet, Merl tripped and landed on his butt.

His eyes glazed for a moment, but he forced himself back up, growling curses. The crew around him cheered him on.

Bobbing and weaving, taking a quick step back, then darting in again to land another left jab to Merl's face, Ethan kept up a steady barrage of blows with his fist, forearms, and elbows. He chopped at Merl like a logger felling a tree, working on inch after telling inch. Still moving, Ethan stepped in beside the man before Merl could turn to face him. Ethan kicked the backs of Merl's knees, causing them to collapse beneath him.

When Merl tried to push himself back to his feet, Ethan flipped the fighting knife over in his hand. The bright blade glittered in the sunlight, then came to a rest with the tip resting lightly under Merl's chin.

"No," Ethan said, gazing into the man's hate-filled eyes. "You've had enough."

"I'm just . . ." Merl wheezed, "just gettin' started. Ye must be . . . pretty tuckered out by now."

"If we keep at this," Ethan stated evenly, "I'm going to have to hurt you. Maybe you'll even make me kill you. I don't want that, but if I have to kill you, I'm going to do it now." He paused. "Do you understand me, Merl?"

"I understand ye," Merl said, grimacing.

Warily, never taking his eyes completely off Merl, Ethan stared down the rest of the crewmen who had been ready to charge the stern of the ship. Creel and most of the others made no secret of how they felt.

"I signed papers back in Nantucket," Ethan said, talking loudly enough that all the men and the captain could hear him. He kept his words calm and steadfast. "Those papers were signed with men I've known all my life." He took a deep breath and let it out. "Maybe the ship's articles don't mean much to some of you, but they mean something to me. I gave my word when I signed them. When I go back to Nantucket, I want to do it right. I want to go with my head held high. I want to know, and I want those men to know, that I gave this voyage everything that was within my power to give."

"Ye'll die, Ethan Swain," Merl promised. "When we shove yer body into the ocean fer the fishes to take, why then ye'll know that ye gave this voyage everythin' ye had."

Ethan shoved his face into the other man's, taking away his personal space. "Do you think so?"

"Aye," Merl growled, and his bad breath pushed into Ethan's face like wet bread dough.

"Then you're a stupid man, Merl Porter," Ethan accused flatly.

Merl trembled with anger. As big as he was, Ethan was certain that no one had ever before humbled the big sailor as he found himself humbled at that moment.

"There are men," Ethan said softly, "who would slit your gullet for the threat you just made." And he tried not to remember that he'd once been one of them. But those were different times, in a past that now belonged to another man.

Merl swallowed hard.

Ethan swung his gaze on the crew. "Even if you succeed in your mutiny, how many of you are going to be left? Will there be enough of you to assemble a proper crew to sail this ship? Have any of you given any thought to that?"

None of the crew had an answer. Even Creel dropped his eyes when Ethan met his gaze directly.

"And how many of you know how to use a sextant?" Ethan demanded.

Again, there was no answer.

"You're out near the heart of a pitiless sea," Ethan yelled, and for a moment he remembered the dead man he'd found as a boy. "There's no room for mistakes out here."

The men hung their heads and looked impotent. Ethan knew his words were wreaking havoc with the precarious confidence the men maintained of being able to captain their own destinies. When he'd first started as a third mate, Ethan had very nearly decided to stop being a sailor because the mates above him and the captain had treated him like he'd known nothing. But he'd learned.

"Say some of you actually live through the weapons the cap'n and his men bring to bear on you," Ethan said, "and you get charge of the ship. Then what?"

The silence hung over the deck, broken only by the ring of rigging against the masts.

"Even if there are enough of you to man *Reliant* safely—" Ethan said.

"Which I guarantee there won't be," Stroud interrupted gruffly, shifting the musket meaningfully.

"—you haven't even planned your next step," Ethan finished. "What would you do with this ship and all the oil aboard her?"

"We ain't thieves, Ethan," Creel answered.

Ethan turned on his friend and shipmate, knowing that he couldn't back off if he was going to save them from themselves and from Captain Folger. "So what would you do, Creel? Take *Reliant* back to Nantucket?"

"Boston," Creel said stubbornly.

"Fine," Ethan said. "There you are in port, and someone asks you what's become of the cap'n of record aboard *Reliant*. What are you going to tell them?"

"We'll tell them the truth," Merl replied, wiping at his broken lips with the back of his hand. "That the cap'n was a heartless bastard an' we heaved his arse over the side."

A few of the men started to cheer.

Ethan put more force in his voice. "What you'd be admitting to is murdering the ship's officers. Have you any idea of what the dock authority would do with the lot of you?"

Creel didn't flinch. "They'd hang us, lads. As sure as the sun sets in the west, they'd hang us all."

"That's right," Ethan said. "They'd hang the lot of you. Of course, that's only those of you that survived facing the muskets Stroud and his men are holding on you."

"We don't have to take the ship back," Donald Hackett said. He was big and black, one of five slaves who had run away from the South, had counterfeit papers made, and signed on with *Reliant*. Whaling crews always had men like him aboard.

"Take the ship an' run," Creel said, "an' we'd be hunted down as thieves an' pirates."

"You'd be hunted," Ethan said. "Everywhere you went, you'd be hunted." He drove his words like nails into a coffin.

"Ethan has the right of it," Holy said, stepping forward to stand at Ethan's side. "All of you have been so wrapped up in getting your nerve up that you haven't thought past that moment. God placed you upon this earth to persevere, not to become self-destructive."

Holy's words, delivered with quick conviction and the rolling cadence that was his by his training in the priest school, had an effect on the men. They calmed.

Ethan gazed at the crew, knowing he had their attention, knowing he had them thinking. At least that was a step in the right direction.

Creel fixed Ethan. "They killed Timothy, Ethan. They killed him in cold blood."

"Timothy Madison hisself had a pistol," Larson said before Ethan could respond.

"A pistol," Ethan responded, turning to face the man, "that you made sure he could get by standing so close to him while you placed him under arrest."

"He stole another like it," Larson argued.

"That's what you say," Ethan said. "But the truth of the matter is that anyone could have put the missing pistol into Timothy Madison's kit."

"We found it there," Larson insisted. "You were standin' there when we found it."

"Creel," Ethan said, sticking out his hand without looking around, trusting his friendship with the man as well as the commanding presence he assumed. "Give me Larson's pistol."

Stroud moved his musket only slightly. "Have a care there, Swain. Ye make one wrong move, an' I'll put a ball in ye. Devil take me if'n I won't."

"If you kill me," Ethan stated evenly, flicking his gaze to Stroud, "there'll be no saving yourself from these men. They'll turn into hounds that will bring you down."

"Ye're thinkin' pretty high-an'-mighty of 'em," Stroud said. He grinned coldly.

"Aye," Ethan replied. "They're good men. Whaling men, and sailors, every God-fearing one of them." In that, he knew, he gave something back to the crew that he'd taken away while addressing their own lack of foresight and planning.

Folger swallowed hard. "Mr. Swain's right," the captain said. "Mr. Stroud, stay your hand. You shall not fire until I tell you to do so."

"Thank you, Cap'n," Ethan said. "Creel."

"Aye," Creel replied.

Ethan felt the warm metal of the flintlock pistol settle into his hand, felt the familiar heavy heft of the weapon as well. There was a time he'd never gone anywhere without a brace of them. He held the pistol out by the heavy octagonal barrel. "This is the weapon you allowed Timothy Madison to take from you."

Larson stepped forward hesitantly, then raised his hand to take the weapon.

With a trick he'd learned years ago, Ethan expertly flipped the pistol and caught the butt. His fingers slid into place naturally, like a hand slipping into a well-worn glove. His thumb rose and drew the hammer back.

Larson froze in disbelief less than three feet way, his hand almost on the barrel.

But he didn't dive or try to jump away.

Ethan stroked the trigger. The hammer dropped, igniting the powder in the frizzen, which thankfully hadn't spilled free from the pistol. The powder in the barrel exploded, kicking the weapon back against Ethan's palm.

Flames and burning cinders leapt from the barrel. Burning pieces of wadding stuck to Larson's shirt. The flames quickly extinguished and became smoldering embers. Despite the scorched cloth, there was no hole where a ball had gone in, no blood to mark a wound.

"No, Mr. Stroud!" Captain Folger shouted. "Do not fire your weapon!"

Ethan almost grinned at the near hysteria in Folger's voice, but the sick fear still twisted through his guts. Ethan had played out a fierce hand, shoving his own life into the pot, but he'd won. Captain Folger had no desire to be without his first and second mates if it came down to that.

With a flourish, Ethan presented the expended pistol butt first to Larson.

Reluctantly, Larson accepted the weapon. His eyes blazed hatred.

"No ball was seated in the barrel," Ethan stated, returning Larson's gaze. "You permitted Timothy to take an empty weapon. Except for the thunder it would make and the fire it would spit."

"That's not what happened," Larson said.

"Sure it is," Ethan said. He didn't take his eyes from the second mate as he raised his voice. "Stroud."

"Aye," the big man rumbled.

"You wouldn't have shot an unarmed man, would you?" Ethan asked Stroud.

"If'n there was pay in it," Stroud replied, "mayhap. But I didn't know the pistol Madison snatched was empty."

Slowly at first, but together, the sailors who had chosen to stand behind Larson moved away, sinking into the ranks that stood behind Ethan.

"Ye're a-makin' this up," Larson sneered. "Pullin' it outta yer arse."

"You boxed Timothy," Ethan accused. "You planted the stolen weapon in Timothy's kit because you knew he would crack. That way you could execute him and put fear into the rest of the crew."

"Ye're lyin'."

Ethan raised his voice. "Cap'n?"

"Aye," Folger responded.

"I want Larson arrested for the murder of Timothy Madison."

Larson growled an oath and stepped toward Ethan with the heavy pistol raised to club him down. Then he stopped and stepped back as the crew stepped forward protectively around Ethan.

"Ye can't arrest me," Larson said. "This ship needs me."

"Cap'n," Ethan repeated, "*Reliant* needs her crew. She doesn't need a second mate who is a calculating murderer."

"The ball musta come unseated," Larson said, a hint of desperation cracking his words. He glanced at Folger. "Sure. That must have been what happened. The ball came unseated an' rolled outta the barrel."

"We'd have noticed a ball come bouncin' loose," Creel said. "That weapon weren't loaded. An' from the amount of waddin' that come out of it when Ethan fired it, ye had plenty stuffed in there. Mayhap enough extra to keep plenty of powder packed tight so it would make a hell of a bang goin' off."

"Cap'n," Ethan called again, "you need to have Stroud take this man into custody for his own safety. If you don't, he's going to be a walking target aboard this ship. When we get him back to Nantucket, Larson can have a fair trial."

Larson reached around to the back of his pants.

Even as he brought the hidden pistol into view, Ethan drew his fighting knife in a blur. He flicked his knife blade forward, resting the point easily against the man's Adam's apple.

"Don't," Ethan said, "or I swear as God is my witness that you'll choke to death on your own blood." His voice was cold as ice, a chilling whisper that recalled the days of blood that still lingered so menacingly in his past.

Larson froze.

Ethan reached forward and plucked the pistol from Larson's grasp.

"Swain's right, Cap'n," Stroud called from the stern beside Folger. "If'n ye leave Larson loose, somebody'll do for him some night."

"But events might have happened as Larson said they did," Folger said.

"Won't matter," Stroud replied. "Not to them men. An' I don't like the idea of bein' used like that to murder a man. Mayhap it'll be me what puts a blade through Larson's ribs and into his heart. Lock him up, or a kinder death would be fer me to put a ball through his head now."

Silence, interrupted only by the call of the terns and the wind through the sails and rigging, hung heavily over the deck. Ethan felt the water sliding down his body under his wet clothing.

"Very well, Mr. Stroud," Folger said finally. "Take Larson into custody and throw him into the brig below."

"Cap'n!" Larson bleated in protest.

Stroud descended the companionway himself, giving Ethan a grudging look of admiration, then screwed the barrel of his musket to the back of Larson's head. The big man grabbed the second mate's collar in his free hand.

"Jenkins," Stroud roared.

"Aye," a thin man with a musket to his shoulder said.

"If'n any of 'em takes an unfriendly step toward me, kill 'em."

"Aye."

A maniacal light flashed in Larson's eyes as he stared at Ethan. He had to roll his eyes to the side because of the way Stroud held the back of his hair. "Ye think ye've won, don't ye? Ye think 'cause ye've got the cap'n persuaded to listen to ye fer right now, ye've won."

"I haven't won," Ethan replied flatly. "Timothy is still dead, and for no good reason."

"The man was a thief."

"He was one of my boat mates," Ethan replied. "Maybe he was other things, but mostly he was that."

Larson spat at Ethan. The spittle hit Ethan's cheek, and he wiped it away with his wet shirtsleeve.

"You've made yourself a powerful enemy there," Holy Jordan commented quietly at Ethan's side.

Ethan thought of the crew and the captain. *I've made more than one enemy today,* he told himself. He turned and gazed back at the whale tied up alongside the ship. Terns had settled on the dead creature's back and were ripping away at the meat. They flapped their wings and cried out to scare their kin away.

"Cap'n," Ethan called, looking back at Folger.

"Aye, Mr. Swain," the captain called back. He still looked slightly shaken.

"We've still got a whale to render."

Folger looked thankful for the reminder. "Aye, Mr. Swain. That you do. Get those men working."

"I will," Ethan promised. "But I'll want to break open a cask of wine from the hold this evening."

Folger pushed his chin up and rolled his head from side to side, obviously not comfortable with being dictated to. "As you will, Mr. Swain. I'll defer to your judgment in these matters."

Until you can find some way to take that away from me, Ethan knew, but he said, "Thank you, Cap'n. After taking the whale like we did, a celebration is in order." And a drink or two always settled a rowdy crew. As long as he made certain none of them got out-and-out drunk, he hoped he would buy himself some time to think and plan.

"*'Ware ship!*" the lookout cried from the crow's nest above. "*'Ware ship!*"

"Where away?" Ethan barked before he could stop and let Folger ask the direction. A ship in these waters was not a casual thing—especially if that vessel took an uncommon interest in them.

"Off the port bow. She's not flying any colors, Ethan."

Ethan ran to the bow. He gripped the ratlines and pulled himself up onto the railing, followed immediately by Creel.

The ship was a big one, a three-master with a full spread of canvas and running with the wind. She flew no flags, and she was making for *Reliant* with all due speed.

CHAPTER 8

Pacific Ocean 3° 28' S. Lat.—107° 12' W. Long.

POISED ON *RELIANT'S* bow railing, Ethan stared out at the mystery ship. Then his mind started racing, turning all the angles of everything that might go wrong. "Cap'n Folger," he shouted over his shoulder, "we need to make ready to stand against that ship and flee if we must."

Folger glared at the ship. "I don't want to give up that whale, Mr. Swain."

"No, Cap'n," Ethan called back. "Neither do I. Every barrel of oil we get from that ship puts us that much closer to Nantucket. But there's a war on, Cap'n, and we know British privateers have been seen in these waters."

The captain hesitated only a moment. "See to it, Mr. Swain," Folger ordered. "Get your crew squared away."

"Aye, Cap'n." Ethan pushed away from the railing and felt the blood rise in him again.

"It'd be better if'n we had muskets and pistols," Creel growled at Ethan's side.

"After what just happened," Ethan said, hurrying along the deck, "you know we're not going to get them."

"I know," Creel said. "That damned ship just makes me wishful of them, is all."

"Stroud," Ethan called out.

Stroud stood staring at the approaching ship, her sails still in full bloom. He held Larson by the hair of the head and kept the musket barrel centered on the base of the second mate's skull. "What?"

"How good are your men with those weapons?"

Stroud glanced at Ethan, taking a little insult at the question. "Good enough. Why?"

"I want you to talk to your men," Ethan said. "When we identify the captain of that ship, should hostility arise, I want them to target that man and keep firing till he's dead. If the captain's shot dead, then maybe the crew will give up the fight."

Stroud's eyebrows rose a little. "Ye're a surprisin' man, Swain."

"Have someone else put Larson in the brig below. I need you to stay on the deck. You've got an eye for trouble that's coming, and you'll know it when you see it. I want your eyes up here with me."

"Aye." Stroud called one of his men down, then quickly lashed Larson's hands behind his back with a piece of rope from a short length tied around the railing.

"Ye're makin' a mistake!" Larson bellowed, eyeing Ethan. "I can help ye!" When Ethan didn't respond, he shifted his gaze to Stroud. "Dammit, Stroud, are ye just gonna tie me up an' ignore me? I can help you!"

"I reckon we can help our own selves," Stroud replied. "An' if'n ye address me in such a tone again, ye're gonna be spittin' up teeth."

"Holy," Ethan called, "get the men armed with cutlasses and knives, then have them prepared to repel boarders."

"Aye." Holy turned and was gone, his voice braying instantly, echoing Ethan's cries to get the crew into motion.

Ethan loped back to *Reliant*'s stern. He waved Creel toward the prow. "Man the forward gun," Ethan ordered.

With the war breaking out between the English and the Americans in June of the previous year, some of the Nantucket whaling investors had equipped their ships with cannon. Most of the investors hadn't bothered with the expense, or with giving the British a possible reason for boarding and commandeering their ships, but *Reliant* had been equipped with two eight-pound cannon rescued from a battleship that had limped nearly to Nantucket before going under.

"Load it with grapeshot," Ethan ordered, "and you'll only fire if I tell you to."

"Aye," Creel called back.

Ethan ran to the stern cannon and untied the knots that held the waterproof tarp over the weapon. He called to his gun crew, relieved that all of them were already there.

Putting his back into the effort, Ethan helped the gun crew turn the cannon around to face the approaching vessel. When the cannon was set to his satisfaction, Ethan stood ready.

"Clear," Ethan said.

The gun crew and Stroud, a half step behind because he had never drilled with the gun crews, stepped back from the path of the cannon's recoil.

Ethan held the slow match in one fist, aware of the gradual burn. A slow match only burned a length of four or five inches in an hour's time. Some washed the twisted hempen rope in a lye of water and wood ashes, but Ethan had always preferred soaking the slow match in a solution of limewater and saltpeter. Embers blew away over the top of his fist in the gentle breeze.

For a time, silence rolled over *Reliant*'s deck.

The sun baked heat into Ethan's flesh, but his wet clothing kept him cooled and made him feel heavy and sluggish. More than anything, he wanted a cutlass at his hip and a brace of pistols belted across his chest. Those old weights were familiar to him, and he regretted that he could miss them. His life would have been better if he had never known them.

Or Teresa, he added grimly, certain he was glad he'd never see her again. But he was surprised at how sharp the pang of loss was. Though it had been over two years since he'd last seen her, there were many nights her memory came to his bed and left the sheets drenched with sweat and his fitful sleep laced with misery.

Sails dropped aboard the approaching ship. Slowly, the vessel reduced speed. White, curling breakers burst over her prow. The ship's crew stepped to the vessel's starboard, lining the railing. Other men hung in the rigging, and two men stood in the crow's nest with a spyglass. A musket barrel peeked above the crow's nest lip.

Ethan knew that if the men had one musket with them, there were others.

Gracefully, riding low and fat-bodied in the water, the ship came to a stop on the other side of the whale. A flock of terns erupted from the huge corpse to fill the air between the ships with a cloud of fluttering wings for a moment.

"Ahoy the ship," a deep-voiced man bellowed from the other ship's prow.

Folger squared himself and stood in full view of the other ship's crew. Sunlight splintered from the brass buttons of his coat. "I'm Captain Simon Folger of the good ship *Reliant*."

"Aye, Cap'n," the man called back. A grin split his homely face. Beard growth shadowed his cheeks, and tattoos marked his thick, scarred arms. He wore pantaloons and a light vest. Sun and sea had bronzed his skin, but Ethan thought the man might be of mixed blood as well. "We be the crew of *Sunfisher*, kept under the watchful eye of Cap'n Thomas Fisher of Virginny."

"You're a long way from home," Folger said.

"Aye, Cap'n," the man agreed. "As is any sailin' man what hopes fer profits."

"Or men with big appetites," Ethan said, raising his voice so he could be heard between the ships. The rolling slaps of the waves against the whale's body echoed in the hollow between the ships, as regular as a man beating a drum.

The man switched his attention to Ethan.

Ethan felt the cold weight of the man's impersonal stare. Both of them knew he'd violated protocol by speaking over and around Captain Folger. Ethan guessed that the captain would have something to say on the matter later, but for the moment Folger said nothing. But Ethan had wanted the other ship to notice the manned cannon.

"Them guns is uncalled for," the man said.

"These are unfriendly waters," Captain Folger said. "And there is a war on. British privateers roam these waters."

An unhappy expression twisted the homely man's features. His brow wrinkled.

At that moment, another man stepped forward, coming from the thick sheaf of men standing along the ship's deck. "Captain Folger," the man said in a thick Southern accent, "I am Captain Thomas Fisher." He doffed his plumed hat and bowed smoothly, an articulation of fluid movement and gentility. But he never took his eyes from *Reliant*. "I assure you, Captain, that you have no reason for overzealous diligence or fears for your security in the presence of this ship, these men, or myself."

The cadence and resonance increased the unease vibrating within Ethan. He knew the man, and his name was not Thomas Fisher. His true name was Jonah McAfee, and Jonah McAfee was a known and feared pirate in many places in the Atlantic and the Caribbean.

"Stroud," Ethan said in a low voice.

"Aye."

"If this goes badly, I want that man dead."

Stroud hesitated. "We don't even know if that man is the real cap'n. That could be someone just pretendin' to be the cap'n."

"That's the cap'n." Ethan never took his eyes from the man, feeling as though he'd suddenly come face-to-face with a snake.

"An' how would ye be a-knowin'—"

"Damn it, Stroud!" Ethan put fire in his voice when he glanced at the man.

Stroud rankled, thought about saying something, then rotated his head on his thick neck and nodded. "Aye then. The cap'n he is." He turned and signaled to his men. All of them nodded.

"I'm glad to hear that, Captain Fisher," Folger said. "These are hard times for sailing men."

McAfee shaded his eyes and glanced at the whale. "Aye, these indeed are hard times, but it seems as though you've had a bit of luck."

Ethan's skin prickled at the silken, honeyed tones of McAfee's voice. Some nights, when Teresa wasn't in his thoughts and some nights even when she was, Ethan still heard McAfee's correct accent and bloodthirsty orders.

Jonah McAfee stood a little taller than Ethan, a ramrod man with broad shoulders and a rapier build. He could have put on twenty pounds and been the better for it, but for all his indulgences in foods and wines, McAfee never seemed to put on weight. The sun and the sea had turned his blond hair almost bone white, an ash color that contrasted starkly with his dark skin and wide-set dark green eyes that glinted with clever cruelty.

The left side of McAfee's face was slightly darker than his right, scarring burned into the skin from a powder magazine that had gone off too close. The powder burns had left the skin largely unblemished except for the slight discoloration that had left him with a permanently dirty face. He tried to cover some of the damage with a Vandyke beard.

His clothes showed care and craftsmanship, good black broadcloth over a white shirt and ruffled tie. The sword at his left hip was a saber with a wide blade and a stirrup grip. The black onyx in the handle gleamed from use and from care.

"We've had luck," Folger agreed, nodding at the whale, "but we've still got a lot of work ahead of us. We need to get back to it."

"I understand, Captain Folger," McAfee said. "We were only concerned about the welfare of you and your ship."

Liar! Ethan thought, but held his tongue. McAfee was the most guileless liar he had ever seen. He tried to keep his head turned down and away from McAfee so the other man might not recognize him. Even after all this time, he felt certain he knew how McAfee would react if he recognized Ethan.

"You see," McAfee said, "it's not often my crew and myself chance upon a ship sitting idle upon the sea. We didn't recognize that you were harvesting a whale until after we sailed closer."

But Ethan knew the only things forestalling McAfee's attack on the ship were the cannon and the crew across *Reliant*'s deck.

"Of course," McAfee continued in an easy voice, "after my crew and I saw that you and your crew were well, we could hardly sail away without stopping by to properly introduce ourselves. Perhaps we might have a gam."

A gam meant two or three days of feasting and talking, of crews intermingling freely aboard each ship while goods and stories were traded. Ethan's stomach rolled at the thought of allowing McAfee or his men aboard *Reliant*. Such an event would be like putting wolves among the sheep. As tough as Stroud's bullies were, they were not anything at all like the devils that McAfee crewed with.

"We can't, Cap'n Folger," Ethan said in a low voice. "We've got the whale to tend to. Having those men aboard would only slow us." He didn't intend for his words to carry to *Sunfisher*.

Folger glanced irritably over his shoulder, then turned his attention back to McAfee.

At the railing, McAfee stared stone-faced at Ethan. Cold apprehension filled Ethan. It was possible that even after all the time that had passed the man might recognize him.

And if he does, what then?

Ethan had no answer. He kept his fist tight about the slow match, feeling the occasional warm brush of an ember across the back of his hand.

"Unfortunately, Captain," Folger said, "we have too much work to do here. Harvesting a whale is bloody and hard effort."

A few of the sailors around Ethan mumbled under their breath. The derisive comments didn't go far, though, and if Folger heard any of them, he gave no indication.

"Understandable," McAfee agreed good-naturedly. "Perhaps another occasion?"

"I shall look forward to that encounter," Folger promised.

"How do you stand on supplies?" McAfee asked.

"For the moment, we are doing well enough."

McAfee nodded, and for a moment he stared harder at Ethan. Steeling himself, Ethan kept his face averted and forced himself to keep breathing.

"I find myself embarrassingly short of coffee and flour," McAfee admitted. "Perhaps we could manage a little bartering before we take leave of each other's company."

"I wouldn't like to see a gentleman sail in short supply," Folger said. "I can spare a few barrels of flour, but they are regrettably full of weevils."

"Weevils will be no problem. I've got men who would rather eat weevils than feel their stomachs wrap around their backbones. What of the coffee?"

"Out of my personal stores," Folger replied. "As one gentleman to another."

"And what would you have in return?"'

Ethan waited, knowing that McAfee might only be curious about what kind of prize he might be setting free.

"Meat," Folger answered. "Fresh meat if you have it."

"I'm ashamed to admit it, but we've been down on our luck concerning meat," McAfee said. "We've been fortunate enough to catch a few fish now and again, but we've been days without red meat, and likely to go days more."

"Aye," Folger said. "We're away to the Galapagos Islands soon enough to try our luck there."

McAfee smiled. "You'll find plenty of turtles there. Not as good as beef or venison, I'll warrant, but tasty enough if you've a skilled cook."

"I do," Folger said.

"I can offer you barrels of sugar or rum," McAfee said. "They're good enough to barter for anything else you might need. Including ship repairs should you need them."

Folger accepted the offer without hesitation.

Ethan mulled over the offer. Sugar and rum were two key products in the slave trade. Rum was made in the American states, then traded to African slavers, usually one indigenous people that captured members from another tribe they constantly warred with. The slaves were brought back to the West Indies and other places and traded for sugar and molasses.

In 1808, five years earlier, the fledgling United States government had outlawed transatlantic shipments of slaves. Despite the ruling, domestic slaves—men, women, and children born into slavery in the United States—were still bought and sold on blocks throughout the South. Besides the domestic slaves, though, illegal importation of new African slaves still continued. Men who captained slave ships could make small fortunes for themselves if they could stay clear of legal troubles, didn't get found out, or didn't have their ship taken over during a slave uprising aboard.

With renewed curiosity, Ethan considered the fat-bodied merchant ship McAfee commanded. Maybe the ship was a prize from some earlier success, but as he thought about the rum and sugar, he thought maybe the ship was something else.

For a brief time, Folger and McAfee dickered over the amounts to be exchanged.

"Good," McAfee said when they'd finished. "I'll get a boat loaded and have the sugar and rum brought over to you."

Ethan looked at Stroud. "Tell him no."

"What?" Stroud grumbled.

"We don't want that man or any of his men over here," Ethan said. His skin prickled and tightened at just the thought. "Tell him no. Tell him that you'll send a boat over because *Reliant*'s deck is covered in blood."

Stroud remained where he was.

Placing a hand on the man, Ethan shoved Stroud into motion. "Now."

Stroud stumbled forward. "Cap'n."

In obvious disbelief, Folger turned and stared at Stroud, then shifted his eyes to Ethan.

"Maybe it would be better if we sent a boat across, Cap'n," Stroud said.

"Why?"

"So one of McAfee's men don't get on board," Ethan said. "You can't trust this man." He spoke in a hurried, low voice so that his words didn't carry to the other ship.

"Why would that matter?" Folger asked in the same quiet tones.

"Because then they could be havin' a better look at the ship," Stroud stated gruffly. "He has a point, Cap'n. Not to mention that the man might be after sendin' someone here what might try somethin'."

"Like what?"

"Like takin' ye fer instance," Stroud said. "Or outright just killin' ye."

"They wouldn't—"

"They might," Stroud growled. "It's yer choice, you bein' cap'n an' all, but me father always taught me that a cautious man lives a lot longer than a brave one. An' that a foolhardy man is just a candle blowin' in the wind."

"Is something wrong, Captain Folger?" McAfee called.

"No," Folger said. "I'm going to send one of our boats to you. Our deck is all fouled with the whale's blood and blubber."

"You're doing us the favor," McAfee said. "It hardly seems fair that you put a boat crew out for us."

"I," Folger said, "insist."

McAfee was silent for a long moment, almost too long to be comfortable, then he nodded. "As you will, Captain Folger."

"Damn you, Mr. Swain," Folger swore in a quiet tone. "You have embarrassed me before this man. I'll not soon forget it."

Ethan kept silent. Having one more thing for Folger to add to his list of ill feelings wasn't very troublesome. Having McAfee recognize him was something else entirely. He remained at the cannon, making certain that Creel did the same at the other end of the ship.

The boat was quickly loaded with flour barrels and small chests of coffee. Folger even threw in a bottle of whiskey from his own private stores as a gift. McAfee reciprocated, adding a few slim volumes from his personal library that he said were novels and histories.

The crew aboard *Reliant* returned to rendering the whale. Before the boat cast off from the whaleship, the tryworks were bubbling and casting off thick clouds of black smoke. The smoke twisted like a writhing snake across *Sunfisher's* bowsprit. Ethan watched the ship, never stepping away from the cannon nor losing sight of McAfee, who remained on the deck. As he watched the ship's captain, Ethan recognized the habits McAfee had—especially the feigned disinterest. But Ethan knew that McAfee watched *Reliant* with hawk's eyes.

As the boat crew reached *Sunfisher* and began unloading the supplies, the rendering team working the cutting stage managed to harvest the whale's head, cutting the top section from the body and from the lower jaw. After hooking the head securely, the crew used the block and tackle to lift the head and swing the bloody hunk of meat and bone aboard. As soon as the head was shored up so it wouldn't roll around, men with saws and knives attacked, cutting through the bone at the top of the head.

The case, called so by whaling men, at the top of the head contained the spermaceti, the most valuable part of the whole animal. Milky white in color, the spermaceti was the purest oil in the whale and always fetched the highest price at any port. With luck, the whale would net three hundred and fifty to four hundred gallons of spermaceti. The lower jaw, called junk, would be harvested as well because the oil contained in that part of the head contained oil that wasn't as good as the spermaceti but was still better than any taken from the rest of the blubber.

Other men set to work removing the whale's teeth. They dropped the teeth in big wooden buckets. Later, the teeth would be doled out to anyone having the skill or patience to carve them into scrimshaw they could sell once in port.

When the longboat was packed again with the promised rum and sugar and the books McAfee had added, the crew aboard dropped their oars into the sea and pulled hard. One of the crewmen working on the whale's head climbed inside once the case was opened. Other men handed him buckets and, one by one, he filled them and passed them back out.

"Captain Folger," McAfee called across the whale's drifting and bird-covered carcass.

"Aye," Folger replied.

"I will pray for you and your men, that your hunt for whales goes swiftly and that you always be fortunate."

"Thank you. I will pray that your own endeavors are rewarded."

Without turning, McAfee gave the order to set sail. Sailors raced to drag canvas up into the rigging. Within minutes, the sails bellied full again and caught the wind. During the talks, the wind had shifted somewhat, and as *Sunfisher* crossed *Reliant*'s stern, a stench rolled over the whaleship.

"By God," Stroud roared at Ethan's side, reaching up to pinch his nostrils closed, "what in the deep pits of Hell is that stench?"

As the sickening wind riffled through Ethan's hair, nausea settled into his stomach. Images tumbled unbidden through his mind, taking him back to the final days with McAfee and Teresa. He remembered ships crammed with the sweat-slick and sickness-encrusted bodies of frightened men, women, and children all chained together. Sometimes corpses had been chained among those poor unfortunates, not yet taken from the dank, mildewed holds and thrown into the heartless sea.

So is that what your life has come to then, Jonah McAfee? Running slaves? No more the proud pirate? Ethan stared at the ship, watching as McAfee crossed the deck and walked into the ship's stern. McAfee raised his hand and waved an abbreviated salute; a cocky, mocking grin limned his face.

At first, Folger lifted his own hand in response, then must have guessed that the gesture was not meant for him. The captain turned and glanced over his shoulder.

"That man knows ye," Stroud commented.

"No," Ethan said. "He must have mistaken me for someone else." Guilt tumbled through him, and he worked to remind himself that he was someone else.

"Might be a bad thing," Stroud mused. "Him thinkin' ye're someone he knows, I mean. Despite his airs, that man doesn't seem like a man to get to know."

Ethan never responded; never said anything, never made a move. He remained by the cannon with a sour fist clenched in his stomach until *Sunfisher* was out of sight and Folger descended to the ship's deck and entered his cabin.

McAfee had recognized him, but the ship's captain had chosen to sail away. Despite how they'd left it between them, despite the way that Ethan had ultimately betrayed McAfee, the man wouldn't come after him if he didn't attack immediately.

Or would he?

Ethan didn't know. McAfee had always been a man of deep and dark desires, a man who hadn't let anyone or anything stand in his way. Ethan remembered the way the ship had sat low in the water, realized then that *Sunfisher*'s cargo holds had probably been full. McAfee wouldn't have wanted to lose the cargo.

The man's decision to sail away didn't mean that he wouldn't return later and try to kill Ethan. He'd tried to kill him before. With grim realization, Ethan knew that he was even less safe aboard *Reliant* now that McAfee knew he was aboard. The crew wasn't happy with him, Folger hated him, and a vicious pirate, with a reputation for bloodletting, who had marked him for death knew where he was. There was no margin for error.

He gave the order for the gun crew to unload the cannon, then went down the companionway to oversee the gathering of the spermaceti from the whale head balanced on the deck by hooks attached to the block and tackle. Every barrelful they could render put them one more barrelful closer to home. He didn't want to see a single drop wasted.

CHAPTER 9

Easter Island, Chile 27° 9' S. Lat.—109° 26' W. Long.

SEATED IN ONE of the chairs inside the tent he'd claimed as his surgery and study, Bullock surveyed his guest.

The old man sat awkwardly in another chair. He showed an unaccustomed familiarity with furniture but still acted as though the chair might slide out from under him at any moment. His native name was a string of incomprehensible syllables to Bullock, but the old man stated that he preferred to be called Malachi, as he'd come to be known as in the white man's world.

Katharine sat in another of the chairs to one side, out of the immediate circle of conversation Bullock sought to create with the man. She held the journal and drew rapidly with her clever hands, blocking in images. Perkins stood near her, his musket in the crook of his arm.

"What do you know of this creature?" Bullock asked.

The old man repeated the cacophonous sounds he'd uttered earlier when he'd first named the creature. Then he spoke in English. "Death-in-the-Water came among us the night the sun fell from the sky."

Bullock considered the old man's answer. Based in science as he was, he didn't know much about mythologies outside the required Greek and Roman legends and stories taught at university.

"Death-in-the-Water has been here since the beginning time?" Bullock asked.

"No," Malachi answered. "Only since the sun fell into the sea."

"He's talking about the falling star, Father," Katharine said quietly.

"Yes," Malachi said, nodding. "I have heard some who called it that. My people, the people who lived here during that before time, believed that was the night that Death-in-the-Water first came among us."

"How did it come among you?" Bullock leaned forward, drawn by the rapt intensity of the story.

"There are some," Malachi said, "who believe the sun had a rider that day. We have heard stories of strange beings in the white world that rode chariots across the sky and carried the sun with them."

"Apollo," Katharine whispered.

"Is that what you believe? That something arrived in these waters with the falling star?"

Malachi shook his head. "I don't know what to believe. There are some who say that the sun falling into the ocean disturbed something on the sea bottom."

"What would have been disturbed?"

"Some say that the volcanoes on this island are made to erupt by a giant serpent that dwells within the earth. One day the serpent will be angered and destroy this place, tear down all the lands and let the seas again wash over them."

Something from space, Bullock thought to himself, *or something heretofore undiscovered that had risen from the ocean depths—a sea monster.* If he hadn't seen the grievous wounds young Warren Johnstone had borne, the idea would probably have seemed ludicrous to him. Or, at least, more ludicrous.

"When did the legends of Death-in-the-Water begin?" Bullock asked.

"After the sun fell from the sky."

"Never before?"

"No. Death-in-the-Water was never there before."

"There are no other legends about Death-in-the-Water?"

"No." Malachi thought for a moment as if searching for the right words. "This creature, whatever it is, isn't native to this island or to these waters."

"How can you say that?"

"Because nothing like it has ever been seen before."

"Do you know what the creature looks like?"

"No."

"Then how can you say there is a creature? Or that there is only one?"

"Because only one has ever been seen."

Exasperation chafed at Bullock's patience, aided and abetted by the lack of sleep the previous night. "If the creature has been seen, then why can't it be described?"

"The description is always that of a whale," Malachi answered. "Except that whales don't have legs to grab their prey."

"What legs?"

"The creature possesses legs. Like those of a squid or an octopus."

"Then how do you know what has been seen isn't a squid?" Bullock asked.

"Because the people who have seen Death-in-the-Water have always said the creature looked like a whale. We know that Death-in-the-Water can't be a whale because whales don't do to men what you saw done to the man you found on the beach last night and buried this morning."

"No," Bullock agreed, "whales do not leave men in that kind of shape. Nor can they pluck them from ships as poor Mr. Johnstone said he was taken." The professor sat back in his chair and gazed out the tent door. The shadow against the tent wall told him that a man stood outside, and Bullock had no doubt that everything he talked with Malachi about would be reported to Captain Mayhew.

"What about squids, Father?" Katharine asked. "Perhaps this is a new type of squid no one has seen before."

Bullock shook his head at his daughter's suggestion. "No squid carries venom." Then he remembered Perkins's story about the venomous squid he'd come across in Australia. "That we know of in these waters."

"Even squids have mouths, Professor Bullock," Malachi said. "We have found men that have been attacked by squids. They have sucker marks on them, and occasionally bite marks have been found on them. None of the victims of Death-in-the-Water have ever been found bitten except by fish and eels and birds when they floated to the ocean's surface before coming in to shore. Death-in-the-Water has no mouth."

"That's nonsense," Bullock said. "Every creature has to have a mouth."

"I do not know," Malachi admitted. "These are only things that I have been told. I came here today, after you found the man last night, to tell you. And because one of the men who watches this camp said that you told the ship's captain you were here to find Death-in-the-Water."

Surprise lifted Bullock's eyebrows. "People are watching this camp?"

"Of course." Malachi nodded. "The people who yet remain here are very afraid of you. They have known nothing but terror and hardship from the Europeans, Americans, and South Americans."

"Where do you think the creature came from?" the professor asked. "Beneath the sea or from the depths of space?"

"Professor Bullock," Malachi said, "I don't believe in a serpent lying inside the earth under the water that can create volcanoes. And if such a creature existed, I don't believe that a piece of the sun plummeting into the ocean would awaken it."

"Then . . . space, is it?"

Malachi sipped his tea thoughtfully. "Do you know what we call this island?"

"*Te Pito o Te Henua,*" Bullock replied immediately.

"Do you know what the name translates to?"

"No, I'm afraid I do not."

"The Navel of the World," Malachi replied. "Our legends of this place, dating back even before our people came from their previous countries, told us that this island would offer the rebirth of the world. Our view of the world at night is of the heart of the star group your sailors call the Milky Way. Thousands of years pass between such events, but this island does line up with the Milky Way. My people have always felt an umbilical connection with the Milky Way. My people believe that things pass back and forth to this island, from here to the stars, and from the stars to here. That is why the re-creation of the world was believed to be taking place here."

"I didn't know that," Bullock admitted. He made notes to himself to research the subject the next time he was around a proper library. He doubted the information would be contained in many books, though, and figured he would be writing letters to peers as well to find proper reference.

"I've talked to sailors upon occasion," Malachi said, "when we thought we might be able to trust them here, and when I was trying to make my way home from New York after I was sold there. They have found new fish and new animals in these areas that they haven't seen before. And there are creatures here that many people have never seen the like of. British scientists, before the war with France and the United States, spoke of coming here to study the animals and fish and plants."

"You think new species are being created in these waters rather than only now being discovered?"

"Yes." Malachi was silent for a moment. "Or perhaps they are arriving from somewhere else. That can be the only explanation for Death-in-the-Water. Never has such a creature existed in the sea before."

Bullock sat back in his chair and listened to the furniture creak ominously beneath him. The old man's explanation for what had happened was secondhand at best, but fitted many of the particulars of the stories the professor had read while aboard ship.

"Have your people ever hunted Death-in-the-Water?" the professor asked.

"Yes."

"They never found the creature?"

"The ones that returned did not," Malachi said.

"Just because they didn't return doesn't mean that the creature got them." A proper scientist was a sterling devil's advocate.

"No," Malachi agreed. "There are slavers, and there are the considerable dangers of the sea itself, but mostly I think there is Death-in-the-Water." He finished his tea and stood. "I will take my leave now."

"I would make you an offer, Mr. Malachi," Bullock stated.

Malachi looked at him.

"Go with us," the professor said. "I can have the captain leave food here for your people in exchange for your time."

"Your offer is generous," Malachi said. "Whatever food you could spare would be welcome." He shook his head. "But I don't want to go out on that sea." He glanced at Katharine. "Were I you, Professor Bullock, and I had any command over that vessel that lies in the harbor, I'd order it back home as soon as I set foot on board. Years ago when Death-in-the-Water first came to this place with the falling sun, the creature was smaller."

"Smaller than a whale?"

"As long as we have known it," Malachi said, "the creature has always worn the mask of a whale. The whale form is bigger now, but not much. However, Death-in-the-Water has become stronger and faster, and more knowledgeable about killing. In the years before, the creature has hunted fish and other whales. The bodies of those creatures have been found washed up on the beaches. Death-in-the-Water has even killed and eaten sharks. We have found their bodies washed up on the shore."

"All this eating despite the fact that the creature has no mouth," Bullock said.

"Every creature," Malachi said, taking no offense, "feeds. We don't know how Death-in-the-Water feeds. But we know it eats. The giant clams found on the sea bottom are a particular favorite of the creature. Their empty shells float on the water and sometimes reach this place."

"Why are the clams a favorite?"

"We don't know, but we do know that Death-in-the-Water's constant hunting has all but killed them out of our waters. And we know that Death-in-the-Water now hunts men."

"Because your hunters have not returned?"

"And because of the man you buried today," Malachi agreed. "Death-in-the-Water has learned not to fear men. Or perhaps it has grown tired of hiding from men. Now the creature hunts them as food. That's why I thought you should get your daughter out of here and to safety."

"We've got muskets enough," Perkins said bravely. "And cannon enough, too, should it come to that."

"Enough to stop a monster?" Malachi asked in a soft voice.

"Aye," Perkins snarled.

The old man nodded as an adult would at the prideful claims of a child. He turned back to Bullock. "I will pray for your safe passage, Professor Bullock, and for the safe passage of your daughter. Thank you for your hospitality."

Bullock followed the man out of the tent and watched Malachi walk back toward the highlands rising from the camp. A foreboding chill rattled through the professor's brain, tangling up in the old man's words. *Enough to stop a monster?*

"Do you think what Mr. Malachi said was true, Father?" Katharine asked. "That the creature has learned to hunt people?"

"I think," Bullock replied, "that it was no accident young Warren Johnstone was swept from the safety of the ship he had been on." He raised his voice. "Mr. Perkins."

"Aye."

"Please send someone to inform Captain Mayhew that we'll be raising anchor as soon as we can break camp."

"DAMNED WASTE OF supplies if ye ask me," a sailor growled.

Bullock stood on *Brown-Eyed Sue*'s forward deck and supervised the unloading of the barrels and crates he'd sanctioned to be left on the craggy coastline. Only a few ash piles and the lonely grave marked the fact that the camp had been there hours before.

Captain Mayhew came forward to stand at the professor's side.

"Have you come to protest my decision to leave supplies for Malachi and his people?" Bullock asked. After his talk with the old man and the information they'd exchanged—both about the creature and about the dire straits the island people were in—the professor had felt incapable of simply sailing away without doing something to alleviate the distress the island's inhabitants were presently undergoing.

"Would my protest change your mind?" Mayhew asked.

"No."

"Then I have not come to protest."

Bullock leaned tiredly on the railing. Beneath his feet, the ship rolled a little over each wave, rising and falling almost imperceptibly. He had never yet spent a day when he did not notice the ship's movements.

"I was told that this creature hunts men," Mayhew said.

At least the captain's spy network was in keen operation. "Perhaps. And perhaps I was only told a bit of growing superstition about the creature that has no truth to it."

"Either way, the possibility makes your chosen venture a bit more entertaining."

Bullock shifted his gaze from the group of men straining at unloading the supplies into one of the longboats to the captain. "This morning you felt there was no creature, that the stories I told you were all superstitious ramblings."

"I still feel that they are," Mayhew replied, "and the sooner I prove that they are, the sooner I'll be rid of you and can get on with an honest captain's work."

"I am not the enemy, Captain Mayhew."

"To me you are, Professor." Without another word, Mayhew strode away.

Bullock willed the anger inside him to dissipate. Getting into a verbal argument or, heaven forbid, a physical altercation with the captain was only a waste of emotion and energy. After being up all night under such rough and injurious circumstances, he had neither to spare.

"You should rest."

Turning, Bullock found his daughter standing beside him. "I cannot," he confessed. "Perhaps as soon as we are under way. I thought you were resting."

"I couldn't sleep," Katharine said. "There's too much to do with all the notes we took."

"We've days of nothing but sailing to do ahead of us. There will be time to get caught up then."

Katharine turned and glanced out at the sea. The sun spilled yellow-gold across the emerald water. White foam swirled at the tops of gently rolling waves. The ocean looked peaceful and still.

"Do you think the creature is out there?" she asked.

"Something killed young Warren Johnstone," Bullock answered. "Whatever it was, it's out there."

CHAPTER 10

Pacific Ocean 3° 28' S. Lat.—107° 12' W. Long.

ETHAN DAUBED HIS quill pen in a bottle of ink. He studied the journal page in front of him. Under his parents' tutelage and against his own protests, he'd developed a fine hand for writing. The words, black ink scratched across slightly yellowed paper, flowed with the uniform regularity of a marching army as he wrote.

Ethan sat in the galley after breakfast. His next watch didn't start till the afternoon, and he'd chosen to catch up on the expanded log entries he wanted to make.

The near mutiny, the loss of Timothy Madison, Larson's incarceration in the ship's brig, and the encounter with McAfee and *Sunfisher* had occurred four days before. Two days later, the cutting teams had finished harvesting the blubber from the whale. Stripped of flesh, the picked-over carcass had been released and dropped through the sea. The birds had no choice about giving up on the corpse, but the sharks had followed the remnant toward the sea bottom.

For the moment, *Reliant* continued to lie at anchor. Although the fires under the tryworks had never gone out, and thick black smoke continued to billow across the decks and stain the sails and choke the lungs of a man unfortunate enough to be caught downwind, much of the whale's flesh remained in the cargo hold, cut up into foot-square Bible leaves for faster boiling.

From Ethan's current estimate, concurred with by the other experienced hands, at least another day's work remained of converting the blubber to oil. When it was all done, the hold would be over three-quarters full.

At best, they were only another good-sized whale away from finishing up. At most, only two more whales would be required.

But there can be a long time in between whales, Ethan reminded himself. Then again, another whale could find them before they weighed anchor.

He pushed those thoughts from his mind. Whatever would come would come. A yawn creaked his jaw open before he realized it, and he covered his mouth.

"Ye should be gettin' some sleep these days, Ethan, what with the whale bein' all cut up an' all."

Startled, not knowing Cook had walked up behind him, Ethan glanced at the man.

If Cook had a name, everyone had forgotten it. Cook stood only an inch or two over five feet, and looked to be all ears, hands, and feet. He was bone-thin, which should have been a disconcerting sight because a man who didn't sample his own cooking was definitely suspect. A simple wooden peg held his long gray hair back in a queue. He was sixty if he was a day, and he'd spent more years aboard a ship than on dry land.

"I am getting caught up on sleep," Ethan replied.

"Well now, ye don't look it."

"Too many things to do, Cook."

"An' all of 'em needs doin' at oncet, I know."

"So it would seem."

Cook took a pie down from one of the cabinets. He sliced a thick wedge, plopped the slice onto a platter, and brought the dish over to Ethan.

"Apple pie," Cook said. "Good and thick. I've a slice of cheese I can put on top for ye if'n ye want."

"No," Ethan said. "I couldn't eat another bite." Truthfully, he'd put away salted beef, fried potatoes mixed with onions, and biscuits covered in thick gravy only minutes ago.

"That's from one of them pies I made for supper," Cook said. He cleared the breakfast platter Ethan had used. "None of them other men are gonna get a bite of them pies till this evenin'. I'm makin' an exception fer ye. Don't make light of the offer. Generosity like this, why it ain't often tendered."

Ethan stared at the flaky brown crust and inhaled the brown sugar and cinnamon scent of the baked apples. He took up his fork and prodded the pie. The thick caramel-colored juice oozed onto the platter.

Cook returned with a coffeepot and warmed up Ethan's cup.

"Why?" Ethan asked.

Cook looked somewhat disconcerted. "Because of what ye tried to do fer us agin the cap'n."

Bile soured Ethan's mouth and took the edge off his hunger. "I don't want to listen to any mutinous talk. A man has already died because of it."

"Nor do I," Cook replied. He took his pipe out of his apron, tamped in tobacco, and lit up. A blue-gray smoky haze quickly enveloped his head. "A lot of this crew is green, Ethan. An' maybe some of 'em don't much like workin' as hard as the cap'n makes 'em. But the cap'n's the cap'n, as I always say."

"Aye," Ethan said.

"Ye see, that's what these young sailors an' these stupid an' hardheaded sailors ain't got figured out yet. Someone's always gotta be in charge of the ship. Ain't nobody in charge, why there ain't nobody safe. Soon as the ship reaches shore, though, all of that can change if'n a man don't like his lot none."

"I know," Ethan agreed.

"Cap'n Folger, he don't figure on bringin' any of this crew back aboard *Reliant* after this here voyage."

Ethan didn't say anything, but he'd been suspecting as much.

"But ye see, Ethan, that there's his mistake. If'n a ship's investors see that every man jack aboard a ship signs ship's articles with another ship as soon as we put into port, why they ain't gonna take too long to figure out what's causin' them losin' experienced hands. Ain't no investors gonna want to send a ship full of greenhands out searchin' for whales, an' they're gonna be highly suspicionin' the man what lost them their crew."

Ethan was silent.

"The ship's investors," Cook said, "why they're gonna be holdin' Folger responsible for losin' that crew."

Glancing away from the older man, Ethan said, "I lost them, too."

"Mayhap," Cook agreed. "But they remain out there to be won back."

"I broke their trust the moment I hit Merl."

"Ah, but lad, ye won their hearts when ye dived into the sea after Timothy."

The image of Timothy getting his head torn off by a shark ripped through Ethan's mind for a moment. He pushed the memory away and concentrated on the pie. If Cook had ever made a finer apple pie, Ethan didn't know of it.

"Ye're in rough waters this voyage," Cook said. "If'n ye was to go along with them what mutinies, why the ship's investors ain't gonna want to have ye ever cap'n a ship fer them. But if'n ye don't support the crew enough, ye'll never have a man that's worth his salt sign ship's articles with ye. An' if'n ye ain't got a crew, ye won't have no cap'n's berth either."

Ethan looked up at the older man. "Is that supposed to be an encouraging speech, Cook?"

"Just a-layin' out them cards ye've been a-starin' at these past few days," Cook replied. "I ain't tellin' ye nothin' ye didn't already know. That's why ye're a-keepin' them two sets of books like ye are."

Surprise vibrated through Ethan. The fact that he was keeping two sets of personal journals was a secret. No one was supposed to know. He'd been doing that ever since he'd returned to whaling. With Captain Folger, the need for two journals—one open for the cap'n's inspection and the other that detailed everything that transpired in his own terms—had been necessary.

"Ye ain't the only mate what's kept two sets of books," Cook confided.

"Who else knows?" Ethan asked. He'd been careful to work on each book in a different place. He worked on his personal journal in the galley on mornings after the crew had finished the breakfast mess. The primary journal, the one that Captain Folger could see anytime he wanted, was worked on by the navigator's desk.

Cook shrugged deprecatingly. "Only me. Ye ain't got many on this crew what's been around as long as I have. I just wanted ye to know that, should push come to shove an' ye're havin' a hard time with the investors, why I'd be proud to step up fer ye. That's all." He started to turn away.

"Cook." Ethan offered his hand, "thank you. Not many men these days offer to stand for another when they don't have anything to gain for it themselves."

A smile curled Cook's lips as he took Ethan's hand. Excitement glittered in his eyes. "Ye're a right 'un, Ethan. Ye are. I always knew that about ye before ye up an' dived over the ship's side for poor ol' Timothy. Now ye just finish that pie up, an' I'll leave ye be."

For a moment, Ethan felt some of the darkness lingering in his heart slacken pace and clear off like clouds under a blazing sun. Perhaps things would level off a bit, and perhaps they would take their final whale or two in the next few days. It was something to hope for.

He finished the pie and thanked Cook again. With the logbook under his arm, he headed up the companionway onto the ship's deck. The moist brine air of morning greeted him, and the sound of a sail popping echoed like small hand claps off in the distance. He gazed up, checking the rigging and the lines, searching for the errant bit of canvas.

He wished they were under way. Every time he looked up into the rigging and saw the sails swelled with the promise of the wind, he was that boy who had grown up in Nantucket watching ships in the harbor, chasing after sailing men for the stories they would tell a young, impressionable lad. Lands yet remained to be discovered, and the sea was a wide-open world of wonder.

Every spare moment he had gotten away from his mother's worry, his father's shop, and his sister's spying eyes, Ethan had hung around the Nantucket docks. He had listened to the stories the sailing men told, carefully examined the scars they offered as proof of their incredible tales of monsters, magic, and sinister pirates, and looked at every object they brought in from the sea and the foreign ports they visited.

While listening to the sailors, Ethan had also met Cyrus Coffin, a retired merchant captain who had made his fortune as master of a trade ship. Cyrus Coffin had taken whales in his day as well, but he had made most of his money working for himself, knowing foreign markets and seasons and spotting new buyers for goods he could fill his hold with.

Ethan had started a journal, filling the pages with lore he heard from sailors. But he also put in details of their successes of trading handcrafts they made themselves or purchased at one port and marketed at another. Ethan's father, himself a speculator of goods while serving aboard cargo ships, had passed on knowledge of trading to Ethan, of things to watch in men and markets. Ethan wrote down the things that Cyrus Coffin told him, the things his father told him, and the stories of trade and goods and ports he heard from the sailors. His mother, ever diligent about the need for neat penmanship, had compromised in her writing lessons and read every entry he had made in that journal.

Writing got to be a welcome habit. The entries allowed him to be alone with his thoughts, to think and to plan and to dream. The original journal he had filled all those years ago was at his mother's house in Nantucket. The entries described the kind of ship he would build for himself, the places he would trade and what he would trade there, and the stories he wanted to investigate to find out if they were true or not.

Ethan still wrote journal entries. When he had a book filled, he never failed to mail it home. His mother and his father sent letters, letting him know they read his journals and were quite fascinated with everything he was seeing and doing. But the journal entries he wrote now weren't the hopeful dreams of a boy. They were solid and factual, something that his mother had pointed out a few times and seemed disappointed by, but he no longer dreamed as big.

Just out of Boston, in January of 1811, a storm had blown up, verging on becoming a hurricane. The winds had snapped the mizzenmast and left it tangled in the mainmast and foremast rigging. Captain Rodham, who had been master of the vessel, had panicked. Rodham had been Ethan's age at the time, and not nearly as seasoned a sailor. Rodham's father had underwritten the ship, passing off investments to the men he did business with.

Ethan had sent sailors up in the rigging to cut the broken mast free, damaging much of the rigging in the process but ultimately saving the ship. Rodham, fearful that the men were making the situation worse because the ship had reacted violently to their actions, had, ordered the men down. Ethan had tried to reason with the captain, but Rodham was past the point of logic, screaming obscenities and threatening to shoot any man who did not obey him. Ethan had punched him senseless, then lashed Rodham inside the longboat in case the ship was unsalvageable.

Later, the crew had testified that Ethan had acted to save all their lives, the ship, and the cargo carried in the hold. The seasoned men of the mariners' court who had listened to the story believed that Ethan had saved the ship, but he had also disregarded the authority of the ship's master. Perhaps, if Rodham's ego had not been so badly stung, he would have dropped the charges with the agreement that Ethan say nothing of the story. Instead, Rodham had pressed the charges with the full weight of his wealthy family name behind it, and a black mark had been entered into Ethan's seaman's papers.

That mark had not only probably ended Ethan's chances of a captaincy, but it had also kept him from a berth on any kind of real sailing ship for four months. After the review board's decision, he had worked as a longshoreman and fisherman in Boston for four months. His father had finally learned of his plight through an acquaintance, and word had been passed along the Nantucket community.

Not many people were interested in taking on a first mate who had struck a captain, but the investors in Nantucket had been insistent. The war with England had started again in June of 1812, and many men were reluctant to take to sea because they would have to face Lord Nelson's navy as well as British privateers. Simon Folger had had no choice about his selection of first mates, but he had chosen the other two mates, all with the eye of getting rid of Ethan the first chance he had.

Still, Ethan continued to write down information in his journal, especially the new possibilities of markets in the Pacific. It was his dream, and even if it had left him, he didn't know how to walk away from it.

And that black mark, damning as it was, had not created as much damage as knowledge of the time he had spent with McAfee and Teresa.

"Packnett," Ethan called up to a young man lazing in the rigging.

"Aye, Ethan," the young man called back down.

"That fore tops'l's luffing," Ethan said.

"Aye. I'll get right to it." Packnett twisted in the rigging, managing hand- and footholds easily as he made his way through the canvas sheets like a monkey.

The other men on deck eyed Ethan cautiously. Even Creel had been somewhat distant in his dealings with Ethan. And Merl Porter had been filled with sheer hatred.

Frustration chafed at Ethan. He had a few books down in the cabin he shared with the other mates, volumes that told tales of the sea that he'd read a number of times and could enjoy time and again, but he didn't like staying cooped up inside the ship. He felt the need to be on the ship's rolling deck, to feel the wind in his face and the sun against his skin.

Maybe you're not meant to be a cap'n, he told himself with black anger. *Maybe all you were ever meant to be is a ship's mate.*

But he wouldn't accept that. He had captained a ship before, and he'd led men. When he'd first talked of leaving that ship, Teresa had laughed at him. She'd told him that being a captain, a man to be feared and honored and respected, was in him. He couldn't easily walk away from being a captain after he'd had a taste of it.

And that's been true, hasn't it? That's what Boston was all about. You couldn't leave command in the hands of others.

He pushed those thoughts away. The incident was behind him. He had to survive the voyage now, and he had to watch his step.

"Mr. Swain."

Ethan turned at the sound of his name and spotted Stroud coming toward him. Stroud was another reason Ethan had been spending more of his free time on the ship's deck. With only a limited amount of seafaring experience, Stroud lacked judgment that the crew and the ship might depend on.

Over Stroud's shoulder, a line of dark rain clouds scudded through the blue sky. Earlier that morning, when Ethan had first taken the deck, the clouds had been smaller, farther away. If the dark mass was a storm front, it was definitely overtaking *Reliant*.

"Still won't leave the ship in the hands of others, will ye?" Stroud asked.

Aware of the way the other men of the crew watched them, aware, too, that they would report to the men that hadn't seen Stroud talking to him, Ethan stood his ground.

Stroud offered his hand.

Ethan took it, but felt like the gesture damned him in the eyes of the true sailing crew. Curiously, since they had faced down McAfee and the confrontation between captain and crew had been suitably banked, Stroud had become friendly toward Ethan. Despite the overtures and the need for a friend, Ethan still wasn't certain how he felt about the other man's behavior.

Perhaps Stroud recognized his own shortcomings as mate and recognized that Folger had hired him primarily for his bodyguarding ability and seamanship. With a choice between having the captain manage the ship by himself or with Ethan, Stroud had chosen to serve as go-between for Ethan and Folger. In a way, Stroud's efforts brought humor to Ethan because he recognized them as an abbreviated form he was trying to manage with the captain and all of the ship's crew.

Still, Stroud's own efforts and concerns impeded Ethan's progress and kept the crew suspicious of him.

"I couldn't stay in the cabin," Ethan said.

Stroud nodded. "Ye've noticed the storm front behind us?"

"Aye."

Stroud stood at Ethan's side. "I think it's gaining on us."

"I agree. But maybe it will blow itself out before it comes upon us."

"Do ye think it will?"

"I can hope."

Stroud rubbed his broad, whiskered chin with a sound like a rasp chewing wood. "I ain't never cared none for bein' caught in a storm at sea."

"Neither have I. Did you need something?"

Stroud swiveled his gaze back to Ethan. He hooked a big thumb over his shoulder. "Not me. Cap'n Folger."

Ethan nodded. "Thanks." He crossed the deck and walked toward the stern. After taking the companionway down, he rapped on the door.

"Who is it?" Folger bellowed.

"Ethan Swain, Cap'n."

"Come in."

Ethan opened the door and stepped inside. As usual, Captain Folger sat behind his desk.

"I thought we might take a moment this morning and talk," the captain said. A logbook lay open before him. "I was just writing up the events of the past few days. It has taken some time. Those days were quite remarkable."

Ethan gazed at the script that flowed over the pages.

"I thought I might talk with you as I progressed on these entries." Folger stared at Ethan with dead eyes. The captain brought his hands together, steepling his fingers. "I want to make certain I write the—correct—sequence of events that happened four days ago."

Wariness throbbed inside Ethan, pacing like a bored tiger in a cage. He didn't know if Folger was threatening him, baiting him, or merely taunting him.

"No comment?"

"No, Cap'n."

Folger heaved a dramatic sigh. "That's a disappointment. You waxed so eloquently only four days ago."

In that moment, Ethan despised the man more than he had the whole long voyage. "Perhaps you're being too generous, Cap'n." He tried to keep his voice flat.

Folger locked eyes for a moment. "Perhaps I am, perhaps I am. Still, you did save several foolish men from their deaths. The bloodletting that you prevented would have been a fierce and unrelenting one. I won't brook an act of rebellion against my authority. These men just haven't been made into believers yet."

A muscle twitched in Ethan's cheek. He kept his jaw stubbornly closed. "Aye, Cap'n."

"Most of those men owe you their very lives, wouldn't you say?"

"No, sir," Ethan replied. "I wouldn't rightly say that." He knew it was the wrong thing to say. Simply agreeing with the captain would have been better. But he couldn't do it.

Folger's eyebrows rose in surprise. "And why not?"

"They chose to save themselves," Ethan replied. "I only pointed out to some of them that it was possible."

Nodding slightly, Folger said, "A gallant answer. And yet, I have to wonder where all of this gallantry comes from." He reached into the desk for a moment, then brought out the ship's articles. He unfastened the strings that bound the portfolio together and rummaged among the papers for a moment. "You were born on Nantucket, to a family of rather common means."

Steeling himself and the immediate angry impulse that filled him, Ethan distanced himself from the obvious insult.

"Your father was a sailing man, but he was no captain."

"No."

Putting on a show of perusing the few densely written pages that described the performance and duties of Ethan Swain, able-bodied seaman, Folger said, "Your father was a middling successful shipwright."

"He still is, Cap'n."

Folger inclined his head. "Quite right. So he is."

"As for middling successful, my father raised his family and saw each of his children successful in turn."

Folger regarded Ethan. "Really? I find mention of your older sister, who seems to have married well and moved to Boston with her husband, a younger brother who is at the College of William and Mary, and two younger brothers who work with your father."

"Aye, Cap'n," Ethan said because Folger's silence left him no choice.

"Does your father count those children successful?"

"Aye, he does."

"I was told," Folger said, leaning back in his chair, "that your father didn't care to raise sailing men. That you signed on to a ship at age thirteen without his blessing."

"Without his blessing," Ethan replied, "but with his permission. And I was twelve at the time, Cap'n."

"Why didn't he want you to take to the sea?"

"My father said the sea took a man too far from home."

"Didn't he want you to return to Nantucket and help him?" Folger tapped the papers. "According to these documents, you've a fair hand for replacing or repairing parts of a ship."

"Aye."

"Then why didn't you stay?"

Ethan hesitated only a moment. "Because I love the sea, Cap'n. I love the feel of a rolling ship's deck beneath my feet, to watch canvas bell out full-bellied with the wind, and to know there's adventure waiting somewhere out here."

Folger waved the comment away. "Romantic nonsense. The sea is a job, Mr. Swain. That's all."

"Aye, sir."

"Do you think you have found much adventure out upon the sea?"

Ethan lied. "No, Cap'n."

"Some would consider taking whales to be adventurous work."

Ethan shrugged. "Taking whales is dangerous and bloody work, and maybe the first few times you tie onto one it is exciting."

"But you don't think so anymore?"

Meeting the man's gaze squarely, Ethan said, "Three men are dead because of the last whale we took, and Bill Fedderson is likely going to lose his arm. No, Cap'n, I don't look on the taking of whales as an adventure. It's hard, dangerous work."

"What you signed on to do, yet," Folger said smoothly, rubbing the fingers of one hand over the back of the other, "that's not all you want, is it? You'd like to be captain of a ship yourself one day."

Ethan hesitated.

"Oh there's no reason to deny it, Mr. Swain. I can see that want clearly writ upon your face."

"Aye," Ethan declared.

Folger shook his head wearily. "How do you propose to become a captain?"

"By putting in time, Cap'n."

"Do you know many ship's mates—or even junior officers for that matter—that actually make their way up to a full captaincy?"

"I'm only interested in one," Ethan said.

Folger barked mean-spirited laughter. "To be so worldly in many respects, you remain quite naive."

Bristling with anger, Ethan barely managed to curb his tongue. He remained silent with effort, feeling his legs shake.

"Few men are ever chosen for the mantle of captain from within the ranks," Folger said. "Men are born to command. They don't learn it."

Almost Ethan loosed his anger, but he knew once he started he wouldn't let up and would say a number of things that he couldn't take back.

"The gift of command is recognized early in such men," Folger said. "They are chosen men, groomed from the day they can stand on a ship's deck, and molded into proper captains." The captain cleared his throat. "So it was with me. I started on board a ship with my father, quickly bested both his skill and his experience with sailing, and was made captain of a merchant ship."

Ethan stood quietly, determined that he wouldn't let Folger's words tear down his hopes for a ship he could call his own. *You can have this ship, Ethan.* Teresa's words came to him then from the past. *You can have this ship, and you can have me. Am I not everything a man could ever hope after? You can have me and this fine ship. Just promise me that you'll name the ship after me and that you'll always be mine.*

He had promised, and he had loved her. Right up until the moment he loathed the very sight of her.

"Mr. Swain," Folger said sharply.

"Aye, Cap'n." Ethan's jaw ached with the effort of maintaining self-control. Timothy Madison had died for no good reason. Captain Folger might as well have pushed the man into the water himself and held him under for the sharks to get.

"Are you paying attention?"

"Aye, Cap'n."

Harumphing indignantly, Folger didn't appear convinced. "How many years have you been at sea?"

"Fourteen, Cap'n."

Checking the papers in front of him, Folger said, "That's not precisely true. It states here that you were gone from sailing for a seven-month period."

That was a lie, but a carefully crafted one. "Aye," Ethan answered.

"You were"—Folger peered more closely at the papers—"a farmer it says here."

"Actually," Ethan said, "I worked on a farm."

Leaning back in the chair, Folger put his fingers to his lips and stared at Ethan as though he could see through him. "Why, pray tell?"

Ethan's face burned a little in embarrassment. He didn't know what Folger would think, and he had learned that a lie had to hew closely to the truth in order to maintain its integrity. Telling the lie would also tell the truth to a degree, and he suddenly felt more vulnerable and exposed than at any time during the voyage.

"There was," Ethan said, "a young woman."

"Why did you leave her? Was"—Folger noted the papers again—"tobacco farming ultimately not to your liking?"

Surprisingly, even after the last few years and how things had turned out with Teresa at the end, the emotion within Ethan was as sharp and as uncertain as broken glass. As the emotion slipped and turned inside him, it slashed and cut at him.

"She died, Cap'n," Ethan said in a choked voice.

The answer evidently startled Folger. He had been looking for a weak spot, perhaps that the young woman had left him for another. "I'm sorry for your loss." He sounded like he meant it, but he also sounded like he didn't know what to do with the information.

"Thank you, Cap'n."

Folger poured more coffee from a small silver service to his side. He did not offer any to Ethan. "There is one other matter I'd like to discuss with you."

Ethan nodded.

"That captain we encountered four days ago—" Folger made an obvious effort at trying to remember.

"Cap'n Fisher," Ethan said. "This ship was named *Sunfisher*. The information is in my logbook entry for that day."

"Of course it is." Folger leaned forward in anticipation. "Was it my imagination, or did Captain Fisher know you?"

Ethan's heart thudded inside his chest. "I didn't know him, Cap'n. I don't think that he could know me."

"You've never sailed with him before?"

Careful, Ethan cautioned himself. A lie was best with no unequivocal absolutes. "I've sailed with a number of men at different times. Perhaps he was a passenger. Perhaps he was a captain that I once saw in a tavern. I don't get to know a man much unless I work alongside him."

In those words, the truth of how well Ethan knew Jonah McAfee came bearing the acrid stench of gunpowder and the iron taste of spilled blood. His knowledge of the man resonated in the quiver of muscles in his forearm as he remembered the force and clang of blade against blade.

I should have killed him, too, Ethan thought bitterly. But he knew the choice hadn't been his to make. McAfee had been the better swordsman; Ethan had been forced to use all his skills just to escape death at the man's hands. Even then, the sea should have dragged him down. Instead, by some miracle on his part and conniving on McAfee's part, they both yet lived.

"That man knew you," Folger said softly. "As sure as I'm sitting here, I know that to be true."

"I don't know a Captain Fisher," Ethan said, and that much was true.

Folger continued to stare at him, as if he were going to tear down Ethan's half-truths and near lies with the sheer force of his will.

"Will there be anything else, Cap'n?" Ethan asked.

Letting a long moment pass, Folger leaned forward again and dipped the quill pen into the inkstand. He looked away, studying the names and figures on his logbook. "You think I'm overly harsh on these men, don't you?"

"Aye," Ethan answered.

"Have you ever considered why?"

Because you're petty and vindictive, Ethan thought, though he didn't say that. "You want to run a tight ship."

A curved, mirthless smile fitted Folger's lips. "Oh, it's more than that. I want to run a very *profitable* ship. These men signed on in Nantucket for a lay of this ship's profits. If they leave the ship before the voyage is finished and the holds are all filled, they lose that lay. Anyone that we take on after the voyage starts gets a smaller lay. Like young Robert Oswalt, for instance. The less that has to be paid out, the more profit this ship earns. The more money *I* earn."

The view was a cruel one, but Ethan knew the assessment was correct. "Cap'n, a trained crew can be invaluable."

"This crew is *not* invaluable."

"If you filled the deck with greenhands, we might not finish this voyage."

"This is a ship. A ship may be captained, and the captain determines the crew's abilities. He makes a weak man strong, and he makes a strong man invaluable."

"But the harsh treatment of the crew only to drive them from their lays is hardly fair."

Folger grinned and pointed his quill pen at Ethan. "You see, that attitude of yours—that willingness or need to be *fair* to the crew—is what will keep you tied to a mate's position for the rest of your career at sea. Investors can't be bothered with what is fair; they can only worry about something that proves profitable. Those men, by the good graces of the investors who raised the capital to put into *Reliant,* have had a place to sleep and eat for the months that they've been aboard this vessel. That's all they're owed."

Ethan pushed his breath out between his teeth and forced himself to remain calm. "Not all the investors feel that way. I know some of them. They're good men. They wouldn't want to take advantage of—"

Slamming the desk with both hands, Folger stood and leaned forward. His face purpled with apoplexy. "By God, sir, do not presume to tell me what those men think or don't think!"

"Begging the cap'n's pardon," Ethan said in a firm voice, "but you don't know how open you're leaving this ship and yourself."

Folger remained on his feet, swelled up like a toad so that he took up as much room in the cabin as he could. "Leaving this ship and myself open to what? Mutiny? We've already faced that one four days ago, and the men all know how I will react to that." He smiled cruelly. "And they know how you will react to it—unless you've changed your mind?"

"No, Cap'n," Ethan answered because he knew that was the reply Folger wanted to hear. But inside, he knew that was the only answer there could be. A mutiny would still rip the ship apart and endanger them all. *Only a few more weeks,* he told himself. *Surely no more than a few months at most.*

"Then I propose that we just believe I know what I'm doing, that it's for the best of the investors and for the best of this ship, and let's leave it at that."

"Aye, Cap'n." The acquiescence almost caught in Ethan's throat.

"See to helping me keep this ship together," Folger said, "and you'll find yourself very well off when we make port with our cargo. You'll no longer be docked the cost of the whaleboat you lost."

Ethan remained silent.

"My advice to you," Folger said, "is if you make friends in this world, make sure they're friends you can afford. The riffraff and sailor trash aboard this ship are barely human. None of them are men you'd want to take at your side should you ever get the chance to go before a board of investors and seek to persuade them to let you helm a ship they owned."

Sadly, Ethan knew that was true. Most mates who made captain had to break old friendships.

"You can't be friends with the men and expect to be an officer," Folger said. "The division between the two is like whale oil and that sea out there. They just don't mix."

"Aye, Cap'n."

"Another thing," Folger went on. "I'll be following up on this Captain Fisher of yours. You were much too quick to react to the man. If you truly didn't know him." He paused, as if waiting for Ethan to confess.

Standing stock-still, aware of the gentle roll of the deck beneath his bare feet, Ethan made no reply.

"Well then, if that's the way you'll have it," Folger grumbled.

It is, Ethan thought.

"You're dismissed," Folger said.

Ethan turned and opened the door.

"Whatever your agenda is," Folger warned, "be advised that I'll be watching you."

"Aye, Cap'n." Ethan stepped through the door, went up the companionway, and gratefully walked into the sun and the breeze. Even with Folger breathing madly down his back, he felt reinvigorated. There had to be a way out of the mess he was in. He couldn't forever be held accountable for the bad things he had done. Or could he? The Quakers preached hard and long against the wages of sin, but if a man did penance, there still remained the prospect of salvation and redemption.

CHAPTER 11

Pacific Ocean 18° 34' S. Lat.—108° 72' W. Long.

BULLOCK WAS TIRED from spending hours peering out at the sea. His eyes felt burned from the harsh sunlight and the long days of searching the ocean since they'd left Easter Island. The previous day, they had found the whale pod they now kept under observation.

Every day, he was up before the sun awaiting first light, and only when the sun drained from the sky did he go belowdecks to work on his notes and papers until he couldn't keep his eyes open any longer. He and Katharine also carried out further research using the papers and journals he'd been given for the voyage in hopes of finding some small detail he'd missed, one that might offer up some clue about the elusive and deadly creature they hunted.

You're sitting out here now, he couldn't help thinking, *like a fisherman's bait. And you've got Katharine sitting and waiting with you.* The thought filled him with chill apprehension.

At the moment, the sun dipped low in the western sky, but sunset was going to be interrupted by the fierce and dark storm that had gathered within the last hour. Lightning flashed in the dark clouds, and thunder approached at a more rapid rate, letting him know the storm would soon be on top of them.

Bullock was also deeply entrenched in a good-natured argument with Perkins. The first mate had been amazed at the knowledge of the sea the professor had exhibited and had demanded to know where he had gotten such knowledge. Bullock had mentioned several of the books he had read on the sea, and Perkins had advanced the belief that scientists—excepting Professor Bullock, of course—would never venture out onto the sea.

"If you can't see scientists doing such a thing," Bullock stated calmly as he could, "then I suggest you reconsider your thoughts on such men."

"Fine," Foster challenged, turning toward Bullock. He was one of the old hands aboard ship, and wasn't impressed by much. "Then ye tell me, Perfesser, who such scientists are that might climb aboard a ship like this."

"Mr. Foster," Bullock said, "surely you have heard the names of Meriwether Lewis and William Clark."

"Them are the two what mapped the lands the French sold to us," another sailor said.

"Correct," Bullock said, warming to the subject. "Do you know what kind of men Lewis and Clark were?"

"Military men," Perkins answered without hesitation.

"Yes," Bullock agreed. "But they were much more as well. Which is why President Thomas Jefferson, in his infinite wisdom, chose them. Both of those men were scientists."

A general disagreement rose from the sailors clustered around Bullock, in turn drawing the attentions of several other bored sailors. The coming storm had drawn all the wakeful men up onto the deck and set them to peering out in concern at the cloud-laden skies and streaks of jagged lightning.

"They were scientists as well as military men," Bullock said. "Meriwether Lewis was an accomplished botanist, and William Clark was a natural observer and a trained mapmaker. Do you know what the men in Lewis and Clark's command called themselves?"

"No," Perkins answered for all of them.

"The Corps of Discovery. *Discovery*, gentlemen, not war. They ventured forth into those far-off places to learn things about the land that President Jefferson had purchased from Napoleon and the French. Most of the men among that group wrote in journals, telling about the things they saw and drawing still others. I've had the chance to see copies of many of those journals."

"Those men were scientists, too?" a young sailor asked.

"No sir." Bullock smiled. "They were very much men like yourselves. Men who watched and sought understanding. Men who could find their way around the written word and discovered a need within themselves to write about the things they saw."

"So Cap'ns Lewis an' Clark trained 'em to be scientists?" Foster asked.

"No, Mr. Foster, they did not. Actually, Captain Clark, though a keenly observant man, struggled often with spelling and grammar, including a graceful use of the written language," a woman's voice answered.

All heads turned toward Katharine as she approached the group. The wind plastered her heavy black wool dress the length of her legs all the way to her ankles. Her hair whipped in disarray, and, for a moment, when the lightning flashed through the sky, her face appeared as blue-white as a china doll's. She carried a cup in both hands, one holding it and the other covering it.

"Evenin', miss," Perkins said. Then remembering his wool cap, he reached up and doffed it. "Ye really shouldn't ought be up on the deck, Miss Bullock."

"Nonsense, Mr. Perkins," Katharine stated casually, as if the weather were no concern in the slightest. "I've discovered during this journey that I'm at least as surefooted on a ship's deck as you are."

The other sailors guffawed at Katharine's barbed comment, and Bullock was certain that Perkins's ears burned.

Katharine handed the cup to her father. "Coffee?"

"Thank you," Bullock said. He felt cold and soaked to the bone.

"It's only half a cup," Katharine apologized. "Navigating the companionway in these waters was more difficult than I had imagined."

Another horrendous crash of thunder rolled over the deck, so loud that Bullock had at first believed he'd gone deaf with the blast. Hearing returned slowly, dawning first with the sound of the waves smashing against *Brown-Eyed Sue*. The ship pitched more violently. At times, the waves were high enough to obscure sight of the whale pod. The huge mammals lay huddled together, awash in the hammering sea.

"Returning to Professor Bullock's story," Katharine said, lifting her voice over the sound of the waves and the rolling thunder, "most men that went with Lewis and Clark's Corps of Discovery, so named by Sergeant Patrick Gass in his published journal, found their letters and journals were well received by publishers, universities, and scientists."

Bullock looked at the gathered sailors. There they were on a ship that felt like it was foundering—at least, to his way of thinking—and Katharine was recruiting men who could add to the knowledge they sought to gain. She was already working with a man named John Maxwell, who had shown a desire to write about their adventures.

"Ye think if'n we was to write about the things we seen, that we might get famous?" Foster asked.

"Perhaps," Katharine answered. "At the very least, you might get paid something for your efforts by one of the universities that will be interested in what takes place in this part of the Pacific Ocean. Those of you that have seen Easter Island have already seen things and places that many scientists and college professors haven't."

Foster clawed at his beard with hooked fingers. Bullock saw larceny glint in the man's eyes.

"What brings you up here?" the professor asked his daughter, as she joined him at the railing.

"I wanted to see the whales," Katharine replied.

"You saw them earlier."

"Not at sunset." Katharine pulled a shawl up over her head to block the salt spray. A moment later, rain splashed across the ship. "Nor did I see them during the storm."

"Seeing them during the storm isn't such a good idea," Bullock pointed out.

"And I know," Katharine went on smoothly, "that some sketches of the whale pod nestling together under a tropical storm will liven up a presentation when you get the opportunity to speak of it back at university."

"Don't you have enough to do?"

"Not as long as you're still working on this." Katharine's voice suddenly raised an octave. "Look. There's a baby whale."

Drawn by the evident delight in his daughter's voice, Bullock glanced back out at the whale pod. The sky had grown so dark that shadows seemed to reach up from the water and cling to the sky with thick, ropy tentacles. It wasn't hard to imagine the sea reaching up to seize the sky and pull it down into the depths.

Out to the left, a small baby sperm whale swam near its mother. With the uncertain darkness grouped around the pod and no real reference for how big the adult females were, Bullock could only guess the baby's size. Usually they were twelve to fourteen feet in length at birth, and weighed in at two thousand pounds. The baby swam under the water, no doubt to suckle from its mother.

"Did you see it, Father?" Katharine asked.

"I did." Despite the tension and fatigue that haunted him, Bullock couldn't help but take joy in his daughter's smile. Every time he seemed to forget how wondrous the world could be, she would come to him and share her perspective about something. Even if the subject was something the professor was overly familiar with, watching his daughter's reaction made the experience seem new again.

Lightning flashed again. The harsh glare ricocheted from the dark heavens to the shifting surfaces of the ocean, creating momentary pools of silvery fire against the water.

"Yonder comes another whale." Foster pointed astern of *Brown-Eyed Sue.*

Bullock shifted and stared at the white-capped water, squinting against the rain and the sudden whip-crack of zigzag lightning that seemed to set the foam afire. At first he didn't see anything and thought perhaps Foster had been mistaken about seeing another whale. Then he tracked the waves and saw them break over the unmistakable square head of a full-grown bull sperm whale.

"Them females don't like the idea of the male gettin' close to 'em," Perkins said.

A pair of females left the pod and circled around to intercept the approaching male. Bullock knew that most males would have accepted the rebuke and gone away. This male, however, never slowed. He was almost at top speed when he rammed the two females. So great was his speed and his weight that he broke the defensive line that the two females had made and drove them backward. A fierce shake of his head and tail and he was through them.

The sound of the meaty impact rolled over Bullock and the ship's crew, broken for a moment by another harsh blast of thunder.

"Look!" a man cried. "That whale's attackin' them other ones!"

Bullock stared in stunned fascination. From all the studies he'd undertaken in preparing for the missions he'd been assigned in the Pacific Ocean, he knew whales to be gentle animals by nature. One attacking, without provocation by whalers, seemed unheard-of. Especially when a male was attacking others of its kind.

But the male did attack, swimming cleanly through the sea, cresting the ten- and twelve-foot waves. In another moment, the male was among the frightened females and calves. The male's great fluked tail rose and fell, slamming into females with bone-breaking force. The male rolled over and opened his lower jaw. Conical teeth ripped along the side of a female.

"God in heaven!" Foster squalled, only to have his next words covered over by an echoing blast of thunder.

The females didn't have a chance. Their numbers should have been their strength. Instead, being clumped together as they were only made them easy prey for a rapacious hunter. Already, four of the females moved sluggishly, obviously injured. The male didn't slow his attacks. He swam past the pod and came around in a wide circle to attack again.

Bullock watched as the male whale plowed through the pod again.

"What would make him do such a thing?" Katharine asked.

Tightening his grip on the railing, bending his knees slightly to ride out the heaving deck, Bullock shook his head. "I don't know."

The male slapped and bit again. One of the females attempted to stand against him, but the male's larger size and speed dominated her efforts. The female was summarily battered to one side. The sound of the horrendous impacts rolled over the ship.

"What the hell is going on, Professor Bullock?"

Turning from the sea battle, Bullock spied Mayhew striding across the deck. The captain pulled on a greatcoat and yanked his hat down to better shield his eyes from the driving rain.

"A rogue male whale is attacking the whale pod we had under observation," Bullock explained.

Mayhew left the railing, marching to the stern and bawling orders. In a short time, the stern cannon that would be used for defense against an unfriendly ship trying to sail in behind *Brown-Eyed Sue* and steal her wind was stripped of protective tarp and readied for action.

"Professor," Mayhew cried out.

White-hot lightning blazed across the sky. Thunder followed, so near and so loud that the noise shook the timbers beneath Bullock's feet as he led Katharine to the portside stern companionway. In his haste, he dropped the ceramic coffee cup, and it shattered across the steps.

In the flickering glare of a lightning strike, Mayhew's face looked lined and hard. "What is it that made that bastard go rogue?"

"I don't know," Bullock shouted back over the sound of the storm.

"Does it have anything to do with this . . . *thing* we've been sent to look for?"

"I wouldn't know, Captain Mayhew. Not yet, anyway. But I mean to." Bullock stared across the open sea at the battle that continued among the whales. The females remained unable to defend themselves or their young. "I should like to observe that whale more closely if I could."

"Would you care how many holes we've put into it, then?"

Bullock stared at the great beast rampaging through the whale pod. "Try and have a care that you don't put any more in it than you have a need to, Captain. That's all that I ask." Images of the falling star dropping into the ocean cascaded through his mind. He strove to control the giddy fear that ricocheted within him. He remembered Malachi's words, reminded again of how the mysterious creature's appearance in the waters was tied to the falling star.

Could there have been a connection?

Bullock's rational mind wanted to deny that. But the instincts that nature had instilled within him clamored at him to run before his life was forfeit.

This is the Pacific Ocean, the professor reminded himself. *There is nowhere to run, nowhere to hide.*

"The mother and the baby are coming this way," Katharine said.

Staring through the darkness, Bullock barely made out the mother whale racing slightly behind and to the right of her baby.

"Why don't they dive?" Katharine asked.

"Because the baby can't go deeply yet," Bullock answered. "The baby is still new to the ocean. Even if they did, they couldn't dive more deeply than the male."

"Mr. Tyler," Mayhew called out. "Is that weapon ready to fire?"

"Aye, Cap'n, but I can't guarantee the fuse." Tyler, young and robust, his chin covered with whiskers, blew on the slow match he held cupped protectively in one hand.

"Just steady on your course, Mr. Tyler. Mr. Perkins."

"Aye, Cap'n."

"Keep those men at that portside railing in case we need to turn that damned beastie back."

"Aye, Cap'n."

"And put a man on the anchor line," Mayhew went on. "I don't fancy being an easy target here in case we need to move quickly."

Perkins gave his orders. A skirmish line quickly formed along the port railing.

"They're coming dead for us, Cap'n," Tyler called from the stern cannon.

Staring out into the water, Bullock watched as the mother and the baby swam straight for *Brown-Eyed Sue.*

"They don't see us," one of the gun crew said.

"Or they only see us as safe harbor," Bullock replied.

"The male sees them," Katharine said.

Looking back past the mother whale and the baby crashing through the waves whipped by the storm, Bullock saw the huge male wheeling away from the broken and battered pod to give chase. In only heartbeats, it became clear that the female and her baby were only prolonging the inevitable. In their panic, both whales swam straight for the ship.

Perhaps, Bullock thought, they believed the ship was a shoal, or even another whale. The waves came high enough to interrupt sight of the whales, and they came high enough to sluice across the ship's deck. Perkins's skirmish line shivered under the assault of cold water, but they held their posts. At Perkins's urging, several of the sailors held their lanterns over the railing and waved them back and forth in an effort to scare off the whales.

Instead, the whales came on.

"Mr. Perkins!" Mayhew roared. "Cut that anchor line!"

Glancing toward the ship's bow, Bullock watched as the sailor posted there swung an axe over his head. The lanternlights glimmered dully against the axe head, but the lightning bolt that sizzled through the dark heavens made the edge gleam like silver for an instant.

Brown-Eyed Sue twisted and jerked like a fish fighting the line. Then, suddenly, the ship was free. And in the next instant the rogue male caught up with the fleeing female. He batted at her with his huge head, then snapped at her with his lower jaw. The sharp, conical teeth raked the mother whale's side. She turned to intercept the male, but he butted her again, knocking her out of the way as he pursued the baby.

"Professor Bullock!" Mayhew roared. "Get your daughter clear of that railing!"

Only then did Bullock realize that Katharine had unwittingly stepped into the cannon's field of fire. The professor hurried across the deck, caught his daughter by one arm, and got her moving away from the railing.

"Mr. Tyler," Mayhew said. "Fire on that damned creature as soon as you have your shot."

"Aye, Cap'n." Tyler bawled more orders to his crew. Together, they adjusted the falconet, pulling the weapon into line to make the shot.

Bullock stood at the stern railing, one arm protectively around his daughter, knowing she would be lost if she slipped over the side. He cursed himself, knowing he should have made her go below. Then, as the huge male whale closed on the ship, he realized that she would have run the risk of being trapped below if the creature holed the hull.

"Set yerselves!" Perkins shouted in warning.

Roping Katharine within his embrace, Bullock clung to the ship's stern rail-

ing with both hands. He was surprised when Katharine grabbed hold of the railing herself with one hand, then knotted a fist in his jacket with the other.

Just then, a huge trough of water scooted under *Brown-Eyed Sue*. The ship
sank like a stone between the waves. The next oncoming wave was a solid mass
of water that looked as though it would swamp the ship. Bullock braced himself
for the deluge.

The baby whale broke free of the water, swimming furiously. Then something seized it and yanked it back into the roiling mass of the ocean.

Light from the wildly swinging lanterns illuminated gossamer strands that
coiled around the young creature. Or perhaps it was only the way the light fell
over the baby whale's hide.

Bullock's mind somehow managed to catalog that oddity in the midst of
thoughts that he was about to die. In the next instant, *Brown-Eyed Sue* lurched
violently and started up the next swell of the ocean.

The baby whale broke free of the wall of water and seemed to hang in the
air for a moment, but Bullock knew the young creature was in actuality flying
across the distance on a collision course with the ship.

Lightning flashed on the gossamer strands that lay across the baby whale's
body. Then the creature struck the portside railing and crashed through. The
fourteen-foot-long body writhed as the baby whale bounced against the ship's
deck. Two hapless sailors got caught in the path of the baby whale, then were
swept from the deck as the whale rolled and broke through the starboard railing
to land in the ocean again.

Katharine screamed, demanding Bullock's immediate attention. The professor glanced up at the towering wall of water just as the male sperm whale
crashed through. For a moment, he believed the beast would land in the middle
of the ship.

"Fire!" Mayhew roared.

Somehow—later Bullock was never exactly sure how—Tyler and his men
fired the cannon. Yellow-and-orange flames leapt from the weapon's muzzle
only a few feet from the professor and his daughter.

The whale swelled to enormous dimensions, then whipped its body. Presenting the other side of its face, the whale showed massive white-and-gray web-
like scarring from something that had burned it years ago. An albino white blind
eye stared at Bullock impossibly from the pitted crater of its face.

It hates us, Bullock thought in that instant, and he was certain of the whale's
intent. The creature hated them with an almost supernatural awareness. Perhaps it

hadn't sought them out; but now that it had found them, it hated them. The professor had never met anything other than a human being that was capable of such direct emotion. Never had he seen a whale so *conscious* of the world around it.

The falconet's muzzle flash gleamed in the male whale's eye, and the wallop of thunder rang over the ship's deck between the high waves. Bullock didn't know if the ball hit the creature or not, nor was he certain if the handful of Perkins's men who had retained their weapons and had presence enough of mind to fire had hit the whale either.

In the next moment, *Brown-Eyed Sue* hurtled farther up the rising wall of water, moving just out of the whale's reach. Bullock hung on to Katharine, desperately hoping they could last through the increased intensity of the storm.

And he fervently wished that the male whale were gone.

CHAPTER 12

Pacific Ocean 3° 28' S. Lat.—107° 12' W. Long.

ETHAN WAITED ON *Reliant*'s deck, swept by the storm winds that whipped in from the east and steeped in the shadows of the moonless night. He watched Creel's approach with some reservation. For the last four days they hadn't talked any more than was necessary for ship's chores.

"Thank you for coming," Ethan said.

After a brief hesitation, Creel nodded.

"You know what needs to be done if we're going to save Bill's life," Ethan said.

"Aye," Creel said. "I know. Don't like it none, though."

"Neither do I." Ethan felt cotton-mouthed at the prospect. "Have you ever done something like this before?"

Creel shrugged. "A bit of finger here an' there. An ear that couldn't rightly be saved. A few toes now an' again. But never a man's arm."

"We don't have a choice."

"Aye. I've seen Bill's arm. It's set up with infection. Ain't no comin' back fer it. Even had we a real surgeon."

"No," Ethan agreed, and he wished that they had been able to sign a surgeon aboard. Even one of the drunken quacks no longer certified to perform surgery in a community would have been welcome. At least that way he wouldn't have been facing the savage butchery left before him.

"Have ye seen Bill's arm?" Creel asked.

"No." Guilt stung Ethan with the admission. "I haven't been brave enough to go see him."

Creel regarded Ethan for a moment. "It's not yer fault his arm's in the shape it's in."

"He was on my boat," Ethan said. "Under my command."

"Weren't no way ye could have kept Bill from harm that day," Creel said. "Lines durin' a hunt, ever' sailin' man knows he's got to keep hisself clear of 'em. Just wasn't Bill's lucky day." He spat over the ship's side. "Just like it ain't ours tonight."

"Can you do this?"

"I can stand it if'n ye can."

Looking at the man, feeling the incredible distance yawning between them, Ethan wished he could talk about the other things taking place on the ship. But he couldn't. "Is Bill still awake?"

"Was."

"I'd hoped he was passed out by now," Ethan said. If Bill were passed out from all the whiskey he'd sent, the situation facing them all would be much easier.

"He ain't passed out," Creel responded, "but he's drunk right enough."

"Does he know we're coming for his arm?"

Creel shook his head. "I ain't told him, an' Holy ain't told him. But Holy, it's been hard on him because Bill keeps askin' him if the arm is gettin' better. Holy, ye know how he is, Ethan, how he won't lie none, why he just ups an' says how the arm is gonna be better any day now."

"It will be better," Ethan said. He steeled his resolve. "After tonight, it will be better. Let's go find Robert."

Creel took the lead down the companionway, and they began searching the ship. Robert wasn't in his berth in the prow cabins with the black sailors, nor was he in the ship's stores or the galley.

"Gotta be below," Creel said, as they started down into the hold.

Ethan paused and took a lit lantern from the hook screwed into the wall at the top of the stairs. They descended through the second deck where the men slept and down into the hold proper.

Reliant pitched and yawed slightly from the repercussions of the distant storm. They sailed under reduced canvas, enough sail up to put them always ahead of the storm front but not so much that getting overtaken by the storm gusts would wreck the rigging if they got caught in a blow.

Ethan swayed on the narrow companionway, shoulders brushing against either side until he passed through into the cargo hold. He stopped a few steps down and lifted the lantern high.

Shadows retreated from the stacked barrels of whale oil that had been put away during the voyage. The barrels lay on their sides, stacked neatly within frameworks made of ship's timbers, one layer upon the other and all tied together with thick rope. Stone ballast, lifted from Nantucket's rocky shores, littered the floor.

The thick stench of rotted blood—so remindful of what Ethan was sure he would encounter in only a short time—cloyed his nostrils and mixed with the gamy odor of the squares of whale blubber still waiting to be boiled. Pinpricks of light danced in the hold, reflections of Ethan's lantern playing out against rats' eyes.

"May have to have us a rat hunt afore long," Creel said, as they continued down the stairs.

"Remind me in the morning," Ethan said. "We'll set it up." Having the rat hunt would also give the men something to do, and take them away from Folger's hard eyes for a time. The captain seldom came down into the hold if he didn't have to.

Ethan continued through the hold. *Reliant* swung back and forth, but he stepped in time with the changes, finding the natural rhythms within the currents sweeping across them. The barrels laden with oil creaked against the timbers and strained against the ropes tying them in place.

"Ain't like Robert to just up an' disappear," Creel commented.

Ethan silently agreed. He also couldn't think of a single reason why Robert would be in the cargo hold. None of his duties would take him there.

Rats squealed as they ran away. Occasionally their heavy claws scraped against the wooden floor or against the oil barrels.

Just as Ethan was about to give up hope of finding Robert, although he had no idea where he might look next, a thud sounded from a nearby row of barrels. Ethan spun at once, bringing the lantern up to bear.

The bull's-eye lantern threw a shaft of light over two figures huddled in the shadows at the back of the row. Robert stood with a knife at his throat and the man wielding the weapon at his back.

"Just leave offa this now," the man warned. "This here ain't no business of yers. Just between me an' this man-child, it is."

Although he was only able to see a portion of the man's face standing behind Robert, Ethan recognized him as one of Stroud's gang of ruffians. Ethan turned the lantern so that the light could reflect from his face without blinding him. "Do you know me, Webb?"

Webb tightened his grip on the sixteen-year-old boy. "Ain't none of yer affair here, Swain."

"Let the boy go," Ethan commanded. Sickness twisted his stomach as he realized what Webb evidently had in mind for Robert.

Webb twitched nervously and stepped backward, dragging Robert with him. "Let it go, Swain."

"Ethan," Robert whispered.

Ethan swung the lantern back to Creel, who took it at once.

"Stand back!" Webb roared. "If'n ye don't, why I'll kill this here boy!"

Ethan drew his long-bladed knife. "Harm one hair on his head," he promised in a cold voice, "and I'll gut you without killing you outright, pull your tripes out with my own bare hands, and throw you into the water for the sharks, Delmer Webb."

Webb pulled his hand tighter against Robert's throat. The heaving and pitching of the ship's deck caused him to nick the younger man's flesh. A worm of blood slithered down Robert's throat.

Quick as a lightning stroke, Ethan flipped the knife over in his hand, brought his arm back, and threw the weapon. As long as the knife was and as short as the distance was between Ethan and his target, the knife flew straight and true, not even trying to turn.

The heavy hilt slammed into Webb's right eye. The man shouted in pain, and his head snapped back. Before he could recover, Ethan gripped the wrist holding Robert prisoner and yanked the blade from the younger man's throat.

"Move!" Ethan growled. The black rage was upon him then. Facing what he was going to have to do to save Bill Fedderson and confronted with the evil that Webb had intended for Robert, Ethan didn't even try to stop himself. He kept hold of Webb's weapon hand and stepped around Robert, shoving a hip into the younger man and sending him sprawling out of the way.

Webb held his free hand to his bleeding eye and yowled like a scalded cat.

Stepping forward, Ethan lifted a knee into the man's crotch, hearing hard bone slap against weak flesh. Ethan head-butted Webb in the face, then kneed him in the crotch three more times, driving him back and up against the hold wall. He shook Webb's weapon hand, knocking the knife free. Maintaining his grip on Webb's wrist, Ethan drove his fist into Webb's bloody face. He kept hitting Webb, trying to drive his fist through the man, picking him up when he fell, then bracing him against the hold and hitting him again and again.

"Ethan! Ethan! Fer God's sake, man, leave off afore ye kill the poor whoreson!"

Breathing hard, Ethan grew dimly aware that Creel and Robert both had hold of him, their arms looped around his as they strived to keep him from continuing to beat Webb. The man was unconscious, held up only by Ethan's strong left hand.

"Ethan!" Robert cried, tugging at his left arm.

Releasing his hold on Webb's arm, Ethan watched the man fall to his feet. Even tired and winded as he was, the black anger throbbed at Ethan's temples.

"God almighty," someone said. "Did ye see the beatin' Ethan gave ol' Webb?"

"Liked to beat him within an inch of his life, he did."

"Ain't ever seen nothin' like that."

"Ethan," Creel called.

Taking another shuddering breath, aware that he was covered in sweat, Ethan stepped back and shrugged out of Creel's death grip. "Let go."

"Ye're sure?" Creel asked uncertainly.

"Aye," Ethan responded. "Now, damn you, let go." When Creel released him, he bent down for his knife and shoved the weapon home in his boot. He turned and looked back out into the cargo hold.

Five men stood behind Creel and Robert. One of them was Merl Porter, who still bore bruises and scratches from the beating Ethan had given him four days ago. Merl took a step back when he met Ethan's eyes.

"Ye men," Creel commanded, "grab aholt of this here poor wretch an' get him up to the brig. Put him in with Larson. If'n he still feels like havin' a go at somebody in the mornin', let Larson deal with him."

"I don't think there's any chance of that happenin'," one of the men commented.

Robert looked at Ethan fearfully. "Are you—are you all right?"

Ethan glanced at his right hand. Small flaps of skin over his knuckles ridged up from where they'd torn loose while he'd been hitting Webb. But most of the blood that covered his hand and arm belonged to Webb.

"I'm fine," Ethan said, and he felt ashamed to admit that. He pushed himself apart from the rage and the fear that clamored within him. "We've got to see to Bill. Are you ready?"

Robert nodded. "I am. But are you?"

For a moment, Ethan wished he could have hung on to the anger that had filled him. When the anger was upon him, he could do anything. Teresa had found that out.

"Let's do this," Ethan said. Without a backward glance at Webb, Ethan strode across the deck and went up the stairs leading to the belowdecks area. Robert kept pace at his side with the lantern.

At the crew's quarters amidships, Ethan stopped outside the private berth where Bill Fedderson had been hidden away since the accident. The black bag containing the surgeon's tools sat outside the door. He thought of the saws and sharp knives neatly laid and kept in the bag. Over the years as first mate, he'd learned an uncommon familiarity with the instruments.

Taking a deep breath, trying desperately to clear his mind of the violence he'd just been a part of and struggling not to think of the further violence he was about to become part of, Ethan opened the door and stepped through.

Bill lay abed. The bed in the infirmary was set up for surgery, made attached to the floor and not hanging from the rafters as most hammocks did. His right arm was swathed in yellowed bandages with dark splotches to show where the blood and pus had almost leaked through.

A foul sickness clouded the air inside the small room, winning easily against the smell of smoke from the lantern hanging against the wall by the door. Ethan knew the horrid odor came from Bill's arm.

Propped on his side on his uninjured arm, Bill glanced at Ethan, then at Creel and Robert behind him. His eyes brightened with fear. Finally, he shifted his gaze back to Ethan. "Surprised to see ye here, Ethan," Bill announced in a tight, hoarse voice.

"Good evening, Bill," Ethan said. He tried not to look at the bandages that held the mutilated arm.

"Figured ye'd have come to see me afore now." Bill licked his lips both nervously and drunkenly. He'd been hitting the whiskey bottles pretty heavily. One of the bottles, half-full, sat wrapped in the bedding within easy reach.

"I would have, Bill," Ethan said, "but the cap'n's kept me hard at it."

"I'd heard that, too." Bill tried a grin, but it looked bright with fever. "But at least ye're here now."

"I am," Ethan agreed. His stomach roiled as he considered what he was going to have to do. Over the past few days, he'd reviewed the procedure for removing Bill's diseased arm several times. All in all, the procedure wasn't any harder than cutting up a chicken for frying.

Bill glanced from Ethan to Holy, who sat on the floor with his back against the wall, then back again. "So what are ye a-doin' here?"

"I came to see how you were doing." Ethan stood inside the door. Both of them knew he wasn't invited.

"Doin' fine," Bill answered. "Healin'. Gettin' better day by day."

Ethan nodded. "That's what I'd heard."

"Won't be much longer afore I can take over duties again," Bill said. "I just been dawdlin' a little. Tryin' to take advantage of the cap'n's unaccustomed kindness."

"I don't blame you." Ethan made his voice cold and distant. He felt Creel standing behind him, blocking the door. His fist, elbow, and knee still hurt from the impacts against Webb's body. "I had the chance to take it easy, I'd be for it, too."

Robert crossed between Ethan and Bill, keeping his eyes lowered as he went to stand by Holy.

"What's wrong with ye, Robert?" Bill demanded. "Ye're actin' like I was a leper or something."

"He's had himself a bit of a scare, he has," Creel said, before Ethan could think of something to say. "Ol' Webb tried to get a mite fresh with him down in the cargo hold a few minutes ago."

A sour scowl darkened Bill's face. He popped a cork from the whiskey bottle. "Damn Webb's eyes. I never thought he was worth the powder it'd take to blow him up." He looked at Robert. "Don't ye worry about that 'un, boy. Soon as I git me fightin' strength back, why I'll give that bastard a proper wallopin'."

"Already been done," Creel said. "They're probably gonna be movin' Webb into the room with ye."

"If'n they do, by God, I'll promise ye that the bastard never gets a night's sleep," Bill crowed.

Ethan noted the fever in the man and how it had left dark shadows under his eyes over wax parchment cheeks.

"Now that's something to drink to," Creel said. "Ye gonna be generous with that bottle then, Bill? Or are ye gonna be a Greedy Gus?"

Bill grinned. "I'll be generous. Why, Robert done brung me another 'un after this 'un." He passed the bottle to Creel.

Creel took a deep draft of the amber-colored liquid, then handed the bottle to Ethan. Taking the bottle, Ethan felt the heaviness and stared into the amber depths. How long had it been since he'd had a drink? He couldn't remember. The nights that he'd spent in the embrace of whiskey or gin ran together like paint on a water-doused fresh portrait. He'd sworn off the stuff, hadn't touched a drop since he'd left Teresa in Port Royal.

"It would be better if ye drank with us," Creel said softly. "Bill don't like to drink alone."

Ethan knew from past experience that Bill was completely comfortable drinking alone, but the man drank more fiercely when he drank in the company of others. Drinking became a competition then.

"Even Holy's set aside his religion fer tonight," Bill said.

Glancing at Holy, Ethan only noticed then that the man's gaze was slightly bleary.

"Don't you worry about me," Holy said in a thicker voice than normal. "I ain't gonna let ye down, Ethan."

Looking at the four men around him, Ethan remembered the hardship all of them were about to undertake. He thought about the black surgeon's bag out in the corridor. Then he lifted the bottle in a salute to Bill.

"Your health, Bill," Ethan said. He brought the bottle to his lips and drank deeply. The harsh dry blast of whiskey burned and numbed his tongue and mouth, then boiled down his neck fiercely enough to take his breath away. Tears sprang to his eyes, and for a moment he thought his lungs had collapsed and wouldn't inflate again. He opened his mouth and coughed explosively.

Bill laughed uproariously, slapping his knee with his good hand and holding his injured arm close to him for protection. "There now. Give me the bottle afore ye drains it. Hurry up, now." He stretched his good arm out and snapped the bottle from Ethan's hand. Upending the bottle, he drank the whiskey down, leaving large bubbles to flow through the amber liquid and burst when they reached the whiskey's surface inside the bottle.

"Holy said Bill had been a-pacin' hisself," Creel whispered in Ethan's ear. "Keepin' hisself just this side of drunk is what he's been doin'. With us here, though, he ain't gonna be able to hold hisself back. Me an' ye, we'll drink a little, then hand the bottle back to Bill each time. He'll consider outdrinkin' us a challenge. When he's drunk, then we'll take him."

Ethan nodded. The plan was a good one. And none of them needed to be completely sober for what they had to do.

CHAPTER 13

Pacific Ocean 18° 34' S. Lat.—108° 72' W. Long.

"CAPTAIN MAYHEW, WE need to recover that whale calf's body." Professor Bullock, with a rain coat pulled tight against him for protection from the driving rain, stood in the ship's stern beside the captain.

Occasional lightning still stabbed spears like bone white ribs through the black clouds, and in places the flat surfaces of the swirling sea reflected the light. The ship's rigging and sails creaked and snapped in the harsh whipping winds that greedily sucked the warmth from a man's flesh. The mainmast keeled over slightly, and Bullock knew the thick pole had cracked less than a foot above the ship's deck. A few of the men were still aloft salvaging sailcloth from the mainmast in case the whole timber came down. The ship wasn't beyond repair, but she was crippled for the time being.

"Professor Bullock," Mayhew stated in a harsh voice strained by over an hour of yelling orders, "I've lost a man tonight—"

"I'm well aware of that," Bullock agreed, cutting the captain off because they had already covered that loss several times. One of the two men that had been knocked into the ocean by the whale calf's hurtling body had been recovered. There had, so far, been no sign of the other. "But it's been over an hour since the attack, Captain. I submit to you that stopping long enough to haul the corpse of the whale calf aboard won't greatly delay any rescue attempts made by this crew, this ship, or by you."

Bullock bent over the railing, with Katharine beside him, and peered into the water. Lightning flared across the sky, webbing like the veins on the backs of an old man's hands, and was mirrored in the black sea.

With the net securely in place, the men used the block-and-tackle assembly to winch the dead whale calf onto the deck. At Bullock's instruction, the sailors played lanternlight over the corpse.

Even softened somewhat by the blurry yellow glare of the whale oil lanterns, the ropes of acid-eaten wounds that crisscrossed the whale baby looked hideous. Despite only an hour's passage since the attack, the poor creature's flesh had already begun dissolution, making it look as though days had passed since its death instead of minutes. Pockets and pustules of grayish green jellylike ichor sagged in the weakened flesh like mushroom growths. The hempen strands had burst some of the venomous pockets, and the vicious liquid snarled through the net slowly as honey.

"Bring it onto the deck," Bullock instructed.

"T'hell with it," one of the sailors whispered. "Better to throw the damned thing back in the drink, says I."

Bullock knew several other sailors agreed with the first. "Captain," the professor called out, aware of how precariously the whale calf's body hung above the sea.

"Clarence is still carrying injuries from the last brush we had with that venom."

Distant thunder crackled over Bullock's head. The rain drenched him, soaking through even the heavy slicker he wore to soak his clothes. "Captain, the presence of the venom only proves that the monster we're looking for was here. We have encountered it and came away far better off than that poor whale calf."

"But not better than ol' Maxwell," one of the sailors grumbled.

"No," Bullock agreed.

Mayhew shook his head. "This thing is evil."

Bullock thought furiously, willing the right words to come to him.

"Captain Mayhew," Katharine said, stepping up beside her father, "whatever we're after in this sea is not some biblical evil thrown out of heaven by a host of angels, nor does it have some especial powers or province—except that which we choose to give it because of our fear or lack of understanding."

Looking at the faces of the sailors, Bullock was grimly aware that none of those men were completely certain they hadn't crossed paths with some unholy creature of Hell.

"You don't know that the beast we encountered tonight hasn't marked us for its own," Katharine said. "Or that it might not choose to pursue us and feed off of the unwary along the way."

Mayhew's face hardened. "See here now, miss. I'll not have any mention of nonsense like that."

"It's not nonsense, Captain Mayhew," Katharine said. "You've seen the journals. And you've seen the letter from the president. We weren't sent here on a wild-goose chase. The proof of that hangs out there in that net."

Bullock watched the men, seeing the unease shift back and forth in them like the contents of a mop bucket on a rocking ship's deck.

"Now that we have bearded the monster," Katharine said, "let my father try to discover more about it. Whether we destroy the creature, or others come in our stead to destroy it, we need to better understand what they or we may be facing. Men are going to be plying these waters in earnest someday for whales, and the people that financed this ship—and your commission, Captain Mayhew—are going to want to know that we did our part in this matter."

Mayhew held Katharine's gaze only for a moment before glancing at Bullock. "Mr. Perkins."

"Aye, Cap'n."

"Hoist the damned thing aboard."

The orders were given, and the boom arm swung around carrying over two thousand pounds of whale. When the net was safely over the deck, Bullock asked the men to hold their positions. He took a lantern for himself, not at all surprised when Katharine did the same.

Crouching, Bullock examined the whale calf's back. The creature was held upside down in the net. Even as he watched, the corpse's flesh weakened still further, breaking down and sagging. Pockets of venom, aided by gravity and the ship's rough ride on the sea, found each other as they coursed through the flesh. They collected in one huge pustule at the bottom of the creature.

"Mr. Perkins," Bullock called. "Could I get a bucket please?"

"Aye."

Perkins returned in short order with a tin bucket. Bullock pushed the bucket under the venom blister distension.

Rocking unsteadily on the ship's deck, Bullock leaned forward with a scalpel. The professor slipped the blade's point into the blister sac. The pustule membrane split at once, shredding like it had exploded, and the great mass of venom dropped into the bucket and across the deck.

Steam rose up from where the vile liquid landed on the rain-soaked deck.

In the next moment, the mop bucket collapsed. Surprise hammered the professor when he realized that the venom had eaten through the tin and left jagged edges.

The blob of venom remained intact rather than diffusing across the wet deck. *Brown-Eyed Sue* rolled across a wave, and the tilting deck sent the venom blob scurrying toward the other side of the ship. Men pushed and shoved each other out of the way, screaming and cursing.

In disbelief, Bullock watched as the ship crested another wave and the venom smacked up against the cargo hold. In seconds, the iron collar around the battened hatch melted beneath the venom's corrosive effects. As the surface tension gave way to the rain and the tilting ship, a tendril of the venom leaked into the hole left where the iron had been.

"Hell an' damnation, Cap'n!" Perkins yelled. "That vile stuff is eatin' through the ship's iron!"

"More'n that!" another sailor cried out. "The damned stuff is eatin' through the nails in the deck!"

Mayhew strode forward and seized a lantern from one of the nearby sailors. He directed the beam down toward the area the venom had crossed.

The holes where the nails had been looked like black cavities.

"If that blasted stuff reaches the ship's hull at the bottom of the hold," Perkins said, "it could eat all them nails out an' sink us right to the bottom."

Mayhew cursed and sprang for the stern companionway.

Bullock turned to the whale calf's corpse and saw more pustules gathering, sliding malignantly through the dead creature's flesh. If they dropped to the deck, the current terror facing the ship's crew would be compounded.

"Mr. Morton," Katharine called, grabbing the net holding the whale and trying in vain to swing the load over the ship's side. "Help me, please."

Bullock went to join his daughter's efforts, adding his considerable strength to hers, then feeling the burden shove over the ship's side.

"Cut it free," Morton yelled. "Cut the damned thing free an' let it drop into the water."

Bullock wheeled on the sailors. "Don't you dare!" the professor thundered. "Don't you dare release this specimen while there is still so much we can learn."

The sailors froze in their tracks.

"Go with the captain, Father," Katharine said. "I'll stay with the men here and keep watch over the whale."

Bullock hesitated, hating leaving his daughter facing such a grim situation. But there was no choice. Before he could turn to give chase to the captain and the other part of the crew, another huge blob of venom dropped free of the whale calf's corpse. The blob missed the ship and dropped into the sea, a ghostly patch of gray-green for just an instant before disappearing into the depths.

In addition to being corrosive to metal, the fluid was obviously heavier than water. Bullock filed the observation away, then turned and ran to the bow companionway.

He fled down the rain-slick steps, slipping and almost falling twice, landing with jarring thuds. The sound of men's hoarse and fearful voices echoed through the cavernous ship's hold ahead of him.

Racing through the forecastle cabins where the lower-ranked ship's crew bedded when not on watch, Bullock reached the secondary hatch. The cover had been left off so that the sailors could go belowdecks as they needed to in order to shift the load during the storm. Lying at anchor on the turbulent waves had caused several minor incidents that had required immediate attention.

The professor stood on one side of the hatch while Mayhew and the crew milled around from the other side, completely encircling the opening. They all had their lanterns directed into the cavernous hold. The beams raked over the crates, barrels, and bags that held the expedition's supplies.

Bullock pushed through the sailors. He knelt and watched as the green-gray mass tracked across the floor.

Dark water swirled an inch or two deep in the hold. The mass rolled beneath the water, looking like a massive slug.

"We've got to get that up from the hold," Mayhew barked. "That hull isn't just held together with trunnels. There are nails in those planks as well."

Bullock knew that sailing men preferred treenails, *trunnels,* as they were called, because nails rusted and allowed rot to fester in a ship. Usually iron nails were used on easy-to-reach areas above the waterline.

The mass continued to slip back and forth at the stern. The lanternlights made it glow.

"Get buckets," Bullock instructed.

"That damn stuff eats through buckets," Horace, one of the mates, said. He was big and blustery by nature, but fear was eating into him.

"Line the buckets with canvas," Bullock said. "The venom doesn't eat through the hemp nets. It shouldn't be able to eat through canvas."

The men stared at him, and he felt their anger and frustration.

"You'll need canvas to wrap around your feet and legs, too," Bullock said. He forced himself to remain calm and to think logically through the problem. "Elsewise the venom will attack your exposed skin. Three or four layers will suffice, I should think."

Bullock stood aside as Perkins led his group of men down the ladder into the cargo hold. Once the last man had started down the ladder, Bullock lowered himself and started clambering down the rungs as well.

At the bottom of the ladder, Perkins assembled the crew, instructing them to wrap the canvas bits around their feet and legs. He also made them hold their lanternlights on seven different pieces of the venom that they spotted.

Bullock reached the bottom of the ladder and stood on the uncertain deck. Cold brine slopped over his ankles and filled his shoes. The stench of half-rotten food, worm-eaten wood, barley, and animals filled his nose. He swept his lantern across the water at the bottom of the hold.

In an instant, he suddenly realized he was below the waterline. He glanced up at the sloped sides of the hull, knowing that if the wood should suddenly give that he was already submerged and well on his way to a watery grave.

Bolstering his reserves, the professor turned his thoughts and dark imagination from that grim possibility and concentrated instead on the pursuit of the venom. He took up some of the short pieces of canvas that lay atop a nearby crate and wrapped them around his feet and legs, emulating the sailors' actions. At the end he added more wraps around his left hand. He wouldn't risk his right.

Howling and screaming curses, the crew pursued the venom with a vengeance. They scraped up bits of the green-gray substance with shovels and dropped them into the two canvas-lined hogsheads Perkins had ordered prepared. Cautiously, as if approaching a live thing, the men closed ranks on the final venom blob.

The venom wavered under the inches of water, spreading out as wide across as two pie plates. The mass coiled unpleasantly, as if it was breathing, but Bullock knew that couldn't be true.

It's not alive. The professor was surprised how many times he had told himself that as he followed the men.

Perkins growled orders and cautioned his forces. The men made tentative contact with their shovels. Several of the blades were pitted and jagged, showing the corrosive effects of the venom. They pushed and shoved on the mass with their shovels and failed time and time again to get under it.

"Pour the contents of one hogshead into the other," Bullock said. "Free up one of the barrels, then tip the empty one over and shove the venom inside it."

Grumbling at the professor, the sailors followed Perkins's orders. They pushed the empty barrel next to the venom and tried to herd the mass into the container. Metal hissed and bubbled when the shovels contacted the mass, and acrid smoke that burned Bullock's nose curled up in gray wisps.

Without warning, a muffled *crack!* came from under the water. With all the light on the mass, Bullock saw the plank under the venom suddenly tear loose, creating a hole nearly a foot wide and almost two feet long. The plank swept under the mass and hurled it into the face of a sailor who had been shoving it toward the overturned hogshead.

The sailor screamed—once—as the venom hit him in the face. The blob was turgid then, as if it had congealed in the cold brine swirling through the ship's hold. The mass lay on the man's face like a plaster, staying with him even as his legs went out from under him and he toppled into the water.

"We've sprung a leak!"

"Someone get the cap'n!"

"Get that damned thing off Carson!"

Two sailors ran for the ladder while the others stood mutely by as Carson fought for his life. Frozen by the terrible sight of the venom eating into the man's face, Bullock stared helplessly.

In the space of a drawn breath, the venom seeped into Carson's eyes and burned them, making them melt like wax on a candle. The man quivered as though palsied. His back reared and shoved his hips from the wet deck until he appeared about ready to break in half. The flesh of his face gave way, parting in greasy strands like honeycomb freshly ripped from a beehive. Light gleamed from the blood-streaked skull revealed beneath, glinted from the gold teeth in his jaws.

Carson fell back as motor control left him. Bullock hoped that the man's life had ended before that, or that the agony had been so overwhelming he had felt nothing in those final seconds before death took him.

Water continued pouring through the hull where the plank had given way. Perkins squalled orders, getting the men moving.

Bullock kept hold of Perkins's shoulder. "I need your help, Mr. Perkins."

"What? I got no time fer this. If'n we don't plug up that hole, we're all gonna be on the bottom come morning." Perkins tried to pull away, but Bullock's grip was like a vise.

Bullock gestured at the dead man. "Help me get that poor unfortunate into the hogshead while the venom yet remains adhered to him."

Perkins gaped at the suggestion. "That's a man there. Not some chunk o' wood."

"I'm quite well aware of that, Mr. Perkins. But at the moment, that man's body is the only thing keeping the venom collected so that it may not run rampant through this crew. The samples we took from Warren Johnstone's body were obviously very diluted. We have no way of knowing how long such a dilution takes, and if your men are going to be down in this hold working to repair that hole, they don't need to be worried about this as well. Do they?"

"No."

"Then for God's sake, man, let's get this done. Hold the barrel for me. I'll attend to the body."

Perkins held the hogshead in the swirling water while yelling at the men working to temporarily plug the leak.

Using his strength and setting himself, keeping himself calm despite all the confusion and clamor taking place around him, Bullock threw his right arm under Carson's body and closed his left fist in the man's sodden shirt inches below the venom. He threw Carson's corpse across his hip, guiding the body with his right hand, and shoved the dead man headfirst into the barrel.

"God forgive us such harsh treatment," Perkins muttered.

Bullock barely heard the words above the men's voices. He gripped the barrel in his two arms, ducking his head to avoid the dead man's feet. Glancing around, the lighting made uncertain with the way the ship pitched and the hurried movements of the lanterns, he didn't see any venom droplets that had been scattered by his lifting of the body. He hoped they'd gotten all of the venom, feeling certain that even a spoonful might be enough to incapacitate or kill an unwary victim. The lantern he'd been carrying bobbed in water that had crept up to his calves. So far, the light hadn't been extinguished.

Wrapping his arms around the barrel and squatting, Bullock lifted the barrel with the dead man in it. Knowing that some of the sailors around him were staring at him in shocked surprise, the professor strode to the nearest crates that he judged would safely remain out of the rising water for some time. He deposited the barrel on the crate, then watched as Perkins and his crew battled to save the sinking ship.

CHAPTER 14

Pacific Ocean 3° 28' S. Lat.—107° 12' W. Long.

BILL FEDDERSON SANG sea shanties at the top of his voice. His whiskey-slurred words reverberated within the small room as he sat in bed with his injured arm tucked up under him. His good hand was wrapped tightly around a half-empty bottle of whiskey that he showed every intention of finishing.

"Saints preserve us," Creel snarled in a hoarse whisper, "that bastard is gonna drink us all under afore he passes out."

"Aye," Ethan whispered. "He will at that." He squinted at Bill, who was raptly engaged in coaxing Holy and Robert into singing a stanza of a raucous debauchery with him.

Holy shook his head slowly, sitting calm as could be with one knee crossed over the other. He held a glass of whiskey in one hand. Robert, flushed and flustered, struggled with the words.

"How drunk are they, do you think?" Ethan asked.

Creel smothered a belch. "Holy can pace hisself. I'd say he's fair to middlin'. But young Robert there." He shook his head. "I ain't never seen him drinkin' anythin' stronger than grog."

Taking a deep breath, Ethan struggled to gather his scattered wits. He hadn't been drunk in a long time, and he knew he was now. Not enough to impair what he had to do, but enough so that he knew his edge was off.

"Everything's ready?" Ethan asked.

"Aye. Robert done brought up a bucket of coals an' set it up outside the door with them irons we're gonna need to burn Bill's stump closed so he don't up an' bleed to death after ye take his arm."

Take his arm. Inside, Ethan shuddered at the words.

Bill roared another stanza, letting Robert join him.

"He ain't gonna make it if'n ye wait," Creel said, as if sensing Ethan's indecision. "Since we been here these past hours, I've seen them red lines in his arm creep up deeper into his shoulder. They're spreadin', too."

"What in hell are ye two a-jabberin' about over there?" Bill demanded. He stared at them.

Ethan knew that Bill full well suspected what they were talking about, and what they were about to do. But he also knew the man wanted to be lied to. Every man about to be turned on by his friends wanted to be lied to.

"We was only discussin' whether the cap'n mightn't miss one more bottle of whiskey," Creel answered, filling in the silence that suddenly loomed over them.

Bill upended the bottle he held, draining the last of the sloshing amber contents. He flung the empty bottle to the wall, causing Robert to duck hastily to one side. Thankfully, the bottle didn't shatter, only hit the wall with a dulled thud and dropped to the floor.

"Well, we'll have to be a-findin' out," Bill declared, " 'cause I ain't ready to call it a night yet."

Ethan moved toward the bed.

"What are ye a-doin', Ethan Swain?" Bill asked.

"You wanted to sing," Ethan said. "I thought I'd come sing with you."

"Ye?" Bill gazed at him with open skepticism. "Ye who ain't so much as whistled a note since I been a-singin'?"

"I've never claimed to have the voice you have." Ethan moved to the side of the bed.

Bill dropped his good hand to the bed beside his left thigh and reached under the blanket.

"Watch it, Ethan!" Creel barked.

Ethan was already moving, though. The gleam of the knife in Bill's good hand caught Ethan's attention for just a moment. In the next, he caught Bill's wrist in his left hand and twisted hard. Bill groaned and fought against Ethan, digging his heels in against the bed and almost breaking free.

"Damn ye to Hell, Ethan Swain!" Bill yelled. "I ain't a-lettin' ye do it! Ye ain't a-takin' me arm! God damn ye, ye bloodthirsty bastard! Ye ain't—"

Shoving Bill's arm down to the bed, Ethan doubled his right fist and slammed a straight punch into the man's jaw. He rolled with the punch, getting all of his shoulder and most of his weight behind the effort. His knuckles collided with bruising force, and the sound of flesh against flesh echoed in the small room.

Dazed by the blow, somehow possessing the stamina to stand against the punishment, Bill hung on to the knife and redoubled his efforts to cut Ethan. The wounded man called on devils and angels to aid him.

"Damn ye, Ethan!" Bill roared. "If ye try to do this thing—if I recover— why ye'll have to grow eyeballs in the back of yer head, ye will—for one night it'll be me there—and ye'll go into the sea with a knife 'twixt yer ribs!"

Ethan drew back his fist and hit Bill again. This time the knife came loose, spilling against the bed. He released his hold on Bill's wrist and swept the knife to the floor. Before he could grab the man's hand again, Bill clawed at his face, almost gouging an eye out. Blackened nails tore bloody ridges down the side of Ethan's face.

Abandoning any pretext at civility, Ethan threw himself onto the bed. "Creel. Holy. Robert. Help me." He struggled to keep Bill's body pinned under his.

The other three men joined him on the bed. The five of them turned into a wrestling match punctuated with curses. Bill head-butted Robert in the mouth, bursting his lips and sending him staggering back. Only a heartbeat later, Bill bit Holy's arm. Crimson stained Bill's teeth and stubbled face.

Ethan hit Bill in the side of the head, dazing the man long enough to get Holy released. Before Bill could recover, Ethan seized him by the hair of the head and yanked his head back.

Bill snarled and snapped at the air like a rabid dog. Creel kept him on the bed by stretching across his thighs. Vile curses and threats spewed from Bill's mouth in an unceasing torrent.

"I'll kill ye!" Bill screamed. "I'll kill ye all! God strike me dead if'n I don't!"

"Robert," Ethan said as calmly as he could while raising his voice over Bill's foul torrent.

"Aye." Robert stood unsteadily and wiped at his broken mouth with the back of his hand.

"Hold Bill's head."

Robert came around the bed and tried to hold Bill's head down gently.

"His hair," Ethan said, holding tight to Bill's hair. "You've got to hold him by the hair of his head if you're going to get the leverage you need."

Robert closed his fists in Bill's hair.

"His good arm, Holy," Ethan said. "Take hold of his good arm and keep him down."

Pale and uncertain of himself, Holy did as he was told. He prayed the whole time. "The Lord is my Shepherd . . ."

Listening to the litany of curses coming from Bill and the prayer that Holy clung to, Ethan stood up from the bed. Holy crawled into the bed with Bill, throwing his body over the wounded man's and holding him in place with weight and strength. The prayer grew louder, mixing with the curses that Bill kept up. Only his wounded arm was free, and he either didn't want to use the limb or the wound had rendered it useless.

Keeping himself centered, not daring let his thoughts get too far ahead in their consideration of what he was about to do, Ethan went out to the hall. He brought in the black bag and the bucket of coals that kept the flat irons heated.

Bill gave up on his cursing. He craned his head around and looked at Ethan in wide-eyed terror. "Ethan! No! Ye can't just cut me arm off! Please! Please, don't do that!"

Ethan would have preferred the cursing. At least with the cursing he could feel a little anger at Bill. Feeling pity gave him nothing to work with. He refused to speak.

Holy, obviously realizing what effect Bill's eyes were having on Ethan, shoved himself up farther till he was on top of the wounded man's head. He covered Bill's head with his body and kept on praying, starting in on the same psalm again.

Bill bucked, nearly heaving Creel off and catching the big man in the forehead with a knee.

"Best be at it, Ethan," Creel said. "This ain't gonna be easy on none of us."

Ignoring Creel as well, Ethan opened the black bag. Gleaming knives lay strapped to the side. He took one out and passed it through the flame of a lantern wick till the edges glowed red. Taking up the bottle of whiskey inside the bag, he poured the contents over the blade, cooling the metal with a liquid hiss.

He took Bill's arm in his, holding the knife by the hilt between his teeth. Bill pleaded and begged, and Ethan fought to hear none of it, to feel none of it. He used a leather strap from the black bag to make a tourniquet. He passed a wooden peg through the knot and twisted the leather tight enough to bite into the flesh.

Satisfied the blood flow to Bill's injured arm had been cut off, Ethan removed the bandages, unveiling the wounded arm. The flesh showed red with fever, blue and green with gangrene, threaded with yellow-and-white pus pockets.

There was no question but that the arm had to go. But where?

A one-armed sailor couldn't expect much in the way of work. But Ethan knew if he could save the elbow, Bill might be fitted for a hook that would at least be somewhat serviceable. However, if he didn't cut enough of the diseased flesh and bone away, the gangrene would set in again, and even more of the arm would be lost. Saving Bill's life again would mean another horrific amputation.

"Ethan!" Bill yelled. "Ethan, for the love of God, please don't take me arm!"

Then, focusing on the fact that the arm felt weak, dead and useless as a rotted branch on an otherwise healthy tree, Ethan slipped the heated knife from his teeth. He gripped the blade tightly. With the stink of the rotted flesh in his nose, Ethan sliced into Bill's forearm just above the midpoint.

An inhuman cry of agony and defeat blistered past Bill's lips. The sound was only partially muffled by Holy's body and continued prayer.

Relentlessly, knowing he was committed, Ethan shoved the knife through Bill's flesh. He reached the bone, then went around it, severing muscles, tendons and arteries. Blood gushed over his fingers, obscuring the sight of what he was doing while at the same time revealing the horror of what the task was. The tourniquet held. After the initial rush of blood, no fresh blood gushed over Ethan's hands.

When he had cut through the flesh all the way around to the bone, Ethan grabbed the flesh and pushed. The meat fell away much like the skin of a rabbit. Flesh worked as a unit, like a suit that held to a man only because the whole piece worked together. That was why flesh slid over bone so easily.

Ethan dropped the flesh glove to the floor. He dropped the knife as well. Reaching into the black bag again, he took out a carpenter's saw, set the jagged teeth to bone, and began to saw.

Bill screamed, then went silent.

Ethan felt the man's arm go totally limp. Face covered in sweat that trickled down into his eyes, he glanced over at Bill.

"He's still alive," Holy said. "He's still alive, Ethan. He's just passed out, is all." He nodded toward the wounded arm. "Best you keep on doing what you're doing."

Ethan raked the sweat from his brow with the back of his arm. "Creel."

"Aye."

"Hold this arm for me. Let me get at it more properly."

Creel took hold of Bill's skeletal fingers, having difficulty securing a hold with all the blood. But he managed.

Without a word of warning, Robert backed away and dropped to his knees. He threw up over and over as Ethan sawed through the arm bones with short, grating strokes that sounded like a blade against a whetstone. The awful noise filled the room. The arm sawed through cleanly. Bone was far softer than any wood Ethan had ever worked.

Creel dropped the arm in disgust.

"The irons," Ethan whispered hoarsely. "I'll need the irons. And I'll require a needle and thread."

One at a time, Creel handed over the three irons. Ethan used each one to burn the flesh of Bill's stump, cauterizing the bleeding arteries. When he felt he'd done all he could do, he took the needle and thread.

"Creel," Ethan said, feeling more at home with the needle. He couldn't guess at how many miles of canvas he'd sewn since taking to sea.

"Aye," Creel responded.

"Take hold of Bill's arm," Ethan instructed. "Pull the flesh down over the bone. I've got to sew everything together here to prevent any further infection."

Pale, and with shaking hands, Creel bent to the task. He circled the bloody stump of Bill's arm and tugged down.

As soon as he could pull the loose flaps of burned flesh together, Ethan pushed the needle home and pulled the waxed thread through. He took care to set his knots properly, as if he was setting canvas that would have to take a blow, but he worked quickly as well, knowing every drop of blood he saved was precious.

When the stitches were all done, and Ethan was satisfied, he poured whiskey over the amputation to keep the germs away. Then he took up the plasters he'd made ready for the wound's dressing. The plasters he'd cooked himself from a recipe given to him by a surgeon aboard his second whaling ship. Consisting of white lead, pork lard, and olive oil, he'd also worked in henna and attar of roses mixed with wax and lard to combat inflammation. He placed the plasters on the stump with deliberation, sealing the wound off from all exposure. Once the plasters were in place, he wrapped the limb in bandages.

Bill looked wan and worn lying in the middle of the bed. The blankets were twisted up around him from where he'd fought them.

Creel busied himself with putting the tools back into the black bag. Blood spattered the floor around the bag.

"Ye did what ye could," Creel said quietly. "The rest of it—" The big man looked at Bill on the bed. "Why that's between him an' his Maker."

"What—" Robert choked on his question. His lips had swelled hugely. "What—what are you gonna do with his arm?"

"Throw it over the side," Creel said. "Bill wakes up, an' he will, he ain't gonna want to see it none." He picked up the flesh and bone and shoved them into the bucket of coals.

"Somebody needs to stay with him," Ethan said. "We'll take turns. Make sure he has plenty of laudanum. As much as he feels a need for these first few days until we see if I've done the job or not."

"I'll take first watch," Creel offered. "After what we just been through, I don't think I'm much fer sleepin'."

Ethan didn't think he was either, but he wanted out of the cramped room and away from the sight of the man he'd just finished maiming for life.

"He'll forgive you, Ethan," Holy said, as if he'd read Ethan's thoughts.

Staring back at Holy, Ethan said, "I wouldn't." Then he turned, took up the black bag and the bucket containing Bill's amputated arm, and headed through the door.

CHAPTER 15

Pacific Ocean 11° 15' S. Lat.—102° 09' W. Long.

JONAH MCAFEE—CAPTAIN of *Sunfisher,* a privately owned vessel since he'd killed the previous captain for her and hung his body from the 'yards for the birds to get at for weeks before finally throwing the rotted corpse over the side—stepped out of his private cabin and made his way up on deck.

The sun was less than an hour old, and there was no sign of the storm that had ravaged the sea during the previous evening and part of the night. As he stepped up the stern starboard companionway, McAfee glanced into the rigging and saw that sailors were already hard at work repairing the slight damage *Sunfisher* had suffered.

Tall and imposing in black leather boots that stood out starkly against his white pants and blue coat, McAfee took the quarterdeck. He'd deliberately chosen the colors to allow the mistake that he was an American officer. Pirates would steer clear of him, and merchant ships would give him the benefit of the doubt.

Only the day before a British ship commanded by Captain George Harrington had confronted McAfee. For a time, the pirate captain had felt certain the Britisher was going to try to take him. And maybe, if Harrington hadn't recognized him as a pirate, he might have tried. Instead, Harrington had smiled and commented on the fact that sharks weren't aggressive cannibals by nature for a reason.

"One healthy shark won't choose to kill another healthy shark, you see," Harrington said. "But if one showed weakness, the other would smell the blood and have no choice but to obey the dictates of its predatory nature and attack. I smell no blood on you, Captain McAfee. And you smell no blood on me."

Surprisingly, they had talked for a while after that, each speaking of conquests that had been taken in the waters they shared. Some of the talk on both sides was filled with lies and grandiose embellishments.

As an added benefit, McAfee had told the British captain of the whaleship *Reliant,* stressing that her hold was very nearly filled with whale oil. When Harrington asked him why he wasn't pursuing the whaleship himself, McAfee had stated that he had cargo to deliver. If Harrington didn't find *Reliant* in the next few days, McAfee vowed to beat him to her. Harrington had taken the challenge.

McAfee had learned of two possible prizes that had interested him. The information had come from a Spanish packet ship. The ship had been running from Cadiz, Spain—where Napoleon Bonaparte's brother Joseph maintained an unsteady rule over the country as King Jose I—to the Spanish colonies in California.

The captain aboard the packet ship had been something of a pirate in his day as well. McAfee had noticed the man's avaricious eyes several times during the meal and the rum that they'd shared. The Spanish captain had casually mentioned two targets for a man hungry enough not to mind a little blood on his hands.

One of the ships had been the whaleship, *Reliant,* and a research ship called *Brown-Eyed Sue.* The Spanish captain had learned of the ships through his travels through legitimate ports and from contacts with other ships in the area. As a show of gratitude for the information, McAfee had given the Spanish captain a half dozen bottles of rum and the two ugliest slave women among the five that *Sunfisher* carried.

McAfee had no idea what a research ship was, or what one might be doing in this part of the Pacific. The whaleship had sounded immediately more lucrative. The pirates had struck out in the direction of the whaleship at once, cutting back and forth until they had caught sight of the smoke from the tryworks a day and a half later.

Only Ethan Swain—*God damn him*—had set the whaleship to rights and got everyone aboard ready for action.

McAfee forced his breath out, willing the anger inside him to turn to ice. Anger worked best for a man when he could be so cold the feeling would crystallize and allow him to make almost emotionless decisions, yet decisions that would lay open a victim's weaknesses. There was no aphrodisiac so strong as seeing a man humbled before him. Especially if that man was a hated enemy.

Ethan Swain had gained such a position in the pirate captain's world by stealing Teresa Santiago from him two and a half years earlier. Teresa, McAfee was convinced, would have been the love of his life. Her father, before Napoleon had deposed King Ferdinand VII from the Spanish throne and put his own brother Joseph on the throne in 1808, had been a smith and fencing teacher to the royal court. Teresa had been an apt student, and her father had doted on her, which was one of the reasons Ethan believed she had been as mad as she was. Her father had died alongside Ignacio de Allende in 1811 fighting for Mexican independence.

Fleeing from Spain, Teresa had ended up in the Caribbean in pirate towns. Rather than making her way by selling her body as so many women did, she chose to become a thief. For the year and more she drifted through the haunts of pirates and privateers, Teresa was a very successful thief who had left a long line of dead men behind her.

McAfee had felt certain that Ethan Swain had never seen that in the woman he had fallen in love with. For nearly seven months, Teresa had managed to curb the lethal madness that had fired her. All because she had somehow fallen in love with a man who was still more of a boy than a man at the time. The memories plagued McAfee. The fates had conspired to bring him both Ethan Swain and Teresa Santiago at the same time, and as a further devilry, to make them attracted to each other.

Swain had always seen McAfee as his jailer, and Teresa had been the fallen angel. Her sad stories of being deposed from the Spanish courts must have delighted and intrigued Ethan, and brought out the brave little boy in him that would have delighted in being her champion. She'd known exactly how to manipulate Ethan—until the very moment that such manipulation no longer worked.

The bitterness at the memories swelled within McAfee. Acid burned at the back of his throat. Teresa had very nearly driven him mad as well. He had given her all that he could, and yet she had chosen the boy sailor they had rescued and impressed into service aboard the pirate ships they controlled.

McAfee pushed the rage away. He had learned to master it. He gazed around his ship, as much a part of her as if the shipwright had built him at the same time she had stood up from her keel.

Amos Gilley, *Sunfisher's* current first mate, looked up from amidships where he was working on one of the cannon. He was a fierce giant of a man with whiskers, colored black and white like a skunk, that enhanced his round face. He gave orders to the men working with him, then turned and came up the companionway to join McAfee.

"Didn't know ye was up an' about, Cap'n McAfee," Gilley said.

"Good morning, Mr. Gilley," McAfee replied. Despite the fact that he ran a pirate ship—he never thought of it as a slave ship despite the stench—McAfee kept a tight rein on chain of command. "Have there been any sightings of the research ship?"

The research ship was a poor second choice to the whaleship, but McAfee wanted to take a prize. The slaves would stand on the blocks in Callao, but the temptation of an unknown prize that might be easily won was strong in him. Especially if, as the Spanish captain had noted, a white woman was among the ship's crew.

"No, sir." Gilley ran a big hand across his broad face. His china blue eyes were so widely spaced he appeared bovine. "Could be the storm last night threw the ship off course."

"And it could be the sea, Mr. Gilley." Depending on the lay of the sea, a man in the crow's nest could see for miles when the sea was at rest, or ships could pass within hailing distance of each other, both hidden by deep troughs.

"If that ship is out here, Cap'n," Gilley declared, "we'll find her fer ye."

"I trust that you will, Mr. Gilley." McAfee stood on the quarterdeck like a proper officer, with his hands clasped behind his back. He was freshly shaved around the Vandyke beard, but he knew the damnable powder scarring showed its worst early in the mornings.

"That whalin' ship we passed up back a few days ago," Gilley said tentatively. "We could go back fer her. We're due for a new moon a few days from now. Gonna be black as sin."

"I've decided to let that one pass," McAfee said. "For the moment. Perhaps Captain Harrington will have the good fortune to take that ship as a prize."

"Me an' some of the crew been talkin'," Gilley said in a conspiratorial tone. "That whalin' crew, why they've had a few more days to get the work done on that whale. There's got to be more barrels of oil fer us to—"

McAfee turned sharply on the man. "Mr. Gilley, do I make the decisions about where and when this ship goes?"

The mate's face blanched white with anger, but there was a lot of fear as well. "Aye, Cap'n. I meant no offense."

McAfee let out a breath and made himself relax. "No, Mr. Gilley, I know that you meant no offense. It was only your greed talking, sir." He turned from the bigger man and gazed back at the rolling green of the ocean. "Were it not for your greed, we'd have nothing at all in common."

Gilley guffawed, choosing to take the statement as a joke.

McAfee had intended it as no joke. Greed was the only thing that provided a common ground between him and his crew. Only the fact that he was clever enough to feed their greed and his own bound them to him. And only the knowledge that he would kill on the spot any man that dared stand against him or refuse an order kept them from his throat.

"There's a man aboard that ship," McAfee stated, "who will make us pay dearly for any attempt we might advance on that vessel. He's not one to give up easily."

"They'd have only gotten off maybe a shot or two apiece afore we'd been among 'em. We'd have cut them down like cotton stalks, Cap'n."

"That's what you think?"

"Aye, Cap'n. Ye trained us good an' proper, ye did. Why, we've taken prizes bigger than that there whalin' ship."

Disregarding the attempt at pandering praise, McAfee pinned Gilley with his eyes. "What do you think that man had loaded in those falconets?"

Shrugging, Gilley said, "I don't know."

"Grape," McAfee said. "Or broken glass if he'd had enough time to get that. And he wouldn't have allowed his men to fire from a great distance."

"We'd have still took 'em."

McAfee shook his head mirthlessly. "Would you have been leading those men during that gallant charge, Mr. Gilley?"

The mate bristled. "I ain't afear'd of no whalin' man."

"Ethan Swain isn't a whaling man," McAfee said. "He's a warrior, a man used to taking the measure of an opponent's life with his blade. Or snuffing out a man with a pistol ball through the eye as casually as you might extinguish a candle." The pirate captain had seen the man do both things while he'd been forced to serve aboard the pirate ships. Ethan Swain had willingly fought other pirates and privateers, which was what McAfee had targeted at the time until his luck turned on him and they'd had to take a merchant ship. That was when Swain's true colors had risen to the forefront.

"Sounds like a good story, Cap'n. Fit fer tellin' over a glass in a tavern, but not—"

"I trained him," McAfee stated. Memories spun inside his head, unleashing the turmoil that still festered within him. "He came to me when he had nothing. Clothing that wasn't hardly worth the time it took to wash. Boots with the soles worn through. He had no money on him, for he'd been robbed just before he'd been beaten and thrown into the sea. I came upon him hours later, when most men would have given in and succumbed to their fate, and still—by *God*—still he fought to live."

The rigging creaked overhead, and men hailed each other, coordinating the work they were doing.

"Swain was more dead than alive when we pulled him out of the sea," McAfee said. "I'd half a mind to leave him there, thinking he was already dead. But Teresa said that she saw him move."

"So ye saved his life?"

"Aye," McAfee replied. "That was potentially the greatest mistake I've ever made in my life."

"What was he?"

"A sailor," McAfee said. God damn him for a fool. "Just a sailor who'd been down on his luck. He'd been sick when his ship hauled out of Port Royal. The captain hadn't allowed him to remain on board, fearing some tropical contagion that would vet his crew. When he recovered, Ethan Swain signed on with the first vessel he could get, not knowing that the crew was an unscrupulous lot who moved contraband under the captain's nose to avoid paying taxes."

"Swain found out about they was smugglers an' they threw him over the side?"

"They knifed him as well."

"It's a wonder the sharks didn't get Swain."

"Well, they didn't, and damn them all for not being more able at their job."

"So that was how you got to know this man?"

"That was how I met Swain," McAfee said. "I got to know him because I kept him aboard my ship."

"This ship?"

McAfee shook his head. "No. Another ship. I called her *Wind Dancer*. She had a figurehead on her that resembled a woman dancing, her hands thrown into the wind."

Gilley scratched his chin. "I heard of that ship. Didn't know ye were the cap'n of her. Always heard it was a woman pirate was cap'n of her."

"I was captain," McAfee said harshly. "If you ever hear tell of *Wind Dancer* again, Mr. Gilley, you damn sure set the record straight on that matter."

Looking away abruptly, wincing from the severity of it, Gilley nodded. "Aye, Cap'n. That I surely will."

McAfee made himself breathe. His throat was so tight in his anger that he felt strangled. "I was captain of that ship, but it was Teresa Santiago that men remembered after they met her."

"I heard she sailed away one day," Gilley said. "Went to loot a ship an' caught her a prince from Europe. Folks said she went to demand ransom for him, held him an' threatened to have his head sent back to his father the king. Then I heard tell that she fell in love with him—an' his royal treasure—an' he up an' made an honest woman of her."

A memory of blood and the foul stink of gunpowder splashed through McAfee's mind. "No." The answer was simple and straightforward, and his tone clearly indicated that he didn't intend to elaborate on it.

"So ye know this Swain from back in them days?"

"Aye. He was just a sniveling sailor who didn't have a pot to piss in nor a window to throw it out of. I took him in." But it had been at Teresa's insistence. "And I taught him the trade of the black flag. I stood beside him in fights and kept his ass intact. When the time came and we took another ship, I made him captain of that one."

"He ain't cap'n now."

McAfee remembered how Ethan Swain looked standing behind the falconet aboard *Reliant*. The last time McAfee had seen the man, he'd looked dead. "No. In the end, he turned on me."

"Why?"

"Over a woman," McAfee said. "Over his own stupidity. At any rate, until that day I saw Ethan Swain aboard that whaleship, I'd thought him dead."

"Why would ye think such a thing?"

"Because," McAfee said, "I shot him. Dead center in the heart. I saw the wound myself." In a flurry, the memory of everything else that had happened flashed through his mind. "I watched him tumble over the ship's side and cursed because I could revenge myself no more upon him. Nor had I time to properly enjoy such a thing. It was over, Mr. Gilley, in a twinkling."

"Except it's not, Cap'n," Gilley said after a moment. "That man's still alive.

An' ye know whereat he can be found. Ye can have yer revenge upon him, an' this time ye can do it more right."

Anticipation burned like hot coals in McAfee's stomach. The promise of such an event was a sweet siren's call.

"Perhaps, Mr. Gilley," McAfee responded. "Perhaps I shall. But it will be at a time of my own choosing when I can make the most of the encounter."

A hoarse yell broke through the relative calm of the press of canvas. *"Cap'n! Cap'n McAfee!"*

Tracking the voice, McAfee spotted a sailor's head jutting up from the cargo hold.

"They's some of 'em bastids what's got loose, Cap'n!" the sailor yelled.

The call to action got McAfee's blood up instantly. He gripped the hilt of the rapier at his side, drawing the weapon smoothly even as he started down the companionway.

"Mr. Gilley, break out muskets for the men."

"Aye, Cap'n."

"And, by God, tell those men that if they fire without order from me—or kill any of those slaves without my command—that I'll have the heads from their shoulders."

"Aye, Cap'n." Gilley sprinted away, fumbling for the storehouse key in his pocket and yelling orders.

At a run across the tilting deck *Sunfisher* presented as she carried over the waves, McAfee drew one of the three brass-barreled flintlock pistols he carried on a belt across his chest. He thumbed the hammer and drew it back. Before he'd stepped out onto the deck, he'd recharged all three pistols. It was a ritual he performed every day, and that attention had saved his life on more than one occasion.

Peering past the sailor clinging to the ladder extending down into the cargo hold, McAfee spotted a half dozen slaves attacking two sailors with feral intent. The rest of the slaves, forty-two of them in all counting the three women, sat in chains that held them to the ship's deck. Manacles covered their wrists and ankles. Scabs and bloody places where the scabs had been picked off or worn away under the irons gleamed in the meager daylight that invaded the hold.

"Get back down there, Mr. Howell," McAfee commanded. "Damn your eyes but you'll not show fear before those cursed heathens aboard my ship."

A huge welt showed on Howell's homely face, extending across his forehead above both deep-set eyes. Blood tracked one cheek. "Cap'n, they's armed! They got me knife! An' they got Waller's and Davison's, too!"

The six free slaves turned to look up the ladder and at the hatch. They'd been inside the hold since McAfee had picked them up in Havana and would have remained there until the ship dropped them off in Callao, Peru in only a couple days. Two of them held knives that gleamed with the blood of the two sailors at their feet.

One of the crewmen kicked violently. His hands clutched at his slit throat. His fate was sealed. The other man lay huddled up with his hands over his head.

Howell clung to the ladder.

Kicking Howell in the face with his heavy boot, McAfee watched the sailor tumble back from the ladder and fall twelve feet to the lower deck. Howell yowled and tried to get to his feet at once.

One of the armed slaves buried his knife to the hilt in Howell's back. The sailor squealed like a stuck pig.

Cool and calculating, McAfee stepped over the the side of the hold and dropped the distance to the deck below. He landed, falling naturally into a squatting position. He retained his holds on his weapons.

The armed slave nearest McAfee raised the knife, holding the blade along his forearm. All of the slaves McAfee had picked up in Havana were unwanted by most slavers. The men were from an African tribe on the West Coast, all of them fierce warriors. Harsh scarring marked their faces, and huge, dangling, hoop earrings had mutilated their ears, leaving them twisted and tattered.

The other slaves still chained to the long iron poles that ran the length of the ship hooted and yelled. Their voices and the clank of the irons filled the cargo hold with thunderous noise.

The slave stepped toward McAfee and screamed at the top of his lungs.

Moving smoothly, McAfee raised the heavy flintlock pistol in his left fist. He pulled the trigger.

Smoke puffed up at once from the frizzen, then the detonation cracked through the din of screaming and yelling. The .58-caliber ball caught the slave just below his nose. Teeth splintered, bright ivory chunks scattering just before a rush of blood filled the slave's mouth and the ball blew out the back of his skull.

Even as the dead man fell, McAfee set himself and whipped the rapier around in a glittering arc. The keen blade bit into the side of the next slave's neck as he threw himself at the pirate captain.

The slave wrapped his arms around McAfee's knees, locking them together. Barely remaining on his feet, McAfee yanked his sword free of the man's flesh. In the next moment, he swung the heavy flintlock pistol down across the back of the man's skull. Bone shattered.

As the man dropped, McAfee whipped the rapier back around, turning aside the other man's knife only inches from his face. Before the slave could recover control of his weapon, the pirate captain skewered the man through the throat, slicing neatly through his Adam's apple.

Shoving the spent pistol back into the belt that covered his chest, he drew a second pistol and cocked the hammer. He lifted his left foot and kicked the dead man free of the rapier.

Still caught up in the cold bloodlust that fueled him, McAfee pointed the second pistol at one of the three remaining slaves who rushed at him. He squeezed the trigger. Blue-gray smoke and yellow flames belched from the octagonal barrel.

The ball caught the man in the forehead and emptied his skull over the two slaves standing behind him.

Neatly taking a side step McAfee led with his right foot, dropping his arm across his body, then whirled with the rapier extended in a backhanded blow. The blade slashed across the fifth man's throat even as the fourth slave toppled to the deck. Gore splashed out over McAfee, but didn't slow the pirate captain at all.

The sixth slave turned to run. McAfee struck at his unprotected back, piercing the man's heart with expert precision. Keeping the dead man in motion, the pirate captain flung him over the nearest row of slaves chained to the deck. He yanked his sword free as the chanting and yelling quieted. Only then did the stomach-turning stench of the hold nearly overwhelm him. He breathed shallowly, suffering as little of the stink as he could.

Howell groaned, moaning for help.

McAfee ignored the stricken man. The pirate captain glared at his cargo.

"Mr. Gilley," McAfee said.

"Aye, Cap'n."

"Get this garbage off my ship before it turns rancid." McAfee kicked the body nearest him.

"Aye, Cap'n. What of our men?"

"If they're dead, throw them over as well. If they still live, tend to them."

"Aye, Cap'n."

McAfee clambered back up the ladder and climbed out onto the main deck. His heart felt lighter, the anger at Ethan Swain's unforeseen survival a little more distant.

He crossed the ship and took his place once more on the quarterdeck. Perhaps Ethan Swain had escaped his wrath for a time, but the pirate captain knew that when the chance presented itself, he would rectify that.

Gilley mustered a group that lowered a cargo net into the hold. Once the bodies of the dead men were loaded into the net, the load was hauled back to the deck and dangled over the sea.

Without warning, *Sunfisher* heeled over from a large impact below the waterline.

McAfee barely kept his feet. Apprehension filled him. None of the maps he'd studied showed any kind of reefs in the area where they currently were.

Just as he started to think that *Sunfisher* had collided with a sunken ship drifting only a few feet beneath the sea—or at least some part of a vessel, which was known to happen—and not yet resting on the bottom, the ship was hit again.

That was deliberate. The cold realization crystallized in McAfee's thoughts.

The pirate captain gazed at his crew. Several of the men had fallen to the ship's deck. Others had grabbed on to railing or masts. One man dangled by a foot caught in the ship's rigging ahead of the foremast.

Holding on to the railing, McAfee made his way to the port side and stared down into the water. There, through the depths left sparkling silver against the green sea, a great shadow drifted alongside *Sunfisher*. Incredibly, the thing paced the ship with apparent ease—and obvious intent.

"Over here!" McAfee shouted.

The mass, certainly longer than the ship, shifted. In the next instant, the thing struck the ship again.

Sunfisher heeled over even harder than before. The prow lifted from the water, then slammed back down.

"Mr. Gilley!" McAfee roared.

"Aye, Cap'n!"

"Hoist sail!" McAfee glanced over his shoulder at the crewman standing at the ship's wheel. "Helmsman."

"Aye, Cap'n." Edgars was a seasoned sailor, used to taking orders while moving quickly.

"Bring us about," McAfee said. "Put us into the wind. Let her have her head and run."

"Aye, Cap'n." The helmsman spun the big wheel.

The wind caught *Sunfisher*, swelling her sails as crewmen filled the lines with canvas. The ship moved from a lope to a gallop.

McAfee peered down into the water, watching as the great mass of whatever pursued them receded for a moment. Then the thing changed course and caught up to the ship again. The creature—for surely McAfee believed the impossible thing must be—slammed into *Sunfisher* again, sending a shiver through her.

Praying that the hull held, McAfee drew his third pistol. He still hadn't fired the weapon. Extending the pistol, he waited till the gray bulk became clearer, an indication that the creature was surfacing.

Then the creature rolled to its side, presenting an evil black eye set in a crater of pitted skin that looked charred and left ragged from a bad burn in the past.

McAfee squeezed the trigger, praying that his aim would be steady on the heaving deck as *Sunfisher* hammered across the waves. The frizzen smoked, then the pistol bucked, but the ship chose that moment to twist violently between the combined assault of the wind and the sea. McAfee knew he'd missed the creature's eye, but he was certain he'd struck the great beast. However, even a .58-caliber round wouldn't do much.

He shoved the pistol back into place, only noticing then that he held the rapier naked in his right fist. "Mr. Gilley! Arm the crew with harpoons!" Harpoons would do more damage than musket balls, and there was no way to get a cannon aimed at the beast.

"Aye!"

"Stand ready to skewer this damn thing!"

In the space of a moment, four men stood ready with harpoons along the portside railing. The whale, for that was what McAfee believed the creature to be, rammed the ship again.

"Harpoon that damn whale before it breaks my ship!" McAfee yelled. He hung on to the railing and rode out the blow. "Mr. Gilley, get a man down to that hold! Check us for leaks!"

The crew hurled the harpoons. Three of them stood up from the whale's gray flesh. Then the whale submerged, diving deeply into the sea.

Nervous anticipation filled McAfee. Even with three harpoons in it, the whale hadn't been hurt too badly. But maybe it had been enough to—

Sunfisher rose from the water, tilting sickeningly for a moment, then came back down into the sea with a stomach-turning splash. The ship wallowed like a drunken pig, then the ballast set her to rights again. Timbers creaked and rigging snapped like rotted string. Loose canvas slapped the breeze.

The man hanging from the rigging dropped like a stone and smacked against the deck. His left leg was bent impossibly beneath him, and McAfee knew the limb was broken. When the ship heaved again, the man slid toward the starboard side. Only a quick grab prevented him from falling into the sea.

Left unattended, the boom arm swung wildly, yanking the corpse-laden net to and fro.

"Belay that boom arm, Mr. Gilley!" McAfee shouted.

Gilley issued orders, and three sailors sprang to seize the boom arm.

The creature came up under *Sunfisher* and rocked the ship again.

"Empty that damned net!" McAfee ordered. "Get the weight off the end of that arm!"

One of the sailors slashed the restraining lines with his knife. The rope parted, and the net dropped. On the way down, the hemp opened, releasing its gruesome cargo.

The corpses plunged into the sea, six black men and two white. They disappeared into the white froth of the water that trailed in *Sunfisher*'s wake.

The whale slammed the ship once more, again from underneath.

The damned beast knows it's protected there, McAfee thought. He didn't like the idea that the whale could possibly be so smart. He'd always thought of whales as stupid creatures, much akin to cows. And upon reflection in light of the attack on his ship, he preferred to continue thinking of them in that manner. There were too many whales in the sea, and they were much too large to comfortably think of them as enemies.

Tensely, McAfee awaited another attack, praying that the ship held together.

A long moment passed. Sailors stood on both sides of the ship with harpoons in hand. One of them helped the man with the broken leg back aboard.

In the distance, the corpses crested the waves and floated.

McAfee paced the quarterdeck from starboard to port and back again. He saw nothing in the water. The breeze pushed through the sails and the rigging, and the slap of the waves against the ship's prow rolled back over him. Everything looked calm.

"Somethin's gettin' the bodies!" a man yelled from the rigging.

Turning, McAfee stared back across *Sunfisher*'s stern. He shaded his eyes with his sword arm.

The bodies crested another wave, which carried them farther away, but as McAfee watched, one of the bodies jerked, then disappeared. For a moment he thought it was only the sea taking the dead man down. Then he saw the wave crest again and the way the corpse jerked.

Something has gotten hold of it from underneath the water.

The wave crested again—and another body disappeared.

Sheathing his sword, McAfee ran to the stern rigging and hauled himself up. The wind pushed at him as he looped his arms through the ropes and set his feet. He took a spyglass from the inside of his jacket and peered at the dead men.

When the wave crested again, only one body was left. One more wave, then even that body was gone.

A few minutes later, a sperm whale surfaced and blew even farther out than the bodies had been. As the water shot up in a tall geyser, McAfee glimpsed the creature's head and spotted the charred burn scarring.

"Mr. Gilley," McAfee called down when he saw the mate step up onto the stern deck. "Have you ever known an unprovoked whale to attack a ship?" He had heard stories of whale attacks himself, but generally those attacks had been by whales seeking to elude whaling men or responding to attacks.

"No, Cap'n."

McAfee studied the horizon, but he could no longer see the whale. But the whale might no longer be on the surface either. A strong sense of unease wove through his thoughts.

"Mr. Gilley, until I tell you otherwise, post extra lookouts during the watches."

"Aye, Cap'n."

McAfee climbed from the rigging, but he didn't feel relieved. If the whale chose to attack them again, for whatever mysterious reason had prompted it to the first time, there was no guarantee that the damnable creature would be seen even with the extra watch.

McAfee released his pent-up breath through his nose. "Helmsman."

"Aye, Cap'n."

"Resume our previous course to Callao. If *Brown-Eyed Sue* is out on these waters somewhere, I want her found." McAfee focused on the ship he hunted. Taking that prize would help him step away from having to let Ethan Swain and the whaleship go. *For the moment,* he promised himself. *Only for the moment. No one escapes my wrath.*

CHAPTER 16

Galapagos Islands 1° 23' S. Lat.—90° 48' W. Long.

CHARLES ISLAND, PART of the Galapagos Islands stuck out in the Pacific Ocean off the coast of Peru, was a haven for whaleships. Not all of the islands had fresh water, and all of them were ungenerous when it came to fresh fruits and vegetables that could be eaten and not make a man sick, but Charles Island had water. The land also had giant turtles, named after the islands, that were a source of fresh meat for sailing men. Once the whale had been harvested, tried out, and the oil put in barrels and safely stored in the hold, *Reliant* had made for the islands instead of Callao. They'd dropped anchor out in the harbor two days earlier and begun resupplying.

After hours spent hunting giant terrapins, Ethan stank of his own sweat and was covered in the fine white powdery sand that covered Charles Island's beach and continued up the island even under the desperate plants and vegetation that had taken root. He was tired, and his left heel was stone-bruised from a short fall over the uncertain island terrain, which was filled with treacherous sand and crumbling earth.

"Bill got out of bed?" he asked. He shifted the straps across his shoulders, which supported the hundred-pound terrapin he'd captured this time into the jungle.

"Aye." Creel matched Ethan's steps and carried a terrapin nearly as big as the one Ethan packed.

Ethan smiled a little at that. "Then he's getting better."

"Oh, aye." Creel rubbed a big hand across his face. "Ol' Bill gets any better an' ye don't figger a way to get him to fergive ye, why ye might want to start sleepin' with one eye open."

"I'll remember that." Ethan followed the path through the scrub brush they'd followed into the trees. "What about the infection?"

"Holy says it's almost gone." Creel fell into step behind Ethan along the narrow path.

"He's changing the dressings often?"

"Three times a day. Me an' Robert is helpin' out with it now."

"That's good." Ethan had been forced to change the dressings himself the first day. Dealing with the stink of the infection and the gory sight of the inflamed wound had been difficult, but he'd forced himself through worse things. In the end, Bill's violent behavior toward Ethan had forced him from his nursing duties. But he'd explained to Holy, who had reluctantly volunteered to take over, how to cleanse and dress the wound.

Robert and Creel had refused at first, claiming viewing the dreadful wound had made them nauseous.

"Takin' care of Bill," Creel said, "why it ain't so bad after ye kind of get used to it. An' the stink ain't so bad this last day or two."

"Good," Ethan said. "That's another sign he's healing. You're seeing to it he gets plenty of laudanum?"

"Aye. He gets what he needs. Holy an' me, we agreed to start weanin' him back a bit. Got so Bill was drinkin' more'n he was eatin'. That ain't no way fer a man to get his strength back."

"How is he doing with that?"

"Oh, he don't like it none. But I offered to wallop him along his gourd if'n he kept at Robert about it overmuch. Me an' Holy, why we don't feel bad tellin' Bill no 'cause we know how bad too much laudanum can be fer a man, but Bill knows that Robert feels sorry fer him."

Ethan shifted the terrapin across his back again. They walked on together in silence for a time.

In the distance, *Reliant* stood at anchor in the harbor. The blue-green sea around her was rocked by slow, rolling curlers spitting white foam that crashed against the harsh rocks lining the beach. Her sails were furled, and she looked hollow and empty-limbed, like a tree back on Nantucket Island in the winter.

The ship looked lifeless, and that thought haunted Ethan from the first shore party he'd taken part in the previous day. *She has no heart,* he realized again. *No heart and no pride. Cap'n Folger has killed her spirit.*

Ethan felt immensely responsible. As first mate, keeping crew morale up was chiefly his responsibility. But to achieve that, he was supposed to have the ear and the concern of the captain. To win a crew over properly, a first mate had to win the captain over. And to win a captain over, a first mate had to win the crew over. In the past, until Boston, he'd prided himself on being able to do those things. Those skills were what he had felt certain were going to make him captain. But now he had neither.

One had to come first: the captain or the crew. But which?

"Ethan," Creel said in a soft voice.

"Aye."

Creel hesitated. "I'm beholden to ye as a friend. That's why I'm gonna tell ye what I'm gonna tell ye."

Cold dread spread across the back of Ethan's neck. He glanced at Creel, certain he knew the words that were about to come.

"Me an' Holy an' Robert," Creel said, looking away and unable to meet Ethan's gaze, "we been talkin'. We know Cap'n Folger's gonna steal our lays from us if he can. An' we think he can."

Ethan wanted to argue because he knew Creel expected him to, but he suddenly found he didn't have the heart for it.

"Now our lays of the ship's profits," Creel said, "even were we to finish this voyage, why it wouldn't be much. A whalin' man's lot, it ain't ever much. Ye know that."

"Aye," Ethan said.

"So what we decided is this," Creel said. "First time Cap'n Folger puts in to a decent port, an' he'll have to at some point, we're gonna jump ship."

Anger stirred in Ethan, but he couldn't sustain it even within himself. He couldn't blame the men.

"You shouldn't be telling me this," Ethan said. "I'm first mate. I've got a duty to tell the cap'n."

"We don't much figger he cares," Creel replied.

Ethan let out a breath. He knew that Folger wouldn't care. Not as long as he believed he could hire on another crew. And any port that the men jumped ship at would have other sailors just as eager to sign on with another ship themselves in the belief that whatever problems they found would be better than the ones they fled.

"The reason I'm tellin' ye," Creel said, "is that me an' Holy an' Robert been thinkin' that maybe ye'd like to come with us."

Ethan's answer was immediate. "I can't." With the trouble he'd gotten into at Boston, jumping ship even from a captain like Folger would end all his chances at any kind of legitimate sailing career.

"Dammit, Ethan," Creel growled. "Ye don't owe that man anything."

"Cap'n Folger didn't let Stroud and his men kill you when you stood up against him," Ethan reminded.

"An' ye did him a good turn by stoppin' the crew from killin' him an' Stroud is the way I see it." Creel shook his head. "That battle that day, why it coulda gone any way." He paused. "Come with us, Ethan. We have ye negotiatin' terms fer us aboard the next ship, why I know we could do better fer ourselves. An' fer ye, too."

"I can't," Ethan replied.

"Cap'n Folger ain't gonna help yer case to get to be cap'n of a ship. If that's what ye're thinkin'."

Ethan let that pass.

"So what are ye gonna do when ye get back to Nantucket an' all they up an' offer ye is another mate's position?"

"I don't know." That was the truth, and it was one of the most frightening things Ethan had admitted to in a long time.

"Is that what ye want fer yerself?"

"No." Ethan didn't trouble himself to point out that continuing to be a mate wasn't something he had in mind for himself either.

Creel started to argue, then gave an exasperated sigh. "Holy told me that's what ye'd say."

Ethan nodded. They kept walking, and the struggling terrapin seemed to weigh heavier with each step. Even with the freshwater and supplies the shore party gathered from the island, they would still have to make a legitimate port soon to take on other provisions.

Overtired from all the stress he'd been facing for the last few weeks aboard *Reliant,* and concentrating on keeping his footing in the loose soil, Ethan missed the whisper of movement around him for a moment, hearing it almost too late. The only thing that saved him was the fact that the attackers weren't willing to kill him out of hand with a firearm.

Scattered pebbles and a puff of dry powdery sand caught Ethan's attention. He spotted the shadow closing in on him from behind.

"Creel!" Ethan shouted. "Look out!"

The big man started to turn, but the flat of a musket butt caught Creel alongside the face, splitting his cheek open. Dazed but still conscious, he dropped to his knees.

Ethan wheeled, crouching awkwardly with the weight of the squirming terrapin spread across his shoulders. He seized the flintlock in both hands and held the weapon before him.

Four men stepped out of the shadows where they'd been in hiding till Ethan and Creel had passed. The men wore white breeches, boots, and red-and-white cotton shirts with red stocking caps that marked them as British navy men. Gold and silver hoops bobbed in their ears, letting Ethan know none of them were officers. Officers didn't wear earrings. All of them had bayonets mounted on their muskets.

The lead man swung his bayonet for Ethan's head.

Moving quickly, Ethan blocked the blade with the flintlock. Metal rang, and the shock of the impact sent tremors followed immediately by numbness up into Ethan's hands and forearms.

Before the Britisher could withdraw, Ethan pushed the blade away with the flintlock, then swung the brass-plated butt into his attacker's face. Teeth shattered, and the man's mouth spread into crimson ruin, his jaw hanging crookedly.

"Creel!" Ethan shouted, as the three other men closed on him.

One of the attackers lifted his musket and pointed it at Ethan. Spinning, Ethan ducked his head and presented the turtle to the man, praying that the man wouldn't hit him in the back of the legs or the back of the head.

The shot rang out. Ethan felt the shock of impact through the turtle. He stayed in motion, dipping his left hand down for the knife in his boot and coming up with the weapon in his hand.

"Damn you!" one of the men swore at the one who had fired. "Cap'n Harrin'ton's liable to have our arses fer firin' afore he allowed it!"

Harrington? The name drew instant recognition from Ethan. Captain George Harrington was a British officer stationed in the Pacific. From his own experience, Ethan knew there was no real difference between being attacked by a pirate or a privateer. Whatever name they wore, whatever flag they flew, those men were interested solely in theft and murder. Personal booty or profit for the king of England, a man who had what they wanted got just as dead for not surrendering it. And even then they might not hold back from murder for the sheer pleasure of it.

Slipping the knife blade under the rope around his right shoulder, Ethan cut through the rope on his right shoulder, quickly following through with the rope on his left. Cut free of the shoulder harness, the terrapin crashed to the ground. A huge wound gaped in the back of the terrapin's shell, spilling bright blood over the dusky green and mottled brown dust patterns.

Ethan kept the knife in his left hand, then took up his musket again, spinning and bringing the weapon to his shoulder. He pulled the musket back to full cock.

Another attacker fired his musket, and black powder smoke obscured his face.

The round whipped by Ethan's ear. He squeezed his own trigger, aiming for the center of the black powder smoke.

Caught dead center in the face by the round, the attacker stumbled backward. His legs went out from under him, and he sat down beneath a tall prickly pear cactus. He was dead before his final breath left him. His spent musket clattered to the ground beside him.

The man with the broken jaw struggled to get up from the ground, but his legs and arms had gone rubbery.

Creel tried to get to his feet as well, but he was still reeling from the blow he'd received. He fumbled for his musket, jerking the weapon up and firing. The ball scarred a rock several feet from the two surviving attackers.

The fourth attacker raised his musket and pointed at Ethan.

Heart hammering in his ears but feeling the old ease he had at facing such dangerous situations, Ethan stood his ground and watched the man's finger. When the knuckle whitened and tightened on the trigger, Ethan spun to his left and dodged backward.

The plume of smoke leapt from the frizzen, then the musket fired a moment later. The ball whizzed through the air and impacted against Ethan's side, striking a rib hard enough to break bone and leave him breathless. Red-hot pain exploded inside Ethan's chest, but he pushed it away. The move had been dangerous because the ball could have caught him across the stomach. He'd seen men gutted by rounds that ripped across their midsections and spilled their intestines down around their feet.

Still in motion, knowing that the other attacker still on his feet was hastily reloading his musket, Ethan swapped hands with his firearm and knife. He ran behind a bush and came out on the other side with the knife raised, blade gripped between his fingers. He whipped his arm forward as the third attacker lifted his recharged weapon.

The knife spun through the air, catching the sunlight. Then the point buried in the man's throat. The quivering hilt disappeared as the musket fired and belched black powder smoke. Dropping his weapon, the man staggered backward, hands gripping the knife and trying desperately to pull the blade from his flesh.

Ethan threw himself forward. The final attacker threw his musket to one side and drew the cutlass from the sash at his waist.

Gunfire crashed in the distance. Ethan knew it came from the beach fronting the harbor where *Reliant* was anchored.

The attacker showed little finesse with his weapon. He swung the heavy blade sideways, aiming at Ethan's midsection. Cut a man badly enough and deeply enough, Ethan knew, and he would seek to withdraw rather than fight.

Reflex born of several different violent encounters at sea and on land thrummed through Ethan. He lifted the musket to block the blow and kept moving, charging into the attacker. The man tried to pull the cutlass back, but before he could get his arm clear, Ethan slammed the heavy butt against his opponent's forearm.

Bone cracked. The blade fell from the man's nerveless fingers. He held his hands up, backing away.

Mercilessly, Ethan pursued him. From the sounds of the gunfire in the distance, the whaleship was under attack. Every opponent left standing was one more who threatened *Reliant* and her crew. Ethan drew the musket back and slammed the butt into his opponent's forehead.

The man went back and down. He lifted his hands defensively, terror straining his bloodstained features as Ethan's shadow covered him.

"How did you find us?" Ethan demanded.

"Cap'n Harrin'ton," the man yelped. "He figgered ye'd come here. He talked with a man named McAfee, who said yer ship was low on fresh meat. Figgered ye'd have to come here."

"Is McAfee here?"

"No."

Ethan felt a surge of relief. If McAfee wasn't there, that meant they were only up against one ship. They had a chance. "Where's Harrington's ship?"

"Up the coast a bit."

"When did you find us?"

"Only a couple hours ago."

A couple hours, Ethan knew, provided plenty of time for the Britishers to get into position to try to take *Reliant*. Blocking out all recognition of the man as anything remotely human, seeing him only as a threat to the ship and his own continued survival, Ethan again hit him in the face with the musket.

The man's skull cracked, and he went limp.

Breathing hard, feeling the blood trickling down his side and the pain that flared through him with every breath he took, Ethan pulled the musket up and looked at Creel. "Are you all right?"

"Aye," Creel growled, touching the bloody wound on his cheek. "Head hurts like blazin' Hell, though."

Ethan lifted his kit and took out a cartridge. He bit the end off, took the ball into his mouth, then poured the powder down into the barrel. He spat the ball into the barrel, not bothering with wadding or using the rod to properly seat the ball. Seating the round helped with accuracy over a distance. The help wasn't much, but Ethan knew from the sounds of the action out in the harbor that everything was close.

"Reload," Ethan commanded. "We've got to get back to the ship."

"Who are these bastards?" Creel asked. He stood a little unsteadily and reloaded his musket.

"British seamen under the command of Cap'n Harrington," Ethan answered. He crossed to the man he'd killed with the knife. He yanked the blade free, then turned to the man with the broken jaw, kicked him in the side of the head, and slit his throat.

Creel swore.

Looking up at Creel, Ethan saw the man had gone white and was staring at the convulsing man kicking his life out on the ground.

"Ye killed him! An' him hardly able to take care of hisself!"

"He would have killed us," Ethan said. "There's no telling how many others he's caught in ambush and killed. This wasn't an innocent man, Creel."

Creel's distinction over killing a man in battle or killing him cold was a reminder of the distinction between the crew and Ethan. For all their rough ways, not many of them had seen how little human life went for.

Ethan cleaned his knife on the dead man's shirt, then sheathed the blade in his boot again. Blood still trickled from the wound in his side, but the flow was already slowing. He grabbed the four muskets dropped by the men he'd killed, loaded them quickly, then slung them over his shoulder.

"Let's go," Ethan said. He trotted past Creel, his mind already occupied with what needed to be done aboard *Reliant*. He swept the harbor with his gaze.

Black smoke eddied above the ship's deck, proof that Stroud and his men were in position and mounting a defense. Several Britishers had risen up from the hills on the east side of the island. All of them were armed with flintlocks. Out beyond the beach, four longboats rowed furiously for the ship from the southwest, coming up behind *Reliant*. None of the sailors aboard the whaleship seemed to know the danger they were in.

CHAPTER 17

Galapagos Islands 1° 23' S. Lat.—90° 48' W. Long.

"HURRY!" ETHAN CALLED. He burst free of the scrub line and ran across the beach. His feet pounded through the sand with loud crunches, and chunks of rock threatened to turn his ankles.

The whaleship's shore party emerged from the south, running for the ship with men at their heels. There were seven sailors. Two were missing from the nine who had been assigned to fill barrels of fresh water and gather terrapins.

"The longboat!" Ethan yelled. "Gather at the longboat!" Air burned the back of his throat as he ran. He felt the sand give way underfoot. Musket fire pocked the white sand beach.

The longboat sat on the beach twenty feet from the waterline, where the shore party had pulled it. Two of the sailors reached the boat first, but one of them spun around abruptly, hit by one of the balls flying through the air.

Ethan glanced down at the wounded man and discovered it was Harkness, one of the men assigned to help Cook. The musket ball had slammed into Harkness's left hip, leaving a ragged and bloody wound but not one that was debilitating.

"Get up," Ethan commanded. He fisted the man's shirt and hauled him to his feet.

Harkness swayed, favoring his wounded hip, but he stood.

Other men arrived, all of them cursing and trying to take cover behind the boat.

"Get your muskets loaded!" Ethan yelled. "Get them loaded now!" He brought his musket to shoulder and took aim on the nearest Britisher, squeezing the trigger and putting his shot in the center of the man.

The Britisher went down, tumbling in a loose heap that took down the man next to him.

Balls cut the air and slapped the sand on the beach. Two rounds tore splinters of wood from the longboat but didn't penetrate.

Ethan dropped the empty musket and unslung one of the four hanging from his shoulder. He took aim again and fired.

The ball caught a Britisher in the center of the chest. The man ran for a moment, then his legs quit working, dropping him into the sand on his knees. He reached for his chest, then sprawled forward.

"Load and fire!" Ethan commanded, dropping that musket and choosing another. "Load and fire if you want to live!"

The sailors hunkered down behind the longboat and opened fire as Ethan changed weapons again. He jerked the musket up and pointed it at the dozen or so Britishers who ran at them. A man fell, joining the three others put down under the combined fire of the sailors' weapons.

Another man went down a heartbeat later, then the sound of the shot rolled over Ethan from behind. Either Stroud or one of his sharpshooters had accounted for the latest victim.

Sand exploded up from the beach under the feet of one of the other men in the pack. As the sand and dust scattered, Ethan shifted to his last loaded musket and saw the iron jaws of a mantrap close over the leg of one of the Britishers.

The teeth clamped on tight above the man's calf. He screamed in agony. Crimson spread over his leg as he tripped and fell. Slavers used the traps to catch men in Africa and along the South American coast as well as the various islands in the Pacific Ocean. The mantrap's chain was attached to an iron bar or a stone block buried on the beach.

Ethan reloaded and ordered his men to do the same.

"One more volley, lads," he told them, feeling the old familiar grin fit to his face. He had faced men and weapons several times while he'd been on McAfee's ships. "One more volley on my command, then we grab the longboat and head for water. Ready?" He lifted his weapon and took aim at the Britishers spread out along the beach in prone positions that offered smaller targets.

The British seamen lay in wait, and Ethan knew they were waiting for them to discharge their weapons.

"Fire!" Ethan yelled.

The muskets cracked in a rapid volley, most of the shots coming within the space of a heartbeat. Spurts of sand and dust kicked up from the beach.

Ethan had no way of knowing how many Britishers were hit. He turned and yelled at the sailors. "Get to your feet! Grab the boat! Push!"

The men sprang to their feet, used to listening to him, and grabbed hold of the boat. Together, they shoved the longboat into the water. The bottom slid smoothly across the hot sand.

The Britishers came up in a mass, surging from the sandy beach and launching themselves in pursuit.

Ethan kept yelling at the sailors, giving them a constant barrage of orders so they didn't have time to stop and think and perhaps freeze and die in their tracks. In only a few steps, they were in the water. Another few steps and the incoming waves surged up over their waists.

Stroud and the musketmen aboard the ship fired into the British seamen, finding two more targets. But a line of black powder smoke along one of the northern ridgelines told Ethan that the Britishers had musketmen of their own in position.

Musket balls splashed into the water nearby. One ball scored the longboat's coaming and threw splinters into the air. Another crashed through the longboat's bottom and allowed a spurt almost the width of a finger to start flooding the boat.

"Into the boat!" Ethan ordered.

The sailors fought the waves and the boat and each other as they hauled themselves aboard.

Ethan shoved himself aboard. He took out another cartridge as he knelt in the middle of the longboat. Without looking, already knowing the names of the men around him, Ethan divided the men into two groups, ordering half to row for the ship and the other half to load their weapons. Under his commands, they pulled and fired into their attackers, driving the last of the men back.

Loaded again, still staying low to avoid the musket fire coming from the shoreline, Ethan gazed at *Reliant*. Stroud was clearly visible on the deck, giving orders to his men. But no one had seen the boats coming up from the south and bearing down on the whaleship.

Ethan stood in the longboat, keeping his balance with difficulty as the men fought the rollers that crashed over the longboat's bow. Water flooded the boat from the waves as well as the hole left by the musket ball.

Cupping his hands, Ethan shouted for Stroud. A man's voice carried farther over water than it did on land.

Stroud turned.

"Boats!" Ethan yelled between his cupped hands, then pointed.

Stroud turned, saw the approaching boats, and ordered his men to turn their attention to the rapidly advancing craft. As a result, the group scattered along the beach grew more bold and started firing on the retreating longboat.

Ethan kept his attention locked on his men, marshaling his forces. "Row, you dogs! Row with all you've got because your lives depend on it!" He reloaded as he spoke, chose a target, and fired, getting lucky with the shot and catching one of the Britishers in the foot. The impact knocked the sailor down. "You're strong men, by God, and I'll have all I can out of you, or I'll cut your throats myself!" He took out another cartridge and reloaded. "The rest of you men, damn your eyes, keep your powder dry and shoot those bastards!" The commands came easily to him, surfacing from the past, so close now that it only seemed like yesterday instead of three and a half years.

The musket team fired, filling the air with black powder smoke. More British seamen raced down from the hillside overlooking the beach.

Ethan knew if they'd been caught on the beach, they would have all been taken prisoner or massacred outright. He fired, reloaded, and fired again.

As the longboat closed on the ship, the sight of the boats closing on *Reliant*'s starboard side was lost.

"Creel," Ethan said.

"Aye," Creel responded.

"I want the sails aloft as soon as you get on deck. Take the men from this boat and see that it's done."

"Someone needs to man them deck cannon," Creel said.

Despite the uneven footing provided on the longboat, Ethan turned on the man in an eye blink. "Creel, don't you question me. Not one word."

Creel swallowed hard, and Ethan knew his behavior was likely to destroy whatever bridges their joint effort in saving Bill Fedderson's life had mended.

Sipping his breath, Ethan said, "Do this for me, Creel. We've got to save the ship first, and the only way to do that is to get her moving."

Stiff-necked in hurt pride, Creel nodded. "Aye. I'll do her fer ye."

Then the longboat smacked into *Reliant*'s port side. A cargo net hung over the side.

Ethan tied the musket to the cartridge bag and swarmed up the ship's side. His bruised and lacerated side felt like it was on fire. As he reached the deck, he saw one of Stroud's gunners go back and down with his face ruined by a ball.

By the time Ethan put his foot on the deck, seven Britishers swarmed up *Reliant*'s side, clambering up a boarding net they'd brought with them. Stroud faced the boarders, calmly reloading his musket. He pulled the weapon up as a man with a bayonet raced at him, then squeezed the trigger and put a ball through the man's head. Dropping the musket, Stroud pulled two pistols, cocked them, and fired one after another, first the left then the right, in measured cadence. Both balls found targets. In the next instant, he reversed the pistols and used them like clubs, but the invading British seamen seriously overmatched him.

Ethan crossed the deck, spotting Folger from the corner of his eye. The captain stood on the quarterdeck flanked by two of Stroud's men. Folger took deliberate aim with a pistol and fired, but Ethan didn't know if the shot struck home or not.

In the next instant, Ethan was across the deck, pulling the musket around and ramming it into the stomach of a British seaman about to stab Stroud. Ethan squeezed the trigger, mortally wounding the man, then reversed the musket and slammed the butt into the man's throat.

Still on the move, pressing into the thick of the knot of men forcing their way onto *Reliant*'s deck, Ethan used the musket to parry a cutlass carried by one of the British sailors. He lifted his foot into the Britisher's groin as hard as he could, dropped the musket, and captured the man's arm in his hands. A vicious twist freed the cutlass. Before the heavy blade could hit the deck, Ethan claimed the weapon as his own.

"Stand with me, lads!" Ethan yelled as he blocked a blow aimed at his head. "Repel boarders! Push these bastards off our ship!"

Weight resting on his toes, shoulders balanced precisely over his knees, left hand thrown out behind him to better control his blade and his body, Ethan faced his opponents. The cutlass became a live thing in his hand, battering aside weak defenses, riposting thrusts, sliding over guards to find vulnerable flesh behind. Blood covered him in minutes, some of it his own but much of it from opponents he'd sliced and hacked.

Dodging a blow coming in straight from the shoulder, Ethan caught himself on his sword hand, then fisted an opponent's breeches. When he came up, Ethan yanked the man's feet from under him, and sliced up through another man's groin. Before the man could get to his feet, Ethan slashed him across the back of the neck, severing his skull from his spine. The man shivered and died.

Another Britisher had a pistol up and pointed in Ethan's face. Ethan dodged to the right, folding his right arm in as he took a step forward. The pistol boomed, spitting out fire and a pall of black smoke. Unlimbering the cutlass, Ethan slashed across the inside of the Britisher's extended arm. The pistol toppled to the deck as blood spewed from the grievous wound.

Still moving, using the edge the Britisher's shock gave him for a moment, Ethan grabbed the man's shirt with his free hand, planted his feet against the heaving deck—noticing then that *Reliant* fought against her tether as Creel and his sailors filled the rigging with sails—and ran the British seaman back toward the rail. Shoving the man over the railing, Ethan pushed him into two other British seamen climbing the boarding net. The wounded man knocked the two others from the net, and all three dropped with bone-breaking force onto the small boat below.

Whirling, his mind staying two or three steps ahead of his body, reading the action by instinct and reflex, Ethan swept the deck with his eyes. Dead men sprawled across the blood-covered wood. Stroud and his marksmen had accounted for several of the dead or wounded sailors, but many of them bore horrible cutlass wounds that Ethan had delivered.

His breath rasped against the back of his throat. He was grimly aware that the ship's crew had stepped back and let him work on his own among the invading Britishers. Several of *Reliant*'s crew stared at him in openmouthed astonishment.

Spinning, Ethan cut through the ropes holding the boarding net to the whaleship's side. Musket balls crashed into the ship's hull and whizzed by his head as the net fell back into the sea. Off *Reliant*'s starboard, four small boats rocked in the water as the men aboard fired and reloaded their weapons.

"Creel!" Ethan yelled.

"Aye," Creel responded.

"Weigh anchor," Ethan barked, striding across the deck to the stern companionway. "Get us out of here."

Seeing Captain Folger standing at the stern quarterdeck, Ethan suddenly realized he'd overstepped his bounds as mate. The decision to clear the harbor should have come from Folger.

"Cap'n," Ethan said.

"Carry on, Mr. Swain," Folger said in a voice tight with emotion. He held a pistol in one hand.

Musket balls continued to pelt *Reliant* from the small boats. Stroud and his men returned fire, but with *Reliant* pitching violently beneath them, their accuracy was deeply affected.

Ethan hurried to the stern falconet. He started loading the cannon himself and was quickly joined by crew he had trained. When the falconet was loaded with grapeshot, he told the men to load the bow cannon as well.

Setting himself behind the cannon, Ethan took a slow match from one of the men, sighted down the cannon, and took the ship's movement into consideration. He touched the slow match to the powder.

The falconet exploded, throwing a cloud of grape into the air. The deadly missiles slammed into one of the small boats, ripping the sailors to doll rags and turning the boat into splintered remnants.

"Reload," Ethan called out. He grabbed the sponge from the bucket beside the gun and shoved it down the falconet's throat to extinguish any residual sparks that might prematurely set off the next powder charge.

"Sails!" Robert called down from aloft. "Sails south!"

Leaving the reloading to the crew that had assembled around him, Ethan looked out over the sea.

The ship was a low-slung brigantine, a three-master that looked sleek and powerful against the whaleship. She flew a British Union Jack. Her name was *Formidable,* scrolled in neat letters on her prow hull. The name confirmed that the ship belonged to George Harrington, a captain in His Majesty's Royal Navy.

Reliant came about slowly in the harbor.

"Helmsman," Ethan called, "get us out to sea, but let her keep her head as much as you can. If those Britishers get in behind us, they'll be able to steal our wind."

"Aye," the helmsman replied.

Conscious of the pain that wracked his body, the sandy grit that stuck to his skin, and the blood that slowly threaded across his flesh, Ethan took up a position at the stern. The British ship closed quickly on them. Men scrambled in her bow, setting up around the eight-pounder cannon she carried forward.

"Stroud," Ethan said.

"Aye," Stroud replied gruffly.

"I want your men up here. The best of the lot."

Stroud came without argument, accepting Ethan's leadership.

Ethan pointed. "They've got themselves a bow chaser. When they get within musket range, I want that gun crew dead. Every man that steps up there should know he's taking his life in his hands."

"Aye." Stroud brought his men forward along the stern. "We'll get it done fer ye, Ethan."

"Thank you." Ethan clapped the man on the shoulder and turned back to survey the ship from the quarterdeck.

Captain Folger watched him with quiet rage.

Leaning on the railing and looking down at the crew on the deck, then up at the men hanging in the rigging working the sails, Ethan thought, *My God. This is where I should be. This is where I was born to be.*

But he knew his presence on the quarterdeck would be denied to him the moment Folger chose to step back into command. However, Ethan was just as certain that the captain would not usurp command until *Reliant* was free of pirate threat.

"Holy," Ethan called down.

"Aye," Holy called back.

"Clear the decks. Throw the wounded and dead British over the side. Get our wounded below. Put sand on that blood on the deck in case we have to repel boarders again."

Holy looked around. "What if the British wounded can't swim?"

"If you're worried about them drowning," Ethan said in a cold voice, "slit their throats first."

A troubled look filled Holy's face. "Ethan, I can't—"

"I can," Merl Porter said, baring a broad-bladed knife. He started among the British seamen. "Ye take care of the wounded, Holy. I'll tend them Britishers."

Reluctantly, Holy nodded.

Bodies dropped from *Reliant*'s deck as sailors joined Merl. Holy got others moving wounded.

"Helmsman," Ethan said.

"Aye."

"Bring her on around. Take us into the wind." Since the wind came from the north, going into the wind would take *Reliant* back toward the British ship.

"Doin' that will—"

Ethan wheeled on the man. "Do it. *Now.*"

The helmsman spun the wheel. Caught by the full onslaught of the wind,

Reliant shuddered for a moment, then her sails belled in earnest. She surged forward, heading back toward *Formidable,* which had been tacking into the wind.

"Stroud," Ethan said, "I'm going to hold you to taking care of that gun crew."

"It'll be done."

"You might target the helmsman as well. That brigantine has more sail than we do. She'll be the faster ship if it comes down to a race."

"Aye."

Ethan raced forward, sprinting across the deck and leaping over the corpses the crew dragged to the ship's sides. He vaulted up the port companionway to the bow and joined the gun crew.

"I want one shot," Ethan instructed the men. "Grape, before we reach them. Followed immediately by bar and chain as soon as we can get it."

They nodded.

Ethan waited, feeling the excitement thrumming through him. The ships closed, cutting almost silently across the water. The British seamen touched off their muskets, black puffs of smoke visible before the balls slapped the whaleship.

"Clear," Ethan said, satisfied with the falconet's aim. He touched the slow match and ignited the charge.

The falconet strained against the ropes that held it in place when the powder blew. The mass of grapeshot spread out and hammered the British ship. Most of the pellets slammed into the ship's side or holed the sails above, but a few of them caught targets and left wounded and dying men flopping on the deck.

"Reload!" Ethan ordered.

The crew sprang into action, clearing the cannon and seating the next charge as *Reliant* sailed by *Formidable.* Less than thirty feet separated the two vessels. As Ethan had hoped, the British captain had been caught off guard by the desperate move. *Formidable* was only then turning, unable to bring her port or starboard cannon into play. The bow cannon was another matter, but Stroud's marksmen dogged the gun crew, knocking men down. When the gunner finally got his shot off, the eight-pound cannonball hummed over the bow, passing by several feet away.

Reliant's gun crew quickly loaded the charge, then pushed in the bar linked with chain. As soon as they were clear and the falconet was properly aimed, Ethan touched off the load.

The bar and chain exploded from the cannon's throat. Spreading out in the air over the intervening distance, the heavy bar trailed the chain behind, then caught in the rigging as it was designed to do, tearing sailcloth and 'yards away. The bar and chain left a trail of destruction in its wake.

After that, the British ship only made a token attempt at pursuit and fired a few cannon shots that missed by comfortable distances. Navy man and pirate, Harrington and McAfee, one robbed and killed in the name of a king and the other robbed and killed for sport and personal gain. Both of them were hunters skilled in ambush, treachery, and battle.

By rights, the two men were competitors. Any natural predator, Ethan knew, marked its territory. Yet, McAfee had pointed Harrington in *Reliant*'s direction. But in a way it made sense. Even if McAfee didn't have the satisfaction of killing Ethan, the pirate would have the satisfaction of knowing that Ethan was just as dead.

And they were both still out there, both still hunting.

Ethan quietly prayed they would take their next whale or two and be gone from the waters. As big as the Pacific Ocean was, the sea now seemed incredibly small.

CHAPTER 18

Pacific Ocean 19° 11' S. Lat.—106° 45' W. Long.

STANDING AT THE starboard railing a few days after the whale's attack and after the load of slaves had been sold in Callao, Captain Jonah McAfee peered ahead into the water. While in the city, he had learned of Professor Bullock's interest in Easter Island through the gossip in the taverns and had once more taken up pursuit of the research ship. The gold they had gotten from the slaves would see them through a few months that would allow the ship to search purely for plunder. He had kept three of the young male slaves to serve as cabin boys aboard ship.

"Do ye see it, Cap'n?" Gilley asked, pointing at the thing that bobbed in the water and rode the restless curl of waves.

"I've got eyes, Mr. Gilley," McAfee retorted shortly.

The object had been spotted by the lookout through a spyglass. He'd claimed it had been a man's body, but McAfee wasn't convinced of that yet. However, that the object was wrapped in cloth was without question.

The crew deployed the fishing net under Gilley's vulgar commands, trailing it after *Sunfisher*. As the ship passed the floating object, McAfee had a brief impression of a man's shape, but it was lost in the swirl of conflicting water currents from the ship and the sea.

The net was hauled back on board and spilled onto the deck. Fish tumbled out, most of them not edible, but there were a few choice specimens that would end up filleted or in Cook's pot. None of those creatures seized the amount of interest as did the corpse that had been caught in the net. Caught by one foot in the net, the dead man hung upside down and spun loosely, arms akimbo. A death's-head rictus pulled back his wrinkled yet bloated features in a fearful grin.

"God help us," one of the sailors said.

Others cursed, and two men threw up over the ship's side.

McAfee controlled his own feelings of revulsion and sickness with difficulty. The stench, equal parts from the brine and from the rot that clung to the corpse, filled his nostrils. He breathed shallowly through his mouth and could almost taste the death that spread from the corpse.

The dead man looked as though he had been in the sea for months because of the way his skin was desiccated. But McAfee knew that was impossible. If a human body had been in the sea that long, the scavengers would have stripped the flesh from bone. Nothing went to waste in an ocean.

The flesh was shriveled in, like an empty glove, and something had burned it in several places. A puncture wound in the dead man's throat was large enough for McAfee to thrust his fist into.

One of the men leaned down to take the glittering silver chain from around the corpse's neck. As soon as his fingers touched the dead man's flesh, he yelped out in pain and yanked his fingers back. He cursed and screamed for water to soak his hand.

As he watched, McAfee saw blisters rise on the man's fingers.

"Venom," Gilley said.

The corpse swung back and forth with the motion of the ship. The men around the body dodged back, giving the dead man a respectful distance.

"Venom from what?" McAfee demanded.

"I don't rightly know, Cap'n," Gilley admitted. "But that's all it can be."

"Why haven't the fish eaten this body?" McAfee asked.

"I don't know, Cap'n," Gilley answered.

McAfee looked at the other men. No one had an answer. He turned back to the sailor holding his burned hand. "Let me see your hand."

Shaking, obviously in agony, the man held his wounded hand by the wrist with the other hand and extended it for McAfee's inspection. The boils stood nearly a half inch tall and held a clear, pinkish liquid.

"Mr. Cochrane," McAfee said. "Get this man below and get some laudanum in him."

"Aye, Cap'n." Cochrane served as the ship's surgeon and doubled as the ship's torturer, a man good at both his chosen crafts if he didn't get too deeply involved in his cups. He caught the key to the medicinal chest that McAfee tossed him. All of the crew knew that the pirate captain kept careful count of the laudanum and whiskey kept aboard *Sunfisher*. Any man caught drunk or incapacitated suffered the lash. Cochrane already had scars across his back.

"I'll want to be kept apprised of this man's condition," McAfee said.

Cochrane took the sailor away.

Kneeling, knowing that he couldn't afford to show fear in front of his crew, McAfee pulled on a pair of leather gloves. He seized a monkfish from among the specimens caught in the net.

The monkfish's head was almost as wide as its body was long and depressed as though it had been stepped on. Almost eighteen inches long, the monkfish was young and still hadn't reached its full adult length of three feet. The topside was gray-green, and the underbelly was white. Gleaming teeth filled the cavernous mouth.

Holding the monkfish securely, McAfee rose and shoved the creature toward the hanging corpse. The monkfish's head shot forward and the creature buried its teeth in the corpse's flesh.

McAfee released the monkfish and stepped back.

Almost immediately, flesh shredded from the corpse as the monkfish's weight bore it down, but the effect was just as immediate on the monkfish. The massive jaws snapped open. Flesh and fish dropped to the deck. The monkfish's body arced in violent throes as blisters ran throughout the creature.

Then the monkfish was dead, and the meat began to slough from the bone before McAfee's eyes.

The crew cursed again, and several of them made signs to ward off evil.

Curiosity overcame McAfee's fear of the dead body. He took a throwing knife from his boot and cut into the corpse's midsection, then jumped back as a flap of meat pulled open. Vile liquid splashed onto the deck. Thin wisps of gray smoke drifted up but were quickly torn away.

Inside, the man was empty. Nothing remained of his heart or lungs or innards. Only strips of fat and gristle clung to the ribs.

"Somethin' hollowed him out," Gilley said.

McAfee stared at the husk of the body. He glanced up at the man's face, only then noticing that the eyes were missing and holes stared back at him under the blistered lids.

"He's been eviscerated, Mr. Gilley," McAfee said softly, drawn to the remarkable and gruesome truth of the dead man's condition. "That is, I believe, the correct term for this poor bastard."

"Maybe somethin' crawled inside him," a sailor ventured. "Et up his insides, then crawled back out again."

"Back out of what?" McAfee asked.

"There's a hole in his throat."

McAfee leaned forward, keeping his body from the leaking and gaping hole in the man's empty midsection. He jammed the knife between the dead man's teeth and twisted so the blade popped the jaws open.

A bloody, blistered mass of tissue greeted McAfee's eyes. Teeth fell out, forced loose by the knife, and bounced across the deck.

There was no tongue. The roof of the mouth had been eaten away. The white bone of skull revealed the open space inside the man's head.

"It et all his insides," Gilley whispered.

Several sailors continued backing away. A few of them made the sign of the Cross. Others prayed and bit their fingers in fearful benediction.

Slowly, drawn into the mystery, McAfee carefully cut the dead man's clothes from him. Red, blistered weals showed against the corpse's pasty white flesh. At first glance, they looked like lengths of knotted rope had made them. Closer inspection revealed tiny punctures where something had bitten into the flesh.

Something had you, McAfee thought, staring at the body. *But what?*

He turned his attention to the gaping wound in the dead man's throat. If something was small enough to crawl into the man, there was no way it was big enough to eat the man's insides and crawl back out again. If there were more than one thing involved, logic dictated there would have been several holes. And it made no sense at all that a small thing would have made the many trips required to eat everything inside the victim.

McAfee set the knife blade to the ragged, bloodless wound. As he pried at the corpse's flesh, sunlight glinted from the bits of metal flaking from the knife blade.

Drawing the knife back, McAfee gazed at the blade with bright interest. Far from the pristine thing it had once been, the knife showed pits and scarring as if it had known nothing but years of hard, abusive work.

Curious about the extent of the damage, McAfee stepped over to the railing. He reversed the knife so the blade jutted down from his fist. He rammed the blade point-first into the railing.

The blade shattered, scattering into a dozen jagged shards.

McAfee stared at the bone hilt that remained.

"Cap'n."

Turning at the sound of Gilley's voice, McAfee saw the first mate using a wooden shim to push at the dead man's clothing.

"There's somethin' in here," Gilley said. A little more prodding with the shim revealed a rectangular object wrapped in sealskin and tied tightly. With careful deliberation and the use of another shim, the first mate opened the sealskin and exposed the book within.

Protected by the waterproof sealskin, the book remained dry.

Choosing to believe that if the book was dry it was then free of whatever venom still resided within the corpse, McAfee knelt and retrieved the book. The tome had been handmade, a roughly assembled aggregation of crudely cut pages that were stitched together with a sailor's knots. The front and back covers were made of scrimshaw. A half-finished bas-relief carving on the front showed the masts and sails of a boat that hadn't yet been rendered.

Curious, McAfee flipped the scrimshaw book cover open. The first page was rendered in a child's scrawl. A picture of a whale—a sperm whale with a badly burned eye and horns like Satan himself—occupied the center of the page.

McAfee's heart sped a little. Then his eyes fell on the book's title:

Pursuit of the Monster.

Then, below:

This Bean The True Akount Of John "Jack" Maxwell In His Own Hand Whilst Servin A Board The Prowd Siense Ship Brown-Eyed Sue An Chaisin A True Monster From The Deeps

Captivated, recognizing the name of the ship *Sunfisher* currently searched for, McAfee turned the page and began to read.

Easter Island, Chile 27° 17' S. Lat.—109° 24' W. Long.

THE TENT BULLOCK worked in held the sharp smell of chemicals and death.

Almost two weeks had passed since *Brown-Eyed Sue*'s encounter with the rogue male whale. Because of the hole in the bottom of the ship, the voyage had been filled with long hours of anxiety and harsh labor as the bilge pumps had been in continual operation. Although Captain Mayhew had been of the firm opinion that the ship would hold together long enough to return to Easter Island, simply knowing that there was a hole letting in the sea had been draining to Bullock. Thankfully, Bullock had had the whale calf's corpse and the unidentified venom to work with. Still, several times a day he had regretted bringing Katharine.

"Sail! There's a sail on the horizon!" a man shouted outside the tent. "Someone find the cap'n! Tell him an' Perkins there's a ship out there!"

At first, Bullock was going to ignore the shouts that suddenly started up outside the tent. He was not a popular figure among the men in recent days. Someone had started the rumor that the venom carried a disease that would kill them all. And the men who didn't believe that believed that the Easter Islanders had cursed them. All of which was because of Bullock.

Then the professor realized that his daughter was not in the tent with him. In fact, he couldn't remember the last time he had seen her. Or even what time it had been. He felt even more guilty when he realized that he couldn't remember if he'd even spoken to her.

Bullock took time to cover the glass container of venom he had been working with. As yet, the samples hadn't lost potency. They were just as strong, undiluted, as they had been when first introduced into the whale calf's body; just as strong—and just as dangerous.

The professor ducked through the tent opening and stepped outside into the blazing afternoon heat. The tent bore the full brunt of the sun and trapped the heat inside. Outside, the breeze coming in from the sea felt much cooler.

Brown-Eyed Sue stood hove to over to Bullock's right. Captain Mayhew had ordered the crew to tie lines to the rock formations jutting up in the harbor, then used the leverage to pull the ship over on her left side to expose the hole underneath. The hole had been quickly patched and the resin was setting up in a controlled and dry environment. Mayhew expected the replacement wood to be solidly in place by morning. Replacing the sheared mast was more complicated, and couldn't be attempted until the ship once more sat level on the still water of the harbor.

Sailors working on ship's canvas, net, and rope along the beach stood and lifted their weapons. All of them carried muskets. During the past two days they had been on the island, all of them had been on alert for the indigenous population, but none of the natives—including Malachi—had been sighted. The empty barrels that had been left at the previous camp suggested that the goods that had been left had been put to use.

Other sailors on the ship came to the ship's right side railing and the rear railing. Muskets bristled as the men hunkered down and took cover.

In the distance, sails stood like thin white feathers painted against the bright blue sky above the pale green of the sea.

Bullock shaded his eyes, but he couldn't make out any telling details about the ship.

A young sailor trotted by carrying a small net full of clams and crabs. The sea creatures clacked as they banged against each other.

Bullock raised his voice. "Mr. Krieg. Do you know where my daughter is?"

Krieg pointed back toward the center of the island. "Up in the hills. I been keepin' an eye on her. So have Jonesy an' Tomlinson while we's keepin' watch over things. We hain't let her get far from our sight. Jonesy and Tomlinson, they's still up there with her."

Turning, Bullock gazed up the hillside and spotted Katharine sitting almost a hundred yards away. She held an artist's pad on her lap. No doubt, Bullock knew, she was working to bring their notes up to date as well. She was just as driven as he was.

For the first time, the professor realized how vulnerable *Brown-Eyed Sue* was as she was hove to on her side. Her cannon couldn't even be brought to bear to defend herself against an aggressor. Captain Mayhew, pragmatic soul that he was, had insisted on placing two cannon on the beach, with a supply of powder and balls laid in. Bags of sand created defensive walls on three sides of each cannon.

"Mr. Krieg," Bullock said, gazing at the sails in the distance. "Do we yet know who the arriving ship is?"

"No. I 'spect Cap'n Mayhew is rightly anxious about it." Krieg spat and watched the ship. "I had to guess who them men was, I'd say they was of no account. Only slavers an' fools come to this island because every sailin' man knows there ain't nothin' worth havin' here."

"I shouldn't wonder then, Mr. Krieg, that the captain of that vessel is probably thinking the same thing about us."

The young sailor suddenly realized what he had said and floundered to correct his *faux pas*. "I mean, only slavers, fools, an' science ships."

Bullock offered the young man a brief smile to let him know no offense was taken. "Even so, Mr. Krieg, we don't appear to be in good company."

"Prolly not," Krieg replied. "Prolly not at all."

"FATHER."

Bullock finished the word he was writing in his current journal, lifted the quill from the paper, and replaced the writing instrument in the inkstand. He blew on the paper to dry the ink, then turned from the table where he sat under the sweltering shade of the tent.

Katharine stood in the doorway, artist pad and three journals under her arm.

"Yes," Bullock said.

"You've heard about the ship out in the harbor?"

"Yes. *Sunfisher,* I believe she's called."

Katharine nodded. "I take it you haven't talked with her crew or captain."

Curiosity stirred within Bullock. Katharine wasn't one to interrupt his work for a small reason.

"No," he replied. "Captain Mayhew elected to place all contact with that ship under his purview. There was some concern that *Sunfisher* was a pirate ship since she obviously wasn't a whaleship." He paused and looked at his daughter. "Don't tell me that you took it upon yourself to talk with those men."

"Of course not. However, I have talked to the men of our ship who have talked with *Sunfisher*'s crew." Excitement showed in Katharine's face. "They have seen the creature as well. It attacked them."

"Why?" Bullock asked.

"They don't know. Men were lost overboard during the attack, and the crew believes the creature got them."

"Did the creature pull them from the ship?"

"No. When the creature rammed the ship, the men fell overboard."

"How many men?"

"Two. Maybe more. The stories I get from our crew change from one person to the next, from one telling to the next. Each enhances the tale. I think even the sailors from *Sunfisher* are doing the same thing."

Bullock peered through the open tent flaps. Dusk had settled over the beach. He'd started using a whale oil lantern hours earlier to combat the deepening shadows that filled the tent's interior and to offset the stink of dead flesh from the whale calf that he worked with.

"The captain is on the beach?"

"He has been," Katharine said. "He will be again. For the moment he has returned to his ship to get the body."

"Body?"

"Only a few days ago, the captain and his men recovered the body of Jack Maxwell." Sadness touched Katharine's eyes.

"Maxwell." Bullock searched for the man's name in his memory.

"He was part of our crew, Father."

"The man that was lost overboard during the attack. One that you were working with."

"Yes. According to the reports I have heard, Mr. Maxwell was killed by the creature that you were sent to find."

"How was he killed?" Bullock listened raptly as his daughter relayed the tale—and the variations she'd heard on the tale—of how the unfortunate sailor had been found in the ocean with all his insides missing from his body.

"Captain Fisher was also kind enough to return this." Katharine held out a small handmade book. "This is the journal I was helping Mr. Maxwell write."

Bullock took the slim volume and examined it. "This book survived the attack and the sea?"

"It was wrapped in sealskin and remained with the body."

Bullock was struck again with how matter-of-fact Katharine handled a subject that should have been considered coarse and vulgar by any young lady of genteel manners.

"Captain Fisher's men said that the corpse was eviscerated," she said.

"Eviscerated?"

"That is his word. The sailors who told me said that the sailor he got the story from only repeated what the captain said upon the discovery of Mr. Maxwell's body."

"That's not exactly a word often used by sea captains," Bullock observed.

"Captain Fisher appears to be a gentleman of distinction."

"You've talked with him?" Perhaps it was only the failing light from the approaching dusk outside, but Bullock thought he detected a slight blush to his daughter's features.

"No, but I have observed him." Katharine unconsciously touched her drawing tablet.

"And what are your observations?"

"That he is a gentleman of distinction. His family is from Virginia, and they—as he puts it—dabble in shipping solely because of his interest in seeing the world from a ship's deck."

"His crew said this?"

"I heard him say it to Captain Mayhew when they met."

Bullock felt a pang of protective anxiety toward his daughter. During their whole voyage, she'd never showed more than passing interest in any man aboard *Brown-Eyed Sue* as anything other than an extra pair of hands and a strong back. Yet here, in the course of a few minutes of seeing but never quite meeting this sea captain, she had met a *gentleman of distinction*.

"I see," the professor said. "Perhaps we should go and have a chat with this sea captain of yours."

"He's not," Katharine protested, "my sea captain."

"All the same, this young fellow warrants an interview on behalf of our mission." Bullock rolled his sleeves down and pulled on his coat even though the temperature inside the tent remained sweltering. "Would you like to accompany me?"

"Of course. I'll need to keep notes."

That was not, Bullock surmised, the only reason that his daughter chose to accompany him. For the first time he realized that losing Katharine to the sea might not be the only way he could lose her. But he'd be damned if he lost her to the likes of a sea captain—no matter how distinguished the man was.

"THE BOAT IS coming in," Katharine said.

Eyes burning with fatigue and mind clouded with questions upon questions, Professor Bullock looked up from the journal he'd been reading. As always, Katharine's hand for letters was clear, concise, and uniform. Much of the data was in his words, copied directly from his own journals, or verbatim from the discussions they'd had during the course of their investigation, but much of it was in Katharine's words as well. She had a fine mind, and her grasp of the situation and the methods he—no, he amended, *they*—had employed was excellent.

He sat on one of the chairs the crew had brought from *Brown-Eyed Sue*, which still sat hove to out in the harbor. The breeze cut in from the ocean, cool enough to chill a sedentary man, and so he sat close to one of the three bonfires the crew maintained on the beach.

A large iron pot containing chowder hung over one of the cook fires, two goats roasted over others, and a final fire held a roasting pig. In addition to the goats, *Sunfisher*'s captain had also seen fit to deliver fresh fruit that might not have been fresh as a daisy, but was far from spoiled and very welcome among *Brown-Eyed Sue*'s crew.

The longboat cut across the retreating waves. Full darkness had come upon Easter Island, and the moonlight dappled silver across the foaming heads of the curlers. A lantern swung merrily to and fro from the stern of the longboat, a glowing light encased in green glass that made it look a little like a firefly.

Bullock stood and carefully packed the journal he'd been reviewing into the battered valise beside his chair. He waited while Captain Mayhew's crew walked out into the foam to greet the longboat. Mayhew waited slightly above the waterline, dressed in one of his finest suits.

Sunfisher's captain stepped from the longboat and helped his crew draw the craft onto shore. In the moonlight, his fair hair and beard looked silver. He was not, Bullock realized, an unhandsome man.

The two captains chatted for a moment, renewing the friendship they had evidently struck up earlier.

"Why does his ship sit so far from the shore?" Bullock asked Katharine. *Sunfisher* sat far out to sea, making for a long boat ride to shore. Lanterns lit her up and marked her clearly.

"There is a sickness on board. Captain Fisher is certain that it has run its course through most of the crew, but he still has a few crew who have it. He doesn't want to chance infecting our crew."

After a few more minutes, both captains approached the center of the camp. *Sunfisher*'s crew seemed a rough lot who tended to stay together, but they acted happy to see *Brown-Eyed Sue*'s crew.

Mayhew drew the crews together for a brief prayer to bless the men and the meal they were about to receive. Then Captain McAfee offered up a toast, breaking out the gallon jugs of wine and rum he'd brought as a special surprise. He'd also brought a small table that his men set up on the beach. He invited Mayhew and both Bullocks to join him.

"Professor Bullock," McAfee greeted in a jovial voice and with a boyish smile. He took Bullock's hand in a firm grip, shook, and released it. "It is an honor indeed to meet someone of your distinguished education, sir. I don't believe I've ever before had the good fortune and pleasure to speak with a university professor."

Flattered, not at all expecting such treatment after being around Mayhew and his men for the past months, Bullock smiled, and said, "Thank you, Captain Fisher. Though I've not been a frequent visitor to your state, your candor and enthusiasm make me realize I shouldn't let much longer pass before I visit again."

"Captain Mayhew tells me that you've been given the assignment of finding the monster my ship encountered," McAfee said.

Mayhew scowled. "We have found it, and the sooner we're shut of it, the happier I shall be."

"More precisely, Captain Mayhew," Katharine said, "the creature seemed to have found us."

McAfee laughed and lifted his wineglass in a toast. "Touché, Miss Bullock," he complimented quietly. "And since the creature also found us, I think there is a bond that links us."

"Were there whales around when you saw the creature?" Bullock asked.

"No. It appeared to be by itself."

"I was told that you still have poor Mr. Maxwell's body," Katharine said.

Bullock thought Mayhew was going to strangle at the blunt statement.

"I do have the body," McAfee said. "Kept locked away in a wooden trunk. Wrapped in sailcloth, of course, for—as you and your father have probably noticed—the venom has the disconcerting habit of eating through metal." He picked at his plate. "Would you like to see the corpse?"

"Yes," Katharine said. "Very much."

CHAPTER 19

Pacific Ocean 14° 19' S. Lat.—105° 03' W. Long.

SWATHED IN THE night's darkness, Ethan Swain leaned on *Reliant*'s starboard railing amidships and gazed at *Miller's Crossing*. The ship was a whaler roughly the same size as *Reliant*. She might have been a couple feet longer than *Reliant*, but she was also at least a foot and a half more narrow abeam.

From the looks of *Miller's Crossing* before dusk had dampened the sun and filled the sea with shadows, Ethan had judged her a smart, clean ship. She didn't gleam, but she had a well-cared-for look about her. The ship had enjoyed good fortune, but she'd also been fortunate to have a knowing captain's hand. All of that showed in her lines and in the way the crew behaved aboard her.

Miller's Crossing was also from Nantucket, and she was carrying a full hold of whale oil. If the weather held and the winds were fair, Captain Robson intended to be home in less than two months. Robson was a captain of the old school and wouldn't have put up with illegal passengers, and he had no need of crew. He'd agreed to a gam, the old tradition of meeting and swapping supplies and stories, but had quickly let it be known through his crew that they wouldn't be taking on passengers.

He had readily agreed to transport the letters Ethan had asked him to take to his family. None of those letters, though, spoke of the near mutiny or the encounter with McAfee. His family didn't know of McAfee or Teresa Santiago, and Ethan wanted to keep it that way. Even the attack by the British naval officer Harrington had been kept to a minimum in the letters. Ethan also sent gifts; delicate carvings and perfumes that his mother and sister enjoyed, a clever wooden puzzle he'd gotten from a sailor aboard *Miller's Crossing,* who had been to Shanghai, that he thought his father would appreciate, boots made of good Spanish leather for all his brothers.

Lanterns placed around the amidships and hanging from the 'yards cast a warm yellow glow over the festivities taking place aboard *Miller's Crossing.* The song from the Irish tin whistle one of the men played with skill ended with a smattering of applause, then a man stepped forward with a violin and sawed a lively tune. The combined crews roared drunkenly and began singing.

Ethan recognized the song as one of the bawdy ditties only drunken sailors away from the civilized outlook of townsmen had any business singing. He grinned at the put-on foolishness and antics of the men as several of them started dancing with each other with put-on snobbery. He also hoped that Captain Robson had had the good sense to lock his wife away before the celebration had gotten out of hand.

A splash sounded in the water between the ships. It was different from the crash of the waves slapping the hulls.

Glancing away from the other ship, Ethan stared down into the dark water. For a moment, he thought he saw something moving there, but he couldn't be certain. His eyes hadn't adjusted from staring into the lanternlight aboard *Miller's Crossing.*

Only a moment later, *Reliant* shuddered from stem to stern.

Holding fast to the railing, Ethan peered up into the furled rigging. If he hadn't known better, he might have guessed that a stray gust of wind had caught them. Vague, preternatural unease filled him.

"Ethan," Nate Philips called from the ship's wheel. The wheel had been lashed tight when the anchor had been dropped, but a man always stood ready there.

"Aye," Ethan responded, jogging up the companionway.

"Did ye feel that then?" Nate asked. He was a rawboned young man who had been destined for farming in Portland, Maine, till he'd left his family and signed aboard his first ship.

"Aye, I felt it." Ethan stayed close to the railing, peering down into the dark water. "We hit something. Or something hit us."

Nate peered into the water anxiously. "Mayhap it was just a crosscurrent what took us."

Ethan shook his head. "That was contact."

"Don't make sense that we could run aground out here."

"We didn't." Ethan stepped back to the wheel and took a lantern from the peg by the navigator's table. "Every island out here is marked."

"Mayhap a boat got loose from them that the crew been usin' to go back and forth. Mayhap it got loose an' banged up against us."

Ethan shined the light over the water. "Contact above the waterline sounds different than contact below it. Whatever we touched, it was below the water-line."

When he spoke again, Nate's voice barely rose above a whisper. "I've heard stories about ships of dead men what rise from the ocean floor, come up to drink the blood of livin' men an' to steal their treasure. An' I've heard tell of monsters what live under the sea that rise up come a full moon to eat men."

"Tonight isn't a full moon."

"Mayhap they don't need a full moon. Mayhap monsters still come even without the full moon."

"I've been out on the sea for years," Ethan replied. "I've never seen ghost ships full of dead men or sea monsters."

"Still . . ." Nate said hoarsely.

Reliant suddenly rocked again, and the movement this time was much more fierce. Lanterns swayed up and down the length of her, and rigging slapped against masts. Two lanterns fell and smashed against the deck. The oil spread, quickly becoming a pool of flames that jumped up bright and yellow from the wooden deck.

"Fire!" someone yelled out from below. "Fire!"

Three men ran out onto the ship's deck, crawling up from the hold.

Another impact, the hardest of all, rocked the whaleship, rolling her over hard to port.

Grabbing on to the railing with his free hand, Ethan reeled with the heaving ship's deck and managed to keep his footing. On a primitive level that he had honed while with Jonah McAfee and Teresa, Ethan sensed movement behind him. He started to turn, whipping the lantern around and left hand releasing the railing to dart down for the knife in his boot. Even as his fingers closed around the hilt, a hard, wet mass slammed against him out of the darkness.

Robbed of his night vision by the lantern, he didn't see what had hit him.

He barely hung on to his scattered senses as he plunged overboard into the waiting sea and whatever lay below it.

Easter Island, Chile 27° 17' S. Lat.—109° 24' W. Long.

STANDING ON THE beach under the harsh silver glare of the moon waxing
between scudding cloud wisps, Professor Bullock watched in anticipation as the
longboat neared the shore. The men aboard the craft shipped the oars expertly,
guiding the longboat up onto the sand and rock with a hollow, rasping series of
thuds.

The men aboard the longboat got out. One man took the lantern from the
prow while another fetched up the lantern from the stern. Nimbly, they got out
barefooted in lapping tides up to their ankles, grabbed hold of the longboat, and
pulled the craft farther ashore.

Bullock took note of the pistols and cutlasses *Sunfisher*'s crew habitually carried and felt a vague sense of unease. Most of Mayhew's sailors didn't keep their
weapons close to hand as those men did.

Added to that, the professor had yet to see a man from the other ship's crew
who had the sickness the captain claimed still infected some of his crew. Looking
out at the ship deep in the harbor, Bullock got the impression again that the
ship's captain did not want Mayhew or anyone from *Brown-Eyed Sue* aboard his
vessel.

Raising the lantern he'd carried from the banquet that had been laid out
along the shore, McAfee stepped over to the longboat. "Bring it out, Mr. Gilley."

"Aye, Cap'n." The rough-hewn first mate gestured to his men, then reached
into the longboat for the tarp-covered figure in the bottom of the craft. Without
care or concern, the sailors hauled the package out of the longboat. "Where ye
want it?"

The stench of the corpse, stout enough to stand against even the eager wind
that sailed in from the sea, rolled over Bullock. The professor opened his mouth
and stopped breathing through his nose. The effort helped only a little because
the stink remained overpowering.

Katharine covered her lower face with a sweater sleeve. But she remained
focused on the terrible cargo the sailors carried.

One of the crew retched. He loosed the contents of his stomach upon the
sand and didn't apologize for his loss of control. Then he took his grip more
firmly and stood ready like nothing had happened.

"The tent over there if you please, gentlemen," the professor responded.

Bullock led the way, with Katharine stepping briskly at his side. Crabs scuttled sideways away from their path, staying just beyond the reach of the lanternlight's glow.

Inside the tent, Bullock and his daughter quickly lit the lanterns. Once the wicks burned confidently, they replaced the glass and the makeshift surgery was bathed in golden yellow. The burning whale oil, scented with cinnamon that Katharine had added, helped cut some of the stench of the corpse.

Gilley and the other sailors laid their cargo on the surgery table. The smack of the tarp-covered figure meeting the table surface sounded wet and pulpy.

"You'll want to be careful as you uncover the body, Professor," McAfee said. "I drained most of the venom from that unfortunate soul, but as you've probably deduced yourself, there is no way to comfortably get it all."

"Not without flensing the flesh from the bone," Bullock agreed. "Even then, I can't guarantee that the venom hasn't thoroughly soaked into the bone."

Katharine busied herself laying out the surgical instruments as Bullock carefully unwrapped the tarp.

Captain McAfee made himself at home, putting his hands behind his back and walking around the small confines of the tent while gazing with deep interest at the various jars containing specimens and chemicals.

The dead man's face glared out ferociously in the lanternlight. The venom that had ravaged his body had left his flesh weakened. His cheekbones had pushed through dead and rotting flesh, and his grin was more ivory with the teeth showing through the lips. Gaps showed missing teeth.

"What happened to this man's teeth?" Bullock remembered the man vaguely and believed that Maxwell had most nearly had a mouthful of teeth.

"When I was inspecting the body, I inadvertently knocked some of them out," Fisher answered. "At the time, I did not know the extent of the effects of the venom and the sea toward making his body so infirm. If you need them, I still have the teeth."

"I will need them at some point." Bullock moved the lantern closer and directed the beam inside the corpse's mouth. The damage done to the soft palate and the gum tissue was extensive. "You said your ship was attacked by a whale before you found this man's body?"

"I don't know if there is a correlation, Professor Bullock, but we were ruthlessly attacked by the whale only a week prior to finding Mr. Maxwell's remains."

"I was told that the whale was a rather singular creature, that you would be able to identify it if you saw it again."

McAfee smiled. "I'm told you would be able to identify it again as well." He touched his cheek. "One side of its head is covered with what appears to be burn scarring. According to the crew aboard your ship, you were attacked by the same whale."

"Perhaps," Bullock replied. "We've not yet proven there exists only one such whale."

"I would submit that the possibility of two such whales existing is rather remote, Professor."

Reluctantly, Bullock agreed and continued his examination of the corpse.

Pacific Ocean 14° 19' S. Lat.—105° 03' W. Long.

SOMETHING IS IN *the water. Something big.*

The thought slammed home in Ethan Swain's mind as he plunged through the ocean slightly astern of *Reliant.* Half-dazed from the impact that had knocked him from the whaleship, he shoved his hands out and slowed his descent. He tasted blood from split lips. Below, the sea was black and bottomless. But he wasn't alone in the water, and that certainty spun a web of fear within him.

Floating, waiting, suspended in the water for a moment so he wouldn't attract attention, he gazed up. Moonlight warred against the lanternlight spilling from the two ships. A cloud of illumination seemed spread against the uneven ocean surface, but the light also made that surface seem impossibly far away. Voices sounded distant and distorted as they came to him through the water.

"Man overboard! Man overboard!"

Ethan thought he could make out indistinct shapes running across the decks of both ships. A wave of movement hammered him again, different from the first time he'd experienced the sensation.

Something is in the water.

The circle of movement felt deliberate and predatory. Sharks circled prey till they were certain of strikes.

Kicking out with his feet, feeling bile burning at the back of his throat, Ethan swam for the surface. Movement broke over him again, smashing against his body like a tide crashing into a beach.

Whatever was in the water with him was huge. Swimming in the open water upon occasion had gotten him used to subtle changes in deep water. The sea was a constant mass of shifting currents, layers separated and given life by different temperatures. The sea constantly sorted through itself, turning itself over and over again like a dog chasing its tail because it was too restless to sleep.

Another current pushed against him, like the wake left by a passing ship driven before the wind. His mind spun, thinking perhaps *Reliant* had sailed across a submerged ship that hadn't quite sunk. Wrecks often drifted submerged for hours, days, or weeks. Sometimes years, though he himself had never seen one that had not come apart in that length of time.

He thought of the tangled mess of rigging he'd found when he was just a boy on Nantucket Island. The corpse still on occasion haunted his dreams, but that dead body had plenty of company these days. He pushed such thoughts from his mind as he swam.

His hand broke through to the surface just as his lungs wracked him with their first convulsive heave searching for fresh air. He kept his mouth closed till his face was above the waterline, then he breathed deeply.

Lanterns swept the dark water. Hard yellow light scoured the sea.

"Here," Ethan called when he had enough breath back. He recognized Holy aboard *Reliant*. "Holy. Over here."

Holy swung his lantern and splashed the light over Ethan. "Over here!" Holy cried out. "It's Ethan! He's over here!"

"One of yours then?" another man shouted from aboard *Miller's Crossing*.

"Aye," Holy called back. "Our first mate."

"How many men ye got in the water?"

For the first time, Ethan felt the salt of the ocean stinging his split lips and nose. The front of his face felt aflame. He struggled in vain to remember what had hit him.

"Two," Ethan replied. He treaded water, searching the depths around him. Something was in the water, and he didn't know where it was.

"Who else, Ethan?" Holy called down. He took a length of line from the railing and threw it toward Ethan.

"Nate," Ethan called back. He had trouble speaking through his bruised jaw and swollen lips. "Nate Phillips had the wheel this watch. He's in the water, too."

Recovering his wind and part of his addled wits, Ethan kicked and turned in the water. Wherever Nate was, the man was in trouble: He didn't know how to swim well enough to stay afloat long.

"Watch out, Holy," Ethan said. "Something knocked us in the water. I don't know what it was."

Most of the men aboard both ships drew back, and the press of lanternlights retreated from the ocean. Mutterings came from both crews.

"Ethan!" Nate gasped. "Help . . . can't swim!"

Turning, Ethan scoured the sea, riding up on a small wave and coming back down. The uneven surface of the sea created long pools of shadow that was proof even against the lanterns. With the sound trapped between the two ships, Ethan was unable to tell exactly where Nate's voice came from. Catching another wave, Ethan glanced around, finally spotting the sailor almost twenty feet from his position.

Nate's face was a pallid oval against the black sea. He slid under the water, and his features blurred and took on a grayish cast from the sea's shadow. He stuck his hands up, waving frantically.

"Ethan! Eth—" Water closed over him again and drowned out his voice.

"Holy," Ethan called, starting for Nate.

"I see him, Ethan." Holy shifted his lantern, focusing on Nate.

"Keep the light on him." Ethan kicked and stroked hard, cutting through the waves.

Before Ethan reached Nate, the man went under. Taking a deep breath, Ethan dived for him. The lights of other lanterns had joined Holy's. The combined illumination painted Nate like a shadow against the water as he kicked and fought and dropped down.

Desperate, Ethan shot his hand forward and closed his fingers like iron bands around Nate's wrist. Before he could even attempt to turn them back toward the surface, the drowning man wrapped his arms around Ethan, trapping his arms against his sides. Unable to swim, Ethan sank with Nate.

Without thinking, Ethan opened his mouth to shout at Nate, to tell the man he had to let go and trust him to get them to the surface or they would both drown. Brackish brine filled his mouth, and bubbles spun toward the surface at least six feet over their heads.

Although the darkness that covered the ocean limited visibility, the lanterns still managed to cut most of the incredibly huge shadow from the depths. The shadow was at least eighty feet long, and perhaps longer than that because it looked easily more than half *Reliant*'s length. Long and thick, the shadow swam headlong into the whaleship.

Reliant bucked, rolling hard over to port. The deep basso boom of the shadow's collision with the whaleship rolled over Ethan. The sound was distorted through the water, but carried a physical impact with it that slammed into

Ethan. Even through the water, he heard men yelling and cursing in alarm. He struggled to free himself from the death grip Nate had on him. If he could break free, there was still a chance that he could save them both.

Turning with amazing suppleness in the water, the giant shadow glided toward Ethan. He felt impossibly small. Recognizing the sperm whale's shape, he watched incredulously as the great creature glided only feet beneath him.

The whale turned on its side, glaring up with one eye set on the side of its head. Charred scarring pitted the whale's head.

CHAPTER 20

Easter Island, Chile 27° 17' S. Lat.—109° 24' W. Long.

"I'VE STUDIED WHALES and whaling, Captain Fisher, and I can tell you with certainty that no such whale exists that could do the damage this man shows."

Jonah McAfee mastered the black anger that filled him with the professor's quick disregard of his theory about the scar-faced whale. He released his breath through his nostrils and entertained himself with a quick thought of gutting the professor and making the man identify the parts of himself that leaked out with his dying breath. But the pirate captain shoved that thought aside. At the moment, he was convinced that more profitable avenues remained to be pursued.

"With all due respect, sir," McAfee made himself say, "I offer in my defense only science's own recognition of so much of the world that yet remains to be understood. I've read widely, and it seems to me that the more scientists poke, probe, and pry into what nature has wrought, the more they know is yet to be learned."

"But we are learning," Katharine said.

McAfee directed his attention to her and forced himself to smile. "Aye. But in my readings, I've seen that even men of science often disregard or overlook things that are superficial."

"Most things, Captain Fisher, are clearly more than surface appearance would indicate. Take yourself, for instance."

An innate wariness stole over McAfee. "How so?" he asked.

"You are obviously a Southern gentleman," Katharine said, "while your men are coarse and vulgar. I mean no disrespect, Captain Fisher, only to note that the men you have on your ship clearly don't share your interest in science."

McAfee chuckled. "No, that they definitely do not. But they are a curious lot and would like to know more about what happened to this man. Elsewise, I'm afraid they'll be making up stories about this event, and what might be lurking out here in the deep blue sea."

"You would have objection to that?" Katharine arched her brows.

McAfee knew the woman was interested in him. He always knew when women were interested in him. Even when Teresa had turned to him right before the end, he'd known she was only acting on her interest in him to get back at Ethan Swain, to make Ethan jealous enough to give his heart back into her captivity. He hadn't expected what had happened between them, though.

"I would have objection to that," McAfee said. "Superstition has hindered science for many years, and seamen—all a scurrilous bunch—do the most harm by journeying from port to port around the world spreading the worst superstitions of the lot. Ships' voyages are often filled with idle hours, and sailors' wits are made dull by such idleness. Still, they manage to acquire the necessary skills to tell even a modest tale in a big way."

Professor Bullock cleared his throat. "Have you ever seen this kind of wound before, Captain Fisher?"

"Over the course of my years at sea," the pirate captain said, "I've been witness to many grievous and grotesque injuries to a man's body. There have been any number of cuts, both deep and shallow, and amputations, those that were immediate and those that were necessitated days or even weeks later."

"And puncture wounds?" Bullock inquired.

"All manner of them," McAfee answered truthfully.

Bullock selected a long pair of forceps that had been coated in tar. McAfee noted the selection of coating. He still had some of the venom hidden away aboard *Sunfisher*. Utensils coated in tar might be something he would need at a later date.

"You have noted the strength of this venom," Bullock said.

"Aye. I've found it to be harmful to both men and fish. I've a sailor on board who is recovering from wounds suffered while we pulled this man's body from the sea." McAfee lied without effort.

Bullock grunted and peered through his spectacles. He poked the forceps into the throat wound and pulled at the rotted flaps of flesh. "Good. The victim we saw earlier hadn't been as envenomed as this man, and we had a young sailor who suffered miserably before finally recovering. I thought I was going to have to amputate his hand."

"I don't think my man is that bad." And if he got that way, McAfee had decided, he would shoot him before he'd spend that much time trying to save him.

"Good." Bullock held a small lantern close to his shoulder and peered down into the dead man's throat.

"That is a puncture wound, is it not, Professor?" McAfee asked.

"What makes you think that?" Bullock prodded the wound. The tar sizzled a little at the contact with the envenomed flesh.

"I've seen a number of puncture wounds. Suffered through them, in fact. The bruising around the wound indicates a puncture."

"Most astute, Captain."

"I've probably looked at more wounds than you have, Professor."

"You've been in war, Captain?" Bullock glanced up at him from across the dead man. "If you'll forgive me, I'd noticed the powder discoloration on your face, as well as the scars from knives and musket ball."

Embarrassment and rage fired through McAfee. He hated the discoloration on his face; he had tried for years to rid himself of it, suffering all manner of poultices and magic potions gleaned from his visits to West Africa and to the Caribbean. Before he could stop himself, he turned his side to the darker light of the tent, trying to hide his face from the young woman's view.

"Aye, Professor," McAfee answered.

"You're too young to have served in the first war against Britain, and seeing you here tells me that you're not actively engaged in the war with the British."

"Sir," McAfee said, unsheathing a little steel in his voice, "I fear I must take umbrage with that assessment. The work I do here, the commerce and the shipping, are important parts of the overall war effort. I've also fought two British privateers since I've been working in the Pacific." The declaration was a lie. As Harrington had pointed out when they'd met only a few days ago, healthy sharks didn't prey on each other. Still, it didn't keep him from wondering what booty Harrington carried around on *Formidable*. Harrington didn't seem like a man who would give everything to his king.

"I did not mean to offend."

McAfee smiled. "To offend, Professor, you would have at first had to have had all knowledge about me and what I have done. I only wish to correct an inaccurate picture of what it is I have been doing in these waters."

"I will remember."

"As to the scars," McAfee said, "and the discoloration to my face, I've fought men. Vicious and bloodthirsty men. Pirates and privateers, blackhearts every one. I killed them where I found them, routed others, and pursued still more. Those tasks were not chosen by me, but I did not shirk either my duty or the penance they had to pay for the evil actions they chose to commit. So you see, sir, I do know wounds."

"Well, you are correct in your assessment of this wound," Bullock said.

"The wound at the back of the throat," McAfee said, "also indicates a puncture by some object."

Peering more closely, Bullock nodded. "You have the eye of a trained observer."

"I was a sharpshooter." McAfee felt Katharine Bullock's eyes on him again. He turned to look at her slowly enough that she could look away and pretend she hadn't been looking.

The young woman busied herself with needlessly checking the oil levels of the nearby lanterns. She had done that only moments earlier.

"Have you ever seen a wound like this, Professor?" McAfee asked.

"I've seen punctures," Bullock conceded, "but nothing like this."

"You have to ask yourself why there would be a puncture wound," the pirate captain said.

"And what is your reasoning?"

"To deliver the venom," McAfee said. "And to suck out that poor man's innards once they liquefied."

Bright interest showed in Bullock's eyes. "Yes, yes, I agree completely. But what would do such a thing?"

"Something big and hungry," McAfee said. "Whatever appendage did that damage, it was part of something huge. It would take a large creature to eat a whole man. Even if it were only eating his viscera."

Pacific Ocean 14° 19' S. Lat.—105° 03' W. Long.

THE WHALE'S EYE spun in the scarred crevasse of its socket, and for a moment Ethan felt the creature's gaze focused solely on him. With the light of the moon and the lanterns above, Ethan saw his own reflection in that alien eye.

He was only a shadow, a flicker of movement across its hard-as-glass surface. In that instant, he forgot that Nate had locked a death grip on him and was dragging them both to doom down in the depths.

Then the eye passed, followed by the incredibly huge body. His foot, then his leg, made contact with the whale. The bruising impact set him to spinning and broke Nate's hold on him. The sailor flailed and kicked; bubbles burst from his screaming mouth.

Recovering, controlling the naked fear that ran rampant through him, Ethan ripped his shirt off. He swam after Nate, staying just out of the man's reach. Unfurling the shirt, Ethan pushed the garment toward Nate.

Desperately, the sailor clutched the bit of cloth. Once he was sure Nate had a good hold, Ethan swam toward the surface again. Peering around, he searched for the whale but couldn't see the creature. A moment later, he heard the hollow boom of impact as the whale struck *Reliant* again. The basso explosion sent a shock through the water.

Ethan fought hard, going straight for the surface. *Miller's Crossing* and *Reliant* lay at least forty yards away. He came up through the water facing both ships. *Reliant* rocked unsteadily, twisting against the waves as she lay at anchor and got mercilessly pounded. Spray tinted silver by the moon and gold by the lanterns broke over her gunnels, but she didn't appear to be taking on water.

He broke the surface and came up gasping. Then he kicked out, stroking with one arm while he pulled Nate behind him. The sailor broke the surface as well, pulled up by Ethan's momentum through the water. Ethan kept swimming, heading for *Reliant* as quickly as he could.

The ship rolled in the water, almost recovering just before she was hit again. Sailors squalled curses and called for divine intervention aboard the vessel. Muzzle flashes and the crack of gunshots echoed through the night as Stroud or some of his men fired into the water.

Fire coursed along Ethan's arms and legs from the strain. His face continued to ache. Blood and brine mixed in his mouth from his lips and nose. Wet hair dangled down in his eyes.

Reliant shivered again as the whale struck once more. Three lanterns dropped from the starboard 'yards, spinning over each other and dropping into the sea. A fourth lantern smashed against the deck and started a blaze.

"Holy!" Ethan yelled up as he closed on the whaleship. When he stopped swimming, he knew Nate would go down. The only chance the man would have would be if Ethan grabbed hold of him and somehow managed to keep them both above water.

"Ethan!" Holy shouted from above. He turned and glanced back as the ship rocked. "Get a boat down the falls! Ethan is in the water here!"

"Not a boat!" Ethan choked on water that lapped up over his chin, then managed to spit it out. "Drop a net over the side! Keep the boats out of the water! The whale will destroy them!"

Ethan reached the ship before Holy could round up a net to toss over the side. With his back against the rocking hull, he hauled on his shirt, pulling Nate toward him.

"Nate." Ethan spat water, keeping his chin above the waterline. "Listen to me. When you get here, let yourself go. Trust me." He had to speak loudly over the confusion breaking loose aboard both ships. *Miller's Crossing* shuddered next, taking a direct hit from the rampaging whale.

Nate tried to speak but got a mouthful of water that sent him into a panicked frenzy.

"Nate," Ethan barked. His fingers brushed those of the sailor. "So help me God, Nate, if you lock up on me, I'll slit your throat and peel you off of me."

Another wave of movement sluiced over Ethan. Before he could stop himself, he glanced at the water, trying to see the whale's shadow there and hoping that he wouldn't find it.

Then Nate threw an arm across Ethan's shoulders and buried them in the water. Caught unexpectedly even though he'd known the move was coming, Ethan went down. Another wave slapped against him.

Nate wrapped both arms around Ethan. Fighting panic, Ethan tried to battle his way free. He heard the muted splash overhead. Looking up, he saw the net in the water. He reached for it, felt his hand and most of his arm break free of the sea, and caught hold of the rough hemp. He hooked his fingers through the squares and pulled them up.

Somehow Ethan found the strength to haul them both head and shoulders out of the water. Nate clung to him, choking and gasping.

"God, thank ye, Ethan. I thought I was a deader, I did. Thought I was gone fer sure that time."

"Climb up," Ethan ordered. "Climb up and get out of the water, Nate."

Sobbing and shaking, Nate caught hold of the net and began to climb. "I'm sorry, Ethan. God as me witness, I'm sorry. I didn't mean to grab aholt of ye like that after ye told me not to. I swear to—"

Nate went rigid.

Ethan felt the man's muscles knot as Nate fell against him. Nate's face was a contorted rictus of pain and disbelief only inches from Ethan's own.

"Oh God," Nate whispered hoarsely. "It hurts."

In the next instant, pain scalded Ethan's side. He felt like a burning brand had been laid just above his left hip. He yelled in agony.

"Ethan," Nate gasped. "Somethin's got me!" Then, like a fish caught on a fisherman's line, he was suddenly yanked back. "It's got me! It's in me head! I can hear it! It's talkin' to me! Oh God! Its voice! It's hungry an' scared an' mad an' lost!"

Stunned, Ethan watched as Nate disappeared below the water.

"Ethan!" Holy's frantic voice came from above. "Get moving!"

More cracks of musket fire pierced the night. The reflections of the muzzle flashes burned briefly against the black water.

The harsh noise galvanized Ethan into action. He twisted around and buried his face in the net and began climbing. Nate was gone. There was nothing he could do for the man. All he could do was save himself.

Reliant swung suddenly, caught again in the grip of another wave that rolled her over on her side.

Ethan swung out wide of the ship, then banged against the rough hull. Barnacles scraped skin from his knuckles and the backs of his hands. He clung to the rope, then started up again.

"*Somethin's got me!*" Nate yelled. "Ethan! Ethan! I can hear it talkin'! I can hear—" The frantic words ended in a gurgle.

Primordial fear coursed through Ethan, lending him the strength to make the climb and distancing him from the pain in his side and his hands. He topped the gunnel and pulled himself over with Holy's help.

"Did you see it, Ethan?" Holy asked. "Did you see it?"

Ethan pushed himself to his feet. "The whale you mean?" His voice cracked.

"Aye."

But that's not what took Nate. Ethan knew that. Nate had been hooked by something.

"Are you hurt?" Holy stared down at Ethan's chest and stomach.

Despite the climb up the ship's side, blood covered Ethan's midriff. He wiped at the blood, searching for the gaping wound that had to have been there to unleash so much of the crimson fluid.

"Not my blood," Ethan stated as he swayed on the rolling deck. "It came from Nate."

"Where is Nate? I thought he was with you."

"He was." *Somethin's got me!* "Something in the water got him."

"The whale?"

"Not the whale. Something else." Ethan forced himself into motion. "Come on. We need to see if we can set this ship to rights. Where's Creel?"

"Aboard *Miller's Crossing.*"

Ethan got enough sailcloth up to straighten *Reliant's* heading again. The ship pulled at the anchor, rearing like a proud stallion, and Ethan kept her balanced. If the whale came again, he was determined to do some damage of his own. He stationed crews on both falconets and put the small group of Stroud's men left aboard *Reliant* on watch.

"Mr. Swain," Captain Folger bellowed from *Miller's Crossing.* "What the hell is going on?"

"We were attacked, Cap'n." Ethan shouted through his cupped hands. Part of him was afraid that the whale would return and attack the ship again, but part of him was certain that it had been satisfied with taking Nate. Two other sailors were missing from *Miller's Crossing.* None of them turned up.

"Attacked by what?" Folger demanded.

"A whale," Ethan responded. But he knew that wasn't all of it. No whale he had ever seen could do what that whale had done to Nate.

Something else was in the water.

Ethan stood in the bow with a harpoon clenched in his hands. Aside from the falconets, he knew the heavy harpoon could do the most damage to the whale. Musket fire would only leave small holes in the whale's massive body, but a harpoon could open up veins and arteries and might cause the creature to bleed to death.

The other men aboard *Reliant* stood guard as well. The festive air they had enjoyed earlier from the gam was gone.

"That whale came here after us," Holy said. "Didn't it? Ain't no other reason for it to show up and attack us, is there?"

Ethan gazed at the black water, knowing he'd never see the whale until the creature slammed into the ship again. Luckily, as proof of good Nantucket construction, *Reliant* as yet had no leaks.

"I don't know, Holy," he answered. "And I wouldn't say such a thing so loud. If the other men aboard this ship hear you and start thinking the same thing, we're going to be dealing with a panic."

Holy fell silent for a moment. "So we're going to just wait?"

"Aye," Ethan replied, because there was nothing else they could do.

Easter Island, Chile 27° 17' S. Lat.—109° 24' W. Long.

"GOOD MORNING, PROFESSOR Bullock," the captain greeted in a flat voice.

"Good morning," Bullock responded, suddenly aware of how grimy he appeared next to the immaculate captain. He'd been asleep when Perkins had arrived and told him Mayhew wanted to speak to him out on the beach. Perkins had said he hadn't been allowed to take no for an answer. Worn and irritable, Bullock had gone under definite protest. "I'd like to know what the meaning of—"

"We leaving this place," Mayhew announced. "Within minutes. If our luck holds, we'll be gone while the fog is still upon us and *Sunfisher*'s crew won't see us."

For the first time, Bullock noticed the fog that swirled around the island. The mass was so thick that *Sunfisher* was hidden, and so heavy that moisture coated his exposed skin.

"Why should you care—"

"Because Captain Fisher and his crew aren't what they seem to be." Mayhew nodded toward the longboat.

Two of the men nearest the boat reached in and grabbed hold of a tarp-covered figure. From the outlines and all that he had seen in the past weeks, Bullock knew the tarp covered a body. Still, he was surprised when the dead African man spilled out onto the longboat's bottom. *Not a man,* the professor corrected himself, *a boy.* The corpse didn't look over twelve.

It took Bullock a further moment to realize that the thing that had killed John Maxwell and Warren Johnstone hadn't savaged the corpse. The young African was dead, but whole. Scars from past wounds and whips marred his dark skin. Scabs covered half-healed wounds around his wrists and ankles.

"What happened?" Bullock asked, wondering what part he was supposed to play and what the dead boy was supposed to mean to him. Even after all the months aboard the ship, the professor still didn't know all of the ship's crew.

"We found this boy's body this morning," Mayhew said. "The corpse rolled in with the tide farther down the beach. When one of the lookouts discovered the corpse, Mr. Perkins thought we would be better served if we were to stay quiet about the discovery."

"What happened to him?" Curious, Bullock peered more closely at the body.

"He drownt," Perkins answered.

"Drowned?" Bullock repeated, trying to make some sense of what was going on. "He fell off *Brown-Eyed Sue*? That's terrible, but I don't see what—"

"Not our ship," Mayhew growled. "This man came from that damnable ship, *Sunfisher*."

"How can you know that?"

"Because I know my crew, Professor Bullock," Mayhew responded. "And because I am not and have never transported slaves."

"Slaves." Bullock glanced back at the young corpse and took in the scabs around the wrists and ankles again. The information clicked into place. "This man came from Captain Fisher's ship?"

"I haven't seen another one out here of late. Have you?" Mayhew demanded.

"No."

"Process of elimination. I thought with you being a scientific man you'd grasp that simple logic."

"*Sunfisher* is a slave ship." Bullock was still struggling to catch up.

"Aye," Mayhew said. "And I don't know what she's doing here, but I'd bet my eyeteeth that it's for no good reason." The captain turned his attention to Bullock. "Fisher's had a rather overt interest in you, Professor, but I have to wonder if it might not be your daughter he was most interested in."

The speculation ran through Bullock like a knife twisting in his stomach. Memory of the glances Fisher had turned in Katharine's direction as well as the captain's willingness to talk to her haunted him.

"Fisher can't be here because of Katharine," Bullock said. "He had no way of knowing she was aboard."

"Ships talk, Professor, and we've talked with a few ourselves."

"Maybe this poor unfortunate boy washed up from somewhere else," Bullock suggested.

Mayhew shook his head. "No. That body hasn't been in the water long. Probably escaped during the night, tried to make the beach, failed, and drowned."

The cold, impartial way Mayhew detailed the events filled Bullock with dread. Death was so casually accepted out on the sea.

"I wanted you up and about, Professor," Mayhew said. "With the cloud cover in place and none of Fisher's men immediately about, we might stand a good chance of weighing anchor and getting into the wind before anyone aboard *Sunfisher* gets wise to us. His men on the beach were all drinking deeply last night. We can only hope the same was going on aboard ship as well."

"And if Captain Fisher should see us fleeing this place this morning?" Bullock asked.

"Then we fight ourselves clear of him." Mayhew firmed his jaw. "Whatever purpose Captain Fisher has here, that purpose does not have our best wishes at heart."

Bullock stared at the dead boy, thinking about how Fisher had kept his vessel away from prying eyes. "You believe there are other slaves aboard that ship?"

"I do."

"What are we going to do about them?"

Mayhew's answer was immediate and unflinching. "Nothing."

"But if this boy is any indication—"

"Professor Bullock," Mayhew interrupted, "that dead boy is a certain indicator of what Fisher has in store for us. Trust me when I say that even worse rough treatment would be reserved for your daughter."

Bullock scarcely controlled the sudden fear that overwhelmed him.

"Now please, Professor," Mayhew continued, "do me the courtesy of getting your things together. We shall have to forfeit the tent, but I hope that we can salvage your equipment and notes. To do that, we need to act now."

Bullock nodded, then turned and walked briskly back along the beach. He thought about Fisher, how the ship's captain had affected an easygoing manner and exhibited a fair amount of education. But that appearance was only a lure and a cover for the evil that lurked inside. Monsters, it seemed, were everywhere.

CHAPTER 21

Pacific Ocean 11° 06' S. Lat.—101° 27' W. Long.

"THAR SHE BLOWS!"

Hearing the cry, Ethan pushed himself up from the deck where he'd been working on mending canvas and peered into the rigging. He observed the fear that swept over the crew in anticipation of seeing the whale. To a man, they moved too quickly or too slowly into position.

They were three days out from the spot where they had been attacked and lost Nate. The whale had not returned during the night, and *Reliant* and *Miller's Crossing* had decided to sail together for a while with the advent of morning. Since that time, all of the men had been anxious about taking another whale so close to the area where the crater-faced sperm whale had been encountered. He had reservations himself because of the wound he'd suffered from the creature that had taken Nate. His injured side was a mass of blisters that were only that day starting to look less infected.

"Where away, Robert?" Ethan called up.

"Sou', sou'east," Robert yelled down. He pointed excitedly.

Walking to the starboard railing, Ethan peered out across the expanse of green sea. *Reliant* caught a wave and rode to the top. From the new vantage point, Ethan saw the whale's spout nearly a mile away. He took the spyglass from his hip pouch, extended the sections, and stared at the whale. Then the ship reached the other side of the tall, rolling wave and dropped downward fast enough to twist his stomach.

"Mr. Swain," Captain Folger called. "Is there a whale?"

"Aye, Cap'n," Ethan called back. He felt and saw the tension roll over the crew. "A sperm whale by the looks of it, and a big one."

"Then we'll make for it."

"Aye, Cap'n."

"Signal *Miller's Crossing* and let them know that we won't be accompanying them any farther."

"Aye, Cap'n." Ethan gave Creel the order to signal the other ship, then went to make sure that the whaleboats were in order. With Larson still in the brig and Stroud having no practical experience, Ethan had promoted Creel to one of the other whaleboats and given him a crew. Ethan had also negotiated a higher-paying lay for Creel during the rest of the voyage.

After he was certain the whaleboats were provisioned with sharp harpoons and plenty of line, Ethan turned his attention to the falconets. He ordered both loaded with exploding balls. If the whale they had in their sights was the same scar-faced one they had encountered before, he intended to fire at will into the monstrous creature. They'd harvest what they could find that was left of the beast.

"I'll handle them cannon," a gruff voice offered.

Recognizing the voice, Ethan glanced up from the prow-mounted falconet and saw Bill Fedderson standing before him. Stained white bandages wrapped Bill's stump of a right arm.

During his ordeal and recovery, Bill had lost weight and lost color. He was freshly clean-shaven, letting Ethan know that Robert had visited him that morning before taking his shift aloft. Bill hadn't been able to shave himself properly, and that concession to letting someone care for him had been one of the first he'd made.

Bill tucked his maimed arm in front of him, dropping his other arm down in front as if trying to cover his infirmity. "Are ye daft? Or didn't ye hear me?" he asked in a challenging and bellicose voice.

"I heard you," Ethan said.

Eyeing him fiercely, pride gleaming in his eyes, Bill said, "Manning them cannon ain't overmuch, Ethan. Even fer a cripple. I can beller at a gun crew with the best of them even with one arm."

"What if that's the whale we crossed paths with a few days ago?" Ethan asked. "Are you ready to stand against that?"

"Ye mighta took me arm, damn ye, but ye left me with two good legs." Bill took a step forward. "If'n ye an' them what goes with ye have to face that bastard, it only makes sense to have a seasoned man on them cannon. Ain't nobody on this ship what's got more experience than me."

"No," Ethan admitted. Pride swelled within him as he saw the fierceness in Bill's gaze. "No, there's not."

Bill lowered his voice. "I can do this, Ethan. I swear on my mother's grave that I can an' I will. I may be a cripple, but I ain't a-gonna be a burden to this crew. I won't do it."

"I know you can," Ethan replied. "I expect you to keep the powder dry and help us if it comes to that."

Unshed tears sparkled in Bill's eyes. "I will."

Ethan offered his left hand. Bill extended his own left hand, and they shook. "Welcome back, Bill."

"Thankee. I'll do ye proud, Ethan. Swear to God I will."

Ethan stepped back and released the man's hand. He'd felt the weakness in the sailor's grip, but it was getting stronger. He raised his voice, having a little difficulty because his throat was thick with emotion.

"Bill Fedderson's in charge of the guns," he yelled loud enough for every man to hear.

Several of the sailors hooted and cheered, welcoming Bill back to the fold.

Ethan turned toward the stern starboard whaleboat. His crew, including Robert, already stood ready. He'd paired Holy with Creel. Both crews consisted of seasoned men.

The whaleboats slid down the falls on either side of *Reliant,* hitting the ocean with splashes that kicked up flurries of spray. Ethan went down a rope hand over hand, followed by the rest of the crew. *Reliant* slowed as canvas dropped and was furled, but the whaleboats skipped across the water like flat stones.

Once the crews were aboard, both whaleboats cut loose and took to the sea under their own power. Ethan sat in the whaleboat's stern, his eyes fixed on the prize that they were going to attempt.

Pacific Ocean 13° 57' S. Lat.—104° 02' W. Long.

THE TROPICAL SUN burned down on *Brown-Eyed Sue* as she sat at anchor. Drenched in sweat, feeling parched but in no way ready to abandon his current project, Professor Bullock fed on his excited anticipation as he watched Perkins and the other members of the longboat crew row toward their intended target.

The target coasted along on the ocean's surface, a bluish purple oval about the size of a man's fists stacked one on top of the other. Glossy ribs ridged the top of the oval and ran down the sides, almost reaching the waterline. The ribs glinted silver in the bright sunlight.

When the longboat reached the oval, Perkins yelled to his crew. They spread the net out upon the water, then pulled the Portuguese man-of-war up in it. With the net secure behind the longboat, the crew rowed for *Brown-Eyed Sue*. After the net was affixed to the boom arm, sailors hauled away. The rope creaked through the pulleys. Water spilled from the sodden hemp, and fish jumped in among the seaweed and other debris the net had scooped up.

Carefully, under Perkins's guidance, the men emptied the net across the ship's deck. The greedy wooden planks soaked up the seawater immediately, but the tar finish didn't let the brine penetrate deeply.

The bulbous mass of the Portuguese man-of-war lay limp on the deck. Beneath the creature, long tentacles stretched in lax coils. Judging the size of the coils, Bullock guessed that the tentacles would easily reach over a hundred feet. The crew stayed back as if they feared the creature might suddenly erupt from the deck like some gargantuan spider.

"It's all right," the professor said. "It can't attack you. Once out of the water, the Portuguese man-of-war can't move. The creature depends on the vagaries of wind and the ocean currents. The tentacles aren't capable of independent motion."

"These things move," another sailor said. "I seen 'em. They sail. Just like this one was doing."

Katharine stood nearby, her face writ with concentration. She held a journal and a bit of drawing charcoal. Her hand moved swiftly, surely, and Bullock knew she blocked in images in seconds.

"They do sail, Mr. Harper," Bullock agreed. Harper had gotten to be one of his favorites, a young man with a quick mind and an insatiable appetite for knowledge. If he hadn't been impoverished and signed on to the ship, his time would have been better spent at a university. Katharine worked diligently with the young man on his journal. "Some of my esteemed colleagues believe it was the sight of the man-of-war all puffed up as it is, sailing serenely across the ocean, that initiated the idea of sails on boats."

The men gathered more closely, the way they had on occasion when the nets had dragged fish from the sea and they'd tumbled upon a choice bit of bizarre nature. Often there was some fish pulled from the brine that some sailors hadn't seen, and occasionally there were even fish that none of the sailors could identify. The fact that Bullock could identify all the mystery fish had earned the professor goodwill on part of the crew in spite of his mission, which had brought them out into the Pacific Ocean in the first place.

"The Portuguese man-of-war is a fascinating study in animal architecture," Bullock went on. "Most people look at this thing and only see one creature. Actually, there are four. The bladder you see at the top of the creature is filled mostly with nitrogen, broken down and kept by the body." Crouching down, Bullock took his glasses from inside his shirt pocket and hooked them behind his ears. He slid a stick he had taken to carrying while poking and prodding on specimens collected by the crew from his pants pocket. He pointed at the man-of-war's bladder. "This part of the organism colony that comprises the creature is a polyp. This creature's job is to propel the colony through the ocean by providing a sail for the wind. A layman's term for this part of its body is crest."

Katharine stood behind Bullock and peered over her father's shoulder. She, like the professor, had only seen jellyfish on occasion.

Bullock studied the coiled tentacles. Fish still flopped and gasped on the deck. The professor poked the stick through the coils and uncovered a small fish trapped within the tentacles.

The fish lay unmoving. Striped in orange and white, edged in black, the distinctive coloration marked the fish immediately as a clown fish.

Bullock mopped perspiration from his brow. "The man-of-war also carries a venom. That's how it catches fish, and how it caught this one in particular." He slid the pointer under the fish and revealed that the creature was attached to several tentacles.

The sailors peered more closely.

"The venom is administered through these tentacles." Bullock indicated the longest tentacles. "These are one of the three creatures that make up the man-of-war's lower body colony. These are called dactylozooids. That's from Latin, which translates as 'finger.' They seek out and subdue prey."

Brown-Eyed Sue caught a particularly forceful wave and shimmied. Several of the jellyfish's coils slipped free and slithered across the deck. The sailors yelped and cursed and jumped back.

"These dactylozooids have a unique architecture within them," Bullock continued, touching the coiled threadlike structures within the tentacle he used as an example. "These threads shoot out and inject prey with a venom that paralyzes it. Eating its captured prey takes time, and the longer the prey lives, the better it serves as a food source because the meat stays fresh." He poked at the jellyfish, revealing the thick tube that ran down from the center of the mass. "This is the gonozooid. These animals are responsible for reproduction."

"How does it eat?" Harper asked. "I don't see no mouth."

"A man-of-war has many mouths." Bullock sorted through the tentacles with the stick, finding the slightly thicker, more bulbous growths. "These are the gastrozooids. Each tentacle has a mouth. The gastrozooids secrete liquids that break down the captured prey's flesh. Once the flesh is broken down, the resulting mixture is sucked back into the man-of-war for nourishment."

"By God," a sailor said hoarsely, "ain't that a horrible way to go? I wouldn't want to be et up whilst I was still a-knowin' about it."

Bullock regarded the man-of-war. He remembered the way John Maxwell had been eviscerated, a hollow husk of the man he had been. And he remembered how Warren Johnstone's flesh had been falling off him while he took his last few breaths.

Captain Mayhew bellowed from the quarterdeck. "Mr. Perkins."

Perkins snapped to. "Aye, Cap'n."

"I suppose there's a reason why those men are dawdling board my ship when there's so much work to be done to keep her in shape." Mayhew's countenance looked as though it was carved from granite.

"Aye, Cap'n," Perkins said. "I had some of the crew doin' some fishin' fer the perfesser. Like ye decided to."

"How much longer are you going to be about that task?"

"I'm finished, Captain," Bullock replied. "If I could get Mr. Perkins to see to it the man-of-war is taken belowdecks where I can more properly examine the creature, I'd appreciate your indulgence."

"Mr. Perkins," Mayhew growled. "Get that thing below and get this ship into the wind again."

"Aye, Cap'n."

Mayhew glowered down at Bullock. "As for you, Professor Bullock, I'd like a moment of your time."

"I will, Captain, as soon as I—"

"*Now,* Professor. If you please. In my quarters. Miss Bullock can see to it your specimen is properly stored."

Bullock mopped perspiration from his brow. "Of course, Captain." He removed his glasses and pocketed them. He nodded to Katharine, who immediately took responsibility for transporting the jellyfish.

Bullock followed the captain belowdecks into Mayhew's personal quarters. The small room was neat and tidy, everything in its assigned place.

The captain indicated a chair in front of his small desk.

With grim reluctance, Bullock took the hard wooden chair. The chair was affixed to the floor, and comfort must have been the last thing in mind when it had been constructed.

"Tell me, Professor. Have you ever killed a man before?"

"No."

"It's not something taken lightly."

Bullock kept his composure with difficulty. He tried to figure out where the ship's captain was headed with his line of interrogation. "Why are you asking this?"

"Because I don't think you truly understand the risks you're exposing your daughter to."

"We haven't seen the pirate ship since we left Easter Island. I think that any danger we might have faced there is—"

"Is still there, Professor Bullock," Mayhew snapped. "And you're a self-delusional fool if you think anywise else."

"I resent that remark, and—"

"Resent the Hell out of it if you want to." Mayhew leaned back in his chair. "Even should we make it back to New Jersey without getting stopped by *Sunfisher* or her crew, and even make it back without another chance encounter with this monster you're looking for—"

"The creature is out there, Captain."

Shrugging, Mayhew said, "Maybe so. But besides those dangers, there is one other you should consider."

Bullock waited. His mind churned through possibilities, but he couldn't come up with the direction in which Mayhew was headed. "What other danger?"

"You haven't known many sailing men, have you, Professor?"

"A few."

"Well then, what you have seen of them hasn't sunk in deeply enough."

"I get along well with the crew, Captain Mayhew. At least, in my opinion."

"Aye." Mayhew nodded. "That you do, Professor. But you forget that each of those men, more or less at his base, is a frightful and superstitious man. They don't have years of training at Princeton or some other university to assure them that the world isn't flat. Most men that I've taken on as crew that haven't yet been around the world remain convinced that one morning or night they're going to find themselves sailing off the edge of the world."

Bullock was astounded by such a declaration. "Surely you can't mean that."

"Surely," Mayhew said evenly, "you haven't been blind to that."

"No one can believe that."

"A round world?" Mayhew stated. "And yet we don't fall off when we go underneath it?" He shook his head. "That's unbelievable."

"Not when you take gravity into consideration."

"Show me gravity, Professor."

Defiantly, Bullock took a fresh quill from the box on the captain's desk. The professor took the captain's hand and held it with the palm flat and out. Bullock held the quill up with one hand and dropped it into Mayhew's palm.

"Gravity," Bullock announced with a little pride.

Mayhew waited a beat, then turned his hand over. The quill dropped to the top of the desk.

Bullock stared at the feather.

"Gravity," Mayhew said, "doesn't work underneath something. That's what a sailor sees."

"But that's not how things are," Bullock protested.

"You and I know that, Professor. Most men in this crew don't." Mayhew put the quill away, returning the desk to spotless neatness. "Do you want to know another thing sailors believe in that every captain has to be aware of?"

Bullock waited, feeling all his arguments evaporate inside him. Closed off from the whisper of wind that had coursed across *Brown-Eyed Sue*, the cabin felt nearly twice as hot as the deck under the sun's glare. Hopelessness squeezed the professor's heart.

"Men talk of sea monsters when they're on the ocean," Mayhew said. "It's normal talk. They've heard stories other men have made up and told them all their lives. And they want to learn the best stories to tell the tavern wenches, young lads, and landlubbers when they get into port. But mostly they're afraid they're going to run into one of the fierce dragons or giant squids they've heard of."

"Those things don't exist," Bullock protested. "Otherwise, men would have seen them before now."

"Is that so?" Mayhew reached into his desk drawer and drew out a pipe and tobacco. He filled the pipe expertly and soon had the tobacco blazing well. "Pray tell me what you're out here looking for, Professor. If not something that no man has ever seen before, something that no man has ever before believed existed."

"This thing exists. You've seen the damage that it has wrought to the bodies of the men that we have uncovered."

"Professor, how can you expect the men to remain objective about what we're facing out here if you can't?"

"I am objective," Bullock argued.

"And even you're afraid of what that creature might be," Mayhew declared. "I've seen how careful you are that Miss Bullock doesn't walk the ship's deck alone. For a time I thought it was because you were afraid of how the men might treat her. Then I remembered how you had let her walk the deck by herself before we reached Easter Island."

"That thing is out there." Bullock was surprised at how his voice shook. He was even more surprised to know that the ship's captain was exactly right. "And it eats people. I think it has learned to prey on them."

"By God, sir!" Mayhew slapped the desk with the flat of his palm. "That is exactly the kind of talk I want to prevent on my ship!"

Bullock slumped back in the chair, suddenly realizing the point Mayhew was trying to make.

"If you panic this crew," the captain said, "they'll make mistakes. At the very least. If they get good and panicked, they may well decide that you are unlucky for them. So some night one of them will slip a knife between your ribs and pitch you over the side. I'm betting that they won't be too gentle with your daughter either."

Cold fear spun gossamer threads in Bullock's spine.

"You having them pull things up from the sea—"

"The man-of-war," Bullock said before he even knew he was speaking.

"Exactly," Mayhew said. "That's the kind of behavior that can get you killed, Professor. And your daughter with you."

"But the men also need to look out for that monster," Bullock said. "It attacked us once."

"That was a rogue whale."

Bullock returned the captain's unflinching glare.

"And that attack," Mayhew went on, "came when that rogue whale was trying to devour other prey. Not us. I want that distinction kept in view."

"I understand what you're saying about the crew's morale. I lack a proper perspective on the situation aboard ship, and I shall avail myself of your experience in the future. However, I will not give up trying to make sense of all the puzzles we have uncovered. I will not have my experiments curtailed."

"Fair enough. Keep them confined belowdecks, and my men out of them as much as possible. Be discreet about your discoveries."

Bullock nodded.

"Also, if you need someone to talk to, keep your discourses limited to your daughter. She seems like a capable young woman. And should you find something you can't talk about with her because it's too delicate—or perhaps because you want an outside opinion—feel free to come to me. I think you'll find that I'm not totally ignorant about many things."

"I'm beginning to see that, Captain," Bullock said respectfully. "I only regret that it has taken me this long to do so."

Frantic knocking sounded at the door. "Cap'n Mayhew."

"What is it, Mr. Perkins?" Mayhew asked.

"Lookout spotted sails, Cap'n. Comin' up from the west an' closin' fast. Figured ye'd want to know."

Mayhew growled an oath, reached for his hat, and clapped it on his head. He led the way out the door, and Bullock followed.

When he stood on the quarterdeck with the captain, Bullock peered over the rolling green sea and barely made out the white square sails against the blue sky.

Mayhew extended his spyglass with metallic clicks. He stared through the device without expression or explanation.

"Who?" Bullock asked.

"I don't know," Mayhew answered. "But she's headed straight for us, making better time than we are." He closed the spyglass. "Mr. Perkins!"

"Aye, Cap'n."

"Get those gun crews ready, Mr. Perkins. In case we have need of them." Mayhew turned to Bullock. "Professor, I'd prefer it if you were belowdecks. Should this thing turn bloody, that would be the best place for you and your daughter."

"Of course, Captain." Bullock started down the companionway. He stopped and looked up. "If you should need anything . . ."

"I won't hesitate to ask," Mayhew said.

Swiftly, Bullock descended the stairs, amazed at how quickly the crew surged into their stations. Then he hurried to find Katharine.

"Get more sail up there, Mr. Perkins," Captain Mayhew bellowed. "We'll outrun them if we can."

Bullock sincerely hoped that could be done.

CHAPTER 22

Pacific Ocean 13° 57' S. Lat.—104° 02' W. Long.

"UNFURL THE SPINNAKER, damn you!" Jonah McAfee stood on *Sunfisher's* quarterdeck dressed in a brace of pistols and his rapier at his side. "We're running with the wind! Give me more sail!"

The spinnaker bore a black skull and crossbones emblazoned on a field of white. Unfurled in a peaceful port, the spinnaker would mean the death of McAfee and his crew—if the local constabulary were large enough and fierce enough to take his ship. But on the open sea with only *Brown-Eyed Sue* in sight, the spinnaker bearing the death's-head grin usually struck terror in the hearts of the other crew while inspiring McAfee's own men.

The gun crews rolled out the cannon, loaded them, and had them once more back in place in only a short time.

Sunfisher cut through the rolling sea much faster than *Brown-Eyed Sue.* McAfee had trusted the ship would. *Sunfisher* was his pride and joy, the best ship he had owned over the last few years of his career as a pirate.

He stood on the quarterdeck as the ship rolled and heaved beneath him. His stomach twisted with the ocean. Blood slammed against his temples as the ship crashed into a wave and was driven upward, then his senses swam around him as the ocean and the ship fell away beneath him in the next instant and dropped the ship twenty feet and more, only to be caught up again by the next wave.

The lines creaked and the sailcloth snapped like angry pups chewing at their tethers. Still, *Sunfisher* held her fierce grip on the wind.

For nearly an hour, *Sunfisher* pursued *Brown-Eyed Sue*. Standing on the quarterdeck, McAfee took a beating from the ship as well as the spray that crashed over the gunnels and whipped back over him. By the time he caught up to his prey, he was half-drenched, and the drying brine had left a white rime on his clothes. He commanded the ship's helmsman, angling *Sunfisher* in behind the other ship and stealing her wind away.

As soon as the other ship started to slow and the sails sagged a little from the yardarms, the stern cannon fired. The cloud of smoke boiled up before spume of water shot up from where the cannonball slammed into the sea. The sharp basso thump of detonation a few seconds later rolled over *Sunfisher*'s deck.

"Mr. Gilley," McAfee roared. "Fire the chase guns as you see fit. Get me a hit."

The chase guns fired. One of them missed, but the other slammed into *Brown-Eyed Sue*'s stern. Coaming and the railing shattered into kindling, and the gun crew toppled backward.

"Helmsman," McAfee called, "bring us alongside the port side of that ship."

"Aye, Cap'n."

"Mr. Gilley, ready the starboard cannon. Fire on my command." McAfee glared at the other ship. At the moment, he hated the ship as much as he would any enemy.

"Guns!" Gilley squalled in warning.

Gazing at the portside railing, McAfee saw the cannon peering out from the firing holes along the other ship. Less than sixty feet separated them as he ran up alongside the other ship.

"Drop sail," McAfee ordered. "Match speed."

The sailors up in the rigging quickly complied. *Sunfisher* slowed, dropping speed till she was running only slightly faster than her prey.

"Stand ready!" McAfee yelled.

In the next moment, *Brown-Eyed Sue* fired her guns. The ship's port side disappeared in a haze of black smoke the cannon belched out behind the balls. Several cannonballs hammered *Sunfisher*'s starboard side and stern, but most of the shots sank into the sea, both short and over the target.

McAfee stood without flinching as the series of shivers ran the length of his ship. He was the mark of defiance the other men had to live up to. *Sunfisher* hadn't been mortally wounded. He'd had ships shot out from beneath him before, and he knew what those occasions felt like.

"Ready!" he yelled.

"All ready!" Gilley bellowed back.

McAfee waited, standing on deck and getting *Sunfisher*'s feel as she dived into a trough, then came back up cresting another wave. Less than fifty feet remained between the ships. He waited, letting *Sunfisher* start the slide back down the other side of the crest.

"Fire!" McAfee yelled.

The starboard cannon went off in one continuous string of rolling thunder. Black smoke filled the air in choking clouds that swept back over McAfee. *Sunfisher* jerked and heeled hard over to port.

"Reload!" McAfee ordered.

The gun crews scrambled on the deck, pulling the cannon back by thick hawser ropes, then swabbing the smoking muzzle out and throwing fresh powder charges into the gun.

Running with the wind as she was, *Sunfisher*'s deck didn't clear of black smoke as much as she normally would have if she'd been firing from a stationary position. The smoke and the stink clung to her.

McAfee peered through the rolling smoke mass. His eyes burned from the acrid stink, but he saw that the cannon fire had shattered *Brown-Eyed Sue*'s port side. Several of her guns were out of commission, and a number of the gun crews lay prostrate or writhed in agony, visible through the holes blown in the ship's side.

A direct hit, more or less, McAfee realized. His crew had gotten as lucky as they were good. He raised his voice. "Mr. Gilley."

"Ready, Cap'n."

"On my mark." McAfee waited till *Sunfisher* was once more sliding down a wave crest with *Brown-Eyed Sue* dead in her sights. "Fire!"

The cannon thundered again, blasting out a salvo of cannonballs that ripped into *Brown-Eyed Sue*'s guts. An explosion belowdecks told McAfee that at least one cannonball had found a bag of powder.

"Prepare boarders!" McAfee drew his sword in his right hand and a pistol in his left. He scrambled down the companionway, joining Gilley and the crew amidships.

The helmsman drove *Sunfisher* into *Brown-Eyed Sue*. The impact cracked more timbers. The two ships came apart, rolling separately over a wave. Then they slammed into each other again.

McAfee kept his feet with difficulty. Several pirates managing the gang-planks toppled to the deck in a cursing mass.

"Get up, you cur dogs!" McAfee yelled.

Sunfisher slammed *Brown-Eyed Sue* once more. This time the pirate helmsman managed to stay side by side with the ship. The pirates lined up, getting three gangplanks laid across the railing. One of them ran across a broken section of railing. Another toppled between the ships, plunging down into the narrow strip of ocean between them.

McAfee stepped up onto the nearest gangplank, feeling the bloodlust rise in him as it always did.

One of the sailors grabbed the gangplank's end and set himself to shove the timber from the ship. McAfee raised his pistol and shot the man through the head. Blood flew as the man stumbled backward and sat down. Life drained from his blood-streaked eyes before he fell back.

McAfee shoved the empty pistol back in his chest strap and drew another pistol. He took one more running step, then hurled himself over the sailor with the cutlass in front of him. When he landed on the deck, the pirate captain rocked on his feet, spun, raised his sword arm, and thrust his rapier into the sailor's back to pierce his heart. He kicked the dying man from his blade and turned to face another sailor. The pistol came up automatically in his hand. He squeezed the trigger at point-blank range and saw the hole appear in the man's forehead.

The dead man stopped his headlong rush, opened his mouth to scream in rage or pain, and loosed his last breath.

McAfee kicked the dead man from his path. He spotted a sailor setting himself coolly behind a musket, his motions deliberate and unhurried. McAfee threw himself forward and down, meeting resistance as *Brown-Eyed Sue* heaved up on a wave.

The sailor's musket ball tore through McAfee's clothing and ripped through the flesh at the back of his neck. Death had only been a whisper away. McAfee stopped and cut back toward the man with the musket. He palmed another pistol as he slashed at the man's head. The sailor blocked the blow with his musket but was left unprotected against the pistol the pirate captain thrust up under his chin. McAfee pulled the trigger and closed his eyes against the spray of blood that followed.

When he opened his eyes again, McAfee blinked blood away. He shoved the third pistol into his chest strap and drew one of the two he had shoved into his waist sash. He roared curses at his men, urging them on.

The pirate crew swooped down onto the sailors like starved crows. Sunlight glinted from their blades as they rose and fell, but the mirror brightness was soon lost as crimson covered steel.

In only a handful of minutes, blood covered the deck. Footing turned slippery and treacherous. The effect was something McAfee had experienced several times. He kept his balance easily, shortening his stride and keeping his weight centered above his hips and knees. Teresa had taught him the art of the blade. He remembered the toss of her black hair and the daring smile she always wore— just one short step from the brink of madness.

Then the memory soured as McAfee remembered that Teresa had also schooled Ethan Swain in the sword. They had spent hours on the deck or on a beach when they'd taken to port after a successful haul. Hours of swordplay had been followed by hours of love play.

Black anger boiled up inside McAfee at the memories. He disarmed the sailor who had tried to stab him from behind. Instead of simply running the man through, the pirate captain slashed him three times in an eye blink, laying open his stomach, chest, and throat. The man stumbled back, choking on his own blood and trying to hold his innards in.

Musket balls rained down on the pirates from the quarterdeck. Two pirates went down with serious injuries.

On the move, McAfee took cover behind the mainmast. He glanced around the deck as he shoved his rapier back into its scabbard. Reaching into his cartridge pouch, he took out a ball and powder load and glanced at the quarterdeck.

Captain Mayhew led an organized group of men who held the quarterdeck. Several of them had evidently seen military action before because they kept up a rate of fire that cost the pirates dearly.

McAfee reloaded his pistols, biting through the cartridges to free the balls and open the paper powder compartment. He poured the powder into the barrels and spat the balls into the muzzles, seating the loads by pounding the butts against the mainmast.

Gilley and a dozen other pirates had taken cover behind the dead men scattered across the deck. Others had taken up positions behind the deck hatch. *Sunfisher* sailed beside *Brown-Eyed Sue,* still bumping occasionally and sending blows that rocked the ship violently.

"Get your muskets ready, Mr. Gilley. I'll be wanting to rush that quarterdeck. I expect you and three men you choose to accompany me." McAfee fisted two of the pistols.

None of the pirates in hiding looked happy about the prospect. The men with Captain Mayhew on the quarterdeck held their fire for the moment, but their marksmanship showed in the divots raked from the deck and the hatch by the musket balls.

"If those men falter, Mr. Gilley," McAfee promised, "I'll shoot them myself. And you. For choosing unwisely."

"Aye, Cap'n," Gilley growled.

McAfee yelled orders over to the pirate crew left aboard *Sunfisher*. Men spread out across the deck, taking up shooting positions. Above them, the black flag flew straight and stiff from the mainmast, proudly showing off the skull and crossbones.

Raking the pistol hammers back with his thumbs, McAfee yelled, *"Now!"*

Two falconets mounted in *Sunfisher*'s prow filled the air with grapeshot that peppered the quarterdeck. On the heels of those deafening explosions, the musketmen aboard both ships also fired their weapons.

McAfee left the mainmast and streaked across the deck. The rapier slapped against his thigh. He ran up the companionway, pistols extended before him. A man stood at the top of the companionway and raised his musket. Firing on the move, McAfee put a ball through the man's heart. The musket fired, loosing a ball only inches above McAfee's head.

The pirate captain dropped the spent pistol and drew another. Reaching the top step of the quarterdeck, he turned and fired into the knot of men taking cover there. A few of them stood to get better shots and were picked off by pirate sharpshooters.

McAfee stood his ground, dropped his spent pistols, and pulled two more. Fearlessly, he fired pistol after pistol into the middle of his opponents. When he was out of pistols, he ripped the rapier from his side and marched into the men as they pulled swords of their own.

None of the men among the group was even close to being his equal. The swordplay turned into a rigorous bloodbath, but a bloodbath all the same. The main problem lay in navigating over the corpses that fell at his feet. That, and withdrawing his blade from the bodies of the falling sailors.

Gilley and the others arrived up the portside companionway and attacked from the rear. In seconds, the group of sailors who had tried to hold the quarterdeck with their captain had been decimated.

Flicking his rapier under Captain Mayhew's chin, tilting the man's head back, McAfee asked, "Would you be interested in the courtesy of surrendering your ship, Captain?"

"Go to Hell." Mayhew stood his ground without fear. "I should have stayed around the island after we found out you were a slaver. Waited for you to come back. Then, when you were talking to Professor Bullock, put a ball through your head and buried you where you fell."

A cruel grin fitted itself to McAfee's face, pulling tight against his cheeks. "That was," the pirate captain said, "an ingenious plan. You should have stuck with it." He rammed the rapier point through Mayhew's throat, then twisted the blade viciously, creating a wound that even the best surgeon would never have been able to staunch in time to save the man's life. Instinctively, Mayhew grabbed the blade with both hands. The keen edge bit into his palms and fingers.

Keeping Mayhew pinned with the sword, McAfee walked the man to the ship's stern, then forced him over the broken railing. With nothing but the savage sea beneath him, Mayhew slipped from the blade and dropped into the water.

McAfee turned to his men. "Mr. Gilley. Get the men organized. There can't be many of these wretches left that need killing. Make certain these men remember that Professor Bullock and his daughter are not to be harmed. I want them alive and in one piece."

THADDEUS J. BULLOCK, Professor of Biology of Princeton University in New Jersey in the United States of America, sat in the stifling dark of a small storeroom with a pistol in his hand that he prayed to God he didn't have to use in the next few minutes.

And if I don't use it, what then?

Bullock stared at the black wall in front of him. Somewhere in those shadows was a door that was cunningly hidden. Captain Mayhew had commanded Bullock to take his daughter and stay there till the pirate ship had been repulsed. Judging from the hellish cannonade that had taken place on deck, followed by the close sound of musket fire and men's screams of anguish and rage and pain, the pirates had not been repulsed. Mayhew hadn't been able to hold the other ship back.

"Katharine," Bullock whispered.

"I'm here," his daughter replied. "We need to be quiet."

"I just—I just want you to know how sorry I am that I brought you into this." Bullock's voice was tight in his throat.

"You didn't bring me into this. I wouldn't have let you leave me at home."

"I didn't mean for it to come to this."

"You couldn't have known."

"Even if they don't find us," Bullock said, "we don't have a chance, Katharine." Even facing death, he could never hold on to an unfounded hope. His mind was too logical, too orderly. "By now, Fisher's men have killed the crew. You've heard those sporadic gunshots. Even if they don't find us and we live, we can't sail this ship by ourselves."

"Being alive," Katharine said, "offers a much better chance than being dead."

In the darkness, Bullock took a fresh grip on the pistol he held. He had only one ball between them and death, and there were surely more pirates than that. Captain Mayhew had provided a cartridge pouch, but the professor knew he would only have time for one shot under the best of circumstances once they were discovered. He would never be able to reload for another shot even with the experience he had with firearms. If they remained undiscovered, they would be facing a slow death at sea if no other ships noticed them and stopped to offer aid.

Footsteps sounded in the room outside the hiding place.

Bullock lifted the pistol. He was amazed at how steady his arm was because his stomach was tied in knots.

Light flared into the hidden room around the door. Even as well put together as the hidden space was, room remained between the joints. However, the light was noticeable from the dark interior while it wouldn't be noticed from outside.

Then a knife blade ripped into the space. The screech of the tight contact between metal and wood ripped through Bullock's ears loud enough to make him wince in pain. He held the pistol steady, willing his trigger finger to relax slightly.

The knife blade turned, prising the door from the frame. Fingers wrapped around the door's edge and pulled it open.

A man's head and shoulders burst into the doorway. The door was only partially open.

"Perfesser Bullock," a man called out in a taunting singsong outside the room. "We knows ye're in there."

The man shivered in the doorway. Lanternlight shone from behind him and stabbed into Bullock's eyes with blinding intensity.

"We've come fer ye, Perfesser," the man continued. "An' we've come fer the pretty young missy as well. Gonna show her a good time."

All vestigial remorse fled Bullock's heart. He aimed at the center of the man's head, finding the target easily enough with the lanternlight marking him, and squeezed the trigger.

The muzzle flash lit up the small enclosure like a lightning strike. The deafening report left a ringing in Bullock's ears.

"Oh God!" a man yelled. The man in the doorframe shuddered. "He's done went an' shot me, lads! He's a killer, this one is! I'm kilt! I feel me blood spendin'!"

With a final convulsive shudder, the man toppled into the room. The lanternlight in the outer room spilled over the dead man sprawled at Bullock's feet.

Confused and frightened, Bullock stared down in disbelief. In a moment of crystal clarity, he recognized the dead man as one of the crew of *Brown-Eyed Sue*. He also saw that the shadows had masked the fact that half the man's head was missing, blown out by a big-bore musket or a cannonball fragment.

Bullock's ball had made a small bloodless hole in the man's right eye next to the bridge of his nose. There was no blood because the man's heart hadn't been beating at the time he'd been shot. The professor continued to hold the discharged pistol on the dead man.

"Aye, an' that's good shootin', Perfesser. I wouldn't have thought ye'd have it in ye like that."

Bullock glanced up at the big pirate who filled the doorway. The man wore a mocking smile and gold hoops in his ears.

"Name's Gilley," the big pirate rumbled. "Maybe ye remember me from Easter Island. I'd like ye to come peaceable-like. I don't mind thumpin' ye, but Cap'n McAfee, he wants ye more or less of a piece."

Bullock raised the pistol.

Gilley grinned more widely. A wolfish hunger darted in his eyes as he stared over Bullock's shoulder at Katharine.

Stepping forward, Bullock drew the pistol back and slammed it at the man's head like a club. The move caught Gilley by surprise. The heavy barrel slammed into Gilley's temple, splitting the skin with a meaty smack.

The pirate yowled in pain and took three steps back.

Blind with fury and frustration, Bullock went after the man. He curled his left fist and drove a hook into Gilley's midsection. The pirate's air exploded out over Bullock's shoulder. Bullock drew the empty pistol back and slammed the barrel into Gilley's forehead. He was barely aware of the movement of other men around him. He wanted to scream in rage, but fear kept his voice choked down in his throat. His thoughts were only of Katharine, of the horror she was going to experience at the hands of the pirates.

For one brief, insane moment, he thought he should have saved the pistol to use on her once they were discovered. He couldn't imagine killing Katharine, but the death he would have given her would have been merciful next to what was going to happen.

He saw the pistol in Gilley's waist sash. The curved handle held scars and showed dully where the finish had worn off. But it was only inches away. He slammed the pistol into the pirate's face again, a glancing blow off a cheekbone that ripped flesh, then dropped the empty weapon. He clutched the front of Gilley's shirt and held on to him, pulling himself close. He reached for the pistol, closed his fingers around the butt, and yanked the weapon free.

He felt the urgency of the moment and knew that he was going to draw fire from the other pirates as he turned with the pistol in his fist. He thought of Katharine, forced away hesitant thoughts, and knew that his murder of her was the last merciful thing left in the life that he had given her.

He spun and brought the pistol up.

Suddenly, Captain Fisher—or McAfee, Bullock remembered Gilley saying—was there. The pirate captain held a musket. Bullock got a clear view of the weapon, then the brass-plated stock came down at him, catching him flush and squarely between the eyes.

Bullock's senses left him in a rush.

CHAPTER 23

Pacific Ocean 13° 57' S. Lat.—104° 02' W. Long.

WATER HIT PROFESSOR Bullock in the face, sending a wave of panic cascading through him. For a moment, he thought he was drowning. He choked and coughed, then opened his eyes, finding himself lying on a ship's deck under the sun. The side of his face and head throbbed with unbelievable pain.

The pirate captain stood before him, a small grin painted tightly on his powder-stained face. A rapier was sheathed at his side and he held the brass-plated musket in one hand, the butt resting on the ship's deck beside him. Sunlight glinted against the polished metal.

"Wake up, Professor Bullock," the captain said.

Agony flashed through Bullock's face. His thoughts were confused, distant from him. His throat was dry and his tongue felt like leather. "My daughter."

"She's well." The pirate captain hunkered down, still holding on to the musket. "So far."

"If you hurt her—" Bullock tried to go on, but words failed him. He pushed up from the ship's deck.

As lazily as a cat taking a mouse, but just as blindingly quick, the pirate captain backhanded the professor.

More pain knifed through Bullock as he went back down. He almost blacked out from the intensity and barely managed to hang on to the threads of consciousness.

"Don't make that mistake, Professor," McAfee said. "That would be so ordinary. Too ordinary for the likes of you and me. I think we can agree on that."

Cautiously, Bullock sat up, remaining seated, his knees drawn up. He wiped blood from the corner of his mouth with the back of his hand. His face felt like it was on fire.

"My daughter."

"My name is Jonah McAfee. Perhaps you've heard of me."

Slowly, Bullock shook his head.

"Pity," McAfee said. "It would have been better if you had known of the atrocities I've committed as a pirate. At any rate, I assure you that I am not given to idle threats."

Bullock looked around the ship. Dead bodies, those of the crew of *Brown-Eyed Sue* and others that must have belonged to the pirate crew, littered the deck. The corpses rolled as the ship crashed through the sea's waves, taking on a macabre semblance of life.

"I believe you," Bullock said.

"I want to know more about the creature that you're hunting. I've already taken the liberty of transferring all your research and notes to my ship."

Bullock quelled the fear inside him with effort. A sour bubble of sickness burst at the back of his throat. He was dealing with a madman. Why would McAfee be interested in the creature? And if he already had all the research work, it wouldn't be long before McAfee knew he didn't need him.

"I want to see Katharine," Bullock said.

A small, cruel smile fitted McAfee's lips. "Stubbornness. Not a good thing to have, Professor."

"I want to see Katharine now," Bullock said, wishing his voice didn't crack so badly. "Otherwise, I am going to push myself up from this deck and make you do your worst. Captain."

McAfee's eyes slitted. "A man should always have a care about what he asks for." He stood and stepped back out of reach, keeping the heavy musket between himself and Bullock. "Mr. Gilley."

"Aye, Cap'n." Gilley's voice sounded hoarse and slurred. He stared at Bullock with piggish, angry eyes. Thick purple bruises already marked his face. A lump stood out from his jaw. Blood flecked his lips.

"Have Professor Bullock's daughter brought on deck," McAfee commanded.

Gilley walked away and gave orders to some of the men. In short order, Katharine was brought from belowdecks. She looked a bit worse for wear, but she didn't appear injured in any way.

Tears filled Bullock's eyes as he saw Katharine. Knowing that she was alive was a relief, but it also filled him with sudden terror. If his daughter were already dead, then he would not still have her life to lose.

"Katharine," Bullock said.

"Father!" Katharine fought to get free of the two men who held her. They held her wrists and laughed as she struggled without success.

"Hold her there," McAfee ordered.

The men stopped and restrained Katharine only a few feet away. She stamped one man's instep. The man yowled in pain, then backhanded Katharine and knocked her from her feet.

Without a word, Bullock erupted from the deck. His mind whirled at the effort and black holes appeared in his vision. His stomach heaved again. Before he got his balance, McAfee slammed a fist into his face. The professor lost control over his body but his mind remained with him. He fell, toppling to the deck.

Razored steel caught the sunlight for one bright instant, then McAfee's rapier point was at Bullock's throat.

"You decided to up the stakes of our little game, so I'm going to tell you how we're going to use those stakes." The blade never wavered from Bullock's throat. "I'm going to ask you questions. If you refuse to answer, or if I feel that you are lying to me, I am going to have one of your daughter's fingers cut from her hand."

The pirates pulled Katharine to her feet. Her face was streaked with blood. They bent her arms behind her back and held her hair pulled back, bending her head up to expose her throat. Tears ran down her bloody face, but she never once asked for mercy.

"They're going to kill us, Father," Katharine said in a calm voice.

McAfee crossed to her. He took one of her hands in his, dwarfing hers with his own.

"Perhaps," the pirate captain mused, "I should take one of your fingers now. To prove to you and your father that I am serious about this endeavor."

"You are a coward," Katharine replied in a surprisingly even voice. "And a bully."

McAfee scowled. "I'll make a bargain with you as well, girl. If you can't shut up, I shall cut an ear from your father's head. What do you think of that?"

Katharine said nothing.

McAfee laughed in amused delight. "It appears that I have made a believer, Professor. How about you?"

"You didn't have to take this ship and kill the crew," Bullock replied. "I told you everything I know about the creature when we were on Easter Island."

"Impossible." McAfee shook his head angrily. "You're lying."

"I'm not lying." Bullock returned the man's gaze. "I could make up things to tell you, Captain McAfee. I could invent a name for the creature. Perhaps even a whole family history. But that would all be a lie." He paused. "I think you would know when I was lying. I can't afford to lie to you. Even if you were going to kill us in the next few minutes, I would prefer that Katharine not experience anything unseemly before—" His voice broke, and he lost control of his emotions. He wept.

Brown-Eyed Sue bucked suddenly like a horse trying to throw a rider. Timbers cracked below; the noise sounded muffled and distant, but the vibration shook the ship. Katharine fell to the deck. One of the pirates dropped as well, and the other remained standing through sheer effort.

"It's the creature!" someone yelled. "It's found us!"

The pirates quickly lined the railing and peered down into the water.

Seizing the moment, taking advantage of the fact that the pirates' attentions were turned toward McAfee as the pirate captain yelled orders, Bullock surged to his feet. Even big as he was and battered, the professor moved more quickly than any of the pirates believed him capable of.

Bullock slammed into the nearest pirate, ducking down to drive his shoulder into the man's midsection and lifting him bodily from the deck. The pirate yelled and flailed helplessly as he sailed back over the railing.

The second pirate swung his cutlass, then checked the movement. Only his hesitation about killing Bullock saved the professor's life. Bullock stepped into the man, curling up one big fist at his knee on the other side of his body and backhanding the man with all his strength. Bone broke in the professor's hand. He thought he heard the snap, but it was lost amid the crack of the hull.

"Cap'n!" the second pirate squalled. He was dazed from Bullock's blow, scooting drunkenly back on his butt as he kicked out with his feet and elbows.

Bullock closed on the man, feeding on the unrestrained rage that filled him. He grabbed the man by the shirt and lifted him easily, swinging and throwing the man over the railing as well. The professor guessed that neither man knew how to swim, and at the time he didn't care.

Brown-Eyed Sue violently rolled once more, jerking on a tangent as she was hit again.

Losing his footing on the treacherously tilting deck, Bullock fell to one knee. He caught himself on his hands. His broken one felt like he'd seized hold of a burning brand.

Only a few feet away, *Sunfisher* jerked from an impact as well. The pirate ship swung sideways, or perhaps *Brown-Eyed Sue* swung sideways, and both vessels slammed into each other. The crash of ship against ship was deafening. Coaming and railing fragments scattered across both heaving decks and became a hazard.

"Get them!" McAfee yelled, pointing at Bullock and Katharine.

Most of the pirates had fallen like tenpins, and nearly all of those showed no real desire to stand up on the shifting ship's deck. The cargo net above them was loaded with a cannon that slipped free of the hooks and came careening down. The cannon caught one man flush and crushed him beneath its weight.

McAfee unlimbered a pistol and took rapid aim, tracking Bullock's movement across the deck. Smoke squirted up from the frizzen pan and the explosive report cut through the cacophony of men's voices and ship's destruction.

Bullock expected to feel the pistol ball rip through his body and was pleasantly surprised to see splinters jump from the mainmast only a few feet from him. If the mast hadn't been there, or if he'd been slightly to the other side of it, McAfee's ball would have caught him dead center.

Chest heaving, trying to regain his lost breath, the professor grabbed the cutlass dropped by the first pirate he'd heaved overboard. His broken hand curled around the hilt awkwardly because of the swelling that had already manifested. His mind raced as he dealt with the problem before him.

"Look out," Bullock said to his daughter. Overhead, the longboat swung in its davits. The professor followed the ropes, noting where they were secured to the mainmast. He timed *Brown-Eyed Sue*'s pitch with the longboat's swing over the railing, then slashed with the cutlass.

The ropes parted instantly, and the cutlass blade buried in the mast. The davits whined as the longboat dropped down. The boat slammed into the weakened railing and smashed through.

McAfee drew another pistol, still yelling at his men to get the professor and his daughter. Most of them ignored him and looked to staying low on the jerking deck.

"Come on, Katharine." Bullock caught his daughter's elbow and pulled her toward the starboard side of the ship. He didn't hesitate when he reached the edge, just took the next step and kept going. He felt Katharine hesitate just a moment, but he kept his grip tight on her arm. Her weight shifted suddenly, going with him, and he knew she had followed his lead and leapt over the ship's side.

CHAPTER 24

Pacific Ocean 13° 57' S. Lat.—104° 02' W. Long.

AS HE FELL, Bullock marked the longboat's position in the ocean. With the ships still crashing through the waves, driven by their sails and the wind, the longboat was already fifty feet to stern.

Bullock hit the water and released Katharine's arm. He'd taught her to swim as a child, and she was even more skilled than he was. He spread his arms and legs and kept his dive shallow, turning immediately for the surface. Once he broke through, he shook the water from his eyes and glanced around desperately.

"Katharine! *Katharine!*"

Both ships kept sailing away, locked in a tight embrace as the crews fought to keep them close. The clatter of the wooden hulls banging against each other echoed over the ocean. Bullock spotted McAfee aboard *Brown-Eyed Sue*. The pirate captain had made his way to the ship's stern and raised two pistols. He fired both just as the ship was hit again. Both balls went wide of the mark, striking the water with liquid slaps.

"Katharine!" The brine made Bullock's voice hoarse. He pushed at the water, trying to turn rapidly. *"Katharine!"*

"Father. I'm over here."

Turning toward the sound of his daughter's voice, Bullock spotted her only a few feet away. "Oh my God, darling. I thought I had lost you."

"No. My dress was too heavy to swim in. I had to kick free of it." Her pale shoulders, bare except for the short sleeves of her undergarments, stood out against the emerald green water.

"I didn't think," Bullock apologized, suddenly realizing how heavy the garments must have been after they had become sodden. "I should have known you would have trouble. I could have killed you."

"You didn't. Your quick actions saved us." Katharine struck out swimming, making for the longboat floating in the distance. "Come on, Father. We have to hurry. The creature is in the water with us. Even the longboat might not be protection against it."

Bullock swam with her. His broken hand throbbed painfully, feeling as though shards of glass twisted inside. She arrived at the longboat first and quickly hauled herself aboard. Crouched on her knees, her hair hanging over her shoulders, she reached out for him and helped him crawl aboard.

Chest heaving from his exertions and the stress he'd been under, Bullock got to his knees in the center of the longboat. At twenty-five feet in length, the longboat was hardly an island, and definitely no safe place for them to be. Only then did the enormity of his actions slam into the professor. He didn't even know where they were.

Katharine remained beside him, her arms wrapped around herself to ward off the chill from the breeze. "You had no choice, Father," she said, reading his thoughts as she so often proved capable of doing. "If we had stayed on that ship, he would have killed us. Even should we die at sea, our deaths will be far better spent here than with him."

"We're not going to die out here," Bullock promised.

As if in counterpoint to his audacity at making such a declaration, *Brown-Eyed Sue* suddenly jerked to a stop in the ocean as if she'd bottomed out on a reef. During the time the vessels had been running mostly parallel, the pirates had been leaping the distance between the two ships. It appeared that most of the pirates had made the distance and were back aboard *Sunfisher*. But even as Bullock watched, a few of the pirates fell into the water between the two ships.

Sunfisher passed the stricken ship by, and pirates hung to her rigging for dear life. Bullock thought he spotted McAfee aboard the pirate ship, but at the distance and with the rolling waves between them, the professor couldn't be certain.

At a dead stop in the water, *Brown-Eyed Sue* came apart and quickly sank into the depths. Bullock hadn't seen ships die before, but he'd read of them. Sometimes the loss had taken hours, and upon occasion even days were required to take a ship beneath the waves.

Brown-Eyed Sue disappeared in minutes, leaving only flotsam, barrels, and debris to ride the waves in her wake. A solid sheet of sail glided just under the ocean surface like a gigantic devilfish, and disappeared in the space of a drawn breath.

Sunfisher kept sailing, following the wind away from them. Evidently McAfee didn't judge them worth the risk of returning. Before the ship vanished over the watery horizon, the vessel jerked violently to one side, showing that the creature still pursued them.

"Father."

Dazed and numb, Bullock turned to his daughter and found her digging into the longboat's provisions.

"There's food and freshwater aboard," Katharine said. "Surely enough to last for a few days. And there is a sail we can use." She pulled at the furled canvas wrapped around the small mast. "Help me get the mast up." The mast lay in the center of the boat, constructed with cunning locks so that it could be put up and taken down as needed.

"Why?"

"There may be survivors in those waters where *Brown-Eyed Sue* went down."

"They could be pirates. McAfee saw to it Mayhew's crew were killed to a man."

"Even if they are pirates, I won't have them drown if we can prevent it." Katharine ceased her struggles with the mast and looked at him. "Please. I need help."

Reluctantly, Bullock bent to the task of setting the mast and stretching the canvas.

HALF AN HOUR or more later, Bullock held the tiller in his uninjured hand and guided the longboat toward the debris and barrels that had scattered in the wake of *Brown-Eyed Sue*. So far, the wind favored them. McAfee and the pirate ship had not returned, and the professor wondered if *Sunfisher* had met a similar fate.

It would be an end they deserved if they did, the professor thought. Then just as quickly he thought of the chained slaves aboard the ship, who would drown as well, and felt guilty.

Dead men floated in the water. They hung spread-eagled like starfish, only the tops of their heads crowning the water with most of their bodies hidden in the sea much like icebergs.

Bullock dropped the small sail that gently powered the longboat and gazed at the water. The ocean was cloudy enough from the wreckage that depth visibility was limited to only a few feet.

"Help!" a weak voice cried out.

Low in the water as they were, Bullock couldn't at first figure out from what direction the voice came. He gripped the longboat's gunnels and stood cautiously in the center of the boat, keeping his weight evenly distributed.

"Here!" the voice called again.

"I see him," Katharine said. She sat in the prow, helping balance out the longboat. She'd taken one of the three blankets that came with the longboat's kit and wrapped it around herself. Looking to port and ahead, she pointed.

Squinting, Bullock made out the man clinging to a broken spar nearly forty feet away. Waves lifted him, gently rolling under him, revealing him, then hiding him away.

"Help me!" the man cried out. "I can't hold on much longer."

Bullock stared hard at the man. "I don't recognize him."

"He's a man," his daughter replied. "And he needs our help if he's to survive."

"If he's a pirate, perhaps it would be better if he didn't."

Katharine looked at him.

"We don't even know if we're capable of saving ourselves, Katharine," Bullock protested. "Taking on one of the pirates would be a grave error."

The attack on *Brown-Eyed Sue* had left twenty-seven bodies in the ocean that the professor had so far counted. Of course, McAfee and his crew of killers had killed most of those floating corpses. Other bodies had probably been dragged down in the tangled rigging that came down from the ship's masts.

Katharine found a rope in the boat's kit, tied it to the longboat's stern cleat, and threw the line to the man.

The pirate caught the rope. "Thank ye, miss. Thank ye. As God is my witness, ye won't regret yer decision to save me." The pirate clung to the rope, but he clung to the spar as well.

"Let go the spar," Bullock ordered.

The pirate glanced around as fearfully as a cornered rat. "I'm tryin'. God strike me dead if'n I ain't."

Katharine pulled on the line. The longboat came around, the prow turning sideways to present her port side to the oncoming waves. Water spilled over the gunnels, drenching the bottom of the longboat, then the wave caught the craft and pushed it up.

Katharine yelped as she fought to hang on to the rope. Her tenacity nearly got her yanked from the longboat.

"Stop, Katharine," Bullock said. "The longboat's riding too high in the sea. If we get caught wrong, we could overturn. And if you fight the sea and that rope, you're going to injure your hands."

"Perhaps if I had a pair of gloves."

"We haven't any," Bullock said. Anger grew in him, fanned by the fear that filled him. Despite his best efforts, he focused that anger on the pirate. "You're going to have to let go of that spar."

Fright drew the pirate's face in tight, hard lines. "I'm tryin'."

"Do it," Bullock commanded.

"I'm tryin'."

"If you can't," Bullock promised, "we're going to leave you out there to die."

"Father!"

"We haven't a choice, Katharine," Bullock said. He didn't look at his daughter.

One of the dead sailors floated up against the longboat. The dead man's head bumped against the wooden hull with a hollow thud.

"If you fight too hard for this man," Bullock told his daughter in a quiet voice, "we could lose the longboat. If it flips over in the water, we'll never be able to right it by ourselves."

Katharine was quiet for a moment. Tears glimmered in her eyes. "I know." She released the rope. Harsh hemp burns scored her palms in long red stripes. "You'll have to let go the spar."

"I can't, miss," the pirate wailed. "I'm scared. I don't know how to swim."

"Keep hold of the rope," Katharine said. "You can pull yourself in before you drown."

"If I let go, I'll sink."

"As long as you hold on to the rope and climb up it, you can pull yourself to the surface. We'll help you aboard. You can hold your breath that long."

"I'm afraid. God, I'm so afraid." The pirate began crying, snuffling and wiping at his face with a sodden shirtsleeve.

Bullock took out a short, hooked fishing knife from the kit aboard the longboat. He stood in the longboat again so that he would tower above the waves that still pushed at them. "You had best make your move soon. I will not tolerate you putting my daughter's life at risk. Especially since you were one of the men that would have taken her from me."

Cursing, the man abandoned the spar and held on to the rope. A wave rolled over him and took him under at once.

Katharine gasped and leaned forward.

"He's still there," Bullock stated calmly. "Look to the rope."

The rope remained taut as a bowstring.

"As long as he doesn't let go," Bullock said, "he should be fine." He shifted slightly as the wave rolled under the longboat. Movement to the right drew his attention.

At first the professor thought that his imagination was playing tricks on him. Nothing was on the water except the debris, and the sky was empty of anything but clouds. Then he spotted the impossibly large shadow that sailed along just under the ocean's surface.

Cold dread filled Bullock, tracking icy claws down his back. In all his years, in all his travels, he'd never experienced the kind of fear that was upon him. He gripped the knife more fiercely and slowly crouched, hoping that his slight movement didn't draw the massive creature's attention.

"Father?" Katharine said.

"Quiet," Bullock commanded in a far harsher tone than he had intended. His throat felt dry and raw, almost too tight to breathe.

"He's gone under," Katharine said.

The massive shadow slid through the water, closing on the longboat. Even at twenty-five feet, the shadow was easily three or four times larger than the craft.

"Father." Katharine leaned forward and grabbed the jerking rope hanging over the longboat's side. She set her feet and pulled. "Help me."

Galvanized into action by his daughter's plea, Bullock dropped the knife and seized the rope with both hands. His injured hand only loosely gripped the hemp, and hanging on proved burning agony. He pulled with Katharine, bringing in foot after foot of wet rope while the whole time watching the great shadow coast beneath the water.

The creature came straight for them. Its passage created a wave that warred against the ocean's natural current. The wake of the creature ran ahead of it, growing taller and fiercer as the massive body rose toward the surface. As it closed on them, some of the corpses floating in the water disappeared, pulled under by some unknown force. Bullock had no doubt that the creature had taken them.

Abruptly, the pirate broke the ocean surface. Fear cracked the man's face. He drew in great drafts of air. "I thought I was drownt! By God, I thought I was drownt fer sure!" He stretched forth his hand.

Bullock reached for the man, but his eyes were focused on the approaching wake.

Glancing over his shoulder, the pirate looked in the direction Bullock stared. The giant shadow stood out plainly in the water.

"Get me in the boat!" the pirate squalled. "Pull me in! Fer the love of God! I don't want—"

Bullock grabbed the man's extended hand with his uninjured one. No sooner did he feel the man's wet flesh against his own, than he felt the shock of impact pass through the pirate.

"It's got me! Oh God, I hear it! It's in me head! I hear it!" A strangled cry escaped the pirate's lips, followed immediately by a deluge of blood. Then an incredible force yanked at the pirate, pulling him down. His chin struck the longboat's gunnels with enough force to shatter his teeth and unhinge his jaw.

The pirate disappeared down into the ocean as the rope yanked through Katharine's hands. She cried out in pain and went after the rope again.

"No!" Bullock commanded. He wrapped his arm around his daughter's upper body and held her back. If she got caught up in the loose coils of the ropes, he knew she would suffer the same fate as the pirate, and he wouldn't be able to pull her back up.

"It's the whale." Katharine held her torn and bleeding hands with the fingers half-curled. "I saw it, Father."

Bullock said nothing. His heart pounded frantically in his chest.

The rope slack they had pulled in continued to burn over the gunnels. Only a few feet of rope remained. Certain that the longboat could not stand against the impossible strength of the whale, Bullock reached down into the boat and plucked the knife up. He remained on top of Katharine, protecting her as best as he could, and placed the knife's edge against the rope.

The rope tightened on the stern cleat, narrowly missing the professor's hand, as the knife bit into the woven hemp strands. The longboat yanked sideways into the path of a curling wave. As the longboat dragged against the ocean, water poured into it, crashing down over the professor and his daughter.

For a moment he thought they'd been swamped and the small craft filled

with water. Then they came through on the other side of the wave. He kept saw-
ing, knowing the longboat had to be barely able to keep afloat.

The wood around the cleat cracked and split, but the device had been set too
well and refused to tear free. The longboat crashed through another wave as it
scooted across the ocean. More water careened into the longboat, bringing the
depth on board up to inches.

The cold water splashed over Bullock and sank icy fangs into his flesh. He
blinked the stinging brine from his eyes and sawed at the rope. Katharine
remained small and still beneath him.

The next yank changed the longboat's direction slightly, letting Bullock
know that the whale—or whatever the creature ultimately proved to be—had
changed direction. But the rope also parted. Another wave caught the longboat,
but this one lifted the craft high and clear of all but the very tip of the roller.
Spray drummed along Bullock's back, thighs, and head, but the sea came down in
pellets instead of a deluge.

Caught in the ocean current, the longboat slid between the troughs, gliding
sideways down the back of the wave that had lifted it. Another wave came,
threatening to overturn the craft.

Bullock made himself move, scrambling to his hands and knees. "Stay
down," he told Katharine. "We don't want it to see us."

Katharine nodded and lay close to the bottom of the boat. Water lapped at
her chin.

Bullock seized the tiller and pulled, straightening the longboat. With grudging reluctance, the boat came around. The professor thought about putting up
the sail, then quickly discarded the idea. Raising the sail would also raise the
longboat's profile against the sky and water. He wasn't at all certain how intelligent the creature they pursued might be.

He stayed low in the stern and glanced behind where the debris and dead
men from *Brown-Eyed Sue* remained afloat. The giant shadow was no longer visible under the water, but as he watched, the heads of the dead men disappeared
one by one beneath the sea's surface, dragged down by something Bullock could
not see but felt certain was feeding.

Pacific Ocean 11° 06' S. Lat.—101° 27' W. Long.

LEADING THE WAY across the deck, Ethan went belowdecks to the galley. He
was bone-tired and ached in every joint. Cutting in was long, arduous work, and

to achieve the quota they needed during their shift while training Robert, he'd pushed himself hard. He was hungry, but more than anything he wanted a dip in the sea to wash the blood and oil off, and a few hours in his rack.

Robert stayed with him. Trapped in the narrow confines of the galley, Ethan was aware of the blood-stink that time and exposure had trapped within them. No matter how much he'd worked at harvesting, his sense of smell had never gone dead as some sailors claimed happened.

Cook served up steaming platters of biscuits and gravy, piles of terrapin cuts, and some of the potatoes and carrots they'd gotten from the packet ship they'd gammed with.

Ethan washed his hands and arms up to the elbow in a basin provided for that. Then he sat at the table and dug into the meal. Robert, cleaned up as best he could as well, sat on the opposite side of the table and tucked in as well.

They ate without conversation. Neither of them had the energy for it.

Seated on the hardwood bench bolted to the deck, Ethan remained conscious of the injury on his side. Most of the blisters had finally gone away, and daily immersion with salt water had toughened up his skin and made scabs come early. He peeled the scabs away as soon as they came on solid so that he could retain his flexibility and to promote a faster and more complete healing.

Footsteps pounded outside the galley as Ethan was getting another cup of coffee.

"Ethan," grizzled old Fred Draper called from the doorway. "Creel says ye're to come quick."

Wariness washed away the fatigue Ethan felt. He handed the cup to Cook and joined Fred. "What is it?" Ethan asked.

"A boat," Fred answered.

Ethan's thoughts immediately flashed to Jonah McAfee and the pirate ship *Sunfisher*. McAfee and all the old hurt and hate from those times past hadn't been far from Ethan's mind over the past days.

"Any sign of a ship?" Ethan asked.

"None."

"How many people?"

"Two. A man an' a woman."

Ethan grabbed the companionway railing and vaulted up the steps. The wound on his side hurt terribly, but nothing broke open.

Creel met him at the top of the companionway, pressing a spyglass into

Ethan's hands. Smoke from the boiling tryworks eddied across the deck and burned as he sucked it into his lungs.

"The boat's to the sou'-sou'west of us," Creel offered. "Like it an' them what's aboard it are comin' direct from the sea."

"Can you identify them?" Ethan ran to the port side. Sailors who had gathered at the railing made a path for him.

"No," Creel answered.

At the railing, Ethan raised the spyglass to his eye and focused on the single-masted longboat heading across their bows. Both people in the longboat appeared to be dead or passed out. Even with the glare of the sun behind him and turning the flat planes of the sea to bright gold, he could see that both the longboat's passengers were burned beet red from exposure.

The sail belled out, catching the wind. A glance at the tiller showed Ethan that it had been tied in place to keep the longboat following the wind.

"Did ye see the tiller, Ethan?" Bill asked.

"I did." Ethan collapsed the spyglass.

"They come all this far, from wherever they come from, on just hope an' a prayer," Bill said.

"Could be plague victims," someone said. "Coulda got the plague an' the cap'n up an' throwed 'em off the ship."

"In a longboat?" Creel shook his head. "If'n that had been the case, the cap'n woulda chained cannonballs around their feet an' heaved 'em into the salt."

"Maybe they're thieves," someone else said.

"An' they come all this way to steal a longboat so's they could go skippin' across the ocean?" Bill cursed the man sourly.

"Ethan," Holy said, joining Ethan at the railing, "that boat is going to miss us. We've been yelling. If those people are still alive, they're too far gone to wake and steer for us."

Ethan stepped away from the railing. "Creel. Get me a boat and a crew ready. We're going after them."

"Aye." Creel turned and gave orders.

Ethan approached the stern, where Captain Folger stood on the quarterdeck. "Cap'n."

"Aye."

Aware that he had an audience and that Folger already knew what he planned on doing, Ethan said, "I'd like permission to go after that boat."

Folger hesitated only for a moment. Stroud and his men still maintained a loose guard over the captain.

"Very well," Captain Folger replied. "You have your permission. Just get this ship back on an even keel in the next few minutes."

"Aye, Cap'n." Ethan turned smartly and jogged back to the railing.

Creel already had the longboat in the water and a crew was setting up in position. "Permission to go aboard with ye?" Creel said.

"Denied," Ethan said. "Get these men back to work, Creel. We're losing daylight."

"Fine, Ethan. But ye have a care out there." Creel's face was hard and cold. "Somethin' like this can't be nothin' but trouble, an' that's one thing we'd best be shut of."

"Bill," Ethan said.

"Aye."

"Time to earn your keep," Ethan said as he scrambled down the line to the waiting longboat bobbing in the water. "Creel, rig up a harness and get him into the boat with me."

Landing in the boat, Ethan stared into the distance and watched the boat coming closer yet clearly on a path to miss *Reliant*.

Bill grunted and landed in the longboat's prow. He yanked the knot that held him, and the harness disappeared.

Settling into the prow, Ethan ordered his crew's oars into the water. In a few short minutes, the longboat intercepted the other craft.

"Ahoy the boat," Ethan yelled through his cupped hands.

Neither the man nor the young woman gave any sign that they heard his call.

Bill shook his head. "If'n they ain't dead, Ethan, they ain't in any shape to hear ye."

"Get us alongside," Ethan told the crew. He reached under the seat and took up one of the fresh waterskins they kept the longboats stocked with for chasing whales. A glance at the blistered lips of the occupants of the boat showed him that they had been without water for a day or more.

Even when the sailors caught hold of the other longboat and matched the craft's speed, the two passengers remained unconscious. Nimbly, Ethan and Bill stepped into the other longboat.

"Take the tiller, Bill," Ethan commanded. "Get us back to *Reliant*."

"Aye."

Kneeling, Ethan checked on the woman first. Despite the sunburn and her unkempt appearance, he knew she was a good-looking woman. He laid his fingers against her neck and felt her heartbeat, thankful that she was still alive.

"Well?" Bill asked.

"She's alive." Ethan opened the waterskin and poured a little water into her mouth. She drank slowly, but didn't wake.

Under Bill's expert guidance, the longboat came about and headed for the whaleship. "What about the man?" Bill asked.

Ethan checked on the man as well. But when he placed his fingers against the man's throat, the man shoved a wicked fishing knife at his face. Lifting his arm, Ethan blocked the weak blow.

The man's eyes focused on Ethan with effort. "Sorry. I thought you were someone else."

"It's all right," Ethan said, but he plucked the knife from the man's hand. "We're going to take care of you."

"What about my daughter?"

"She's alive."

The man let out a long breath, and for a moment Ethan thought the man had died. Ethan had to stare hard to see the heartbeat at the side of the man's neck. He poured water into the man's mouth, then returned to the young woman and did the same.

The longboat shuddered, and Ethan knew the craft had struck something in the water. He glanced up, searching the water. The sun lay in front of him, and the low, bright rays reflected with blinding force from the sea.

"Shark," Bill said. "Damn thing came up under us. I couldn't do nothin' about it."

"No," the man said in a hoarse voice. "Not a shark. It's a monster. I saw it." He struggled to push himself up. "It's a ship-killer."

"Get him," Bill said. "Afore he throws hisself overboard an' undoes all this savin' his life we done went an' done so far."

Ethan pulled the man back from the gunnels. "Ease off. It was just a shark."

"No." The man fought desperately against Ethan, but he was far too weak to be effective.

"Relax," Ethan said. "We'll be aboard ship in just a few minutes. You will be taken care of there."

"You don't understand," the man said. He was obviously raving, out of his mind with exhaustion and exposure. "There is a monster in the sea. It comes from somewhere else. They call it Death-in-the-Water. It looks like a whale, but it's not a whale. It's something else. Maybe part of it is a whale, but the rest of it is something else."

"Easy," Ethan said.

"No." The man tried to fight again but wasn't even strong enough to lift his own body. "You don't understand. Truly you don't. I didn't understand—I didn't believe. But I believe now. I saw it. The whale. Not the thing. But I saw the whale. It has a hideous face. All burned on one side. Like McAfee and his powder burns."

"McAfee?" Ethan suddenly felt cold.

"Jonah McAfee," the man said. "He's a pirate who hunts the monster. He's after the monster."

"That ain't no monster," Bill said, pointing with his chin.

Gazing over the gunnels, the man stared in the direction Bill indicated. The triangular fin rose through the water and glided back toward the whaleship. Evidently the hunter had been feeding on the whale's carcass and had been attracted to the motion of the boats in the water.

"Thank God," the man said hoarsely. "Thank God, it's only a shark."

"What about McAfee?" Ethan asked. But it was no use because the man had passed out. Quietly, Ethan went about pouring more water into the mouths of the man and his daughter, keeping the amounts small so they wouldn't get sick. And from time to time, he stared around the horizon, fearful that at any moment he would spot a black flag flying high and proud, and Jonah McAfee standing beneath it looking to finish what had been started so long ago.

The wind seemed to carry Teresa's mocking laughter to Ethan's ears. She had told him that the day would come that McAfee would kill him if he didn't kill McAfee first. Ethan had never believed that, but he had never believed that Teresa would go mad either.

Despite the vision of the sea and of *Reliant* sitting at anchor before him, Ethan saw Teresa standing aboard the ship's deck during the last battle they'd shared. She had held Cat's-Eyes John's head, fingers knotted in his blood-matted hair. Her laughter, God, her laughter haunted him. And if McAfee was still nearby, Ethan knew that he hadn't escaped the penance he had yet to pay for the things he had done.

CHAPTER 25

Pacific Ocean 11° 06' S. Lat.—101° 27' W. Long.

"MR. SWAIN."

Hearing Captain Folger's voice, Ethan looked up at the quarterdeck and spotted the man there. "On my way, Cap'n," Ethan called. He turned to the work crew supporting the two men on the cutting stage hanging over *Reliant*'s side. "Creel."

"Aye," the big man responded.

"Take over here for me."

"Aye." Creel narrowed his eyes as he glanced at Folger. "Ye think the cap'n's givin' credence to them stories the perfesser's been tellin' an' has hisself scared of what's in the water?"

Several of the crew surreptitiously listened to the exchange.

"I don't know," Ethan answered.

"Do ye think there's somethin' out there?" Creel asked.

"There's always something out there, but I don't think it's anything more than what we've already faced." Ethan turned and crossed the deck.

The shadows of the ship's riggings passed over him and showed on the soot- and blood-encrusted wooden surface underfoot. He was aware that all of the men watched him. Even though he didn't want to because he knew the crew would note his own apprehension, he glanced up into the rigging. Three men stood watch over the ship.

He'd increased the watch after the professor's stories, but he'd told the men the reason was because of the threat of pirates. McAfee and Harrington were the primary causes for concern, but Ethan couldn't forget the sight of the whale with the charred face, or the way that Nate Phillips had died practically in his arms before being yanked away.

Professor Bullock had regained consciousness two days earlier, nearly twenty-four hours after they'd rescued him from the sea. Driven by frenzy and the weakness left to him from exposure to the sea, the professor had related the stories of the monstrous whale and the corpses he'd found with flesh falling off, as well as the attack by McAfee and the pirates of *Sunfisher*. Folger had wanted the crew's knowledge about those things limited. That hadn't been possible because Bullock had told the stories to everyone who had come into his room, urging them to leave the waters they were presently in before the creature found them.

On the quarterdeck, Ethan came to a stop at Folger's side.

"Cap'n," Ethan said.

Folger kept his eyes on the crew's efforts. The whale's headless body remained at *Reliant*'s starboard. The head case had already been cracked open and given up its wealth of spermaceti. Only the bits and pieces of blubber on the huge body remained to be dealt with.

"How much longer do you think it will take to finish the whale?" Folger asked.

"We'll be done by nightfall," Ethan replied. "I've still got to get a crew inside the whale's guts to get the ambergris."

Folger nodded. "I want to be under way by morning. Do you foresee any problems with that?"

"No, Cap'n. I'd hoped we could take a couple days at anchor and let the men get rested before we start making demands of them."

"Believe it or not, but that's exactly what I would like to do as well. But we don't have that option. Professor Bullock says he and his daughter directed their longboat toward us the day before they arrived because they saw the smoke coming from the tryworks. If they could see it, so could others. Including that damned pirate captain, Fisher."

"His name is McAfee," Ethan said before he could think to stop himself. Bullock had been very clear about that.

Folger looked at Ethan. "Aye, so I understand. I still get the impression there's more you know about this man than you are telling me."

Ethan took a deep breath and knew he had to skirt the truth. Creel hadn't mentioned the fact that Harrington's man had stated the British privateer had been pointed in their direction by McAfee. "I've heard of McAfee, Cap'n. He gave his name to us as Fisher."

"But you recognized him the day we saw him?"

"I thought it could have been him."

"Yet you didn't see fit to tell me."

"At that point, Cap'n," Ethan pointed out, "we had a mutiny brewing aboard this ship. Since *Sunfisher* left, I never gave her another thought." And that was an egregious lie, but Folger had no way of knowing that.

"What do you think of Professor Bullock's insistence that there is some kind of monster in these waters?"

"He makes a strong case for it."

"By stories alone."

"I saw the whale he has described."

"You saw *a* whale, Mr. Swain. It could have been the whale that we have tied up alongside *Reliant*." Folger pursed his lips. "I should be more convinced if Bullock were able to offer more substantial proof."

"The professor says that McAfee took all of his research materials."

Nodding, Folger said, "I know. In a way, that's very convenient, isn't it?"

"And what reason would Professor Bullock have to lie?"

"Professor Bullock would have us leave these waters and sail for Princeton immediately. He insists that President Madison gave him the assignment of look-ing for the monster."

Ethan said nothing.

"Yet Bullock no longer possesses the letter."

Watching the activity below, Ethan remained silent. The letter had been with the research papers.

"That leaves me in something of a quandary," Folger went on. "Should I take Professor Bullock at his word and proceed with all due haste back to Prince-ton with a cargo hold not quite full? Or should I honor the assignment made by the investors who gave me this ship's command?"

"It's a hard decision, Cap'n."

"Indeed. I have thought that myself for these past two days. You and I, we take a lay from this ship that is in direct proportion to how much whale oil we bring back. To abandon this voyage with the hold not yet full would only take money out of our pockets."

Ethan nodded.

"If Professor Bullock still had his letter from the president, maybe I could see my way clear to return more or less immediately. As he so wishes." Folger corrected himself. "Or rather, as he so demands."

Below, Creel got the gutting crew together. With the head case gone, the whale was more easily lost. If the whale corpse spun free of the lines, the body would sink to the bottom of the ocean like a stone. But the ambergris was too valuable to pass by.

"Yet," Folger went on, "if Professor Bullock is indeed a representative on a special mission for the president of the United States, I'll be damned for not returning under all due speed."

"It is a puzzle," Ethan said.

Folger was silent for a moment, then asked, "What would you do?"

Ethan had known the question was coming and chose a path to avoid it easily. "For the moment, Cap'n, I'd finish up this whale, then I'd put in for Callao."

"Callao," Folger mused. "Why?"

"As we've already discussed, we desperately need to resupply," Ethan said. "And we're shorthanded on crewmen."

"We could be even more shorthanded after we make port. Despite the fact that the ill feelings on part of the crew have muted somewhat, I know they're still there. And if I know that, I know that you know that."

Folger was silent for a time. "I'll take your thoughts under advisement. Thank you for your time."

Dismissed, Ethan made his way back down the companionway and stood at the railing as Creel commanded the crew. Despite his best efforts at staying focused on the present, Ethan's mind kept wandering back to the past. The presence of Katharine Bullock, herself a young woman, had triggered many of those old memories, releasing them from the vaults where Ethan tried to keep them.

Although the air was filled with the stink of the boiling oil, Ethan could smell Teresa's scent heavy in his nostrils—the expensive perfume she preferred as well as the smell of her flesh. He also remembered how her skin looked in sunlight, moonlight, and candlelight. With McAfee in the area, with the growing realization that Katharine Bullock was a fine-looking woman, Teresa's madness seemed to dog Ethan's heels.

"Mr. Swain."

Caught off guard, Ethan turned and saw Katharine Bullock standing behind him. "Miss Bullock," he said, standing a little taller. "A whaling ship's deck is hardly the place for a young lady." In the past, her forays on deck had been limited to the quarterdeck in the captain's or her father's company.

She straightened herself and squared her shoulders. When she had arrived in the longboat, she'd only had her undergarments, which had caused a sensation among the sailors. Folger had made a donation of clothing from the ship's stores, but all *Reliant* carried that came close to fitting her was small men's clothing. Despite the men's clothing, though, the fact that she was female still made itself known, as Ethan was well aware.

He chastised himself that his thoughts had strayed in that direction. He reminded himself of the mistake he had made with Teresa, how he had been drawn into her web of treachery and deceit, which had disguised his own hopelessness at being impressed by McAfee and his crew. Teresa had used her talk of love as a balm, a means of getting him to accept his captivity.

"I assure you," Katharine said, "I have seen much worse than what this ship has to offer." She gazed around. "Though I have to admit that I have never seen it on such a grand scale."

"There's nothing grand about a whaleship's work," Ethan stated. He was suddenly aware of how disheveled he was. Blood and oil covered him from head to toe, and he knew he must stink at least as badly as the tryworks.

"On the contrary," she said, "I know that people depend greatly on the work that men such as you manage to do under hostile conditions. If not for whalers, there would be no oil for lanterns, many fewer candles, and no whalebone for buttons and skirt hoops."

Ethan nodded and took a little pride in her words. "This deck is still a dangerous place to be. Even for an accomplished whaling man. I'd feel much better if you stayed away from this area."

"As you will. I only wanted to thank you. For saving my father's life and my own. I apologize that I didn't thank you earlier."

"You were weak," Ethan said. "I've seen men die from less than you and your father endured."

"My father is a resilient spirit."

"Aye," Ethan agreed. "And so is his daughter."

She looked embarrassed.

"Beg pardon, miss." Ethan cursed himself. The words had flown from his lips before he'd even known they were going to be said. "I didn't mean to be so forward. Forgive my poor manners if I've overstepped my bounds."

"You haven't," Katharine said. "I'm not used to such direct compliments from men I hardly know."

"It's me," Ethan apologized. "I'm a poor hand at anything other than directness. My mother often laments that."

"I would ask a favor of you if I could."

Ethan nodded. "If possible."

"A journal," she said, "and writing utensils. If you don't have that, I'll take any paper you can get for me, and I'll burn my own charcoal."

"That won't be necessary. I've got a small store of writing supplies that I will share with you."

"I appreciate your generosity."

"I'll have those things brought to you in short order."

"I also wish to observe the work you and your crew are doing here. I've never before had occasion to watch a whaling ship at work."

"This work here is harsh and rough. Greenhands who first start to work aboard a whaleship are often plagued with nightmares for days and weeks until they get used to the work."

The block and tackle brought up another thick section of blubber. Blood dripped onto the deck only a few feet from Ethan and Katharine.

"Mr. Swain," Katharine said, "I've helped my father cut open dead men over the past few weeks. I've seen pirates cruelly kill a ship's crew down to a man, shooting them in the head where they lay or cutting them down where they stood. I admit that this work is harsh, but I know what I can handle."

"Very well." Ethan wanted to tell her that her presence on deck would be a distraction to the men, that she would be stared at the whole time she was there, but he figured that she already knew that. Truth be known, she was going to be a great distraction to him. And if he did not make her allowances she would be trapped belowdecks in the stale, stomach-turning air that flooded *Reliant* from the blubber-stocked hold. "I'll see that a chair is brought up and made available to you."

"Thank you for your kindness. Please don't let me keep you from your work." Katharine turned to walk away.

"Miss," Ethan called after her.

She turned back to him. "Yes."

"The . . . whale your father saw?"

"Yes."

Ethan felt suddenly awkward, and he realized that the question he was prepared to ask could be taken as very offensive. "Nothing."

"You're wondering if I saw it, too?" Her gaze was direct.

Ethan took a short breath and let it out. "Aye."

"I saw it," she replied. "In a little while, I will show it to you. My father is a man of science. A most exact man of science. He didn't want to believe in this thing any more than you do, and probably he was even more skeptical than you appear to be. But he isn't anymore." She turned her eyes away from Ethan and gazed out to sea. "That thing is out there. And wherever it is, it is hunting men. It has learned how."

"Thank you. I apologize for any offense I might have caused."

"I take no offense, because even though the story is true, my father and I recognize that it is most incredible," she said, and walked away.

"So what do ye think?" Creel asked, stepping close to Ethan. "Do ye think they're crazy as bedbugs, the both of 'em?"

"No," Ethan said, staring after the young woman. "I don't think that at all." He turned back to Creel. "Let's get this whale finished up. If we're going to be facing sea monsters or pirates or outrunning a storm, I'd rather do it with the wind at my back and a full set of canvas straining overhead."

AN HOUR LATER, Ethan descended to the whale with the second gutting crew. All of them went down carrying buckets.

Another crew worked behind them from a separate cutting stage, cutting into the lower section of the whale's decapitated head. The blubber there was richer in oil than in the rest of the body. Once the meat was gone from the head, the jaw and teeth would be saved for scrimshaw.

A wiry Frenchman named Rudolpho Germaine was chosen to cut through the whale's body to the intestines. With the blubber already removed, the job was not difficult. However, with the whale fully gutted, the remainder of its blood and fluids pouring into the ocean, the sharks and other hunters around the creature went into a greater feeding frenzy. The corpse also took on more water, requiring greater effort on the part of the chains that bound it to the ship. *Reliant* tilted only a little more, and even then not as badly as she had when the whale had first been made fast to her.

Searching through the whale's guts was odious work. Even with a handkerchief tied around his face and scented with vanilla from Cook's stores, Ethan felt his stomach lurch a couple times.

After a few minutes, Rudolpho found a chunk of the gray-white ambergris in the intestine. The cutting stage was lowered, and the Frenchman recovered the cabbage-sized mass and dropped it into the bucket Ethan held. On the open market once the ship returned to port, the cabbaged-sized mass would be worth hundreds of dollars.

Ethan tied the bucket to a rope and passed the ambergris on up. "Bill."

"Aye," Bill called back down.

"Make sure that gets weighed and cataloged. Then turn it over to Cap'n Folger."

"Aye."

The ambergris was so lucrative that Folger had insisted on keeping it in his cabin under lock and key. Even a collection of pinches stolen from the chunks could set a quick-fingered sailor up in style for months of easy living.

Ethan worked for another hour at Rudolpho's side. More chunks of ambergris were revealed in the mass of guts beneath the Frenchman's blade. While passing another bucket up, Ethan spotted Katharine Bullock seated in the stern.

The young woman held one of the journals he had given to her. The expression on her face was one of intense concentration. Her bandaged hands, still recovering from the rope burns she'd suffered while trying to save one of McAfee's pirates, worked with amazing skill and dexterity. Watching her piqued Ethan's interest. With the way her hands moved, it was clear that she wasn't simply writing, and she worked with carbon rather than ink.

"Mr. Swain."

Drawn by the deep voice, Ethan shifted his gaze over to Professor Bullock, who leaned over the railing's edge slightly more forward amidships. For a fleeting moment, Ethan felt embarrassed and wondered if Bullock had caught him staring after his daughter.

"Aye, Professor," Ethan responded.

Bullock indicated the bucket of ambergris in Bill's hand. "I'd like a closer look at this material—the ambergris you've been recovering—if I might. I believe there's something embedded in it."

"I'll be right up." Ethan warned Rudolpho to hang on, then climbed up the fishing net draped over the ship's side. He took the bucket from Bill. "I'll be responsible for this now, Bill."

Bill nodded and walked away, obviously irritated that his routine had been disrupted.

"We'll do this in front of the cap'n," Ethan said.

Bullock spread his massive hands. "Of course."

Ethan led the way to the stern quarterdeck where Katharine was and told Folger about the professor's request. With obvious reluctance, Folger agreed.

Ethan reached into the bucket and took the oily chunk out.

Bullock took the heft of the chunk in one hand, then drew it to his nose. He gasped and pulled his head back in obvious surprise. "I would have thought that something used in the manufacture of perfume would smell better." He passed the chunk to Katharine.

"The ambergris seasons, Professor Bullock," Captain Folger said. "What you're looking at there was just taken from the whale. It's still wet from the whale's fluids. As the ambergris seasons, it dries and become sweeter-smelling."

Nodding, the professor turned the chunk over in his hands, examining every facet. "I am somewhat familiar with ambergris and whales, of course, but I find I am sadly lacking in the particulars of this substance."

"Ambergris isn't just in any whale's intestines," Ethan said. "It's only been found in sperm whales. The story goes that a sailing man saw a whale vomiting up the substance on a beach and went over to examine what it was. There have always been stories about what whales have swallowed. Listen to the tales sailors tell in taverns, and you'll hear of treasure chests and whole ships whales have swallowed."

"What this sailor found was ambergris," Bullock mused.

"Aye. My guess is that a sailor brought the ambergris back as a curiosity and it found its way into the hands of someone who made perfumes."

"Does the ambergris have to remain in this chunk shape until it is processed?" The professor stared at the substance. "There appears to be something within it, and I would like to see what it is."

"I don't want any of that material lost," Folger said. "Ambergris brings a hundred dollars a pound and more, and even a few crumbs add up."

Ethan stripped off his shirt and spread it across the quarterdeck. "Use this," he told Bullock.

Kneeling with genuine effort, the professor placed the ambergris on the shirt. He tried to manipulate the substance, but his broken right hand was still swollen too large to allow the necessary movement.

Ethan crumbled the ambergris, digging out the object that had captured the professor's attention.

"Is that a bone? A tooth?" Bullock asked.

Opening his hand, Ethan revealed eight inches of curved hornlike material. "It's a squid's beak."

Bullock's eyes flicked to his. "What kind of squid?"

"A giant squid. I've heard some sailors call them kraken."

"Kraken are a myth."

Ethan smiled. "Then you're holding an impressive piece of myth, Professor Bullock."

Bullock turned the beak in his hand. He laid it down for a moment to pull a pair of glasses from his pocket. The left lens was cracked slightly in the lower right corner. "Scientists have never captured a giant squid. We've never even seen one."

"There's still some debate over them," Ethan said. "Some sailors don't believe in them either."

"Why?"

"Because they don't want to," Ethan replied honestly. "The sea has plenty of terror for a man who spends his life upon it even when he thinks he knows all the dangers. Admitting that there are more things he doesn't know about is even more daunting."

Bullock looked at Ethan over the top of his glasses. "And what do you think?"

"I've gutted whales before, Professor," Ethan answered. "I've found a few beaks like that during my time rendering sperm whales. On occasion, I've found tentacles inside the whales that were fresh. Even pieces of meat that were ten and twelve feet long."

"From squids?"

Ethan nodded. "Couldn't have been from anything else." He pointed his chin at the ambergris. "Are you done with that?"

Bullock held up the squid beak. "Can I keep this?"

"Aye. It's worth nothing." Ethan bundled the ambergris in his shirt and dumped the chunk and the small pieces back into the bucket for the captain. "If you've got the time and the interest, I'll show you something else."

Curiosity shone in Bullock's eyes. "Of course."

"Cap'n," Ethan said. "Would it be all right if I took Professor Bullock and his daughter in the hold where the Bible leaves are kept?"

"Very well. I entrust the professor's safety to you, but I also hold you accountable for it."

"Aye, Cap'n," Ethan responded. Only after he started down the companionway did he want to kick himself. He knew he should steer clear of the professor and his daughter. He had problems enough without trying to take on any of theirs. Still, Bullock seemed enamored of the secrets the sea possessed, and Ethan enjoyed the idea of teaching the professor things he didn't know. It was a chance to share with the man the love he had for the sea.

Ethan took a lantern as they continued down the companionway belowdecks. He lit the wick and led the way to the main hold.

Katharine coughed and made retching noises as they entered the cavernous room lined with barrels and raw blubber.

"I apologize for the stench," Ethan said. "This might not be something you should try to do, Miss Bullock."

She stiffened her spine. "I can do this. It just caught me off guard, is all."

Ethan admired the stubborn streak that he guessed ran bone-deep in her. He continued on, taking the professor and his daughter deeper into the bowels of the ship.

In the hold, Horace McBain and three other men worked on the blubber. Sharp knives sliced through the bloody and oily meat, cutting it first into sections that measured twelve inches by twelve inches. Later, they would slice those sections into thin wafers that could be easily boiled in the tryworks.

"Horace," Ethan said.

"Aye," the big man said. He gazed lustfully at the professor's daughter, but his knife never ceased moving.

"This whale was scarred," Ethan said, stepping in front of the man to break his view of Katharine. "I want one of the sections that shows the scarring."

Horace called out to the other men. After a brief search, one of the long blanket cuts that hadn't yet been reduced to sections was singled out. Horace and the other cutting crew dragged it into view with boat hooks.

"Here," Ethan said, holding his lantern over the blubber blanket. The light brought out the pattern of close-fitting circular scars.

"What are these?" Bullock asked, inspecting the blubber. He pocketed the squid beak and traced the circular marks with a forefinger. "Wounds left by the chains used to tie the whale to the ship?"

"Battle scars." Horace grinned.

"Have you ever seen the suckers that are on the underside of a squid's tentacles, Professor?" Ethan asked.

"I've had occasion to," Bullock replied.

"Usually," Ethan said, "you only find whales with these kinds of markings in the Atlantic, the Gulf of Mexico, or in the northern Pacific."

"But you found a squid beak in this one," Bullock pointed out.

"A beak, aye," Ethan said. "But no tentacles or meat. Beaks probably stay with a sperm whale for a while. Could be this particular whale ate a squid in the Atlantic or the Gulf and swam here afterward. Some of the old salts I've crewed with have suggested that the ambergris is just the whale's way of purging itself of bits and pieces of the giant squids they can't digest."

"Like a cat's hair ball from preening itself," Katharine suggested. "Or an owl's pellet."

"I'm not familiar with owl pellets," Ethan admitted.

"An owl doesn't have teeth," Katharine said, "so it swallows its prey whole. The food travels through the esophagus and the intestine, then into the gizzard. In the gizzard, the prey is divided into two parts—one part that is digestible and the other part that is not. The part that is not digested is vomited back up by the owl in the form of a rounded pellet."

Ethan was amazed at the depth of knowledge the young woman had. It made him want to talk to her more.

"So the whale gets these marks while the giant squids battle for their lives?" Bullock asked.

"Aye," Ethan said. "That's what the sailors say that I've talked with. They say that the giant squid live on the ocean floor. Only the sperm whale can reach them. But they also say that the giant squids prey on the sperm whale as well."

"Hunters that prey on each other," Bullock said. He studied the scarring while Katharine opened the journal and began to work by the light of Ethan's lantern.

Ethan watched the woman work, intrigued by her swift, sure hand even though her palms were bandaged. Lines formed images on the blank page, quickly becoming a rendering of the blubber blanket.

"I was told of the attack your ship suffered only a few nights ago," Bullock said.

A whisper of winter chill darted down Ethan's back. "Aye."

"*Reliant* was attacked by a whale. You saw it."

Ethan nodded.

Bullock reached for the journal Katharine held. He flipped pages and Ethan was surprised at how much work she had done since he'd provided her the book. The professor stopped on a page.

"Is this the whale?" Bullock asked, offering the journal up for Ethan's inspection.

Coolly, trying to remain detached from the memories that came flooding back, Ethan surveyed the whale Katharine had drawn. One side of the huge head was a mass of burn scarring.

"You drew this from descriptions given to you by the crew?" Ethan asked.

"No," Katharine said. "I drew that whale from memory. We have seen it too."

"We saw it again," Bullock added, "the day that *Brown-Eyed Sue* was destroyed."

With effort, Ethan closed the book and passed it back to Katharine.

"They say you were trying to rescue a drowning sailor that night," Bullock said. "I was told the man was yanked from your arms. Did the whale do that?"

"No," Ethan answered. "A whale couldn't do that. It was something else."

Bullock pointed at the blistered wound on Ethan's side. "The men I found suffered the same kind of injuries as you wear on your side. Where did you get that?"

"From that night," Ethan said hoarsely. Memory of the burning brand that had seemed to lie across his side returned with jarring strength.

"Then," Bullock stated, "I would say you just barely avoided your own death that night."

CHAPTER 26

Pacific Ocean 11° 06' S. Lat.—101° 27' W. Long.

WORKING BY LANTERNLIGHT, all of the men dragging from the days of incredible effort to harvest their prey, Ethan gave the order to loose the chains that held the remainder of the sperm whale's body to *Reliant*. The chains slipped free, and the carcass sank directly into the sea.

Heat from the still-boiling tryworks washed over Ethan. The crews manning the fires and the boiling oil would have to work through the night and for the next several days to finish rendering all the blubber that had been transferred to the hold. As Ethan watched, a net containing four barrels of oil was lowered into the hold while another was being filled. More stood ready to be loaded and lowered.

"Get the men fed and then to bed, Creel," Ethan commanded. "The cutting crews first, then the others. In the morning, work them all into additional shifts to help with the tryworks and the cutting down in the hold. The cap'n wants this ship under sail as soon as possible."

"I will," Creel promised. He looked slightly better than he had in days. "Did ye know the young miss was still up an' about?"

Glancing over his shoulder at the quarterdeck, Ethan saw Katharine Bullock in her chair working at the journal by the light of a lantern. She had been there nearly the whole day, even taking meals there. During the last few hours of finishing up the whale, Ethan hadn't even looked in her direction. He was surprised to see that she was still at her chosen task.

"She's a hardworkin' one, that one," Creel said. "I've heard Nantucket women are hard workers, managin' their husbands' businesses an' family affairs while their husbands are out to sea, but I bet that one would stand up to any of 'em."

Ethan nodded.

"Ye know," Creel said, "was I not a married man, I might be wantin' to get to know that young lass a little more."

"But you are married," Ethan said.

"Aye." Creel grinned. "But you're not, Ethan. An' I've been seein' how she looks at ye. I been seein' how she looks away from ye just as ye turn to look at her."

"You're imagining things, Creel," Ethan protested. "You've been working so hard you've taken leave of your senses."

"Oh? An' do ye think so now?" Creel shook his head. "No. I'm a man what knows the tender love of a good woman. I know when a woman is interested in a man." He glanced up at Katharine. "Might not be for keeps, but it's worth lookin' into."

"I'm a sailor," Ethan objected. "She's a professor's daughter. One who has obviously been keeping up with her father's studies. I'm just an oddity to her." Memory of Teresa, of how different she had been with her being the daughter of a fencing master to the court of Spain, cut into him painfully. Impressed as he was on McAfee's pirate ship in the Caribbean, Ethan had had no business getting attracted to the woman. But Teresa had never been one to take no for an answer. And, truth to tell, he'd thought he'd never get off *Wind Dancer* alive. So he had loved her until the very end, and only McAfee's belief that he was dead had allowed him to live. That and two long days at sea before he was able to float into the beach near Port Royal.

"Ethan," Creel said with a knowing tone. "All that she may be to you is an oddity. I'm only suggestin' that ye spend a little time talkin' to her since it's obvious to me that she'd like spendin' a little time talkin' to ye." He paused. "Mayhap ye might even help her out some. If the rest of the crew thought ye had designs on young Katharine Bullock there, mayhap some of them wastrels would cease to be a-botherin' her the way they been. At the very least, ye'd have someone to distract ye from all them deep thoughts ye're a-havin' about this voyage."

Ethan hesitated. "And what if she doesn't look on my attentions with favor, Creel?"

Creel shrugged. "Then ye walk away an' get mad at me. I figger I'm riskin' the most here. Likely if I'm wrong, you'll schedule me extra shifts down in the hold cuttin' Bible leaves with Horace."

"And doing Cook's pots and pans," Ethan promised.

Scratching his chin, Creel said, "Ye know, now that I think on it agin, mayhap tryin' to talk to the young miss is a bad idea."

Ethan excused himself and walked toward the stern. He climbed the companionway to the quarterdeck.

Katharine Bullock looked up from her journal and met his gaze. "Mr. Swain," she greeted.

"Miss Bullock," Ethan said. "You're working late."

"Yes. I'm trying to re-create as much of the work that my father did as I can. Losing all his research to Captain McAfee during the attack on *Brown-Eyed Sue* has been devastating."

"I imagine that it would be." Ethan turned a hand over at the deck. "May I sit?"

"Please," Katharine said. "Sit wherever you please."

Ethan crossed to the railing almost ten feet from her and sat with his back against the coaming. The gentle rocking of the ship against the ocean waves lulled him instantly, making his eyelids heavy.

"I see that you and your crew have finished with the whale," Katharine said. "I watched as you released the carcass."

"Aye," Ethan answered.

"Has any mention been made of returning to the United States?"

"No."

Katharine pursed her lips and nodded. "Captain Folger hasn't taken my father's story as gospel."

"I think he has, but he just hasn't made his decision known. Taking on the responsibility of a whaleship isn't an easy thing. Showing up with the holds not completely filled would not count as a successful voyage."

"May I ask you a personal question?"

Ethan spread his hands. Despite his fatigue, he found the conversation with the young woman welcome. "You may."

"What draws you to this business?" she asked.

"Why?"

"I am helping my father write about this part of our voyage. We've both agreed that you're an important point in the narrative. We've also agreed that we need to know more about you in order to do justice to your part in this."

Embarrassment flooded Ethan, followed immediately by a touch of panic. "I'm just a common sailor. I don't think scholars would be interested in the likes of me."

"On the contrary. I find you a most intriguing man."

Her directness caught Ethan off guard.

"So I ask you again, what is it that draws you to this business of whaling?"

Ethan chose to fill the uncomfortable silence that might have stretched between them. "If there's a way to it, I'd someday like to be a cap'n."

"Of a whaling ship?"

"No. I've had enough of whaling."

"Then what kind of ship would you be captain of?"

Ethan grinned with self-deprecation and shook his head. "The idea is too big. Too fanciful."

"No idea is too big and fanciful. My father is a university professor. You wouldn't believe all the ideas that he and his fellow scientists have about science and the nature of man. Those ideas, as my father so eloquently puts it, are only— to use your terminology—too big and too fanciful until they are proven."

"If I could," he said, "I'd operate a merchant ship. One that I owned myself. And I would travel from port to port, figuring out the things that would sell."

"A merchant trader."

Ethan nodded. "Aye."

"That can be a very risky business."

"Not if you own your own ship," Ethan said. "That's the biggest cost, and the very thing that makes it impossible for so many men and indentures them to shipowners and investors. The next trick would be to find a crew that would give their all to such a venture. With no shirking and no theft."

"Do you think you could find men like that?"

"They're out there," Ethan said. Talking to her in the quiet of the moment that existed between them proved hypnotic. He'd never told anyone outside his family of his dream. Not McAfee and not even Teresa. It had all seemed so impossible. But for the moment, for the golden moment spun from the amber light beaming from the lantern at Katharine Bullock's side, it seemed so close. In the clear light of day, he was certain the dream would recede so far away he couldn't even think of it. "I've seen men like those that I'm talking about. Do you know why so many men are drawn to the call of the black flag aboard a pirate ship? Or even now aboard privateers given letters of marque by one country or another to prey on the ships of other countries they don't have peace treaties with or are at war with?"

"Because of the booty they are able to steal?"

Ethan shook his head. "No. Because of the freedom. You see, a man stepping aboard a ship in the United States Navy or one like this that is owned by investors gives up all control over his life. He works aboard a ship, day in and day out, at whatever tasks the cap'n assigns. He eats what the cap'n sees fit to feed him, wears what the cap'n sees fit to clothe him in. And when he leaves the ship, he's hardly got any money in his purse for all the hard years he's put in. Maybe he's had bad luck on a voyage. Like Bill Fedderson on this one." For the first time, he realized that he had been talking too much. And he noticed that Katharine's hands had been busy with the journal. "I apologize. I guess I'm over-tired. I usually don't go on like this."

"I find the subject fascinating. But where does a man like Captain McAfee fit in to the type of man you just described?"

"McAfee," Ethan said, "and British Captain Harrington don't fit in to that type of men. McAfee and Harrington are hunters, professional killers who traffic in death and robbery."

"I have formed the same opinion of Captain McAfee, though I've not yet met Captain Harrington."

"If you're lucky, you won't." Feeling the weight of the conversation turn too heavy, Ethan glanced at Katharine's journal. "What are you working on?"

"Sketches."

"You're an artist?"

Smiling and looking embarrassed, Katharine shook her head. The wind caught and captured her hair, dusting it over her shoulders and framing her face, and reminding Ethan that she was a very pretty woman.

"No. I've no eye for art. But I am good at drawing things I see. My father draws as well. Scientists have to be able to capture images of creatures and plants and landscape formations. Even rocks. I've been told I do rocks quite well." Self-consciously, Katharine closed the journal.

"May I see that?" Ethan said, caught up in his own curiosity. "After all, you've gotten me to talk far more than I intended to."

"All right then." Katharine handed the book over.

Opening the journal, the first picture Ethan saw was of the burn-faced whale. His stomach clenched, and for a moment he was back in the water that night with Nate Phillips. He felt Nate yanked from his grasp and felt again the searing pain that covered his side.

Forcing himself on, Ethan looked at several other sketches of the whale. Pages of dead men followed. The damage to their bodies was revealed in horrific detail. "These are the two men you and your father examined?"

"Yes."

Turning more pages, Ethan found illustrations of *Reliant* and her crew. The drawings showed line drawings of the harvesting of the whale, the transfer of the filled oil barrels, the boiling tryworks, and the ocean horizon. Several pictures occupied one page, rendered in miniature, while others filled whole pages. Two pages showed pictures of the whale blubber blanket sporting squid scars and the squid beak.

Ethan recognized himself in some of the drawings. The experience was humbling and embarrassing. He saw how bedraggled and unkempt he looked, and he felt shamed. But even more than that, he knew the face on the page was almost identical to the one he saw in mirrors when he looked.

Concern filled him as he realized that others might recognize his face as well. It was one thing to be seen while in port and have someone mistake him for the pirate that he had at one time been, but it was another to be part of a science presentation that might get him seen by more people. The crimes he'd committed while under McAfee's black flag would still net him death at the end of a hangman's rope in several places if he were caught.

Shaken by the image of the whale as well as the sketches of himself, Ethan handed the journal back to her. "There's something you and your father haven't considered."

"What?"

"You say that McAfee took the research papers you had written. All the papers you had gathered."

"Yes."

"You might try to get word to him," Ethan said, "and let him know that you're willing to ransom them back. If the university or the men who sent you and your father out here are willing to pay. For that matter, maybe President Madison might pay the ransom if he deemed the papers worthy enough."

Katharine gazed at him. "I would have never thought of that. Neither would my father. But how would we get word to McAfee?"

"Have messengers offer a reward in taverns in the Caribbean and in Callao,"

Ethan said. "Send letters. Any place where slaves are offered at auction. I've heard McAfee is in that business these days. Word of the offered ransom will reach McAfee eventually. It may take some time, but it will reach him."

"Do you think he would accept the ransom?"

"That depends. If he thinks he could get more for it somewhere else, he might try that."

Nodding, Katharine said, "I'll talk to my father about it." She started to get up.

"The professor's asleep in the galley," Ethan said.

"He shouldn't sleep there. He should be in bed so he can rest better."

"If you'll allow me," Ethan said, "I'll have it taken care of." He stood, called to Creel, and asked him to send two men to see Professor Bullock to bed.

"Thank you," Katharine said.

"You're welcome. You should probably think about getting some rest yourself."

"I will. I just need to work a little while longer. My mind is so busy that I can't relax."

Ethan sat near the railing again, resting his forearms on his drawn-up knees. He watched her as she worked, admiring the quick way she laid out the illustrations on the pages and the firelight that played on her hair. Before he knew it, his eyes were closed and his body rocked to the timeless surge of the sea beneath the ship.

"You should get to your bed," Katharine said sometime later.

"I will," he said. His senses felt like they were buried in cotton, and he barely drifted back into a conscious state.

"You don't want to leave me out here by myself, do you?" she asked.

Blearily, Ethan blinked at her. "It doesn't seem like a good idea."

Katharine hesitated for a moment, then closed the journal and put her charcoal into a small clasp purse that Ethan had lent her. "Then why don't we both get a good night's sleep and start fresh—and early—in the morning."

Ethan stood with difficulty, feeling the pain in his side. "May I walk you to your quarters?"

"Yes."

In the thick shadows of the night that the lanterns failed to burn away from the ship, Ethan followed her down the companionway to his room, which she now borrowed. Despite his fatigued state, he remained definitely aware that she was a woman in the man's clothing she wore.

She thanked him politely at the door, then he retreated to the quarters he'd been temporarily assigned. Despite his fatigue, he lay sleepless in the hammock for a time. His thoughts remained filled with Katharine Bullock, thinking about the way she held her head and the way her voice sounded.

Then he slept, and in his sleep Teresa returned to him, slit Katharine's throat with her sword, and threatened to spill all of Ethan's secrets out in a journal she was writing for scientists.

He awoke in a cold sweat, his heart pounding and a scream locked tight in his throat. It was a long time before he was able to get back to sleep.

CHAPTER 27

Pacific Ocean 12° 31' S. Lat.—98° 42' W. Long.

THREE DAYS LATER, the storm rose in the south and came at *Reliant* like a thing possessed. Dark clouds turned the world slate gray, robbing the sky and the sea of color. Even the foamy curlers riding the tops of the tall waves only looked slightly lighter than the rest of the ocean. The wind shifted constantly, coming from all four cardinal points on the compass at one time or another. Miniature waterspouts, although only looking small against the whaleship, rose occasionally from the sea and spun away like dervishes, or they collapsed and disappeared after a short time.

Clad in a borrowed rain coat and matching pants, both coated in tar to make them waterproof, Professor Bullock stood on the whaleship's prow with some of the other men under the jib sails that popped and cracked as the wind cut through the rigging.

Although Bullock had tried to convince Katharine to remain belowdecks, as had Ethan Swain, she stood at his side, taking refuge in the small respite his body gave. Bullock hung on to the bow shrouds that ran down from the mainmast. His body swayed and jerked as *Reliant* fought the storm.

All of the ship's crew looked concerned, and none of them remained belowdecks.

Bullock wiped his face constantly, unable to bear the wetness that seemed to hang in the air. He didn't know if the majority of it was the rain or the spray that burst across *Reliant*'s bow.

"Mr. Swain," Bullock said. "Are you sure we're not in the heart of the storm?"

"I'm sure," Ethan replied. "If we were in the heart of it, we'd have been carried away by now."

"You'll understand if I don't feel the same confidence that you do."

Ethan leaned in so he could be more easily heard. "We're riding the edge of the storm, Professor. Maybe even gaining on it a little. I've weathered plenty of squalls before."

"Captain Folger insists that's the case as well, but he's consumed enough whiskey that I don't trust his judgment anymore."

"He's right enough about this," Ethan said.

Bullock took some comfort in the young sailor's words. During the days he had spent watching Ethan with the ship's crew, at the task of sailing the ship, and with the quiet time he spent with Katharine, the professor had developed an appreciation for the man and his skills. The fact that the mate was consuming so much of Katharine's time was irritating, but Bullock had made allowances. The professor had never before seen his daughter so animated in conversation with anyone. As it turned out, Ethan and Katharine obviously found a number of things to talk about. They both had work, too, but they usually made time to talk to each other over meals, or during the quiet of the night when the ship was at rest.

"Has Captain Folger said anything further about returning to the United States?" Bullock asked.

Ethan shook his head. "The cap'n's not an easy man to talk to."

Bullock had seen that for himself. "What do you think he will do?"

"Whatever he chooses."

"And you'll go along with that?"

Ethan nodded. "I'm not the cap'n, Professor."

"And if you were?"

Ethan hesitated. "Professor, this whaleship is no place for you or Kath—your daughter. What I know is this: We're going to try to outrun the storm and get in to Callao, Peru, to resupply. Once we're there, I'll help you secure a berth aboard another ship—a safe ship—that will take you and your daughter back to the States."

"What will you do?" Katharine asked.

"Stay aboard this ship and finish out my contract," Ethan said. "We're only one whale away from having enough oil in the hold to return."

Worry framed Katharine's face, but she didn't voice her concerns.

"These waters are dangerous," Bullock insisted. "Surely you've seen that. That creature is still somewhere nearby. I've told you that it hunts men aboard ships. Staying here makes no sense at all."

"These are the waters we've got to hunt in," Ethan said. "Just like that creature. If we get lucky, we'll get our whale and be out of here in a couple days. Then when you return with the United States Navy to hunt this thing down, this ocean will be safe for my next voyage out here."

Bullock smiled a little.

"Ethan!" the lookout bawled from above.

"What?" Ethan yelled back.

"There's a boat out there!" The lookout pointed forward.

Gazing forward, Bullock made out the longboat as it topped a tall roller. The craft looked small against the sea. At the top of the wave, the longboat stood almost on its prow as it plunged over and shot down. For a moment when the craft disappeared, the professor thought the boat might have capsized and been lost. Then it rose to the top of another wave.

Bullock knew that no one sane would be out in a boat in a storm like they faced. But by that time, Ethan Swain was already organizing the rescue operation.

ETHAN SAT IN the stern of the whaleboat, calling out orders to the crew on the oars. Solid walls of water rose around them, sending the whaleboat spinning, then demanding that the crew work even harder to get back on an interception course with the whaleboat.

Observation by spyglass aboard *Reliant* had confirmed that the longboat had one passenger. However, that confirmation hadn't been able to ascertain if the passenger was alive or dead.

Nearly twenty minutes of hard pulling were required to reach the longboat. All of the crew, including Ethan, were nearly exhausted from their efforts, and they had the return trip to deal with.

The man lay frozen with fear in inches-deep water that cascaded from one end of the longboat to the other as the angry sea tossed the craft. His long gray hair was matted and partially obscured his face. Rough whiskers lined his jaws, cheeks, and upper lip. The wrinkles on his face and the map of veins across his nose and cheekbones identified him as a drinker. If those details had escaped notice, the harsh sour breath and the whiskey bottles in his coat pockets would have given the fact away.

"God help me," the man exclaimed in wild-eyed terror. "I thought I was dead. I surely did."

Robert stood on his knees and lashed the two boats together, stern to stern. It took some frantic paddling to pull the whaleboat around into position along the longboat's side, but they got the job done. Merl Porter, chosen because of his great strength, howled obscenities at the storm one moment, then asked for mercy the next.

Working quickly, drenched to the skin, Ethan secured the two boat prows together. The waves caught and threw the boats, battering them against each other.

"Thank ye," the man shouted. "Thank ye fer comin' after me. At first I was afraid that I wouldn't be seen out here. Then I was afraid that even if I was seen, no one would brave these here rough waters fer the likes of me."

It only took a heartbeat for Ethan to recognize the storm-tossed man and know that his greatest fear aboard *Reliant* had just been realized. The man was a pirate. A man named Henry Cochrane. He was one of the men who had served under Jonah McAfee in the Caribbean when Ethan had still run with Teresa, when he had still been a pirate himself.

Ethan sat back, letting Creel and Merl bring Cochrane into their boat. He hunkered under his rain coat hood and hoped that Cochrane was too drunk and too frightened to recognize him. The safest thing to have done, though, was to shove a knife through Cochrane's heart and throw the body back into the sea. The man was a butcher, a man who lived to torture and torment. He had been a physician at one time, and a murder that hadn't remained concealed had thrown him in with McAfee.

There weren't enough crew to try to save both boats, so the decision had been made to bring the man into the whaleboat and sacrifice the other one to the sea. Once Cochrane was aboard, Robert and Ethan unlashed the lines and shoved the longboat from the whaleboat. The crew dug in with their oars, fighting the sea and the rain and the wind as they clawed for every inch back toward *Reliant*.

Cochrane took the blanket he was offered from the whaleboat's kit and wrapped himself tightly. He rocked back and forth and moaned.

"How come ye to be in the sea?" Creel asked.

"A monster attacked me ship," Cochrane said. His words riveted every man.

"Ye're a cap'n?"

"No," Cochrane said. "Ship's surgeon."

"What ship were ye with?"

Ethan prayed that the question not be answered, that a lightning bolt might strike Cochrane dead in that moment, or that Cochrane would lie big. The man was too drunk and too scared of the storm and the sea to think rightly.

"I was with *Sunfisher*. She's a trade ship—"

Merl Porter surged forward and slammed a big fist into Cochrane's face, spilling the man down the middle of the whaleboat.

"Slave ship, ye mean," Merl spat. "We saved us a damn pirate, boys. Risked our lives for a man shoulda been dead days ago. Best thing fer us to do is heave his ugly arse overboard an' let the storm finish him off."

"No!" Cochrane yelled. "Please!" He held a hand to his bleeding nose. The rain washed crimson down through his gray chin whiskers, staining them red. "I beg ye! I'm no pirate! McAfee impressed me! I never raised a hurtful hand to no one!"

Ethan knew that was a lie. He'd seen Cochrane kill in cold blood.

Merl reached for Cochrane.

Creel grabbed Merl's arm and kept him from hitting the man. Puzzled, obviously wondering why Ethan wasn't taking part in the matter, Creel looked over his shoulder.

Ethan felt trapped. He didn't know what to do. So far Cochrane hadn't managed to recognize him, but the man might recognize his voice.

"There'll be no dumpin' him over the side as long as I'm here in this boat ride," Creel said. "If'n the man had raised a weapon just now, mayhap I'd feel different. But he didn't."

"Ye're makin' a mistake, Creel Turpin," Merl threatened.

"Maybe I am, but it'll be an honest one if'n I do." Creel glanced at Ethan again.

Ethan still refused to speak. If he could just keep silent till they reached *Reliant,* he felt certain Folger would slap Cochrane into the brig. Once there, with luck, Cochrane would never know about him. Folger would order the man cut loose in Callao.

"Ye say a monster attacked yer ship?" Creel asked. "What kind of monster?"

Cautiously, Cochrane sat up and pulled the blanket around him again. He sidled away from Merl. "It looked like a whale, but it wasn't. It come outta nowhere—"

"After ye attacked *Brown-Eyed Sue*, ye mean," Robert said with fire in his young voice.

Cochrane nodded. "After Cap'n McAfee ordered the attack on that ship. Him an' his men, they was takin' goods an' supplies from that ship whilst the monster struck us."

"What was it?" Creel asked.

"It looked like a whale." Cochrane touched his face. "A scar-faced whale. But it weren't no whale. I never seen no whale what had tentacles attached to it."

Ethan listened to the man's words with a mixture of panic, anxiety, and sharp curiosity. A tentacle could well have been what grabbed Nate Phillips that night.

"Them tentacles," Cochrane went on, "they speared through men what was standin' on the deck. Shot through 'em like harpoons, then dragged 'em into the water like a fisherman takin' in his catch."

Merl and two of the other men in the whaleboat crew looked fearfully into the hills of swirling water that rolled around them.

"The creature took half our crew before we was able to turn it," Cochrane said. "It tore *Sunfisher*'s 'yards an' rigging to kindlin'. An' I think it drove Cap'n McAfee mad."

"The creature drove McAfee mad?" Ethan couldn't help posing the question. He still remembered how Nate had said he could hear the creature inside his head. And Professor Bullock and Katharine had spoken of the pirate being taken as having remarked the same thing.

"It did." Cochrane nodded solemnly. He took the whiskey bottle from his pocket and downed a healthy swig. Looking at Ethan, Cochrane wiped his mouth with the back of his arm. "McAfee's insane with anger. He's swearin' vengeance against that monster, vowin' to hunt it down an' kill it. He's plannin' to find a way to make money off of that thing. He's got the professor's papers an' such, an' he thinks he can ransom those an' maybe the creature itself to the president or to the British."

Ethan knew McAfee wouldn't give up the chase then. Only two things drove Jonah McAfee insane with lust: vengeance and the possibility of treasure. In the creature, McAfee had managed to embody them both.

"Even while the ship was bein' repaired," Cochrane went on, "McAfee was huntin' that hellish thing. Me an' a couple other men, we decided we wanted no part of that. So we taken this boat an' jumped in the sea three nights ago. I lost them other two durin' the storm, an' I figured I was lost me own self was not ye to come along an' fetch me up like ye did." He toasted them with the whiskey bottle but offered nothing to drink. "God bless each an' ever'one of ye."

"McAfee is still in these waters?" Creel asked.

"Aye." Cochrane drank deeply from the bottle. "Once McAfee gets a notion in his head, it takes a lot to get it out agin. He's a madman. I seen him insane before, but I ain't never seen him like this."

"He's got to be crazy if'n he's out here in these waters a-chasin' a monster he'd do well to fight shy of," Creel said.

"There's never been anyone as crazy as Jonah McAfee," Cochrane agree. "He's a vengeful man. Never fergets any trespass what's made agin him." He looked at Ethan. "Ye remember what he was like, Ethan. Ye remember how he was down in the Caribbean aboard *Wind Dancer*. Remember how him an' Teresa kilt them people, an' he very nearly kilt ye?"

IRON SHACKLES BOUND Ethan's wrists as he stood in Folger's quarters a short time later. Upon returning to *Reliant,* Merl Porter had wasted no time in telling Captain Folger how Cochrane had been aboard *Sunfisher* and how the man had known Ethan to be a pirate. Drunk and scared, Cochrane had tried to lie his way out of the mess he'd gotten himself into. He'd given Ethan up, naming him as a pirate, never telling Folger and the others that Ethan had been the one who had truly been impressed into service aboard the pirate ship.

Cochrane's story, twisted and garbled as it had been, had been all Folger needed to clap Ethan in irons and bring Larson up from the brig. Folger had made it known that he preferred a mate who was guilty of nothing more than taking a stand against a rebellious crewman who would have shot him if he hadn't been armed with an *allegedly* empty pistol.

Ethan stared past the captain through the stern windows, watching the sheets of rain run down the glass panes. He was afraid and angry and without hope. He hadn't, until that moment, remembered that a man could feel like that all at the same time.

"Do you recognize this man, Professor Bullock?" Folger asked.

In spite of himself, Ethan stared at the professor's reflection in the glass panes behind Folger. The lantern on the captain's desk engraved the images as gray ghosts. Katharine stood at her father's side, and the disappointment and hurt that showed on her face cut Ethan to the quick. She had liked him, and in the end, he had betrayed her trust though he had not intended to.

"I do," Bullock replied in a tight voice.

Stroud and his men filled the cabin. But Donald Larson stood again as Folger's right-hand man. Larson kept a pistol in hand that pointed straight at Ethan's heart.

"Who is he?" Folger demanded.

"We were never properly introduced," Bullock said, "but I recognize him as one of the crew of *Sunfisher*."

"Let the record show that *Sunfisher* is the pirate vessel under the command of Captain Jonah McAfee that was responsible for the destruction of *Brown-Eyed Sue*," Folger said.

Holy Jordan, looking grim and unhappy, sat in the corner of the room with a journal that was the official record of the charges. Holy's quill flew across the pages, and Ethan swore the manacles around his wrists got heavier with every word Holy wrote.

Folger turned to Cochrane, who was also in chains. "State your name for the record."

"Cochrane. Henry Cochrane. But I ain't no pirate, Cap'n."

Folger frowned at the man, obviously irritated at the delay. Although he had wanted the official record prepared, evidently Folger was discovering that the time taken to collect all the statements was getting between him and his bottle.

"If you're not a pirate, then what are you?" Folger demanded.

"I was impressed, sir," Cochrane stated contritely. "I wasn't no pirate by choice. McAfee an' his men, they taken me up from a ship an' forced me to be one of 'em. That was when I met Ethan Swain."

Cochrane gazed at Ethan and looked uncertain, as if not believing Ethan wasn't going to fight his statement.

Ethan didn't see the use in it. He knew Folger, and he knew that Folger hated him and would use any excuse to get back at him. Both of them were going to the brig.

"Was Ethan Swain one of the men who forced you to become a pirate?" Folger asked.

Cochrane hesitated. "No sir. 'Twere Cap'n McAfee his own self."

Folger wasn't happy, but obviously Cochrane didn't want to risk Ethan's wrath by pressing his pack of lies.

"Professor Bullock," Folger said, "did you see Cochrane take part in the boarding of *Brown-Eyed Sue*?"

Bullock studied the man's face.

Cochrane licked his lips.

Staring at the man's reflection, Ethan knew that Cochrane had been there. He wouldn't have missed the killing.

"I don't remember him from the boarding action, Captain Folger," Bullock said. "I remember Cochrane as one of the men that McAfee had carry Maxwell's body to me on Easter Island. As I recall, Cochrane got sick." He glanced at his daughter.

Katharine nodded, but her eyes were on Ethan.

"Cap'n," Ethan said, "you're wasting time here, and you're endangering the crew."

Cruel amusement twisted Folger's face. "More so than by having a pirate for a first mate on this voyage?"

"Aye," Ethan said. "And moreover, you're playing the fool. Cochrane has told you McAfee is in the area hunting the creature. If he's close by, then McAfee has got to be—"

Before Ethan could get another word out, Larson leaned across the desk and clubbed him with the pistol barrel. The weapon slammed against Ethan's temple and turned his knees to water. He dropped, barely conscious.

"McAfee is in the area, damn you!" Ethan said. "That needs to be the thing you deal with the most. For all you know, Cochrane has been sent here to damage the ship." He tried to stand, but his legs had gone to rubber beneath him.

"I jumped ship during the storm," Cochrane said. "I couldn't stand it no more."

"You're a damned liar, Cochrane," Ethan accused.

A flicker of movement signaled Larson's next swing. Ethan tried to dodge and saw Bullock start forward.

Bullock said, "Don't—"

Then Larson's gun barrel slammed against Ethan's head and everything went away. The only good thing was that unconsciousness relieved him of the helpless feeling that was starting to win out over the other emotions warring within him. McAfee was out there somewhere, and Folger was going to get the whole ship killed.

AFTER ETHAN SWAIN'S incarceration in the brig, everything aboard *Reliant* changed in the next two days—including the miserable weather while the

storm continued to gather strength. Folger drank more and became more bel-
ligerent and demanding, empowered by Donald Larson's apparent willingness to
cripple or kill anyone who spoke out against the captain.

But the change that bothered Professor Bullock most was the change in his
daughter. Katharine became quieter and more withdrawn. Where Ethan Swain
had gotten her to talk about things she had seen and done, even gotten to speak
of happy things in her past and things she hoped to undertake in her future,
Katharine had chosen instead to focus on the work they were doing to re-create
the research. She was even reticent around him. Bullock didn't feel that she
blamed him for Ethan's imprisonment, but he did feel as though he had let her
down by not choosing to help Ethan.

In point of fact, Bullock didn't think his attempts would do any more good
than Katharine's own efforts to see Ethan down in the brig. Captain Folger
denied her visitation, and Ethan's boat mates told her that he didn't want her to
see him down in the hold and that it was no place for a young lady.

Ethan Swain, Professor Bullock had decided even after the short time he had
known him, was a person of considerable depth. He was rewriting journal
entries now that included pieces of knowledge Ethan had imparted to him. That
knowledge helped build the hypothesis the professor was shaping toward the origins of the creature they hunted and that in turn had hunted them.

A shout drew the professor from his work.

"Thar she blows!" a man's voice called out from the rings on the mainmast.
"Thar she *blooowwwwwsssss!*"

"Where away?"

"Nor'-nor'west."

Bullock put his journal away and crossed to the starboard stern. Katharine
joined him and gazed out to sea.

"It's a whale," she said.

"You see it?" Bullock asked.

She pointed.

Bullock peered at the sea, finally able to spot the whale floating low in the
water perhaps two miles away. On good days, the professor had learned, men
could often see whales eight miles or more away. That had been another thing
Ethan Swain had taught him.

Below, Larson shouted commands, getting *Reliant* set to anchor. Sails were
drawn up into the rigging, and the ship slowed. In minutes, whaleboats were run

down the falls with crews in them. Larson took the lead boat. All of the men wore rain coats against the deluge of waves that constantly broke over the gunnels.

The whirling storm tore at the ship's rigging, seemingly worse now that *Reliant* was not charging forward herself. Waves crashed against the bows with thunderous slaps.

Bullock walked back to Folger. "Captain, this is insane. You need to call those men back. You can't possibly expect to be able to take a whale and harvest it while this storm blows over us. There isn't time before the storm reaches us."

"We're past the storm, Professor. What you're seeing here is the leading edge of it. In a little while, this bad weather will slide by us without touching us. We may be in for a little rain, but that's all."

"And if the storm isn't so obliging?"

"It will pass."

Bullock cursed the captain beneath his breath as he rejoined Katharine. "The man is a damned fool," he told her.

Katharine nodded. Her eyes tracked the whirling clouds. "The storm is going to be upon us in a little while." She pulled her coat tighter.

Together, they watched the whaleboats splash across the thundering surf, growing closer and closer to the whale. Bullock felt that the craft were going to be swamped at any time, but somehow the boats and the men continued to make it across the sea. He had heard stories of the whalers' bravery in facing the depths, but those stories paled in comparison to watching such men really risking their lives.

Katharine took a collapsible spyglass from her coat pocket. The device had been one of the things Ethan had loaned her. Fitting the spyglass to her eye, she stared at the whaleboats. She stiffened. "Father! It's the whale! The whale with the burned face!"

Taking the spyglass that his daughter handed him, Bullock focused on the whale. There, just barely, because the crashing surf washed over the large creature with such frequency, the professor spotted the charred area of the creature's head between gaps in the fog that rolled in from the approaching storm front. Fear rattled inside him. He turned to Folger.

"Captain! Captain! You've got to call those men back!"

"I will not." Folger glared at him.

"That whale," Bullock said. "That is the whale that broke *Brown-Eyed Sue* apart. Those men are going to forfeit their lives and draw that creature's wrath to us. Look at the face and see how it's burned."

Folger took out his own spyglass. He was quiet for a moment. "I don't see anything."

"That's because you're bleary-eyed with drink," Bullock challenged. "I'm telling you what my daughter and I both saw. The deaths of those men will be on your head."

"So will the success of this journey, Professor," Folger stated sharply. "That whale looks big enough to render out more than enough barrels to fill the hold of this ship. I won't return lacking."

"If that whale attacks us," Bullock pointed out, "you may not return at all."

"Sir," Folger growled, "you will restrain yourself, or I will see you taken from this deck. This instant."

"Captain," Bullock said in a calmer voice as he stepped back, "look at the whale again. Please. There's still time for us to escape."

With obvious reluctance, Folger raised the glass to his eye.

The wind shifted and rose in strength, carrying a deluge of spray that came down as stinging mist. Bullock's eyes smarted from the salt, and in seconds he found himself nearly drenched.

"The whale does have a burned face," Folger admitted. "But there is no way to call those men back. Mr. Stroud."

"Aye, Cap'n," Stroud called back.

"Have the anchor weighed, Mr. Stroud. If things don't fare well for Mr. Larson's and Mr. Creel's crews and boats, I want us out of here immediately."

Helpless, Bullock stood at his daughter's side and watched as the boats closed on the hulking monster floating on the ocean's heaving surface. Even if *Reliant* were ready, there was no reason to believe that the whaleship could outrun the creature.

ANXIETY FILLED THE whale, rousing him to wakefulness. He opened his eyes just as a jagged streak of lightning stabbed through the wine-dark skies. He knew that the *Other* had wakened him, but he didn't know why. He supposed it was because the *Other* wanted to feed. The *Other* always wanted to feed. The only reason that the whale had been allowed to rest was because the *Other* had rested, and because the *Other* knew when it had pushed its host nearly to his limits.

For a fleeting instant, the whale wondered if the *Other* knew he was going to die soon. Or maybe the *Other* didn't have any concept of death.

Over the years that the *Other* had taken possession of his body, the whale had come to realize that the *Other* had somehow lived in the flaming rock that had fallen from the above-water. That flaming rock had been the *Other's* home. When it had sunk beneath the waves, the *Other* had no longer been able to live there.

The whale knew that the *Other* didn't feel comfortable not living in a home. The *Other* thought of itself as *exposed* rather than *homeless*. When it was exposed, the *Other* was more vulnerable. Hermit crabs claimed shells as their own when they outgrew their previous homes. When they were between shells, the hermit crabs hid. Only sometimes, because the whale lacked deep or long thought processes, the whale wondered where the *Other* would go to live once he died or the *Other* outgrew him. Because even if he didn't die, the whale knew that the *Other* would have to leave him soon. The *Other* had grown too large to be contained in the whale's body much longer.

The anxiety rippled through the whale again. In that instant, he knew the emotion was not his own. The *Other* had set the feeling off within him, warning him of danger as it had in the past.

The whale stared at the sea, seeing only the storm through his good eye. His other eye had limited vision because of the burns he had suffered all those years ago. Still, he was able to recognize the shadows that moved at his side as being something other than the sea. He started to turn, then felt a sharp, stabbing pain in his side.

The *Other* screamed within the whale's mind, urging him to get into motion.

Flexing his tail, the whale shot forward and began blowing. His best defense in any fight was to dive deeply, and in order to do that he needed to have his breath ready to hold for a long time.

Another pain bit into his side. He shot forward, gliding through the water. Before he went far, he caught sight of a boatload of man-things pulling at their sticks on the side with his good eye.

During his years at sea, the whale had been chased by the man-things before. Sometimes he had deliberately let them get close at the *Other's* insistence because none of the man-things knew the *Other* lurked within him and was so much more dangerous than he was. The *Other* was as capable and clever as the man-things, and it planned and hunted much in the same way once it had discovered it could eat the man-things.

One of the man-things stood in the back of the boat, and the whale knew what was coming when he saw the long pole in the man-thing's hand. In a flicker of movement, the man-thing drove the cruel spear deeply into the whale's flesh. The line payed out behind the spear.

The whale had no words for the instruments of torture the man-things used, but he recognized them all the same. He had been speared before, but he had always been able to rip free of the lines by diving. He blew again, preparing to dive.

Then he felt the *Other* stirring within him, demanding action of its own. Rather than pursuing the safest course, the *Other* often preferred combat. Several times in the past when the whale would have chosen to flee, the *Other* had commanded him to attack small boats as well as big ships. None of those courses of action came without risk, which the *Other* seemed less and less inclined to admit existed.

In the beginning, the *Other* had only wanted to survive long enough for others of its kind to join it or rescue it. The whale had felt the *Other's* loneliness and fear, and he knew from the memories he sometimes shared with the *Other* that it had been hunted wherever it had come from before its flaming rock had fallen into the water. But the *Other* had been a hunter as well, not just a feeder as the whale was.

Obeying the *Other's* commands, knowing the creature would fill him with pain if he didn't, the whale turned on the boat on the side of its good eye and whacked it with his tail. His sudden blow caught the man-things unprepared. Their boat shivered and came apart, spilling screaming man-things into the sea.

Immediately, the whale ducked his head beneath the water, wanting to dive deeply and force the man-things to rip out the spears they had shoved into his sides. Instead, the *Other* commanded him to open his mouth so it could feed.

He felt the *Other's* tentacles slide from his stomach into his throat, then out through his mouth. He barely saw the tentacles strike the man-things fighting against the sea that covered them.

Then the whale felt the flash of contact of two of them. In the beginning, the whale had only known the surprise, agony, and fear of the contact, never knowing how many victims the *Other* had claimed. But now the whale could distinguish among the individual man-things, even the other sea creatures that the *Other* was sometimes forced to feast on.

The *Other* connected with its prey on many levels, beginning with the physical. The *Other* touched the thoughts of the man-things as well. From even that brief touch, the whale felt the fear and panic of the man-things, but that came through the *Other*, driven into the whale's conscious mind by his connection to the creature that lived within its body.

Besides the fright, the whale also heard memories of the man-things, saw images of their pods and how they lived with each other in the places on the dry land, which at first had been unbelievable to the whale. The whale was certain that the *Other* felt the emotions and thoughts of its food much more strongly than he did.

Sometimes the *Other* had kept its food alive for hours or days, and during that time the whale had been almost overwhelmed and driven out of its mind by the strange and twisted thoughts that were too large for its mind and its experiences. The whale didn't know if the *Other* delighted in its slow execution of its prey, or if it enjoyed the information it got from its food. The *Other* had learned all it could from the whale years ago, and through the whale, the *Other* had learned all about the world below-water and some about the world above-water.

Even as the whale felt the *Other* drag the two man-things into his mouth, he felt another stab in his side from the man-things aboard the other boat. This wound felt different than any other he had experienced.

Freed for the moment from the *Other's* covert control, the whale dived deeply. He felt the harsh pull of the spears in his side as the rope drew tight, but he felt confident he could once more break free as he had in the past.

But only a little way down into the ocean, he knew he was in trouble. His lungs grew tight and felt close to bursting. Unable to continue, he returned to the surface. The man-things in the boat kept the lines tight.

A kaleidoscope of images, thoughts, and emotions whirled through the whale's mind as he breached the surface. Few of them, except the fear and pain, were his. He tried to breathe and found that his lungs wouldn't function because they already felt full. He tried to exhale so he could inhale again, but the effort to exhale was hampered by the fact that the air suddenly felt as thick and unyielding as the sea around him.

The *Other* screamed at him, then unleashed the pain it was capable of to make him yield to its commands. Even the pain, usually so sharp and terrifying, only felt dulled and far away. The whale tried to exhale again but felt only thick fluid shooting from his blowhole.

Then the world around him turned black, and he knew that he was at last free of the *Other* because he no longer felt the cruel creature inside his mind. The last sounds he heard were the screams of the man-things as the *Other* preyed on them.

CHAPTER 28

Pacific Ocean 12° 31' S. Lat.—98° 42' W. Long.

"CAP'N, THEY'VE TAKEN a whale."

Jonah McAfee glanced up at the crow's nest. Excitement and bloodlust warred within him. He kept both controlled with difficulty. "And have they seen us?" They had spotted *Reliant* three days earlier, during one of the worst events of the storm.

"No, Cap'n. Not as far as I can see."

"Thank you, Mr. Rogers. Keep a sharp eye on them." McAfee paced the quarterdeck and felt the thrill of the hunt upon him. Even after days of repairs, rerigging and refitting sails after the creature had hit them, sails which had been torn apart again by the storm and had to be fixed all over again, *Sunfisher* had proven herself a much faster vessel than the heavily laden whaleship.

He'd lost three men and a longboat during the blow, but under the circumstances he still felt fortunate. He would, however, miss Henry Cochrane's cold-blooded ways around torture the next time he needed to question a reluctant informant. Most of the men had calmed down over the last few days. They were convinced that they wouldn't again see the monster that had broken *Sunfisher* up, but McAfee knew differently. The creature was still out there. He could feel it.

The storm's wind picked up, driving fifteen- and twenty-foot waves up from the sea, waves that crashed against *Sunfisher's* bows. The sails flapped overhead. Only enough canvas hung in the wind to maintain the ship's position against the storm front.

"So what do you want to do, Cap'n?" Gilley asked.

"What would you do, Mr. Gilley?"

Gilley considered the question carefully. "If'n it was me, I'd be all for gettin' over there an' takin' that ship now afore that storm lights down on us."

"Then it's a good thing you're not me," McAfee said. "Because that's not what we're going to do."

Gilley blinked.

"You see, Mr. Gilley, if that captain has sent whaleboats out into the sea, it means his hold is not full. Personally, I'd much rather take a full whaleboat as I would one that is carrying only part of a load."

"But that storm—"

"We can weather the storm," McAfee said. "We've weathered several storms in the past." He gazed up at the black clouds, seeing lightning streak through them. "This is just a storm like any other we've seen."

"As ye say, Cap'n."

"Good. You see, those men will start rendering the whale within hours. They'll spend two or three days working on that whale, striving in six-hour shifts, to fill the barrels while they battle the storm as well. By the end of that time, they're going to be exhausted, and the hold will be filled."

A grin fitted Gilley's lower face. "Them men will be all tuckered out."

"I don't know about you, Mr. Gilley, but often in the past I've found that taking a ship is much easier with a simple show of force when the men aboard that vessel believe they've already been asked to give too much."

"They'll fight to live."

"So they will. But if we offer them the opportunity to disembark that ship to the safety of longboats and survive without fighting, I believe they will."

"It's a good plan, Cap'n."

"I know," McAfee said. "We'll back away from them a distance. So far they haven't seen us. Once they fire up the tryworks to start boiling the blubber, the smoke will mark their position clearly for us. We'll have no trouble locating them."

"What about Swain, Cap'n? Are ye gonna let him live?"

"No," McAfee said coldly. "That man will die this time. I'll have his head and feed his body to the sharks a bit at a time to make certain." The pirate captain restrained the anticipation within him. Waiting to kill Ethan Swain was going to be the hardest thing he had done. "When we do this, I'll have my revenge and a ship with a cargo hold full of whale oil. Once the cargo and the ship are sold, I'll have the investment capital I need to find the monster."

"What about them men ye let escape from the whaleship?" Gilley asked. "They know about the monster."

McAfee smiled. "I said they could escape the whaleship, Mr. Gilley. If you'll recall, I made no mention of them escaping *me*. In the water, those longboats will be sitting ducks for our cannon crews."

The wind ripped through the rigging and sails again, causing *Sunfisher* to rock and catch an incoming wave off kilter. The ship's deck rode high, then rolled over slightly sideways.

Through long practice McAfee stood his ground till the ship righted again.

"Storm's shifting," Gilley said nervously. "The brunt of it is gonna be on us in a little while."

"We'll stand through it," McAfee said confidently. "*Sunfisher* has weathered many storms. This will only be one more."

"Me," Gilley said, eyeing the dark clouds, "I'd rather sail out of its way."

"We'll weather it, Mr. Gilley. Make certain the hatches are battened down and the ship is made ready."

"Cap'n," Rogers yelled down from the crow's nest. "I see sails yonder."

"Where away?" McAfee yelled back. He wasn't worried. Ships trafficked through the area on a regular basis, which was why he had guessed that the whaleship would pass that way. If not there, then there would have been another sea route he would have caught them on.

"East," the sailor called. "East-nor'east."

A glimmer of unease dawned in McAfee's gut. Most captains with any true sense and no hurry would have stayed closer to the coastline. He strode back to the stern and climbed up into the rigging a short distance. Unlimbering his spyglass, he searched the ocean in the direction the sailor had indicated, back toward Peru and Callao.

At first, McAfee missed the topgallant sails that the sailor had spotted. Even as he watched, the sails were taken down, indicating that the captain had chosen to weather out the storm as well—or didn't want to be seen. The possibility knitted a ball of worry that rested uneasily in his chest. But he also knew he had gone the furthest by being prepared for the worst.

Scanning the topgallants, McAfee spotted the British Union Jack—containing the crosses of St. George, St. Andrew, and St. Patrick in red and white on a field of dark blue—standing straight in the wind.

"The Britisher," Gilley exclaimed. "By God, what's he doin' here?"

"He's a greedy man who gets well paid by his king," McAfee said, stepping down from the rigging. "There's only one thing he would be doing here."

"So what do we do about this bastard?" Gilley asked.

McAfee glanced at the storm as the winds shifted again. "We watch him like we're watching *Reliant* and this storm."

"An' if'n he don't go away when we're ready to take the whaleship?"

"Then we'll bide our time. They say that vengeance is a dish best eaten cold, Mr. Gilley. It could be that we'll have to find out how true that is. For now, let's get *Sunfisher* back out of the way and see if Harrington is going to be as brave in the face of this coming storm as we are. There is no way I'll allow Harrington to take that ship without a fight."

WITHIN MINUTES, THE storm transformed into a ferocious and ravening beast. The raging winds howled out of the west and blew through *Reliant*'s rigging, and the waves rose up out of the depths twenty-five feet and more to crash over the vessel's bows. The whaleship's upper deck was soaked in a matter of minutes.

Reluctant to leave the deck until he saw the results of the whale hunt himself, Professor Bullock stood wet and miserable and nervous inside a rain coat. The wood felt slippery and treacherous beneath his boots. Katharine stood at his side despite his sharp insistence that she go below.

Together, they had witnessed the whalers' attack on their prey. Evidently Larson and his boats had caught the giant sleeping, or perhaps it had been trying to recover from the grievous injuries that had been dealt it in the last few days. Surely, Bullock believed, nothing made of flesh and blood could withstand all the destruction the whale had done without suffering consequences of its own.

The struggle with the whale had been violent and costly. Five men of the six in the second boat had been lost to the sea before Larson succeeded in thrusting his lance through the whale's lungs. Even then, when the whale had dived beneath the water, Bullock had felt certain the animal was going to get away. It couldn't die so simply, not after all the mystery and death that it had been part of, not without offering some explanation of what had made it different.

Watching the whale surface had been unbelievable. A moment after that, crimson blood flew high into the air while the sailors aboard *Reliant* shouted and cheered the hunters' success. There was no doubt of the kill according to the seasoned sailors aboard *Reliant*.

More than two hours had passed since the kill. Rowing back with the dead whale had proven difficult even though the sea pushed the whaleboat and the carcass in the direction of the whaleship. Finally, though, the crew reached the ship, and the whale was made fast to the starboard side.

An argument ensued between Larson and the crew regarding whether to try cutting up the whale then or wait until the storm had blown past. Larson argued to start right away because, if they waited, the gathering sharks would eat a fair amount of their catch, and at the captain's command, Stroud's musketmen backed up the decision.

Under protest, the crew prepared the cutting stage while other hands managed the sail and brought *Reliant* about so that her port was offered to the oncoming waves, and the ship provided some protection against the harsh sea.

Bullock's stomach churned every time a wave slapped the whaleship's broadside and lifted the vessel. Looking over the starboard side to watch the men work the whale was difficult because the professor had to fight the fear that the ship was going to fall over. He knew the more correct term was knockdown, and described when the ship rolled over on her beam-ends. But he also had to fight the insane fear that the whale would somehow miraculously return to life and shatter the whaleship.

"Don't fret none over it, Perfesser," Creel said as he passed by to help secure the chains tying the ship to the whale. "*Reliant* will stand up to what we're gettin' right now."

Bullock stared into the ocean as the whaleship leaned again and slid a little, feeling like he was going to fall over. But that was merely vertigo making his head swim because the horizon was more out of kilter than ever.

"I'll try to remember that, Mr. Creel," Bullock responded.

"This ship, she's stood up to blows more fierce than this one." Creel hauled on the chain with two other sailors. "Ye got to remember that she's carryin' a lot of ballast, what with all them barrels of oil. They'll hold us steady enough, they will."

Bullock could tell the difference with having the whale tied to the ship immediately. *Reliant* moved a little more slowly as she twisted in the water, but the ship still moved. He gripped the railing tightly.

Creel noticed Bullock's tense stance as he passed back by. "Perhaps ye'd be better off belowdecks, Perfesser."

"No. I'd feel like a rat awaiting drowning." Bullock gazed up at the dark, swirling heavens and the tops of the masts cutting through the clouds of mist. "And when, Mr. Creel, am I to know that the storm has pressed *Reliant* beyond her capabilities?"

Creel grinned. "Why, when us men start abandonin' ship, of course."

"Of course," Bullock replied dryly.

"No need to fret about that either. Why, most of us men can't swim. We won't be goin' anywhere anytime soon. The sea is downright inhospitable to any what's foolish enough to take a longboat out in this." Creel continued on his way.

Minutes later, the cutting stage was lowered over *Reliant*'s starboard. Creel and another sailor named Arnett started cutting into the whale. Blood wept from the wounds they sliced in the dead creature, but the crimson liquid quickly washed away in the heavy mist that fell from the dark clouds. Lightning stabbed white-hot brands through the sky, jagged and flicking quickly as snakes' tongues.

"Hey, Creel," Arnett said, stepping back from the whale on the narrow cutting stage. "Did you just see that thing move?"

"Didn't move," Creel insisted as he inserted the big metal hook attached to the block and tackle hanging over the ship's side. "Ye're imaginin' things, Arnett. Whale's dead. The crews drug it for two hours. If'n it was alive, it woulda done somethin' before now."

Bullock raked mist accumulation from his eyes. The salt spray stung fiercely enough to bring fresh tears.

Arnett returned to cutting.

"Pull," Creel bellowed to the crew working the block and tackle. "Pull. Hard as ye live now, lads."

The block-and-tackle rope tightened and took on the massive weight of the blubber blanket peeling free of the dead whale. *Reliant* tipped over farther and rocked more with the waves. Bullock pushed himself back, leaning away from the railing each time the ship rolled.

The whale turned in the water as its flesh tore free. Pale white bone and red meat showed under the blubber layer. Triangular fins of the sharks that had come to the feast sped away from the corpse as the movement startled them. The wind continued to howl mercilessly. Thankfully, when the ship was turned so dangerously on her side, the port side blocked the wind and the spray.

"Keep on, keep on," Creel urged above the storm's bluster.

Jagged streaks of lightning lit the clouds and cast reflections against the sea. Thunder blasted with deafening intensity.

Folger had been wrong, Bullock realized. The storm had shifted and was no longer skirting them. The force and fury of the elements burst full upon them. The mist gave way to driving rain, with drops as fat as a man's thumb. He drew his coat more tightly around him, but it didn't offer much defense against the spray and the blinding sheets of rain.

A man's scream ripped through the tumultuous noise of the rough weather. Bullock's head snapped around instinctively because the cry had sounded like a mortal one.

Arnett reeled back on the cutting stage and gripped his right arm. He had been leaning on the whale's body, scoring another line of cuts he and Creel would be making. He screamed again, his voice already going hoarse with the effort and the emotion. His knees turned to rubber beneath him as the strength left his body. If Creel had not caught the man by the back of his coat, Arnett would have fallen into the ocean.

Bullock's heart was at the back of his throat in an instant. He peered closely at the whale, looking for any indication of life it had been hiding.

"Pull up!" Creel bellowed. "Pull up, damn ye! Arnett's went an' cut hisself, an' he's like to bleed to death if'n ye don't hurry!"

The men working the ropes on the cutting stage hauled away. The cutting stage rose in jerks, thudding against the ship's hull as the vessel swung over in the sea while the waves crashed against her port side. Somehow Creel managed to keep Arnett and himself aboard.

"Father," Katharine said, "I saw the whale move."

"It couldn't have moved." Despite his fear that the ship was going to tip over or that he was going to misstep and fall over the railing all on his own, Bullock was already moving quickly down the companionway to the amidships working area. "That whale is dead." *God, please, the thing has to be dead.*

"It moved," Katharine insisted. She came immediately after him, plunging down the companionway more fearlessly than he had. "I saw it move."

Bullock glanced at the huge floating corpse. For a brief instant he thought he saw the whale's skin roll or pulse. But it wasn't movement of the whale. Rather, it was movement *independent* of the whale, something that slithered under the subcutaneous meat that had helped hold the whale's blubber to the body. However, he knew that wasn't possible. The motion had to have been a trick of the searing lightning or the sheeting rain.

When the cutting stage hauled level with the deck, Creel heaved Arnett aboard, then clambered up himself. Men gathered around the wounded sailor, their voices rising in surprise, adding fearful curses only a moment later.

"Mr. Jordan," Bullock called over the din of the rising thunder. He had gotten to know Holy Jordan over the last few days of traveling together because the man had helped Ethan treat his wounds and Katharine's.

"Aye," Holy replied.

"Get the medical bag from below," Bullock ordered.

Holy split off from the crowd and ran to the forward hatch.

"Ain't no medical bag gonna help Arnett," Merl Porter mumbled. "That poor bastard's gonna die."

Bullock shoved his way through the crowd of stunned sailors. He couldn't believe the way they were acting. Surely they had seen men with serious wounds before.

Arnett was curled into a ball on the deck. Crimson stained the wood, but was quickly washed away in the heavy mist. The man shook and shivered as if palsied.

Dropping to his knees, Bullock laid a hand on the sailor's hip and rolled him over. Arnett went easily. When the sailor flopped over, the other men stepped back quickly. Many of them cursed or called on God, and a few of them warded themselves against bad luck.

When he saw the nature of Arnett's wounds, Bullock froze.

Arnett's right arm was devoid of flesh up to the elbow. Bloody chunks of meat lay on the deck where he had landed after being thrown there by Creel. Bright white arm bones and finger bones threaded with scarlet lay against Arnett's chest. As Bullock watched, Arnett's left hand gripping his wounded right arm became infused with venom that immediately swelled the flesh. A moment later, the flesh of Arnett's other hand split, ripping free of skeletal fingers and the forearm bones.

"Help me!" Arnett cried hoarsely. His eyes wandered all around, almost spinning in their orbits. Bullock felt certain the man saw nothing at all. "Please! Someone! For God's sake help me! It hurts! It *hurts*!"

Robert started forward.

"Stay back!" Bullock roared.

The command froze the young sailor in his tracks.

Bullock shook his head. "You can't help him, son. No one can help him." The professor only hoped that the venom in the stricken sailor's system had acted quickly to eradicate any real conscious thought of the suffering that was going on.

A red blush crept up under the flesh at Arnett's throat. Within the space of a single ragged breath, the blush filled Arnett's face as well. He never lived to draw another breath. The air went out of him in a rush, but his body remained knotted up from the venom that had coursed through his flesh.

"'Twas the monster," Merl Porter said in a hoarse voice. "Damned thing knows we got the perfesser aboard, an' it done come fer him."

A few of the sailors agreed with Merl.

Despite the horror that filled him at Arnett's death and the continued fear of the storm that raged around *Reliant,* Bullock grew angry at the stupidity some of the sailors chose to exhibit. "You damned fools," he snarled.

"Here now," Merl said. "Ye've got no call to be speakin' to us that way."

Bullock stood, raising himself to his full height. "Until you start speaking with at least a modicum of common sense, Mr. Porter, I'll speak to you as I like. Whatever took the life of poor Mr. Arnett, it was not a monster. It was a creature. Don't spook your fellow miscreants by espousing supernatural origins for this damnable thing."

"Listen to ye." Merl stepped forward threateningly. "Mayhap ye're pertectin' that thing. Mayhap ye made some kind of deal with ol' Satan hisself to keep ye in a nice part of Hell when ye get there. In return, ye just gotta keep a-leadin' that there demon to good an' righteous God-fearin' men it can inflict its pain an' sufferin' on. Just like ye led it to the cap'n an' crew of *Brown-Eyed Sue.*"

"That's insane." Bullock pointed down at Arnett's corpse. More of the man's flesh sloughed off the bone, dropping to the drenched deck and sliding back and forth with the pitch of the ship. "Have you ever heard of such a demon before?"

"No, but I still says ye're responsible." Merl eyed Bullock belligerently. "I've got half a mind to heave ye over the side to feed yer monster, an' to heave yer daughter after."

Hardly had the threat against Katharine left Merl's mouth than Bullock planted a doubled fist in the center of the big sailor's face.

Merl staggered back, unconscious even before his feet failed him, and he landed in a sprawling heap on the deck.

"Here now!" Captain Folger yelled from the stern quarterdeck. "What the hell's going on down there?"

Bullock looked at the sailors spread around him. Since his time aboard

Reliant, he'd learned that most of the men were superstitious about one thing or another to differing degrees. He had no friends among them, but most of them were not direct threats as Merl was.

"Mr. Larson," Folger went on, "I expect you to get full and complete control of that crew."

"Aye, Cap'n," Larson bellowed back across the harsh blasts of thunder and the rolling cannonade of the waves striking the whaleship's port side. He glared at Bullock. "Lads, I think ol' Merl had the right of it. Only I don't think the perfesser is in league with that thing as much as he's a damn jinx." He glanced at Katharine. "I don't think the woman is jinxed, though."

"You're an idiot," Bullock snapped.

"Here now." Larson stepped forward, hands curling into fists at his side.

"Careful, Mr. Larson," Bullock threatened. "If you make me angry, maybe I won't just settle with striking you. Maybe I'll summon that demon out in the water to carry you away."

Sailors around Larson stepped back, creating space between themselves and the mate.

Holy returned, carrying the beat-up black medical bag and shoving his way through the crowd of superstitious sailors.

"It's too late, Mr. Jordan," Bullock said. "Thank you for moving so quickly."

Holy pulled his hat off in one hand and knelt beside the dead man.

"Don't touch him," Bullock said. "I think the venom in Mr. Arnett's body will migrate to your own at the slightest touch. I've never seen the venom act so quickly." Even as he said that, the professor knew the statement was true. Evidently the creature had some degree of control over the amount of venom it used. And there was even the possibility that it used multiple venoms.

"Mr. Turpin," Katharine said. "Did you see what happened to Mr. Arnett?"

Creel shook his shaggy head. "No. It all happened so fast. I saw all the blood an' I just thought he'd cut hisself. Seen men do that afore. E'en in weather what wasn't as bad as we're facin' now."

"Did you touch Mr. Arnett's wounds?" Katharine asked.

Creel brushed at his sodden clothing. "No. At least, I don't think so."

"If he'd gotten touched by the venom, he would know it." Bullock rocked on his feet as the ship rolled over to starboard again. He peered over the railing at the dark water where the whale's body floated. The bloody stripe where the blubber blanket had been cut away stood out boldly against the sea, like the white flesh of a red apple.

"Mr. Larson," Captain Folger yelled from the stern quarterdeck, "get those men back to work this instant."

"Aye, Cap'n," Larson yelled back.

Bullock hung on to the railing and turned to face the stern. Rain pelted his face. "Captain Folger, you can't expect these men to harvest that whale. The creature I told you about is within the whale."

Folger cursed, ignoring the fact that Katharine stood on the deck. "I'm not leaving that whale, Professor. Its blubber will fill Reliant's hold. There's profit to be made today, and—by God, sir—I'm going to make it."

"You're risking these men's lives."

"Superstitious twaddle," the captain roared back. "Whatever killed Arnett was in the water. And whatever that was is gone by now, else we'd have seen it again."

"No, sir," Bullock yelled. "You're wrong. That creature isn't in the sea. It's in the whale."

"Mr. Stroud," Folger said clearly.

"Aye, Cap'n." Stroud stepped forward.

"If the professor doesn't step away from that railing and allow Mr. Larson to get those men back to work, you will shoot him."

Before Stroud could reply, the ship shuddered, breaking the rhythm she had held so far. The deck tilted more steeply. The sound of wood splintering cracked above the angry growl of the storm.

Nausea whirled in Bullock's stomach as he turned to the block and tackle, certain the splintering sound had come from there.

The blubber blanket hanging from the great hook still trailed over the ship's side. Only now the huge piece of meat weighing a ton or more showed direct tension instead of the laxness that had been there before. As the professor watched, the blubber shifted and the block and tackle rigging cracked again. One of the bolts holding the boom arm to the deck pulled free and rattled across the deck for a moment before disappearing into the surging sea.

"Somethin's grabbed on to the blubber!" Creel yelled. "Cut it loose, lads! Cut it loose afore it pulls us over!" He pulled his knife free as he pushed himself through the group of men between him and the boom arm. "Out of the way!"

The storm winds shifted again, picking up power and changing so that they slammed directly into Reliant. The whaleship tilted farther than she ever had before, leaning down so that water roiled up over Professor's Bullock's boots.

"Father!"

Startled, thinking that Katharine had been caught unawares and was now tumbling from the deck, Bullock turned and reached for her. Instead, she had a firm grip on the railing a few feet from him and was reaching for him with her free hand. Her coat blew around her, proof of the fury that raged over the ship.

Reliant rolled again as another wave crashed into her. For one stomach-turning moment, Bullock thought the ship's center of gravity would hold against the sea and the wind and the pull of the thing that had hold of the blubber blanket.

Then *Reliant* rolled over on her side, stabbing her topgallants, yardarms, and rigging deep into the maddened sea.

CHAPTER 29

Pacific Ocean 12° 31' S. Lat.—98° 42' W. Long.

WHEN *RELIANT* ROLLED over onto her starboard, Ethan Swain tumbled head over heels in the brig and listened to the avalanche of whale oil barrels and stone ballast slamming against the starboard hull and anything that got in the way. He thought he heard someone nearby scream, but he couldn't be certain because of the cacophonous din that filled the hold.

Battered and bruised already from the beating he'd been given by Larson while he'd been unconscious, Ethan felt new agony course through him as he fought to get to his feet. The dim light that had illuminated the bow area of the hold was gone, and his first hope was that the lantern had gone out. Otherwise, the spilled oil from the broken barrels would catch fire. In the meantime, he was working blind.

He reached for the iron door, having to reach over his head because the ship had changed orientation. As he felt for the lock, claws ripped across the back of his hand.

Ethan yanked his hand back as his mind summoned up all manner of fright-ful images that the claw was attached to. Only the frantic rasp of his own breathing, the creaks *Reliant* made in her new position, and the distant cries of men reached his ears.

Move, Ethan commanded himself. *If* Reliant *goes down, you're going down with her.*

Cautiously, he reached up again and felt for the doorframe. The iron door remained in place, but the wood around it had splintered. He gripped the broken board and pulled, feeling the claws bite into his arm.

Realizing that the claws had merely brushed against him and that there was no force involved nor any further effort to get through the bars to get at him, Ethan put out his hand tentatively. He felt the claws again and resisted the immediate instinctive impulse to draw his hand back.

A quick exploration of the claws led him to a scaly stump of a leg and to the conclusion that the limb belonged to one of the Galapagos terrapins that had been set loose in the hold. While holding the limb, he felt a warm trickle of fluid run along his hand and down his arm.

Blood, he realized, because the fluid was too thick to be water. Evidently the creature had gotten crushed in the avalanche of falling ballast and oil barrels.

He let go the dead terrapin's leg and returned his attention to the broken board at the side of the iron door. Careful of splinters, he grabbed the board and pulled, breaking the piece free almost at once. Encouraged, he laid the piece at his feet and reached up for another handhold. Even working blind, he had a sizable hole in minutes.

Grabbing the edge of the iron door, he pulled himself up. Before his shoulders passed through the hole, the doorframe gave way under the combined weight of the dead terrapin, a barrel of oil, and Ethan. He fell, barely managing to push away from the barrel, the door, and the eighty-pound terrapin, certain that if either had landed on his legs, it would have broken them. In the hold beyond, more barrels shifted, and for a moment Ethan feared that the ballast and the barrels were going to fall on him and crush him.

He scrambled up through the hole and stood in the darkness. A rectangle of light glowed softly to his right, marking the amidships hatch that led to the blubber room trapped between the cargo hold and the upper deck. Evidently both the upper and lower hatches had been left open while the crew had been taking the latest whale.

"Ethan," Cochrane called from the cell adjoining the one Ethan had escaped from. "Let me out of here." His own cell door was warped in its frame but buried under oil barrels.

Ethan ignored Cochrane and crossed on the starboard hull, which had been the wall before the knockdown. Halfway to the hatch, Ethan spotted a man's arm sticking out from beneath a pile of oil barrels. As *Reliant* rocked on the current, the light from the hatch shifted and showed the man's features to be those of Obed Pettigrew, a middle-aged salt from the Boston area.

Ethan rolled the barrels from the man, but found that it was too late. The barrels had crushed the life from Pettigrew, breaking his chest so badly that splintered ribs showed through his torn flesh.

Even under the dire circumstances that had befallen the whaleship, Ethan knew his presence among the captain and crew wouldn't be welcomed. He knelt and searched Pettigrew's grisly remains. His quick hands turned up a fair-sized fishing knife that would prove useful in a fight if it came to that.

If any of us survive that long, Ethan thought after another wave slammed *Reliant* and heeled her over. Ballast and barrels shifted in the hold again, tumbling toward him. He gathered himself and sprinted for the hatch. His foot slipped in a patch of whale oil that had threaded through the confusion of barrels.

Blubber blankets and Bible leaves lay scattered over the next room. The foul stink that habitually clung to the room seemed stronger, as if the air in the room couldn't flow as well as normal.

Stepping through the next hatch proved to be problematic. Where the lower decks had walls that now translated into floors, the upper deck had nothing but empty space that dropped into the ocean.

Peering over the hatch's edge, Ethan saw that most of the crew had dropped into the water or held on to the railing at the bow and stern that hadn't been submerged. Others, including Professor Bullock and his daughter, had found respite in the rigging and the sails that now lay in the ocean. Several of them called for help. The whale's body floated under the press of the masts, and Ethan realized that the buoyancy of the carcass had been one of the primary reasons *Reliant* hadn't gone completely over on her beam-ends.

As he lay in the open hatch, Ethan saw how low in the water *Reliant* rode. He had been aware of the whaleship's turgidity while sitting in the brig. No one had made an effort to toss out ballast after more oil had been taken on. He cursed Larson and Folger both, knowing neither man had the desire to keep *Reliant* as fit and trim as she could be. Even as the food and other supplies were used up, barrels of whale oil would have helped supplement the loss. For the moment, *Reliant* was a fat sow lying in the water. Occasionally, water slapped up over the hatch and threaded down into her hold. If she got enough of the sea in her guts, Ethan knew they would be in for even more trouble.

Easing out onto the hatch's edge, Ethan reached up and caught the mainmast rigging. He hauled himself up, working across the top of the hemp webbing like a spider.

"Ethan."

Glancing up, Ethan spotted Bill Fedderson hanging on to the iron rings used by the lookouts. "Good to see you're alive, Bill."

Bill nodded. "Like as not, none of us will be for long."

Ethan used his borrowed knife and cut sections of rigging loose at one end. Mending them later would prove no big problem, but for the moment the rigging dropped into the water where the crew struggled to get back aboard *Reliant*.

"Cut loose some of the rigging," Ethan directed.

Bill scooted along the foremast with his legs wrapped around the pole. He took out a knife and cut sections free as well.

"Don't give up the ship yet," Ethan said. "After this blow settles down, we'll get her right again."

"Ain't the blow I'm worried about," Bill said. "That monster what et Nate Phillips that night? Why, it's here, too."

Ethan's heart thudded heavily in his chest. "Have you seen it?"

"No. But it kilt Arnett only a minute or two before we got knocked down."

"How?"

"Venom. Least that's what the perfesser says. I saw Arnett me own self. He come back aboard from the cuttin' stage already a dead man in the makin'." A look of horror crossed Bill's face. "He fell apart, Ethan. The meat just plumb fell offa him."

Ethan thought of the drawings he'd seen in Katharine's journals, and of the wound he'd received on his side. Even now, though his flesh had healed, the scarring was permanent. *Ignore that for the moment,* he told himself. *One problem at a time, starting with the most dangerous.*

As he looked at Folger and Larson in the water, Ethan realized that he was actually stepping from one problem to another. Maybe his efforts were going to save some of the men, but he still didn't know how he was going to save himself from the captain and the second mate.

He continued crawling out on the mainmast till he reached a spot over Professor Bullock and his daughter. Ethan cut more rigging free and dropped the end into the water near the Bullocks. Ethan kept an eye on the whale's body, expecting the monster to come springing from any side of the corpse at any moment.

The storm continued to rage and howl overhead. *Reliant* rolled like a bucking horse, constantly stabbing her masts and 'yards into the water, prevented from completely turning over by the whale's floating corpse.

Ethan waited on the mast and watched as Katharine climbed the rigging. Fear squirmed inside him as he scanned the dark water below her. Several terrapins had fallen from the deck and floated on the ocean. Ethan hoped that whatever might be lurking in the water would choose them as easy prey.

The sails had come unfurled when the masts had struck the ocean. Yards of canvas lay spread across the water in areas, providing dangerous places that some of the crew had gotten trapped under.

"Bill," Ethan called.

"Aye," Bill responded. "Ye'll want to watch yerself, Ethan. We ain't alone out here as ye'd think."

"What do you mean?"

"We took the whale what has the monster in it. Leastways, it's the scar-faced bastard ye said ye saw the night Nate Phillips was lost."

Ethan gazed into the dark water around the whale. "Have you seen the creature, Bill?"

Bill shook his head. "Not me. But it kilt Arnett, and that's fer sure." He gazed down into the water as well. "Mayhap it slithered away in all the confusion, but I can't say."

"I want a head count soon as you can get it. I want to know how many men we've lost."

"Aye," Bill said. "We lost six that I know of. Arnett an' five aboard one of the whaleboats Larson took out after the whale."

"And Pettigrew," Ethan said. "I found him below."

"I'll get it done."

Ethan reached down to catch Katharine's arm. At first, she shied away from him, then finally reached up and caught his hand. He pulled, lending his strength to hers the last few feet. Professor Bullock followed her up.

"Bill was wrong about the creature, Mr. Swain. It hasn't gone anywhere. It's still inside the whale."

"I'll keep an eye peeled, Professor."

"You do that. It's good to have you back among us, son."

Captain Folger and Larson climbed up the mizzenmast rigging. Stroud and his men followed them up.

"Who let you out of that cage?" Folger demanded across the distance separating the two masts. "By God, I'll have the skin from the back of the man that allowed this prisoner to go free."

"No one let me go free," Ethan replied. "Belowdecks is a mess, and the cargo hold is even worse. The iron door was stove in by falling cargo. There are barrels broken open down there, so anyone going inside the ship needs to be watchful with a lantern. That oil will catch fire, and we'll burn up with the ship or drown."

"You're a prisoner aboard this ship," Folger accused. "A pirate awaiting a just hanging when we reach home."

Angry, knowing he had to make a stand, Ethan stood on the mast, balancing himself against the wind that flew over the port side of the ship that still managed to blunt the main effects of the storm. The mast bobbed up and down, but Ethan kept his feet with an easy grace. Katharine and her father clung to the mast, their feet still resting in the rigging.

"No," Ethan replied. "I'm not a pirate, and I'll not be a prisoner anymore either."

"You stupid bastard!" Folger screamed. His face flushed with apoplexy. "How dare you!" He looked over his shoulder at Stroud, who hung in the rigging. "Stroud, shoot that damned pirate through the head!"

Stroud hesitated, clearly torn between the order and trying to keep safe and sound. Finally, he heaved himself up onto the mast and took up a musket from one of his men. He unwrapped the oilskin that had kept the weapon dry, then pulled the hammer back and looked down the barrel.

Ethan stared back across the musket at Stroud. "If you pull that trigger, Stroud, I'll consider that a declaration of war. If you miss, I'll swim across this water and carve your heart out."

"I won't miss."

Ethan held his hands straight out at his sides. "How certain are you that you'll kill me? Because that's what it will take."

For a long moment, Stroud peered down the length of the barrel. Finally, he said, "I'm not afraid of you."

"I know," Ethan said in a hard voice that he had whetted while walking the deck in command of pirate ships, "but you stand with me or you stand against me. Right now in this instant, and in this place where Folger's damnable greed, arrogance, and incompetence has put us."

"Damn you, sir!" Folger yelled. "Incompetence has nothing—"

"Your incompetence," Ethan interrupted in a louder voice, "is exactly why *Reliant* is lying beam-ends in the water instead of standing proud and tall as she should be."

"Stroud!" Folger roared, turning to the third mate. "Fire that weapon!"

Slowly, Stroud lowered the musket, never taking his eyes from Ethan. "No, sir. I don't reckon that I will. He means what he says, an' I ain't in no hurry to die if there's a way we can get out of this. I can't be certain of getting the shot off under these conditions with all the rain, an' I'll not kill another man in cold blood fer ye the way I did Timothy Madison. I've had me fill of that, I have."

Ethan loosed a tense breath. He'd had no choice but to force Stroud to choose. Stroud was the most important cornerstone he would need in converting the crew who suspected him or did not like him.

"He's not an innocent man," Folger protested vehemently. "He's a pirate."

"I have only yer word on that," Stroud said. "An' that of a pirate his own self. Without Ethan Swain allowed to say a word about the matter hisself."

An exultant triumph dawned inside Ethan, but he knew the true success of the moment was as fragile and fleeting as a rainbow.

"One of you other men, then," Folger ordered, looking around at Stroud's sharpshooters.

"Stand as ye are," Stroud growled.

None of Stroud's sharpshooters moved to obey the ship's captain.

"Mr. Stroud," Folger said, "I'll have you brought up on charges of mutiny."

"It's yer cat," Stroud replied. "Ye want it skint, then skin it yer own self. Me?" He nodded toward Ethan. "I'm all fer gettin' outta this alive, I am. An' I ain't a bettin' man, Cap'n Folger, but I figure I know where I'm gonna put my trust. An' it ain't in ye or Larson there."

"But you'll put your trust in a pirate?" Folger acted as if he couldn't believe it. "If you listen to him, you're going to get your gullets sliced through for your trouble."

"Pirate or not," Ethan said, "I'm the best man you have for getting this ship, this crew, and these people out of this alive and intact."

"You're all fools!" Folger roared.

Creel spoke up from the foremast. "Wasn't Ethan what got us in the fix we're in, Cap'n Folger. An' I suspect mayhap he ain't the only man what's chased after somethin' while under a black flag. Now I ain't sayin' that I have, but I've knowed them what has, an' most of 'em are decent men that was just lookin' fer a way outta a bad time."

Larson moved quickly, snatching a musket from one of the nearby men. He started to unwrap the oilskin. "I'll kill the bastard fer ye, Cap'n."

Moving only a little, Stroud pointed his musket at Larson. "Ye'll be handin' that musket back to the man ye took it from, Larson, or I'm gonna empty that jug-eared head of yers."

Slowly, Larson handed the weapon back. "This ain't over, Swain," the mate threatened.

"I reckon it's over enough," Stroud said. "If'n ye raise a hand agin him before every man jack aboard this ship is safe to home, I'm gonna kill ye. Flat out, Larson, I swear to me Maker that's how it'll be." He turned his attention to Ethan. "It's yer crew. Fer now. An' if'n I've made a mistake in me judgment, ye need to know that I'm a man what makes amends for me mistakes."

Ethan nodded. "I'll see if I can earn your trust." He turned and surveyed the water. Only a few men remained in the water. *God help me and help us all, but I live for these moments when everything counts on me and the clock is against me.* "Creel."

"Aye."

"Pick a three-man crew. Get rigging down to those men and get them out of the water. Mr. Stroud, I expect you and your men to keep watch over Creel and his crew, and those men in the water. I don't know what effect a musket ball will have on whatever it is that lurks down there, but I'm willing to find out if it shows itself."

"Aye."

"But I want you to do it from up there." Ethan pointed at the port side of the ship. "Up there you'll have a better vantage point and the relative safety of the high ground."

"Aye."

"Take half of your men at a time. I want the other half keeping cover over Creel's crew at all times. One group covers the other as one pulls back."

"Done," Stroud agreed.

Some of the tension and frustration flowed from Ethan as he assumed command. Being master of a ship was something that he was used to, something that he was born to do—something that he had missed for so long.

Creel picked his team and started moving along the masts to cut new rigging to drop to the sailors still struggling against the sea.

"Bill," Ethan called.

"Aye."

"Get this crew to the top of the port hull. I want a temporary shelter built there that will protect this crew till the storm blows itself out. Use what sailcloth you can scrounge. Cut sails free of the mizzen if you have to. If we have to lose sails before this is over, that's where we'll lose them."

"You're crippling my ship," Folger protested.

"This ship is already crippled," Ethan said. "I'm pruning, trying to save what I can from the wreck you have tried to make of her."

Folger cursed him in a loud voice.

"Holy," Ethan said, stepping out toward the end of the mast where it dipped into the ocean. "I want you and you alone to go inside the ship and assess the damage. I want a list of salvageable supplies and where we can find them."

"Aye." Holy swung down to the hatch.

"I also want to know how much water we'll have to pump out of *Reliant* once we get her up again." Ethan gazed around, slitting his eyes against the driving rain that continued to pour from the slate gray sky. "Robert."

"Aye," the young sailor said.

"You'll come with me. I want to see if there's a way we can get those falconets up so we can use them if we have to."

"Aye," Robert said.

Ethan raised his voice. "Holy."

"Aye." Holy shoved his head back out of the hatch.

"I'll need the cooper's tools when you come back," Ethan said.

"You'll have them."

Looking down, Ethan said, "Professor Bullock, I'll need you to see your daughter up to the port hull. Maybe the weather will be more disagreeable there for a time until Bill gets that shelter made up, but you'll be safer."

"I understand. Thank you."

Katharine stared at Ethan, but he couldn't read anything in her gaze. "So you're going to save the men who would have seen you to the gallows?" she asked.

Ethan felt uncomfortable. "Not all of these men would have done that."

"Even so," the young woman said with that directness she had, "a proper pirate would have killed the captain and the men that chose to stand with him. In fact, that would probably be the safest course to take at this juncture, wouldn't it?"

"I would never have done that."

"Exactly," she replied. Then she started climbing, leaving Ethan and her father staring after her.

The professor pushed in close to Ethan. "My daughter seems to rather favor you," Bullock said. "I know she tried to visit you several times while you were imprisoned to bring you food. Do not disappoint her."

A flicker of anger passed through Ethan but was quickly gone. He smiled at the grim irony. "I think, Professor, that if I don't manage to save us all, we'll all be disappointed."

Bullock paused. "She won't be disappointed if you fail, Mr. Swain. God knows, my daughter accepts failure in people, but she does not lightly put her trust or confidence in people. The thing is, she'll be disappointed if you don't turn out to be the kind of man she thinks you are."

Ethan shook his head. "I'm not the kind of man she thinks I am. I was a pirate."

"And yet, it was a life you walked away from. Why do you suppose that is?"

"Because I killed someone I thought I loved," Ethan stated baldly, "and because I made a mortal enemy in that life."

"Even so, you could have still continued to be a pirate. You didn't. You chose not to. That is what my daughter sees." Bullock clapped him on the shoulder in passing. "Good luck. And if there is anything I can do, please know that you can count on me."

In disbelief, Ethan watched both Bullocks crawl across the mast to the deck. By that time Bill already had a section of rigging stretched across the port hull to provide a way up.

"Ethan," Robert said nervously, "I think I saw the whale move."

Ethan stared through the rigging, his senses alert. The loose sailcloth and the rigging made seeing difficult, as did Creel and the men below. Everything seemed to be moving, including the whale.

"The whale is moving, Robert," Ethan said. "*Reliant* is rolling over on it, and the whale is riding the residual waves."

"Not the whale itself," Robert said. "I swear I saw something moving *within* the whale."

Ethan looked at the line hanging from the block and tackle as he climbed across the rigging and the foremast to get to the bow. The ship's prow stood higher out of the ocean and he hoped to free the falconet there while taking advantage of that. His mind was already busy working out the rigging he'd need to move the small cannon to the port hull. Hopefully, the falconet wouldn't be there long, or even be needed. But if something—some monster, he had trouble thinking of the creature that way, especially since it had to be smaller than the whale—did still lurk in the water, he wanted a capable weapon.

Below, Creel had brought in all the stranded sailors that had grabbed on to the railing and didn't know how to swim out to the rigging where the topgallants thrust into the ocean.

"Creel," Ethan called out as he clambered down to the falconet.

"Aye," Creel shouted back.

"Cut that blubber blanket free of that block and tackle while you're down there. When the storm quiets, *Reliant* may have enough ballast and cargo aboard her to right herself, but we're not going to make her do it carrying deadweight."

"Aye, Ethan."

"Cut through the blubber, Creel. We may have need of that hook."

Creel waved acknowledgment, then set to the task himself.

From the corner of his eye, Ethan tracked movement, following it back to the whale. The dead creature lay buoyed in the water, and nothing looked any different. He turned his attention back to the falconet. Once he had the cooper's tools, he didn't foresee any problems getting the weapon loose from the bow deck.

A hoarse scream of pain ripped from the waterline at the ship's starboard.

Ethan jerked around, his hand slipping automatically to the knife he had thrust into the waistband of his breeches.

Below, Creel and another man stood waist deep near where the block-and-tackle line disappeared into the ocean. The blubber blanket, lighter than the salt water, floated out from the whaleship like a long gray tongue.

The other sailor, Gabe Parsons, reached out for Creel. "Help me! For God's sake, help me! It's got me, Creel! It's got me!"

Creel grabbed the man's hand and pulled. Parsons didn't budge even though both men strained mightily. It was evident that something below the waterline had seized Parsons.

Ethan abandoned his work on the falconet and leapt for the rigging. He made his way through the rigging while carrying the knife naked in his fist. As he went, he mapped his path through the rigging. Evidently the creature felt more comfortable striking below the waterline.

"Stroud," Ethan yelled.

"We're lookin'," Stroud called back. "So far we can't even see so much as a shadow on the water."

The thing, whatever it was, was definitely in touch with the whale. The big corpse moved, changing rhythms as if it fought with Parsons.

Suddenly, a whiplike appendage lifted free of the water. With the way the rain still fell in sheets, Ethan couldn't make out many of the details. The tentacle came set, then spiked forward.

Parsons froze for a moment when the tentacle stabbed through his back. By that time, Ethan was close enough to see the tentacle burst through the unfortunate sailor's chest. Parsons's scream died midway.

Ethan hung from the rigging above Creel. "Creel, let him go. You can't save him."

Fear bloomed dark and full on Parsons's face. But calm followed almost immediately afterward. "It's talkin' to me, Creel. I can hear it. In the back of me head, I can hear it. It's askin' questions. It's talkin' to me. Oh God, Creel, get it outta me head."

The tentacle thrust through Parsons's chest withdrew, and blood jetted from the horrendous wound. A second later, a dark flush spread through the sailor's body. Everywhere the flush spread, Parsons's flesh burst open in gaping cracks that bled black blood.

Creel fell back suddenly as Parsons's arm came off at the shoulder. Yelling in terror, Creel shoved himself backward and pushed the amputated arm from him. Musket fire cracked from the foremast and the port hull. Balls struck the water around Parsons, and two of them hit him.

"Creel!" Ethan yelled.

Reaching up, Creel caught Ethan's hand. Ethan yanked back, digging his feet into the rigging to get the leverage he needed. Creel came up just ahead of a second and third tentacle that slapped through the water and thudded against the deck. Ethan and Creel kept retreating up the rigging, moving as rapidly as they dared.

In the next instant, Parsons disappeared, yanked back under the water by a quick twitch of the tentacle.

JONAH MCAFEE STOOD at the stern quarterdeck and looked through his spyglass. The British ship had set up almost four miles away. With the rough waters caused by the storm, the British vessel was seldom visible through the waves and the rain. McAfee was certain that *Sunfisher* was just as likely hidden much of the time.

But just as he knew Harrington was there, McAfee also knew that the British captain knew he was there as well. McAfee wasn't certain if Harrington knew the whaleship was only a few miles away.

McAfee collapsed the spyglass, suddenly aware of how sluggish *Sunfisher* rode in the ocean. Most captains probably wouldn't have noticed the subtle and tired shift of the ship's center as he did even in the hellish squall that blew over them. The storm had hit *Sunfisher* hard, slamming her with great gusting fists that snapped rigging and tore canvas. None of the damage was extensive, and she had survived much worse, including the attack by the whale-thing after they had taken *Brown-Eyed Sue.*

"Mr. Gilley," McAfee called.

The mate stood on the starboard side of the stern, taking advantage of the shelter offered by the ship's wheel and the pilot who held *Sunfisher* steady and pointed straight into the face of the storm.

"Aye, Cap'n."

"Go below, Mr. Gilley, and let me know how the ship is doing."

"Me, Cap'n?" Gilley wasn't pleased with the prospect. None of the crew spent any more time belowdecks than they had to. A slaver ship could never get rid of the stink of the bodies she transported.

"You, Mr. Gilley," McAfee said. "And I'll have that inspection done now."

"Aye, Cap'n." Gilley made his way down the companionway and disappeared belowdecks.

McAfee waited, anxiety churning in his guts. He knew something was wrong. *Sunfisher* felt—off. He knew no other way to phrase the feeling.

Gilley reappeared in less than a minute. He ran up the companionway, his lantern banging against the railing. He looked frightened.

"Cap'n!"

"What is it, Mr. Gilley?"

"It's the cargo hold, Cap'n. We're takin' on water. A frightful lot of it."

McAfee ordered the helmsman to hold to the course, then led the way back down belowdecks. At the center hatch that opened down into the cavernous cargo hold, the pirate captain peered down, holding the lantern before him.

The light reflected across the lake that had formed at the bottom of the ship. The water wasn't overly deep at the moment, not quite coming up over the stone ballast that littered the hull.

Swearing lustily, McAfee went on down into the hold. The stench of unwashed bodies rose more strongly because of the wet conditions inside the hold. Death hung in the still air inside the hold as well.

"What happened?" McAfee demanded.

"I don't know, Cap'n."

"Where is the water coming from?"

"Starboard," Gilley answered. "Back near the stern."

Despite his misgivings about trudging around in the brackish water that had no doubt sopped up the excrement, blood, and sweat from the hundreds of slaves that had been transported in the hold, McAfee stepped from the ladder. He trudged through the foul water and told himself that all he had to do to get clean again was go topside and stand in the rain a minute or two.

Back in the stern, he pointed the lantern up and played the beam along the hull.

"There," Gilley said, pointing. "Do ye see it?"

McAfee did. As he watched, a fresh deluge of water seeped through the hull and came down in a crooked sheet. Evidently the combined attack by the creature and the constant pounding of the storm had done more damage than he had thought. "Get McCarter and Tanner down here," he told Gilley.

"I'll fetch 'em, Cap'n, but they ain't gonna be able to do nothin' much except slow that down. Even then, we get caught by the waves wrong, an' we're liable to get busted up so bad we'll go down in minutes. Do ye see how them timbers is cracked?"

"I see them, Mr. Gilley, and I understand the trouble that we're in. Get those men. Now."

Gilley retreated, moving quickly.

Standing in the water inside the hold, water that mimicked the waves outside the ship, McAfee listened to the surging currents pounding the hull mercilessly. The sea was relentless, he knew; she would break them and take them if she could. And the fates had conspired to trap him between a storm and the Britisher, with Ethan Swain almost within his reach. And Harrington, if he smelled blood from the broken ship, wouldn't hesitate to attack and take *Sunfisher* if he could as well.

In that moment, McAfee hated Ethan Swain more than he had ever hated the man before—more than McAfee had hated his father, his family, or anyone else he had ever known. Memories of Teresa still tortured McAfee. Especially the memories he had of the times he had seen Teresa swaddled in the sweat-soaked sheets of the bed Ethan had only then quit.

McAfee had found Teresa, had given her more than Ethan Swain had ever given her. How could she not have loved him and chosen to love Ethan instead? The puzzle still made no sense and remained beyond McAfee's understanding.

Every night, he dreamed of Teresa's death, saw again and again how Ethan had raged against her over the prisoners Teresa had decided to kill until she had drawn her blade and attacked even him. The battle had hypnotized the pirates and the crew of the ship they'd been taking as prize. Many times during the past, the pirate crew had seen Ethan and Teresa go at each other across a ship's deck or on a beach where they had put into port, but it had always been training and in sport. No one had known the battle they saw before them was anything more than another practice session until—

Footsteps creaked along the ladder, signaling the return of Gilley with McCarter and Tanner. They waded through the water that sloshed across the ship's bottom.

In little more time than McAfee took to make his own assessment of the situation, both men agreed that no repairs could be done without putting *Sunfisher* in dry dock. Too many of the timbers were cracked, creating fissures that ran several feet.

"Mayhap them fissures was already there from us running against *Brown-Eyed Sue,* or from that attack by the damned whale," McCarter said. He was a lean man from Georgia. A man who had been a thief, then a shipwright, then a thief again when the shipbuilding business didn't pay well enough or fast enough to support his gambling and drinking habit, or keep ahead of his bad luck at cards. "An' this storm, Cap'n, why this storm is like to be the death of us all."

"What would you suggest, Mr. McCarter?" McAfee asked, though he was certain he already knew.

McCarter spat into the water and scratched the back of his neck. "I'd recommend goin' to Callao an' patchin' her up." He shook his shaggy head. "I can caulk her fer now, but that ain't gonna hold with all this rough water an' her bein' damp as she is. But me, Cap'n, why I can't say as how she'd even make a return trip without comin' apart. Maybe we could save her if'n we got her towed."

McAfee took a measured breath and let it out. "With the Britisher lying between us and Callao, going to Callao isn't an option. If Captain Harrington even gets an idea that we're vulnerable, he'll be drawn like a pig to blood."

The three men were quiet for a time. Only the booming crash of the waves against the hull and the erratic rush of sloshing water filled the hold.

"If we're going to make it home," McAfee said, "we're going to need another ship. Whether to tow *Sunfisher* or to transfer to. There's one a few miles away. If we move quickly enough and bravely enough, I can have my revenge, we can have a fortune in whale oil, and we can have a new ship before the Britisher knows what we're up to."

CHAPTER 30

Pacific Ocean 12° 31' S. Lat.—98° 42' W. Long.

"WHAT ARE WE going to do?"

Ethan finished the knot he was working on, then looked up at Professor Bullock. "We're going to live through this. That's the only plan I have. As to the exact manner that we're going to accomplish that, I'm still working out the details."

Professor Bullock took his glasses off and cleaned them. "Not an exact science, is it?"

"It's a work in progress." Ethan sat on the mainmast and peered up at the port hull. Heavy rain continued to fall, and the winds blew hard enough that he had to lean into them to keep from being blown off his perch on the mainmast. He glanced down at the water. So far there had been no further movement within the whale, or maybe it had been so small as to be imperceptible.

Bill had constructed makeshift shelters along the port hull. He'd stripped sailcloth from the mizzenmast and fashioned tents that protected the crew and the Bullocks from the harsher aspects of the storm. Shelter, Ethan knew from experience, helped keep a man's spirits up when he was otherwise facing an impossible situation or task. The port hull and the men were less than ten feet away, but with the canvas canopies and the storm swirling around them, they might have been in another world.

Katharine Bullock and Robert Oswalt pulled a basket of food up from the hatch where Holy and two other men had loaded it. Food was another important morale booster, but Ethan had denied the crew any liquor despite the fact that Captain Folger and Larson drank.

Another tent covered the bow falconet that he and Robert had freed and had others help them haul to the port hull. They had mounted the small cannon to the hull as best they were able, thinking if they were forced to they would at least get a few shots from the weapon before the falconet ripped free of its makeshift moorings. He hoped they'd never have to find out.

In addition to the tents, Ethan had also assigned some of the men—himself included—to securing a fishing net from belowdecks to the portside railing between the foremast and the mainmast. The net had small mesh that would hold a man's foot without slipping through. If the storm continued, sleeping on the hull wasn't going to be possible without risking being tossed or blown into the sea. But sleeping in the fishing net, while not comfortable, was at least possible. Lying out in the open and getting drenched wasn't something he was looking forward to. He only hoped that the net was too high up for the creature inside the whale to reach.

"Do you really think you can get this ship upright again?" Bullock asked.

"Aye," Ethan said confidently. "That part of the plan is the simplest. Like as not, *Reliant* will come up by herself all right. With all the ballast and cargo she's carrying, she won't have much choice once the wind stops blowing. That's why a ship is designed the way she is with a hold separated from the waist and packed the way she is: to make her bottom-heavy so she'll stay upright in squalls and rough water." He looked over his shoulder and up at the dark clouds. "This weather here is just rougher than most."

"I'd never planned on getting that intimate with the details of sailing," Bullock admitted.

"A man going out on the sea," Ethan said, shaking out another piece of rope he'd cut to use as ties for the fishing net, "even for pleasure, he should know how the sea is and how his craft stands up to her."

"Should I ever be so inclined to go out on open water, which I very much doubt after these past few weeks of experiences, I'll keep that in mind."

"At least you're starting to think you're going to get out of this, Professor."

"That," Bullock said, glancing down at the water under the fallen sails and near the dead whale, "remains to be seen, doesn't it?"

Ethan finished another knot. "The real problem is figuring out how to deal with that thing down there." He nodded toward the whale corpse.

Since Parsons had been killed and dragged away, none of the men had willingly left their places on the port hull. Only Ethan's commands and example of doing things himself had gotten most of them moving.

"The whale is dead," Bullock said.

"But that isn't all there is to it, is it?" Ethan asked. "There's something living inside it."

Bullock nodded. "I think so."

"What?"

"I don't know."

"You're a scientist, an educated man, and you've seen what this thing is capable of. You've seen how it hunts, and you know how it attacks. Give me your best guess. I'll start with that."

For a moment, Bullock was quiet. "The one thing I am sure of is that whatever that creature is that's living inside the whale, no one has ever seen its like before."

"That doesn't help."

"There are different possibilities. And I don't know which I cling to more fiercely. None of them make sense or even lend to a working hypothesis. From the reports I've seen, this creature has been hunting in these waters since 1797."

"The year the falling star crashed into the ocean near Easter Island."

Bullock gazed at Ethan. "You knew that? Or you've been talking to my daughter?"

"Katharine told me."

"So you already know the possibilities that exist."

"That the creature is something that has been living on the ocean floor that no one has ever seen before. I have trouble with that one. Men have been going to sea for a long time. New things are found and discovered, but not generally in waters they've been working in."

"But no one has seen the giant squid the sperm whales eat," Bullock pointed out. "If you had not shown me the pieces of beak from the ambergris, I would never have believed you." The professor gazed at the water. "Another possibility is that the creature was somehow inside the falling star and arrived here from somewhere else. That the falling star wasn't a falling star and was instead some kind of container or vehicle that came from a world other than ours."

"I find that one even harder to accept," Ethan admitted.

"As do I. But while I was on Easter Island, I spoke to a native who told me the people there believe their island is the Navel of the World, and that things from other places outside our world show up there with some regularity."

"I've heard those stories, too," Ethan said. "That's why they were supposed to have built the *moai*."

"Exactly."

"But I haven't ever seen anything from other places there. Those people don't even have enough to feed themselves."

"Still, it's a possibility. The only other possibility is that whatever that thing is, it's some kind of supernatural entity."

"A demon from the burning pits of Hell?" In spite of the bleakness of their situation, the ship being knocked down and his whole career as a captain—and maybe his life—being forfeit, Ethan had to smile and shake his head.

Bullock frowned, then smiled himself. "Doesn't sound much better than the other two, does it?"

"No," Ethan admitted. "But there are a lot of elemental things about the sea, Professor. If ghosts and ghost ships and such were to exist, the sea would be a perfect place for them. Kind of like the albatross in 'The Rime of the Ancient Mariner.' It wasn't a real creature in Coleridge's poem, just a figurehead for the bad luck that the sea dealt to the sailor."

Surprise showed in Bullock's gaze. "I didn't know you were interested in literature."

"I read," Ethan said. "My father always told me that a man who wants to make something of himself needed to be a man who knows his way around a book. Sailing as I have, I've met people who have been around books. Some of those people don't know how to talk to common folk, but I've never seen one who didn't have a head full of ideas."

"If we should ever get out of our present predicament, I think I'd like to talk to you at greater length."

Ethan shook his head. "I'm nobody, Professor. I'm a might-have-been. Even if I'd stayed honest and not become a pirate, I'd probably be nothing more than a mate my whole life. Becoming a captain, a legitimate captain with an honest ship under him, that just wasn't in the cards for me."

"Then when you get us out of this, what do you plan on doing?"

"I haven't tried to think that far. Mostly, I'll try to keep from getting my neck stretched." Ethan struggled not to think of the future. Everything looked dismal and dark. He turned his thoughts again to the creature that lurked within the whale. "You think whatever is living inside the whale is a parasite?"

"Possibly."

"I've seen parasites on fish, Professor. If you kill the host, generally the parasite dies, too."

"I don't think that is the case here. I don't think that thing is a parasite in the sense that you're used to seeing."

"If it's not, what else could it be?"

Bullock gathered his thoughts for a moment. "Are you familiar with Portuguese man-of-wars?"

"I've seen them."

"Do you know much about them?"

"You can't eat them," Ethan said, "and if they sting you, it hurts like blazes. The stings will kill some men."

"The man-of-wars are actually made of four different creatures," Bullock said. "Each of them with a different life survival skill, and none of them capable of living on its own. The relationship is called symbiosis—different creatures living together out of mutual need for the other."

"How did those creatures live before they got together?"

Bullock shrugged. "I don't know. Neither does science as we know it."

"Do you think this thing is like that?"

"The whale isn't. We know that from what we know of the whales. They live independently as organisms. They also exhibit family and social hierarchies that are surprisingly more complex than that of herd animals such as deer or schools of fish. But perhaps this creature is. Perhaps it requires symbiosis but is so far from where it usually lives that it seized the whale as the closest replacement it could find."

"And it feeds on men."

"It has learned to," Bullock agreed.

"Why didn't it go back wherever it came from?"

"Simple." Bullock spread his hands. "Because it can't. Perhaps a return is physically impossible, or perhaps it doesn't know how."

"So this thing reminds you of the man-of-war because it lives within the whale?"

"No. That is one facet, but the primary reason is because of the venom that thing uses. The venom is necrotic—meaning it is capable of killing and breaking down flesh and blood-based tissue. Both dead men I have examined, like the unfortunate Mr. Parsons, have exhibited the same response. The man-of-war stings its prey with injectors, then attaches other tentacles to the captured creature that pull its prey's flesh into the feeding areas of its body."

"You think that was what the tentacle was that killed Parsons? That it's down there feeding on Parsons now?"

"Yes," Bullock said. "However, the man-of-war we're familiar with has no real control over its shared body. A man-of-war has to float wherever the wind blows it, and trap and eat whatever fate brings to its clutches. The thing that lives within the whale chooses to hunt, and it has managed to go where it has wanted to through the whale. At least, according to the journals I was given to study for this assignment, and you've witnessed the whale's aberrant behavior firsthand yourself. You've also seen that it has absolute control over its appendages. It is not completely trapped in an unresponsive body."

"Now that the whale is dead, what is going to happen to the creature within it?"

"I don't know," the professor answered.

"It can't stay with the whale's corpse."

"No, but neither may it be able to escape. Or it may not want to."

"Until it finds something else to crawl into."

"Exactly. Its template for survival may include having a symbiotic host at all times." Bullock was silent for a moment. "I also think that if the creature is from some other place than our world, it might have needed the time within the whale to adapt itself to live in ours."

"You think it has changed itself?"

Bullock nodded. "Or been changed."

Ethan surveyed the fishing net strung from the port railing and judged the effort acceptable. He would have liked to have the structure tighter in case they did have to spend the night in it, but under the circumstances it wasn't possible. Still, anyone sleeping there could tie himself in place so he wouldn't end up in a pile at the center.

He wiped rain from his face and thought briefly of joining someone under a tent on the port hull. Despite the inclement weather, he thanked God that the South Pacific never got as cold as the Atlantic.

A few minutes later, Katharine joined them, carrying a small basket of food covered by a piece of sailcloth. "I've brought you something to eat," she said. "Is the net safe to sit on?"

"Aye." Ethan took a pile of loose canvas and spread it over the net. "You can sit there. It won't be comfortable, but at least it will be better."

"Thank you." Katharine unfolded a sailcloth remnant. "I also brought this to shelter the two of you while you ate."

Thankfully, Ethan helped Bullock stretch the canvas over them, making a small dome structure that hung over their heads and shoulders. The basket Katharine brought contained fresh pomegranates, bananas, mangoes, smoked fish, and bread.

Ethan helped himself, surprised at how hungry he was. He scooted the canvas on the fishing net over so he could watch the swirling dark water almost thirty feet below. At thirty-seven feet across her beam, *Reliant* was wider-bodied than packet ships and most merchanters, who depended on speed and fought against the passage of time constantly. Ethan only hoped that thirty feet was a safe enough distance from whatever lurked in the ocean beneath them.

"The crew feels confidence in you," Katharine said.

"It may prove misplaced," Ethan replied. "We're not out of this yet."

"No, but most of them believe that you are the best chance they have of escaping this situation alive."

"What do the others think?"

Katharine hesitated. "That they're going to die."

"Well then," Ethan said with a trace of irony, "I'm certainly better than that."

"None of them want to trust Captain Folger," she said. "Mr. Larson has tried to create some support for the captain among the crew, but each attempt has only met with failure."

Ethan had noticed the few times Larson had gone among the men, but had chosen to ignore it.

"The last time Mr. Larson approached the men, Mr. Fedderson told him that he would throw him into the ocean if he heard Mr. Larson say another bad word about you."

"I apologize."

Katharine looked at him curiously. "You apologize?"

"I apologize for Bill," Ethan said. "I've known him for a long time. He's got a foul mouth when he gets stirred, and I'll wager he was stirred when he talked to Larson."

"He was," Katharine admitted, "somewhat indelicate in his handling of the matter, but succinct nonetheless. But Mr. Larson did understand Mr. Fedderson's message. He hasn't been back."

Ethan peeled an orange and quickly sectioned the fruit. He dropped the peel over the side of the net. The peel fluttered in the wind, flipping end over end, then landed on the dark water with the bright orange side up. He watched the peel intently, but nothing bothered it.

"I have been wondering," Katharine said. "Why are you letting Captain Folger and Mr. Larson drink while you forbade the other men?"

"Because I need the men sharp."

"There's more to it than that." Bullock looked at his daughter. "Mr. Swain is a canny tactician. By allowing the captain and Larson to drink, he's also allowing them to distance themselves from the crew. They'll sit up there and get drunk as lords, not paying any attention to Mr. Swain's rules and direction, and create more ill will for themselves on the part of the crew. Captain Folger and Mr. Larson believe themselves to be showing defiance, when in truth they're showing contempt for the rest of the crew and no cool heads for surviving this situation."

Katharine shifted her gaze to Ethan. "I see. And you planned all that?"

"I didn't plan it. I'm just taking advantage of it."

"Why?"

"Because," Bullock said, "it beats having to kill those two men."

Katharine stared at Ethan. "You would do that?"

"That wouldn't be my first choice," Ethan answered, unable to lie. "Killing the cap'n and Larson might split the crew, make them decide whether or not they trusted me to make the right decisions for all of us or only for myself. Right now I've got the crew all headed in the same direction."

"But you would kill the captain and Mr. Larson if you felt you had to?"

Ethan hesitated, then decided to go with the truth. "Aye. If it meant being able to save you and your father, these men, and this ship."

Katharine was silent for a moment, and the silence stretched into discomfort for them all. Ethan kept his attention divided between the food basket and the water below.

"If you'll excuse me," Katharine said a moment later, "I'll go see if Mr. Jordan can use any further assistance."

Ethan thanked her again for the food, but felt bad about the sudden way she left. He looked at the professor. "I apologize to you, Professor. I shouldn't have spoken so crudely to her."

"Should you have lied then?"

"I couldn't do that."

"And if you had, she would have known. Take that from someone who has tried in the past to lie to her for her own benefit."

"She seems to have high expectations of me."

Bullock nodded. "Katharine has high expectations of everyone, and even higher expectations of those she cares about."

"She shouldn't do that with me. I'll only disappoint her."

"On the contrary, I believe you challenge her. Your mere presence, the dichotomy you represent with your past and with your behavior, are forcing her to come up with a new paradigm for men."

"I don't know what 'paradigm' means," Ethan said, feeling suddenly inadequate as well as uncomfortable with the conversation. Still, the interest he had in the young woman wouldn't let him remain silent.

"A model, if you will."

Shrugging out of the canvas, feeling the weight of the sailcloth where the material had bunched and trapped pools of rain, Ethan stood. "You might tell her for future reference that the only thing she needs to know about men like me is to stay away from them. We're nothing but trouble and probably have only the shortest and dimmest of futures."

"Oh, I'll not tell her that," the professor said. "I learned a long time ago to not stand in the way of my daughter's chosen course. I think it would be very much like trying to stand in the way of yours."

Ethan pushed all thoughts of Katharine Bullock from his mind. The young woman represented too many things that he could never attain. He peered down into the water.

"What are you planning?" Bullock asked.

"We've got two whaleboats left to us after the storm hit," Ethan said. The port whaleboats remained hung in davits and would have to be cut free and managed through the sails or lifted over the port side. The stern whaleboat had gotten smashed when Larson had taken his crew out several days earlier. Another had been lost taking the whale with the burned face. "Those won't be enough to get us to safety. There's one more down there."

The remaining whaleboat lay trapped under a sheet of canvas. Only the outline gave its position away.

"I thought you said we couldn't hope to reach Peru in whaleboats."

"We could hope to, Professor. But I don't think it would happen. Our best chance is to remain with *Reliant*."

"Then why do you need the other whaleboat?"

"Should the ship sink as a result of this storm, which I don't believe it will but I do believe in being prepared, two whaleboats won't be big enough for us to carry enough food and water and passengers to safety with the distance we'll have to travel to the mainland. Even three aren't big enough to do that safely, but three are better than two."

Bullock was silent. "That thing, whatever it may be, is still waiting down there. I trust you'll be careful."

"It's a little late for that."

CHAPTER 31

Pacific Ocean 12° 31' S. Lat.—98° 42' W. Long.

ETHAN LED THE way down the deck of the knocked-down ship. Creel, Holy, Robert, and two other sailors followed him down.

Stroud and his marksmen kept watch over Ethan and his crew from the portside railing and the fishing net strung below, all of them encamped beneath sailcloth to keep their powder as dry as possible. Stroud had taken care to point out that he couldn't guarantee any of the muskets with all the dampness in the air. Only when carefully guarded by oilcloth would the powder stay dry. As soon as Stroud and his sharpshooters set up to fire, they exposed the powder to the dampness, and delaying to take the oilcloth away might prevent a shot that would arrive in time. Still, Stroud had kept an extra musket wrapped for himself and had half his men keep their weapons wrapped. Bill Fedderson manned the falconet that had been removed from the bow. Katharine and Professor Bullock remained in the fishing net with new coils of rope recovered from the ship's hold, prepared to throw them out to provide a new avenue of a hasty retreat from the water if necessary.

The storm continued unabated, as did the pounding rain. The unceasing precipitation was beginning to take on biblical proportions.

Clad only in his sodden clothing and remaining barefooted to better manage the rigging and ropes, Ethan wore his fighting knife—recovered from one of Larson's lackeys—at his hip. He would have felt more confident with a brace of pistols as well, but the weather prevented that.

Ethan kept close watch on the dead whale, wondering if he would even see the whiplike move that might impale him as he'd seen happen to Gabe Parsons. He also couldn't help wondering if he was going to die by the action of something earthly, unearthly, or demonic. What would happen to that spark of him, the essence that the church elders in Nantucket had talked of, if he were killed by something unearthly or demonic? Would the thing seize that part of him and keep it in thrall? Could his death today result in eternal damnation?

Easy, he told himself. *Ship those oars. Stay focused on the task at hand.*

Reaching the mainmast, Ethan climbed from the rigging and stood on the rough timber. His callused feet served him in good stead. He glanced at the foremast and saw Creel standing ready there.

"Are you ready, Creel?"

"As I'll ever be," Creel replied. Like Ethan, he wore a makeshift harness of ropes with another line tied to the back. The theory was that if he fell into the ocean or if the monster sprang at him and he couldn't see the thing, Robert and the other man holding the retrieval line could haul him in like a prize catch. Holy and Samuel Deering manned the rope tied to Ethan's harness.

Without another word, Ethan walked forward along the mast. At twenty-seven inches wide, the mast was not impossible to walk along even in the gale winds. He saw the masthead bob where it touched the ocean, and he knew that the vibrations would pass through the water. Fish always knew when something was in the water with them. Two triangular sharks' fins headed for the spot.

Thankfully, the covered whaleboat was little more than halfway out along the masts. However, *Reliant's* mainmast was eighty-five feet long from rail to masthead, and the distance put him over forty feet from the ship. Along the way, he had to pass by the dead whale lying in the space between the masts.

The pale flesh where the blubber blanket had been removed stood out clean and white as bone.

For a moment, Ethan thought he saw the skin pulse where the blubber had been cut free. But when the motion wasn't repeated, he guessed that it was an illusion caused by the rain and the wind and his own nerves.

Pausing at a point even with the whaleboat, Ethan took out another coil of rope he'd carried over his arm. Rigging hung in the water with the sailcloth, and would have served his purpose if it hadn't been for the thing hiding in the whale. He bobbed more out on the mainmast than he had on the ship, more aware of the ocean's ceaseless fury churning beneath him.

When Creel set up opposite him on the foremast, Ethan threw the coil of rope over to the man while holding on to one end. Creel missed the coil of rope, but it made it over the foremast. He retrieved the rope while Ethan made his end fast. Then Creel pulled the rope taut between the two masts and secured it.

After testing the rope and being encouraged by the tautness, Ethan swung onto the line and started making his way hand over hand toward the canvas-covered whaleboat. The hemp bit into his hands, and hanging at the ends of his arms reawakened all the bruises and aches his body had accumulated over the past weeks. Waves constantly swept across his lower body, pulling at him again and again and causing a frantic anxiety that impelled him to flee.

Mastering his fear, Ethan drew even with the whaleboat and dropped ten feet to the whaleboat. Holy and the other man holding on to the rope tied to Ethan's chest allowed enough slack to make the drop. The boat slithered under-foot and tried to skate away, but he kept his balance and threw himself into the boat's bottom. The sailcloth covering the boat shook and shivered, and the pools of water rattled and sounded faintly tinny in the falling rain.

Ethan ripped his knife free and slashed at the sailcloth over the whaleboat's prow. He hated damaging the canvas, but he knew that once they had the ship upright again it could be repaired. Once the prow was free, he shoved the canvas down in front of the boat. The plan was to tie on to the whaleboat with the spare rope Creel had carried out, then pull it free of the canvas and back to the ship. From there, the crew could pull the whaleboat back around to *Reliant*'s port side and prepare it with the others.

A warning prickle spiked across the back of Ethan's neck just ahead of Creel's shout.

"Ethan! Look out!"

A sliding, whickering noise sounded to starboard. Ethan spun and spotted the slither under the canvas that raced straight for him. He dropped to the bottom of the boat, narrowly avoiding the tentacle that ripped through the canvas and speared straight for his head. Up close, he saw that the tentacle was covered with an iridescent glitter, the same blue-green of a corpse left out too long and gone to rot.

He couldn't fathom how the thing had seen him. Somehow it had known he was there—had sensed him or felt him in some fashion. If he had been in the water, Ethan thought he could have better understood. Fish had the ability to sense things in the water, the size as well as the proximity.

The tentacle came back, flashing straight for Ethan's head. He moved back, and the limb smashed into the whaleboat's bottom with a booming thud. Knife already in hand, Ethan swung at the tentacle, which was at least as thick as his forearm.

The keen blade sliced through thick skin and hard muscle. Yellow ichor sprayed over Ethan, and for a moment he was horrified that the creature had vented its venom over him. But there was no burn, no pain, no sudden breaks in his flesh. He remained whole.

Blood, he realized, wiping at the mess that dappled his chest. The thing had bled yellow blood over him.

Nothing he'd ever seen had yellow blood.

The tentacle continued to slap the water, but the limb seemed to be moving blindly.

"Ethan!"

Glancing up to tell Creel that he was all right, Ethan watched in horror as another tentacle snaked through the air, coming up behind Creel. Ethan pushed himself up and tried to shout, but before his voice ripped from his throat, the tentacle took Creel full in the back.

The impact knocked Creel from the foremast. The tentacle trailed over the foremast and followed Creel into the water like an obscene umbilical cord.

"Ethan!" Holy yelled.

Turning, Ethan tracked two more movements beneath the canvas that closed on his position in the whaleboat. Across the water, he saw the line in Robert's hands grow tight, then Robert and Dickie Louis were yanked into the water. Robert knew how to swim, but Dickie didn't.

In the next instant, the rope harness around Ethan's chest and midsection seized him with bruising force. The air was forced from his lungs as he was yanked up above the two tentacles. He held on to his knife as Holy and Samuel Deering hauled the line in.

Remembering the line that stretched up between the mainmast and the foremast, Ethan looked up in time to grab the rope with his left hand just as he caught against it. Unable to slide over the rope, Holy and Samuel's efforts only trapped him against it, holding him like a fly in a spider's web.

It got Creel! It got Creel!

Holy and Samuel Derring shouted warnings and pulled fiercely, only succeeding in pinning Ethan more tightly to the rope.

Below him, the two tentacles twisted and turned, coming back at him with inhuman speed. Musket explosions sounded in the distance. Musket balls threw spume up from the raging ocean and *thwacked* into the whaleboat. One of the tentacles was hit by musket fire, but that had to have been more by luck than by design. The other tentacle kept coming, joined only a moment later by the first tentacle, which now wept yellow blood from a wound.

Ethan swept his knife through the rope strung between the two masts as well as the rope holding him to the harness. The hemp parted like a cat's whisker under a barber's razor. Holding on to the piece of rope tied to the mainmast, Ethan swung toward the mast. He slid his knife between his teeth just as one of the waves reached up to slam into him. The knife blade bit into his lips, and he tasted salt and sucked drops of blood into his lungs, but he clung to the knife and forced himself not to cough.

Another wave splashed him as he reached the apex of his swing on the other side of the mainmast. He pulled himself up the rope, swinging like a pendulum beneath the mainmast. Gripping the mainmast, he pulled himself up and took the knife from his teeth.

Standing in a bent-kneed crouch to better keep his balance atop the bobbing mainmast, Ethan glanced at the place where Creel had gone into the sea. There was no sign of him. Even if there were, Ethan knew he was in no position to help. Sudden death was alive and moving in the water below.

Creel was gone. There would be no rescue from the jaws of death at the last moment. He was dead—or as good as.

Feeling guilty and angry and scared and ashamed, Ethan turned and fled along the mainmast just as the two pursuing tentacles whipped over the top in pursuit of him. They slammed into the mainmast so hard they sent vibrations throughout the timber's length.

"Ethan! Run!" The command came from over two dozen throats aboard *Reliant.*

Obeying his own fear, certain that the tentacles would catch him at any moment, Ethan ran. The mainmast was only partially finished wood, serviceable but not polished smooth. His callused soles found traction easily, and even the drenching sheets of rain had a hard time clinging to the wood. As fast as his feet slapped against the timber, his heart hammered faster in his ears.

He crossed forty feet in little more than a dozen paces, then threw himself forward into the rigging, where Holy and Samuel were already scrambling to safety. Slipping the knife between his teeth again, Ethan climbed the loose rigging. He didn't turn to see if the tentacles were still behind him; the fearful look on the faces of Bullock and Katharine on the fishing net let him know that.

Within a few short feet of the fishing net, Ethan hurled himself upward. He caught the net's edge in hooked fingers, then swung his body up and around, landing on his back and rolling immediately to his feet. He pushed Bullock and Katharine before him.

"Move," he ordered. "Get above. Now!"

Bullock guided his daughter toward the portside railing.

"Stroud," Ethan commanded. "Have your men fire into the whale."

Stroud roared orders, and the marksmen shifted targets. Ethan knew the musket balls probably wouldn't penetrate the dead whale's blubber, but if the creature inside were sensitive to pressure and vibrations, maybe the impacts of the shots would at least prove confusing.

The two tentacles, one of them still bleeding yellow blood, stopped moving five feet beneath the fishing net where Ethan stood. He stared at them, uncertain whether the tentacles had reached their limit thirty feet up from the waterline, or if the musket balls striking the whale's flesh had proven distracting enough to break the thing's concentration.

"Ethan!"

Looking through the fishing net, past the poised tentacles, Ethan spotted Robert swimming below. The young man's arms and legs thrashed through the water as he made for the ship. For a moment, Ethan thought Robert was going to make it and prepared himself to go down and aid him if possible.

Then Robert jerked in the water, robbed of the muscle control he'd had. A moment later, one of the tentacles smashed through Robert's head. Bloody pieces of his skull flew several feet away. Then the tentacle twitched and yanked Robert beneath the water.

The sailors taking cover on the port side of the ship cursed and cried out in disbelief.

The two tentacles below the fishing net dropped and disappeared under the sea.

"No, you sorry bastard," Ethan stated grimly. "You're not going to take what you want and just return to your hiding place." He turned and made his way across the fishing net, then climbed down to *Reliant's* hatch. He went into the hold and picked up a lantern and a small keg of whale oil that was used to fill the lanterns aboard ship. He also found and took a bottle of the captain's whiskey.

Dripping wet and shaking, Holy met Ethan at the door. The sailor gazed at the keg over Ethan's shoulder, then at the lantern he held in one hand.

"What are you doing, Ethan?" Holy asked.

"All that I can, and all of it too late to save Creel or Robert or Gabe or Dickie or Nate. But I'm going to see it done all the same. Step aside."

Reluctantly, Holy swung out from the hatch.

Ethan used the net system Holy had rigged to transfer some of the other supplies he'd been told to move up to the portside railing area in case the ship went down. Getting the small barrel of whale oil to the fishing net was difficult. In the end, Holy aided him, though he didn't ask any questions or offer advice.

At the edge of the net, Ethan broke open the small barrel with his knife. He walked out along the mainmast, keeping his eyes on the whale below. When he reached a point above the carcass, he upended the barrel and poured the oil over the whale.

"Mr. Swain," Folger called drunkenly. "What the hell are you doing? You can't be throwing away my cargo like that."

Ethan ignored the man, concentrating instead on covering the whale's flesh that remained exposed above the waterline. Close in to *Reliant* as the whale was, the waves that lapped at the corpse were small and didn't crest the top of the mass.

When heated, the whale oil was liquid and poured easily. But inside the barrels, the oil got thicker, almost like pudding, often forming crusts at the top. If left exposed to air, the purer spermaceti and junk oil would turn from straw-colored liquid to white wax.

Once the barrel was empty, Ethan threw it into the water. He expected the creature to strike the barrel with one of the tentacles, but the barrel floated for a time before taking on so much water that it sank to the point it almost disappeared. Ethan uncorked the whiskey bottle and poured the contents over the oil and the whale. The liquid didn't pour in a straight line, but enough of the whiskey hit the oil-smeared body that he was satisfied.

Ethan turned the lantern's dual wicks up, encouraging a cheery double blaze inside the device. Then he drew the lantern back and threw it at the whale's back.

The lantern shattered against the whale's back. Glass shards scattered. For a moment, Ethan thought both wicks had gone out, but the design had been retooled with an eye toward precision. At least one wick, and perhaps both, caught the whiskey on fire and quickly spread in a rolling ball of flame to the slower-burning whale oil.

The scent of burning whale flesh, so familiar because of the constant exposure to the tryworks, filled the air. Blisters came up on the whale's body, then popped and exploded and bled more oil from the corpse that the flames lapped at greedily.

Ethan didn't know for certain, but he hoped that the harvested oil would help ignite the natural oil held in the whale's blubber. With luck, the creature would burn down to the waterline. The flames might even creep inside the body and burn from the inside until the corpse sank and hopefully took the parasite with it.

The answer to that puzzle would never come, though. A moment later, a hole opened in the section of flesh where the blubber blanket had been removed. Tentacles ripped at the section, tearing the hole bigger and bigger, forcing the initial hole to yawn open. Then the thing—a thing that reminded Ethan of the Portuguese man-of-war Professor Bullock had been comparing the creature to earlier—poured out of the whale's body and into the ocean. It seemed to be made almost entirely of tentacles, but there was a central mass as well, though Ethan couldn't discern any details about it. The creature's color was iridescent blue-green, shiny and bright as a fish's scales, deepening almost to black at its center.

"God help us," Holy whispered as he held his position on the mainmast beside Ethan. "What is that thing?"

"I don't know," Ethan replied. He wished he had another barrel of whale oil, another bottle of whiskey, and another lantern because the creature continued oozing rapidly through the large opening in its host and away from the flames that burned the whale. He raised his voice. "Bill, fire that falconet!"

The small cannon boomed, throwing out a spray of grapeshot that sparkled the sea surface and struck the strange creature. Yellow blossoms of blood showed on the blue-green skin. Before Ethan had a chance to guess at the amount of damage done to the creature, it disappeared under the water.

"Did you see that?" Holy asked in a hoarse voice. "It was carrying Creel and Robert and Dickie Louis in its tentacles. Ethan, *they looked like they were still alive!*"

CHAPTER 32

Pacific Ocean 12° 31' S. Lat.—98° 42' W. Long.

NIGHT BLEW IN before Ethan was prepared for it. He hadn't realized how many hours had been lost in preparing the ship for a long stay under the storm, which continued and made everyone's stay aboard *Reliant* even more inhospitable.

Not that there was much chance of rest. After seeing the creature emerge from the whale's corpse, dragging the bodies of their shipmates behind, *Reliant's* crew had gone into perpetual panic mode. Frequently, one sailor or another would scream that he had seen movement in the water, which would cause a sudden deluge of oil poured into the water, followed by a torch that would light a pool of flame that covered the sea over twenty feet each time. After long, tense minutes, the flames would burn out when the oil was exhausted. The sea would return to darkness, and the tension would begin climbing again within the crew. Ethan had been forced to use up some of the freshwater supply to put out fires that had come too close to *Reliant's* deck.

With the canvas and rigging caught up around the whale's bulk, *Reliant* showed no signs of coming up from the ocean. Ethan still believed the ship would right herself, though. All she needed was time—and maybe a little help.

The rain continued, as did the winds slamming in from the west. With the absence of the sun to warm the day, the night turned cold and inhospitable. Unable to take the chill and the wind, *Reliant*'s crew migrated down to the fishing net Ethan had strung between the foremast and the mainmast. They huddled beneath folds of canvas that had been cut free of the mizzen and shared lanterns gleaned from the whaleship's supplies in an attempt to stay warm.

The moon refused to come through the swirling cloud bank, but incandescence somehow managed to thread through. Fog lifted—or descended, Ethan was so tired that he didn't know—and looked like pale fire in the distance. The uneven planes of the sea held a silvery luster that constantly shifted, appearing and disappearing like a magician's trick.

Ethan sat on the mainmast in his raincoat. Fatigue had settled over his mind and dulled his wits, but the fury at Creel's and Robert's deaths and the murder of the other men lay coiled in the pit of his stomach and burned. He kept watch over the water. Barrels of oil, a crate of whiskey bottles, and pine pitch torches Ethan had made from the sap and pulp of pine timbers stored in the hold stood ready in cargo netting that was tied to the mainmast. The pine pitch torches caught fire quickly and could be easily made up.

The whale's corpse had finally sunk into the brine after burning for nearly an hour. The smoke had been thin and quickly torn away in the wind, hardly leaving a fleeting stain to mark its passage. The weight of the whale sinking and hanging from the chains that bound it to the whaleship had turned *Reliant* a little farther, causing great consternation among the crew and no little blame being heaped upon Ethan's shoulders.

"Ethan." Professor Bullock carried a lantern over and sat beside him.

Ethan resented the professor's intrusion but couldn't bring himself to voice that. "Aye, Professor."

"I don't believe the creature is going to leave these waters until we are all dead," Bullock stated quietly so that his voice didn't carry. "I haven't told any of the others."

"It's a fish, Professor," Ethan objected. "A shark gets drawn to a place by the scent of blood, but if there's nothing to eat there, it goes away."

"True, but a shark is an animal. It has limited intelligence."

"And you don't think this thing does?"

"I read all the journals and reports of the attacks attributed to this thing. There was a small packet ship, *Crystal Bell,* which hailed out of New York. She shipped a ten-man crew regularly between the United States and Fort Astoria in

Oregon Territory, carrying cargo and mail and furs brought in by John Jacob Astor's Pacific Fur Company."

"I've heard of the place," Ethan said, hoping to cut the story short. "It was established there a couple years ago."

"Yes," Bullock said, "and the British are very desirous of it because the trade there is brisk and has made Astor a rich man. In fact, some of the investors who sent me on this mission are concerned that Astor will lose that fort to England."

"You had a point, Professor."

Bullock wiped at his face, scraping away the heavy mist. "Sorry. I'm tired, and my mind is always working. I've got more facts and figures in this thick skull of mine than I'll ever use." He sighed. "The point being that *Crystal Bell* was found devoid of life not far from where we are."

"There are pirates in these waters," Ethan said. "British privateers. Any number of things could have happened."

"The ship's cargo was intact," Bullock said. "The ship itself had suffered massive damage. Not unlike what we've seen the creature we're dealing with capable of delivering. The creature is an intelligent hunter. I believe it will stay here, hunting us, until we are all dead or we have proven that it can't take us without further risk to itself or that we are beyond its reach. Just as I believe it did to *Crystal Bell*."

"It's an animal," Ethan said, wishing he didn't doubt his own statement so much.

"So is man," Bullock replied. "Why did this ship stop at the Galapagos Islands?"

"To take on water."

Bullock nodded. "And to take on turtles. Which was served up for meals, as I recall. Those islands are hunting grounds for sailing men. They hunt there to feed. This ship has become such a hunting ground for the creature. I believe it recognizes that. You remember I told you that the whale came back to the area where *Brown-Eyed Sue* went down?"

Ethan nodded.

"As the wind filled the sails and blew the longboat east toward you and this ship, Katharine and I saw the corpses of the drowned and murdered sailors and pirates pulled beneath the waves. I believe that the creature stayed there. Stayed there and fed. Just as it plans to stay here and feed."

Gazing down into the dark water, Ethan said, "It can't reach us here."

"Can't?" Bullock asked. "Or hasn't yet?"

The silence stretched between them.

"Look," Bullock said, "I don't know what you have in mind to aid in our escape from this situation, if anything, but I want you to know that I am willing to help you. In any way that I can. I know you are grieving over your friends, and maybe you even doubt your ability to handle this situation, but you must try." The professor glanced over his shoulder. "These men believe in you. They will follow you if you lead, but they are frightened, and most of them won't act on their own because they haven't trained themselves to."

"I've already gotten three of them killed," Ethan objected in a tight voice. "It was my fault the creature abandoned the whale's body so that it might be even more dangerous than ever."

"You had a good plan. Burning the whale could have resulted in the creature's death or a debilitating injury. It didn't." Bullock struggled to find the words he thought he needed. The lanternlight played over his strained features. "A scientist is wrong more times than he is right. Most men are, too. That's how life is constructed: so that we may make mistakes that we can learn from."

The wind shifted, pushing against *Reliant* from a different direction. The ship creaked, then settled in again.

"If I may be so bold. You have already learned things about what you want to be in life by making mistakes."

Ethan looked at the older man. "You don't know me. You don't know anything about what pushes me."

"Mr. Swain, you have already proven to yourself that you don't want to be a pirate. Else you would have stayed in that life. You have also proven yourself to be a man others can rely on." Bullock hesitated. "What I'm saying is that you're a man of action. You look for command. You relish it."

"And I've gotten men killed who I claimed as friends. There aren't many men that I can say that about, Professor. How many people are my mistakes going to kill?"

"No more," Bullock stated, "than will be killed by your decision to remain passive in these circumstances."

"The creature may go away."

"It may not," Bullock argued. "Every hour that passes while it remains down there is an hour it has to heal and scheme and plan. And to grow hungry again."

"It can't reach us up here."

"Do you really want to take that chance?"

"No."

ONLY A FEW minutes later, Ethan crept through the rigging to the mizzen. He carried an axe tied across his shoulders.

Finding volunteers after what had happened to Creel, Robert, and Dickie proved difficult. In the end, only Holy Jordan had the courage and both hands to follow Ethan. Two more people would have been better, but Ethan accepted Holy's offer.

They cut through the mizzen rigging to arrange quick escapes upward if it came to that. Together, standing with one foot on the lower mizzen and the other foot on the 'yards, they started swinging the axes. The sharp edges cut into the weathered timber with difficulty, sending shivers through its length. Holy prayed the whole time, keeping time with his blows to emphasize his pleas for forgiveness and divine mercy.

"Have you cut away a mast and rigging before?" Ethan asked.

"No." The word came in the middle of prayer.

"When we cut it free, *Reliant* should stand again. The ballast and cargo will pull her up. With as much weight as we're cutting from her, she'll come up quick."

The rest of the crew and the Bullocks had already taken measure and tied themselves into the net strung between the mainmast and the foremast. Ethan had also ordered Stroud to keep the men from throwing oil into the water and setting fire to it until he and Holy were clear.

"You'll have to keep a sharp lookout when the timber gives way. The mast will crack the last few inches after we get through most of it. We'll try to cut the whale's body free of the railing when we get level."

"Aye," Holy said, and kept chopping with the same frantic, powerful stroke that matched Ethan's own.

The water lapped at *Reliant*'s deck constantly. The sound of their efforts carried across the ocean and came back at them from the passing waves ten feet below, interspersed with periods of long silence between waves.

"*Eee-than.*"

The cold voice sent shivers down Ethan's spine as he paused and looked around. He glanced at Holy, who had ceased his prayers.

"Did you hear that?" Ethan demanded.

"Aye," Holy responded. "I did."

Ethan took a better stance on the 'yard and mizzen and held the axe in both hands before him. The axe made a more powerful weapon than the fighting knife he'd sheathed on his leg.

"*Eee-than.*"

This time the voice sounded stronger and clearer, and it was recognizable.

"That's Creel," Holy said.

"Maybe," Ethan admitted. He didn't want it to be true, but he was afraid it was.

"Do you believe in ghosts?" Holy asked.

"No," Ethan answered grimly, and he knew that whatever was calling to him had to be worse than any haunt he'd ever heard of.

"*Eee-than.*"

Motion in the water to port drew Ethan's attention. As the waves shifted and the moon's incandescence hit right, he spotted Creel's head bobbing on the water.

Creel's face was slack and pale gray in the moon's glow. His mouth was open. As Ethan watched, the sea rolled into Creel's mouth and out again.

"God preserve us," Holy whispered. "That's no ghost. That's a demon. Maybe that was no falling star the professor saw all those years ago, Ethan. Maybe it was a demon cast out of Heaven itself and meant for the fiery pits of Hell. Only somehow it ended up here instead of there."

"Stand easy, Holy." Releasing the axe with one hand, Ethan took his friend by the shoulder.

"It's a demon," Holy persisted. "It's only took on Creel's body like a suit of clothes. He's dead."

"I know," Ethan said. "He *is* dead." But he said that more to remind himself than to agree with Holy.

Slowly, the rest of Creel's body emerged from the water till he stood only ankle deep in the calmer water at the bottom of the overturned whaleship. He stood erect, silvery water hanging in his hair and from his unshaven face. His gold earrings glinted at the sides of his head. Immersion in the water had washed away the blood from the wound where the tentacle had ripped through him, but Ethan still saw the torn fabric because the pale skin showed through underneath.

"*Eee-than.*" The voice sounded asthmatic, wheezing in and out. "*Eee-than.*"

Voices from above grew louder. Ethan heard Creel's name several times.

Then lanternlights played over the corpse that walked on water near *Reliant's* port railing.

"*Fear, Eee-than. Be . . . fear.*" The words came out as a command. "*Fear . . . me. Fear . . . me.*"

Musket blasts cut loose overhead. Several balls splashed into the water, and several more struck Creel's corpse.

"*Eee-than,*" the corpse croaked. Creel's head jerked as a ball took him in the temple. White bone showed through gray, bloodless flesh. "*Die, Eee-than!*"

Creel's face and head suddenly shattered, coming apart in gory flaps as the tentacle inside suddenly erupted through and whipped across the intervening distance.

"Move!" Ethan shouted, getting his shoulder into Holy and shoving him toward the rigging. Even as he went into motion himself, dropping the axe and following Holy up the rigging, swaying with the bobbing whaleship, Ethan knew that two tentacles zipped through the space he'd just vacated. He climbed, the hemp tearing at his fingers and toes, as he tried not to think that the tentacles were going to pierce him at any moment.

Liquid poured down in three streams from above. The strong smell told him the liquid was whale oil. Some of the oil spilled over him, drenching him. He kept moving, feeling the rigging twist suddenly. Unable to stop himself, he glanced down and saw that a tentacle had threaded through the rigging squares between his legs, narrowly missing him. He climbed, but watched in horror as the tentacle coiled around and started to come for him. Then another deluge of whale oil came down, drenching him again. Some of the oil splattered over the tentacle as it locked back and prepared to plunge forward like a cobra. When the oil hit it, the tentacle immediately withdrew, whipping away like a scalded cat.

Stroud, Professor Bullock, and Bill hurled pitch pin torches after the oil.

Still climbing, knowing the ropes by touch after all the years spent aloft, Ethan watched as the torches tumbled end over end and smacked against the whale oil that floated on top of the water. The oil caught fire slowly, then leapt across six feet of space, occasionally becoming islands as the currents tore the oily pool apart.

The tentacles retreated, but not before recovering Creel's body and dragging it back under.

Not about to give up any food, Ethan realized bitterly. He hauled himself up to the fishing net and stood gasping for breath.

"It's watchin' us," Merl Porter said. His lip and face were still puffy from

Professor Bullock's blow earlier that day. "Damn thing knows it's got us treed like raccoons. It knows we ain't got no place we can go."

"Pipe down," Bill ordered.

"The hell with that," Merl snarled. "That thing can snatch us offa this ship like a kid snatchin' cherries from a tree. Ain't none of us safe up here. It can get us anytime it wants."

"I told ye to pipe down." Bill took a threatening step forward. "Ye'll pipe down, or I'll wallop a knot on yer noggin that'll be there till Gabriel blows his horn."

"Ye just try it, ye one-handed orangutan," Merl blustered, going for the knife at his side. "Why, ye're just curryin' favor to a pirate son of a bitch what's—"

Bill started forward, rocking across the fishing net. Men scattered away from the two.

Moving fluidly, feeding off the anger and frustration that filled him, pumped from the residual fear that hammered inside his body, Ethan slid his fighting knife from its leg sheath and whipped it under Merl's chin.

Merl froze, his hand still wrapped on the hilt of his knife.

Only the lapping of the waves against *Reliant*'s hull sounded over Merl's and Ethan's harsh breathing. The blood roared in his ears, and he knew he hovered on the edge of taking the man's life.

Fear showed in Merl's eyes.

Controlling the savagery that filled him, Ethan spoke in a calm voice. "Merl Porter, there's only one crew on this ship at this moment. *My crew*. I'll live with them, and, if it should come to that, I'll die with them. I'll fight for them against you and against that vicious beast down in the water there."

Merl swallowed hard, his Adam's apple bobbing past the knife blade.

"If you start to raise a weapon against one of my crew again," Ethan said, "I'll cut that ugly head from your shoulders and throw your body from this ship." He paused and leaned in closer. "Is that clear?"

"Aye, sir," Merl croaked.

"Then step away, and don't give me cause to regret sparing your life."

Visibly shaken, Merl stepped back and nearly tripped over the tangled canvas at his feet.

Ethan didn't take his eyes from the man as he sheathed the fighting knife. "Mr. Stroud."

"Aye," Stroud replied.

"You can uncock that musket now," Ethan said.

Merl glanced over his shoulder, only then realizing that the marksman had centered his sights on his head.

"I thought ye had it taken care of," Stroud said. "Just thought ye might be winded from yer climb below."

"Thank you, Mr. Stroud."

"Aye, Cap'n," Stroud said.

"Cap'n!" Folger yelled in drunken outrage. He stood uncertainly at the top of the port railing, where he'd insisted on staying. "He's no captain! The man's a pirate! Deserves to have his neck stretched! I'm the master of this vessel!"

"I'd be happy to throw him overboard," Bill offered.

Ethan glared across the distance at Folger. "One crew," he said. "That's all. Your choice whether you're in or out. Take your vote now."

Folger glared around at the rest of the crew hunkered in the temporary safety that Ethan had caused to be constructed. No one, not even Larson, tried to take his side. Reluctantly, Folger sat and pulled his makeshift shelter back around him.

Ethan looked at the crew, then at the Bullocks. He silently damned himself. No matter what happened, the die was cast. The mutiny had been bloodless, but it had been a mutiny all the same.

HOURS LATER, ETHAN lay awake in blankets under the sailcloth. The sea below burned yet again after frantic shouts of, "There it is! There it is!" He hadn't seen the creature since he and Holy had gone below to cut away the mizzen.

He peered at the distant eastern horizon, wondering how much longer it would be till morning. Without the moon and the stars, he couldn't even guess. Time dragged, and he felt his heart beating in his chest.

"Mr. Swain," Katharine Bullock called softly. "Are you awake?"

Ethan didn't speak, didn't move.

Katharine sighed. "I know you're awake, Mr. Swain. You've been lying over there for a long time, and you haven't once drifted off."

Giving in, Ethan sat up. "Aye, Miss Bullock. I'm awake. And you should be asleep."

"I can't sleep either. My head's too busy." Katharine sat only a few yards away, huddled up to the mainmast as Ethan was, the sailcloth drawn up to her chin.

"Perhaps you could talk to your father." Ethan looked around the fishing net and saw that most of the men were asleep. He'd posted guards from Stroud's marksmen, and those men were in position near barrels of whale oil.

"I have been talking to him," Katharine said.

Ethan had heard them talking, but he hadn't listened because his mind was turning on his own thoughts.

"He's asleep now," Katharine went on.

"What do you need?" Ethan asked.

"I wanted to talk."

"We are talking."

That observation gave the young woman pause. "Might I come over there? I'm afraid our voices will wake those who are sleeping."

And you don't want the wakeful ones to overhear you, Ethan thought. He felt certain there were more men awake than sleeping. "Can it wait till morning?"

"I would appreciate the chance to talk now."

"Then please join me." Ethan shed the sailcloth and the sodden blankets, then pushed himself up to a sitting position on the mainmast. It felt uncomfortable to be talking to her like he was in bed, though he wasn't even able to sleep on the fishing net.

Katharine brought over her own blankets and sat a few feet from him on the mainmast. "I know Father has already apprised you of the creature's possible intelligence."

"Aye."

"The way that it baited you using Mr. Turpin's body is a further indication of that."

Ethan nodded politely.

"But the way that it used Mr. Turpin to speak to you?" She shook her head. "No one has ever seen or heard of anything like that."

Not for the first time Ethan noticed the way her long chestnut hair hung in ringlets over her shoulders and reflected the dulled lights of the lanterns the crew had hung from ropes across the sleeping area, as if the lights would ward off the darkness and the monster that hid within the night.

"Some have," Ethan said.

She looked at him.

"Holy's of the opinion that the falling star carried a demon to the bottom of the sea," Ethan said. "That it missed Hell and ended up here. In the Caribbean, there's a religion called vodun, where people give themselves over to gods and spirits that take possession of them."

"You've seen this?"

"Aye," Ethan said. For a moment, his head filled with the sound of the hammering drums and the sight of nearly naked men and women dancing in wild abandon, some of them carrying flaming torches. Teresa had taken Ethan deep into the jungles to see the secret places that she had learned of.

"I've heard of the vodun religion," Katharine said. "It's supposed to have come from West Africa, brought by the people enslaved to work on the plantations two hundred years ago. I thought the religion had gone out of practice."

"They still practice it," Ethan said. "But they hide it now."

"Do you believe their dark gods and spirits possess them?"

"I don't know."

"Were you ever possessed?"

Ethan hesitated. *Bewitched,* he thought, thinking of Teresa, *but not possessed.* "No."

"Then you don't know that they were merely faking the effects or suffering from a mass delusion."

"No. But the thing down there wasn't imagination or fakery."

"I am not suggesting that it was."

"Then what are you suggesting?"

"Nothing. I'm trying to put these past experiences into a framework that we can use to understand what we're up against. We know very little about the creature."

Ethan silently agreed.

"Father does have a new theory about why it stayed in the whale so long, though. He came up with it because of the things you revealed to him about whaling."

"Something I told him?"

Katharine nodded. "The information about the sperm whale blubber, the ambergris, and the giant squids has led him to believe that the creature might have been swallowed by the whale and held prisoner. Father believes that the creature was unable to penetrate the squid's blubber layer because of the oil's chemical composition. That is also why Mr. Maxwell's book, wrapped in oilskin, remained undamaged after Mr. Maxwell was killed and . . . dissoluted. Father experimented with the venom he recovered from Mr. Parsons's body. The oilskin surrounds the venom and holds it perfectly sealed in suspension within the oil."

"I didn't know he did that."

"Mr. Turpin recovered Mr. Parsons's body for a short time while you were busy organizing the crew. Father has hypothesized that the creature had never encountered blubber before. If you will recall, the creature emerged from the section of the whale where the blubber blanket had been cut free. If the creature has been inside the whale for sixteen years, maybe at some point it grew too large to crawl back out. Maybe what it first viewed as a home or fort became a prison."

"The creature was able to strike from within the creature," Ethan argued. "That doesn't sound like it was trapped."

"Maybe we're wrong," Katharine said. "It's possible. But while you were on the rigging climbing back up and the whale oil was poured over you, the tentacle pulled back."

Ethan remembered. "But it should have known the whale oil couldn't hurt it."

"The fact remains that it didn't. It fled, pulling back instead of choosing to attack you."

"It also talked," Ethan reminded. "Maybe it used Creel's voice, but it talked."

"The creature might have been using Mr. Turpin the way a hunter would use a moose or duck call."

The thought was more than a little disturbing to Ethan. "How would it know the words? Or my name?"

"I don't know. Maybe it has a sense beyond the five that we understand. The way that animals seem to know danger is around before there is a physical clue."

"But to know my name?"

"Was Mr. Turpin dead when you saw him last?"

"Aye."

"Then it had to be the creature that spoke. How else would you hear your name and the other things that you heard?"

Ethan had no answer.

"When all that is left is the impossible, Mr. Swain, that must be the answer. That is what science is founded on. It then becomes the scientist's job to find the rules that redefine the impossible as possible."

"But this seems more than impossible."

"Have you ever heard of a man named Luigi Galvani?"

"No," Ethan admitted.

"He was a teacher of medicine in Bologna, Italy. In 1780, he used electricity to make the muscles of an amputated frog's leg flex and move. Several sea creatures utilize electricity as part of their defensive or offensive reflexes. Torpedo fish discharge electricity. In 1772, John Walsh experimented with those electric fish. Maybe this creature is electrical in nature as well and somehow that gives it a different means of communication than we are used to. Maybe even a whole new spectrum of senses."

"That sounds even more impossible."

Katharine hesitated. "Do you remember when Mr. Parsons was . . . was killed?"

Ethan did. It was one of the things he was sure he would never forget.

"Mr. Parsons, at the time of his death, believed the creature was talking to him. He claimed to hear its voice in his head."

"So did Nate Phillips."

"So what would cause them to say something like that if it wasn't true?"

"I don't know. Gabe Parsons, God rest his soul, was not an imaginative man." Despite his fatigue and frustration, Ethan found himself drawn into the young woman's conversation. Everything seemed unreal, as if the world he had always known had been turned over on its side as *Reliant* had.

"My father and I believe the creature is intelligent, Mr. Swain," Katharine continued. "But that doesn't mean it's as smart as a human. If the whale did not aggressively swallow the creature, I think concealing itself is one of the creature's defenses. It realized, on whatever level of intelligence you choose to attribute to it, that it was different than anything around it. It chose the whale as a hiding place."

Ethan turned the possibility over in his mind. "So what is the creature going to do now? Find another hiding place?"

"Possibly. We don't know how intelligent it is. We don't know what its normal impulses are. We have to assume that the basic needs—of food, shelter, and safety—are the ones it will immediately address. The creature could be lingering here simply because it knows it will be able to feed for a while. Or, if it is a thing of higher intelligence, it might be waiting to kill us all to protect the secret of its existence."

JONAH MCAFEE STOOD on *Sunfisher's* stern quarterdeck. The night had turned chill and remained wet. He squinted through the spyglass at the bright light that stood out against the western horizon.

The lights, he was certain, belonged to *Reliant*. But why they were all clustered instead of placed about the ship as running light he had no clue.

He kept *Sunfisher* running black, which was a dangerous thing to do in all the fog, but he kept only a light press of canvas into the wind. Since he knew *Reliant* had taken a whale, there was no hurry.

The fog shifted, swirled, and completely disappeared in places. The storm was breaking up and gave every indication it might be gone soon. The rain would probably be another matter. Firing cannon in the rain was problematic. Powder got wet, and balls sometimes jammed in the barrels, requiring effort to get them clear and operational again.

But piracy, especially for a pirate captain in desperate straits, was never convenient. *Sunfisher* continued to take on water despite the best efforts of the crew—even when threatened by their own demise. The ship was riding lower in the water than she ever had unless she was full of cargo. She also handled like an arthritic sow on ice.

Gilley climbed the companionway stairs.

"I hope you've brought me good news, Mr. Gilley," McAfee said in a calm voice.

"No, Cap'n. Afraid I ain't got none of that." Gilley jerked a thumb back amidships. "Got the bilge pump goin' full blast, but she ain't gonna keep up with the water comin' in. McCarter and Tanner says them cracks is gettin' worse. Could be that hull'll go anytime."

"Even so," McAfee said, "she'll carry us through to our prey."

Gilley turned and squinted through the dark fog. "Ye see 'em, Cap'n?"

"I do, Mr. Gilley. Have the crew drop anchor."

"Here?" Panic whitened Gilley's features. "But, Cap'n, if'n ye see that ship, let's go fetch it."

"Not in the dark, sir. We'll arrive with the morning. Sailing in from the east, they'll have the sun in their eyes when we hit them. We'll look like the very shadow of death come calling."

"Will *Sunfisher* make it till then?"

"She'll have to, Mr. Gilley. You can tell the crews belowdecks that I said that. Salvation is at hand, but they have to hold their pace to get us there."

"Aye, Cap'n. I'll tell 'em."

"Well then, Mr. Gilley, I hope they're more enamored of those prospects than you appear to be."

"Aye, Cap'n." Gilley hurried back down the stairs, shouting orders to drop the anchor.

McAfee wiped the lenses on the spyglass and looked through it again. The fog whirled, then parted, and he saw the collection of lanterns against the deck of the overturned whaleship. The lanterns looked like a nest of fireflies in the darkness. For a moment, he could make out the net that had been stretched from the railing between the mainmast and foremast. All of *Reliant*'s canvas was buried in the sea.

"Damn you, Ethan Swain. What have you done to that ship?" McAfee swore. As far as he could tell, *Sunfisher* had managed to give the British ship the slip for the time being. Or perhaps Harrington's vessel had suffered damage from the storm as well.

The fog covered the whaleship again and remained thick for a time.

McAfee's thoughts flew, chased by fear. If something was drastically wrong with *Reliant*, there was no chance in Hell that any of them would survive.

Even as he was thinking those thoughts, a pool of fire ignited in the water in front of *Reliant*. He didn't know what to make of that.

CHAPTER 33

Pacific Ocean 12° 31' S. Lat.—98° 42' W. Long.

"ETHAN, WAKE UP. There's a ship a-comin'."

Struggling through layers of sleep, Ethan came awake with Bill Fedderson shaking his shoulder. The stink of burning whale oil still hung in the air. The fires had continued all through the night.

"A ship, Ethan," Bill said, offering his hand. "Careful of the young miss, there."

As the blood started flowing through his limbs again, lifting the chill of the morning from him, Ethan grew aware of the weight against his right side. He looked down and saw Katharine Bullock's chestnut locks resting against his shoulder. He couldn't remember going to sleep, but they both must have done so while talking.

She woke in that moment, looked up at him with those dark eyes, and looked embarrassed.

"What ship, Bill?" Ethan asked, taking the man's hand and rising stiffly.

Bill pointed to the east. The sun was just coming around the world, penetrating the heavy cloud cover with pink and purple and gold rays. He recognized the ship and the rake of her sails at once. She sailed straight from the east, looking like a shadow cut from black velvet against the dawn.

"*Sunfisher.*"

"Aye," Holy agreed, studying the ship through a spyglass. "I thought I knew her from somewhere."

Renewed anxiety thrilled through Ethan. "Was there any activity on the creature's part last night?" He had been awake for most of it.

"No," Bill said. "I've talked with the lookouts. We passed the night quiet enough. But it looks like the mornin' isn't gonna go that way. Ye know, Ethan, that damned beastie may have up an' jumped ship in the middle of the night, an' now we're up here left high an' dry a-facin' pirates."

Ethan glanced down at the dark water. He remembered the discussion he and Katharine had been having before he'd fallen asleep. Either way he went with the possibilities Katharine had presented suggested that the creature wouldn't leave.

"I don't think so, Bill," Ethan said. "Rouse the men and get them ready."

"Aye, Cap'n," Bill said.

Ethan was as surprised by the address as he had been at Stroud's use of the rank the night before. But he didn't say anything as Bill trotted off to wake the few sailors that still slept.

"Mr. Stroud," Ethan called.

"Aye, Cap'n," the big man said.

"Get your men up on the port side. I want them hidden as best as they can. I want you and two of your men to cover McAfee. The rest will attempt to rake *Sunfisher's* decks. On the next volley, you will listen for my orders. None of you will fire until I give the order. We'll get one chance for you to prove your marksmanship without them knowing we've got you and your men aboard. After that, they'll respect it."

Stroud got his men up and retreated to the port side.

Ethan ordered the other sailors up to the port hull as well, then turned to Bullock and Katharine. "You two would be better off inside the ship."

Bullock nodded.

"Be careful, Mr. Swain," Katharine said.

"I will," Ethan replied. "Holy, get them belowdecks."

"Aye," Holy replied.

Marshaling his reserves, still tired from the previous day and the uncomfortable and short night, Ethan stood at the edge of the fishing net and stared at the approaching ship. He took time to put fresh powder and balls into a musket and a brace of pistols. He wore his fighting knife sheathed at his leg and a cutlass at his waist. He kept the musket in his right hand.

A fine, gray rain continued to fall, peppering the ship and the sea. He hoped that the weather would play in their favor, keeping McAfee's cannon wet and problematic. But dealing with the pirate captain in a hand-to-hand battle wasn't something Ethan looked forward to.

Sunfisher dropped anchor seventy-five yards out. She rose and fell on the waves that picked up again past *Reliant* lying beam-ends in the ocean. Even as he noted that, though, Ethan also noted that the ship rode extremely low in the water.

McAfee, dressed in resplendent attire, stepped into view on the prow. He kept *Sunfisher* turned into the curling waves with her back to the wind so he could move quickly if he chose to.

"Ethan Swain," McAfee said exultantly as he leaned forward on the prow railing. "This is an unexpected pleasure."

"State your business, McAfee."

"Are you in a hurry?" McAfee asked. "From the looks of things, you won't be going anywhere anytime too soon."

"We'll go right along when we're ready for it," Ethan said.

"Is it you that I'm going to be dealing with then, Ethan?" McAfee made a show of peering past Ethan. "I'd heard Captain Folger was master of this vessel."

On the portside railing, Folger stood and rocked drunkenly. "I am."

"Mr. Fedderson," Ethan said without turning around, "sit that man down."

From the corner of his eye, Ethan saw Bill sweep Folger from his feet. When Folger kicked and cursed and swore dire threats, Bill straddled the man while two other sailors bound and gagged him.

McAfee grinned. "So you've gone and made yourself captain, have you, Ethan?"

"You'll deal with me," Ethan said.

"Well, good for you." McAfee applauded. "I knew you weren't cut out for a mate's job even though you managed to fool yourself for a while. Captains are born, not appointed by some group of nervous investors or politicians. They're men who reach out and seize what they want. You and I know that."

Ethan waited. He constantly checked the water where the creature had been. The uncertain light of the newly birthed dawn spread a sheen across the waves that made visibility below the waterline poor. He watched *Sunfisher,* seeing how slowly she responded to the natural roll of the ocean, like she was fighting the sea at every turn instead of conquering it or going with it.

"If I had been you," McAfee taunted, "I think I would have waited till I had found a better ship to take from its captain."

"If you think so ill of her," Ethan said, "I don't know why you came for her."

"I want the cargo," McAfee said. "and I want Professor Bullock and his daughter. I saw them."

"You're going to have to take them then, Jonah, because I'll not give them up."

Rage flushed McAfee's face. "You insolent bastard."

"I was taught by one of the best."

"I can take that ship," McAfee said, "and kill every man jack aboard her." He shouted, directing his attention past Ethan. "Do you bastards hear me?"

None of Ethan's crew responded.

"They know of you," Ethan said. "They know you're a murderer as well as a thief. No man aboard this ship expects any mercy from the likes of you."

"As God is my witness, Ethan," McAfee said, "I'll turn this ship and present you broadsides. You've got that one falconet. I will put that ship on the bottom of the sea."

"Do that," Ethan said calmly, "and you'll lose this cargo and the professor and his daughter."

"Maybe they won't feel as defiant as you."

"It's not a matter of defiance, Captain McAfee," Bullock yelled as he emerged from the hatch. "It's a matter of self-preservation. We've already seen your brand of mercy aboard *Brown-Eyed Sue*."

"Damn you then," McAfee roared. He added several obscene oaths. "We'll come get you, Ethan. You've got nowhere to run." The pirate captain ordered two longboats into the water and filled them with pirates bristling with muskets and swords. Ethan counted ten men in the first boat and eleven in the next. He guessed that was nearly half of McAfee's remaining crew according to the estimates Cochrane had given. Even so, twenty-one men more than matched the number of men he had left aboard *Reliant*.

If they gain this ship, Ethan knew, *we can't stand against them for long.* But he knew that there was no choice; McAfee would see them all dead anyway. He gazed again at the dark water at the ends of *Reliant*'s masts.

Had the monster gone? Was it full or dead or sleeping? Had it been injured by the repeated fire attacks? Hurt but not seen for certain?

There was no way to know. Ethan took a deep breath and let it out. He stood on the fishing net and centered himself as Teresa had taught him. If their luck held, the powder would be dry for their first shots. If Stroud's men were careful, they could keep firing for a while.

The two longboats started across the water. The oarsmen worked slowly and carefully, and all of them were afraid they would be fired on. Musketmen among their ranks took aim on *Reliant,* but Ethan knew they would hold their fire and hope intimidation would win the confrontation rather than provoking a battle themselves.

The dark water remained empty. Ripples spread out from the mast ends.

Damn you, Ethan thought. *Where are you?*

The oarsmen pulled through quickly, sending the craft plunging through the water. They rowed up the waves, then crashed through on the other side.

At the halfway point, Ethan raised his voice and his own musket. "Mr. Stroud!"

"Aye, Cap'n."

"On my mark, then. With as much luck and skill as you have."

"Aye."

The longboat crews took aim at Ethan. Their threat was clear.

Ethan sighted down the musket barrel and aimed for the center of the long-boat. With the way *Reliant* bobbed on the water, he knew he could keep the shot within the craft.

The longboat oarsmen kept pulling through.

"Fire!" Ethan ordered in a loud, clear voice. He squeezed the trigger through and felt the brass-plated butts slam back against his shoulder.

Stroud's men fired immediately after, and the sudden eruption of musket fire took away all other sounds. Musket balls chewed into *Sunfisher's* hull, coaming, and deck. Several of the balls also tore through flesh and blood or smacked into bone.

Already moving, knowing a hailstorm of musket balls was headed his way, Ethan threw himself atop the mainmast. Musket balls ripped through the canvas that covered the fishing net in several places. More shots spun off the mainmast or dug into the wood.

"Mr. Stroud," Ethan yelled, peering down at the longboats. Black smoke obscured both craft for a moment.

"Aye, Cap'n," Stroud yelled back.

"Target the longboats, Mr. Stroud. I don't want a single man to reach this ship or be able to return to *Sunfisher*. The more we kill here, the fewer we have to contend with later."

"Aye." Stroud roared his orders.

Holding on to the mainmast, Ethan shoved the musket aside and drew one of the three pistols. He aimed at the lead boat and pulled the trigger. The hammer fell, but the pistol misfired. He drew his second pistol and fired just as the marksmen raked the boats.

Blood spewed from wounds the pirates suffered, and bodies pitched into the water. Before the echoes of the gunfire died away, tentacles rose from the water under the two longboats. There were at least two dozen tentacles. Several of them speared through pirates, ripping into their bodies and their heads, then yanking them into the water. The other tentacles grabbed hold of the longboats, crushing them into splinters.

There you go, McAfee, Ethan thought, spotting the pirate captain peering around the foremast, where he had taken shelter from the musket fire. *What do you think of your prospects of catching a monster now?*

In seconds, men and boats disappeared beneath the waves.

Shaking himself free of the amazement he felt, Ethan shouted, "Mr. Stroud."

Stroud's voice was a beat late in coming. "Aye."

"Target the ship, Mr. Stroud." Ethan drew his remaining pistol and took aim at *Sunfisher*. He pulled the trigger and watched as a man pitched from the bow a moment later. The shot was lucky, but it broke the pirates' stunned disbelief at what they had seen.

McAfee strode from the foremast. He aimed a pistol and fired at *Reliant*. His crew followed suit a moment later. Musket balls rattled off the whaleship's deck, some of them ringing from the great iron pots in the tryworks where the blubber was processed. A few of the bricks around the tryworks cracked and split off, bounced across the deck, and tumbled into the water.

"Get this ship out of here," McAfee barked. "Now!"

The pirates scrambled to obey, moving through the rigging and the sails.

"Mr. Stroud," Ethan called up.

"Aye."

"Fire as you will, Mr. Stroud." Ethan remained on the mainmast for protection but reclaimed his musket. He knelt on one knee, crouching over to guard the musket from the rain as he took a cartridge from his pouch and reloaded.

With *Sunfisher* already in place to take the wind, the sails filled, and she moved. But Ethan noticed how slowly she tracked across the sea, and he saw that her bow barely rose in the approaching waves. He guessed that she only had a day left in her before the sea took her. Probably less now that McAfee had lost half his crew.

"She's out of range, Cap'n," Stroud shouted.

Cheering broke out among the whaleship's sailors. Probably only minutes before most of them had been thinking they were dead men.

"Are there any wounded?" Ethan asked.

"Two," Holy called back. "Neither of them is serious."

"One," Stroud said. "He'll be fine."

"Professor Bullock? Miss Bullock?"

Father and daughter both answered that they were fine.

Feeling relieved, but knowing the hardest battle yet remained ahead of them, Ethan looked at the shattered debris that floated on the ocean. It was all that was left of the two longboats and the men who had ridden in them.

"Sail!" Bill cried. "I see sails off the bow!"

Turning, filled with an instant sensation of unease, Ethan studied the horizon and saw the tall ship leaning with the wind in the distance.

"What is she?" Ethan asked.

Bill took a moment to answer. "Damnit, Ethan. She's British. Got an English Union Jack flying high an' proud from her."

And that swept away all feelings Ethan had of success and most of his hope for survival. Still, the ship was a half hour or more out, judging by the distance and the way she was going to have to tack into the wind. He started planning immediately.

"ARE YE SURE this is gonna work?"

Ethan glanced up briefly at Bill hanging in the mizzen rigging above him. Bill lowered a bucket containing charges of gunpowder that had been measured for cannon loads.

"It should." Ethan had concocted the plan during the night, but he had planned on using it to kill the creature that lay in wait in the water by *Reliant*. Still, it would serve to help against the British, at least to cut their numbers down somewhat. He lifted three of the gunpowder sacks from the bucket and slapped them into the notch in the mizzen that he and Holy had cut the previous night. He had dried the notch out as best as he'd been able.

" 'Should' don't mean 'will,' " Bill pointed out.

"It's the best I can offer." Ethan wrapped the gunpowder charges in oilcloth he'd saturated in whiskey.

Bill looked in the direction of the approaching British ship. She was only minutes away now. "Mayhap we should try this before the Britisher gets here."

"We're going to try to blow this mizzen free of the ship, Bill. Even if we get upright, the English ship will have speed on us. And cannon. What I have planned is the only way. All we have is surprise, and we need to make every ounce of it work for us. We're in this for all or nothing."

Bill paused, then spoke in a low voice. "They'll kill ye when ye go over there, Ethan. Ye know that, don't ye?"

"Maybe not."

"They will, an' ye know it." Bill hesitated. "Ye should let me go in yer place, Ethan. I'm a cripple. Me an' ye know that. A one-armed man ain't worth much. Ye're a cap'n. Ye can get this crew home if anyone can."

Ethan tied a rope around the oilcloth to hold the gunpowder in place. "You and Holy can get this crew home. Folger knows maps, and if he gets too drunk, Professor Bullock—and probably even Katharine—can read them as well."

"If'n ye die at the hands of them British, I'm gonna kill Larson an' Folger straightaway. Larson for him killin' Timothy as he did, an' Folger for him a-gettin' us in the fix we're in now."

"That'll be on your head then, Bill. But I wish you wouldn't."

"Why should you care for them?"

"I don't," Ethan answered as he clambered back up into the rigging. "But even while I was a pirate, not a single innocent man died by my blade. I take some pride in that, Bill, but I take shame in that, too, because I can't say the same for the crew I shipped with." He drew level with the man. "I want a crew I can be proud of."

Bill offered his hand, tears in his eyes. "Fine then, Cap'n Ethan Swain. I'll respect yer wishes because I respect ye."

Ethan took the hand. "You do that, Bill. Just you see that you do."

"But ye should let me go talk to those Britishers instead of ye."

"I can't. That cap'n is going to want to hear someone that sounds like a cap'n, Bill. You don't. If I'm going to buy us any time at all, I need for that cap'n and his crew to be properly distracted." Ethan took a breath and looked at the British ship sailing toward them. "This is the only way. We can't count on the creature again."

STANDING ON THE fishing net, Ethan surveyed his impromptu battlefield. While he had placed the charges around the mizzen, Holy and his crew had run rope lines out to the end of the mizzen where it dipped into the ocean, and likewise with the foremast. The ropes were taut and straight. Thick knots were tied in the end of both ropes, which stayed eight feet out of the water at all times.

During the placement of the ropes, no sign had been seen of the creature. Professor Bullock believed the creature was still underwater, still feeding on the dead pirates it had taken only a short time before.

Kirkland, the Welsh archer in the crew, stood at Ethan's side. He carried his bow, but left the weapon unstrung.

"Do you see those knots?" Ethan pointed at the ends of the ropes tied to the mizzen and the foremast.

"Aye," Kirkland said.

"Can you hit these kegs at that distance with the wind blowing?" Ethan slapped one of the two five-gallon sorghum kegs he'd had Holy bring up from inside the whaleship.

"Cap'n," Kirkland protested. "That distance there, it's less'n thirty paces, it is. An' those kegs are big."

"You're going to be shooting from a ship riding the sea," Ethan said, "and you'll probably be taking enemy fire during the second shot if you don't immediately attract it on the first."

"I'll hit the targets, Cap'n," Kirkland assured him. "Me life on it, I will."

Ethan looked at Kirkland. "Your life on it," Ethan said, "and very probably everyone else's."

STANDING ON THE stern quarterdeck, Jonah McAfee watched the British ship avoid *Sunfisher* and sail around toward *Reliant*. The whaleship still lay on her beam-ends.

Evidently, the British held some respect for *Sunfisher*. But that, McAfee knew, would change the moment Captain Harrington of His Majesty's Royal Navy learned that *Sunfisher* had lost over half her crew.

"We should make fer the coast, Cap'n," Gilley said.

"We would never make it in this ship," McAfee said.

"I don't think we'll last as long as it takes the British to unload that whaleship, either. What difference does it make if we go down here or while tryin' fer the coast? At least if we try fer the coast, we won't have as far to go in the longboats."

"No, Mr. Gilley, we'll take our stand here." McAfee watched Ethan Swain through the spyglass. "Do you see Swain?"

"Aye." Gilley's tone indicated that he didn't care about Swain or the whaleship.

"You see, Mr. Gilley, your problem is that you don't know Ethan Swain."

"Ye've told me about him."

"Aye, but I haven't told you everything about him. The way he fooled us into getting trapped by that creature? That is the Ethan Swain I remember best. God, I loved him for the cunning he exhibited. I've seen him walk into a roomful of enemies—all of them wanting to kill him, set them at each others' throats, and walk out of that room more or less intact. He only did it once, but by God it was something to see." McAfee lowered the spyglass. "Give the order to get us under way, Mr. Gilley. I want us positioned upwind of the Britisher. In case Ethan pulls another trick, I want us there and ready to capitalize on it."

"*SUNFISHER'S* GETTING UNDER way," Holy announced.

Glancing past the British ship, which was dropping anchor a hundred yards east of *Reliant,* only a little farther than *Sunfisher* had dropped anchor over an hour earlier, Ethan saw that the pirate ship was sailing south, intending to pass behind the whaleship some thousand yards distant.

"He's leavin'," Bill said. "He ain't wantin' no more of this."

"No," Ethan said softly. "McAfee is waiting. He's one of the most patient killers you'll ever have the misfortune to meet."

Holy looked at the British ship. "Her name's *Formidable.*"

Ethan surveyed the eleven cannon visible on the ship's starboard hull, bringing her total to at least twenty-four, including the two chase guns set in her bow. She wasn't a frigate, but she was close. He guessed that the British captain had made the conversion from one of the ships he'd taken as a prize.

"Well, she's rightly named," Ethan said. "How many crew do you make her for?"

"Fifty or sixty," Holy said. "At least."

"Prolly not that," Bill answered. "I heard a goodly number of them fine British seaman was kilt on Charles Island when they tried to sneak up on ye."

Holy looked at Ethan. "Harrington will remember this ship. Maybe he'll even remember you. Are you sure you want to do this?"

"This isn't something I want to do," Ethan said. "It's something has to be done. There isn't another way. Just be ready. And keep your heads."

A group of Britishers walked to amidships. Ethan picked out the captain immediately because of the white-powdered wig and the uniform.

"Hallo, the ship," a young officer called out.

"I'm Cap'n Ethan Swain," Ethan called back. "Of *Reliant,* a whaleship from Nantucket."

"I am Lieutenant Anthony Cross, of His Majesty's Royal Navy," the young officer said.

"If I were you," Ethan said, "I'd have a talk with your navigator and your helmsman, Lieutenant. You're a long way from home."

The British crew laughed at the comment, but a harsh glance from the ship's captain quickly silenced them.

"We're here on the king's business, Captain Swain."

"I'm out here trying to earn an honest man's wages. Have one of your sailors explain the concept to you if you don't know what I'm talking about."

Only a few of the men laughed at that. The British navy was reviled for its practices toward enlisted men. The fact that the British sailors escaped every time a British warship put into port was one of the reasons the English had started impressing American sailors.

"If you'll pardon my frankness, sir," Cross went on, "you appear to be in a bit of a quandary."

"Just got knocked down by a squall," Ethan replied. "We'll have her up again soon enough."

The captain leaned in and talked to Cross quickly. Cross nodded, and asked, "Did you know there is a war on, Captain Swain?"

"Another one?" Ethan put irritation into his voice.

"Aye," the lieutenant answered. "As you are an American citizen, I am informing you that your ship is being seized by the king's navy and claimed as the spoils of war, as well as all cargo aboard her."

"I don't think I much care for that," Ethan said. "And I don't know if you can do that. I remember things didn't exactly happen that way on Charles Island. Maybe you'll be unlucky again."

Captain Harrington stepped to the railing. He looked to be in his fifties, a weathered and fit man who had gone thick in the middle. "Captain Swain, I expect your summary surrender within minutes or I will blow you out of the water where you sit. I do not tolerate cheeky bastards, and the mistakes made at Charles Island will not happen again. Do you understand me, sir?"

Ethan waited, counting the seconds, acting as if he didn't know what he was going to do. Then he lifted his voice. "I've got a marksman aboard this ship who can shoot the eyes out of a mosquito at this distance, Captain Harrington. What do you say to that?"

"Lieutenant Cross," Harrington said.

"Aye, Captain."

"Can you hear me, Captain Swain?" Harrington demanded.

"Aye," Ethan responded.

"Good." Harrington cleared his throat. "Lieutenant Cross, in the event that Captain Swain does have such a marksman aboard his ship, and I am shot dead, your first order of duty as the new master of this ship is to blow that filthy derelict from these waters. Is that understood, Lieutenant?"

"Aye, sir," Cross answered.

A faint smile touched Harrington's lips. "Captain Swain, unless you have two such skilled marksmen, you have five minutes to tender your surrender." He took out a gold pocket watch.

Ethan looked over his shoulder as if torn. He waved, as though he were waving off the sharpshooter he'd claimed to have.

"I did not get to be a captain in the royal navy by being a man afraid of dying," Harrington said.

"I can see that," Ethan replied. "I've got a woman aboard, Cap'n Harrington."

Interest flickered on the British captain's face. "An American woman? A white woman?"

"Aye," Ethan said. "I'd like to negotiate the terms of our surrender, Captain Harrington."

"From the looks of your present predicament," Harrington observed with a trace of a gloat, "you're hardly in a position to do that either."

"As a courtesy between cap'ns," Ethan suggested.

Harrington snapped his pocket watch closed. "Very well, Captain Swain. Do you have a boat left to you capable of making the trip?"

"I do."

"Then come." Without another word, Harrington turned and walked back to the stern quarterdeck as if he wasn't concerned about the possibility of a sharpshooter at all.

"ETHAN," KATHARINE BULLOCK said, "there's no guarantee that this will work."

Ethan clambered into the longboat tied up at *Reliant*'s stern. She was referring to the net that held a layer of whale blubber cut into Bible leaves against the bottom hull of the longboat. The longboat had also been one of the projects in his plan. The theory was that the creature would ignore the boat because of the blubber layer, thinking it was only a whale. There was also the hope that the creature was still full from all the dead pirates it had taken. It was doubtful the creature had left given the way they had seeded the waters with the dead from McAfee's ship.

"If it doesn't," Ethan said as he prepared the sail, "I'll be the first to know."

"Please don't joke." Katharine looked worried, but she didn't look weak. Ethan found that he liked that about her. "Even if you evade the creature, you're going to be stuck on that ship with the English."

Actually, Ethan full well expected to be killed within seconds once the plan was put into play. If he succeeded, he would buy enough time for *Reliant* to recover, get the wind behind her, and he would get killed sometime after that. Of course, *Reliant*'s escape also depended on how desperate Jonah McAfee saw his own situation. There was no mistaking how low *Sunfisher* rode in the water, nor in what had caused her to be in such a condition.

"Not for long," Ethan said, lying. "I should be able to escape during the confusion and catch up to this ship if I move quickly enough."

"And if you don't move quickly enough?"

Ethan smiled at her, wanting to leave her looking brave. "Then I'll catch up to you later."

"Promise?"

Hesitation froze Ethan for a moment. "Promise," he said. He glanced up at Bullock.

"Come, Katharine," the professor said, getting the hint. He took his daughter by the shoulders and led her back up into the shrouds leading to the fish net.

Ethan shook hands with Holy, Bill, and Stroud, then pulled the sail up on the longboat and let the wind catch him. The breeze was strong and pulled him swiftly forward. He knew McAfee was in position to take advantage of the wind as well, which was something he was counting on. When he'd seen *Sunfisher* sail in that direction, he'd actually gotten a little more hopeful.

As the longboat crossed over the section of water between the mainmast and foremast, Ethan's gut clenched. He expected at any moment for the creature to explode up out of the water, spear him with its tentacles, and drag him down. He kept hearing Creel's strained voice in his head.

Eee-than. Eee-than. Eee-than.

He turned his thoughts from that after he got halfway to *Formidable*. There were probably sixty men aboard, and eleven cannon pointed in his direction. And he thought he could seize the advantage in the time allotted between heartbeats.

The plan was audacious. And that was the only reason he thought it might work.

The sail carried him to the ship without mishap. A rope ladder was tossed down.

Four British Marines with muskets leaned over the railing and pointed their weapons directly at him. Lieutenant Cross joined them.

"Climb up, Captain Swain."

Ethan took hold and climbed to the deck. One of the Marines quickly checked him for weapons.

"He's unarmed, Lieutenant," the grizzled Marine announced.

"Thank you, Sergeant." Cross stood at attention. "This way if you please, Captain Swain. Captain Harrington would like to see you on the quarterdeck."

Ethan fell into line behind the young lieutenant. The four Marines flanked him, keeping their muskets at the ready.

Captain Harrington waited on the quarterdeck, staring up at the sunshine that had just started to break through the clouds. "Looks as though we might have a bit of fair weather after all."

Ethan stopped when the lieutenant waved him into place. "Thank you for the courtesy of seeing me, Captain Harrington."

A wolf's smile, full of teeth and devoid of mercy, split Harrington's face. He brought his hands from behind his back. One of them held a cocked pistol. He pointed the weapon at the center of Ethan's face.

"I am not," Harrington said, "a man used to being dictated to. Nor am I overly fond of the drubbing your damned whaleship handed my men on Charles Island."

"No, Cap'n," Ethan said quietly. Fear almost exploded his heart. For a moment he felt certain the Britisher was going to kill him. And if he did, no one aboard *Reliant* had even the small chance he had hoped to provide for them.

"Let's hope that your crew thinks well of you, Captain Swain," Harrington said. "Because we're about to find out."

"Aye, Cap'n," Ethan said as contritely as he could manage. He looked into Harrington's eyes, seeing McAfee's eyes and Teresa's eyes, too. God help him, had that look ever been in his own eyes? So cold and so calculating? If it ever had, then he deserved to die. *But not yet. Please, God. Not. Yet.*

Harrington pulled the pistol barrel back. "Get down on your knees, Captain Swain."

CHAPTER 34

Pacific Ocean 12° 31' S. Lat.—98° 42' W. Long.

HESITANTLY, ETHAN DID as Captain Harrington ordered. He marked the position of the captain and the lieutenant, as well as the four Marines around them. He noted that the lieutenant carried a pistol in a sash at his waist and that the sergeant carried a knife in his boot. They were all cards waiting on the table to be played.

"Lieutenant," Harrington said to his junior officer, "inform the crew and passengers of *Reliant* that if they don't surrender their arms at once, I am going to put a ball through their captain's head."

Cross relayed the message.

Ethan didn't even keep up with the words. From the corner of his eye, he watched as Holy reluctantly led the crew and the Bullocks out onto the fishing net.

"All right," Holy yelled across the water. "We surrender."

Ethan studied them, looking for Kirkland. The Welsh bowman was nowhere in sight. Ethan's stomach tightened, but he kept himself calm. Things would go very fast now. He reviewed his plan, wondering if he had thought of everything, knowing if he hadn't, it was all about to come to an end.

And there was still no way to know what part the creature would play.

"Get men over there, Lieutenant," Harrington ordered. "Have them take control of that ship."

"Sir, that ship isn't going anywhere. If we divide the crew, we may be hard-pressed if that pirate ship decides to close on us."

Harrington's gaze hardened. "That whaleship's cargo is worth a fortune. Part of that fortune—a large part of that fortune, I might add—is going to be mine. I want my interests looked after."

Immediately, Cross called out the orders. Three longboats of crew containing ten men each, letting Ethan know that *Formidable* carried in excess of sixty men because nearly forty more remained on the deck. Most of them were gun crews manning the four guns mounted amidships, two to a side. More would be below in the gun deck.

Ethan watched as the three longboats started across the water to *Reliant*. He half expected their oars to rouse the creature below, and was relieved when the three longboats rowed between the foremast and mainmast, obviously heading for the shrouds hanging in the water there.

Kirkland was a slim shadow that stepped out of the hatch. He nocked a flaming arrow to his bow and bent the weapon back.

"Go!" the Welshman yelled, then waited a half beat while the crew fled back away from the fish net's edge.

Stroud stepped out of hiding at the top of the port hull. He pushed one of the two powder kegs into motion. Held by a rope harness, the powder keg slid down the rope leading to the mainmast. When it hit the knot, the harness stopped sliding suddenly, leaving the powder keg hanging below, rocking slightly from side to side.

Kirkland released the flaming arrow, which streaked across the distance and hit the powder keg. The flaming arrow had been created using oily rags, but even those small rags affected the weight of the arrow.

Flames spread from the arrow to the oily cloth wrapping the powder keg. Ethan had instructed that the keg be broken open so the gunpowder inside could be easily reached. Besides the explosive powder, the keg was filled with broken glass and small stones broken out of *Reliant*'s ballast. The explosion as well as the glass and stones blew over the Britishers, turning many of them into bloody corpses in that instant.

By that time, while Harrington and Cross and the four Marines were frozen, Ethan was moving. He surged up from the deck, knowing if he failed that his life was measured in seconds.

Harrington started to turn back to Ethan. The sergeant lifted his musket and pointed.

Ethan caught the captain's gun wrist, shoved the pistol toward the sergeant, slid his finger over Harrington's, and pulled the trigger.

The ball crunched through the sergeant's forehead and punched through the back of his skull, throwing blood over the man beside him. He staggered back into the man beside him, dead on his feet.

Sliding his hand down the pistol, Ethan closed his fist around the long, octagonal barrel and yanked the weapon free of Harrington's grip. At the same time, he lifted his knee up into Harrington's crotch, connecting solidly.

Over on *Reliant,* Kirkland fired his second arrow, striking the second powder keg solidly. Flames wreathed the keg.

The British sailors in the longboat that had survived the initial blast could only watch in helpless horror as they tried to dig the oars in. The other two longboats had been decimated by the first powder keg.

Beyond *Reliant, Sunfisher's* 'yards suddenly bloomed with wind. The skull and crossbones spinnaker unfurled from the bow, and Ethan knew that McAfee was making his move as well.

Using the captured pistol as a club, Ethan backhanded Lieutenant Cross in the face, splitting his cheekbone open and knocking him from his feet. He dropped like a dead man.

The second powder keg blew, taking some of the mainmast with it but not touching the 'yards. The third longboat escaped destruction, but several of the soldiers aboard it were torn to doll rags.

Ethan set himself and shoved Harrington into two of the Marines, then hurled himself in the other direction toward the dead sergeant. He raked the knife from the man's boot, threw himself to the deck as the soldier who had been standing with the sergeant fired his musket. The shot went just over Ethan's head and dug splinters from the deck.

Coming up in a roll, Ethan extended his arm and slashed the Marine's throat. Blood rained down on him as he stood and grabbed the dying man. He whirled behind the man and felt the shock of impact as one of the other two Marines' shots struck the body. He pushed the body ahead of him, ramming the corpse at one of the Marines standing with his back to the starboard railing.

Sunfisher's skull and crossbones spinnaker drew the ship closer.

Kirkland's third arrow struck the powder charges Ethan had set around the mizzen.

Legs pumping, Ethan slammed the corpse into the Marine just as he fired. The ball cut by Ethan's ear. Then the dead man and the live Marine collided and toppled over the railing. The live Marine screamed all the way down till he hit the water.

The explosion around the mizzen ripped the timber to shreds. Relieved of the weight of the mast and the mizzen rigging and shrouds, *Reliant* came up in the water as the cargo and ballast righted her.

"Fire!" someone yelled.

Ethan felt the deck shudder underfoot as several of the cannon on *Formidable* fired. The ship rolled back. Horrified, thinking that *Reliant* had just taken a fusillade that would kill the group aboard her, Ethan watched the cannonballs strike the water where the longboat filled with dead and dying men still floated. Two of the cannonballs skipped across the water. One of them struck *Reliant*'s deck, bursting the tryworks to bits and toppling the iron pots into the ocean, where they promptly vanished. The other cannonball leapt up into the hatch and knocked Kirkland back out of sight as the ship kept moving up on an even keel.

The remaining Marine on the quarterdeck reloaded his weapon, fingers moving with trained grace under pressure. He lifted his weapon, pouring part of the powder onto the frizzen.

Ethan sprang for the unconscious lieutenant, yanked the pistol from the man's waist sash, prayed to God that the weapon was ready, and cocked the hammer. He aimed on the fly, trusting the secure weight of the pistol and the countless times he'd used a pistol before. He squeezed the trigger and put the ball squarely through the Marine's heart before the man could fire the musket.

Still moving, Ethan dropped the spent pistol and gripped the lieutenant's sword. The blade was a German-made rapier, one of the best of its kind, and gripping the handle felt like shoving a hand into a well-worn glove. The fit was perfect, and the blade flicked through the air like an extension of his body.

Harrington stirred, striving to get to his feet.

Winded from his exertions, Ethan grabbed the man by the arm with his free hand and slid the rapier blade under the British captain's chin.

Several of the Marines amidships had noticed what was going on and turned to aim their weapons at Ethan.

Thankfully, the British captain was tall and wide of girth. Ethan had plenty of room to hide behind the man.

"Call them off," Ethan commanded. "Have them stand down, or so help me God I'll split you open like a melon."

"You men stand down," Harrington ordered.

The crew froze in their tracks.

"That's good," Ethan said. "Real good." He raked in a breath, still breathing raggedly. From the corner of his eye, he saw *Sunfisher* bearing down on the English vessel. To the starboard, *Reliant*'s sails filled. Crew scattered across her deck released the holds they had on the fish net and the shroud lines and dropped the short distance to the deck. Holy directed a crew to the railing to cut free the chains that held the dead whale.

"You're a fool," Harrington said. "You'll never get off this ship alive."

"Then neither of us will," Ethan assured him. "Because you're going to die before I do."

The British crew suddenly ran from the port side as *Sunfisher* hove into view. The pirate ship's sails dropped. She slid into place beside *Formidable*.

Grappling hooks secured the two ships together, and gangplanks spanned the few feet of distance between. The pirates sprinted across the gangplanks and leapt to the British ship. Muskets and pistols blazed, then the fighting broke down into knife and sword battles that rained blood down over the deck.

Hammered by *Sunfisher*'s greater weight caused by the water riding in her hold, *Formidable* scooted sideways in the water. *Reliant* was under way, shorn of her mizzen and most of her canvas hanging in tatters. Unfortunately, the whaleship was relatively uncontrolled at the moment, at the mercy of the sea and the wind.

Reliant caught *Formidable* amidships. The British ship's prow shattered the whaleboat's hull, leaving a gaping hole in its side. Caught in *Formidable*'s forward momentum, *Reliant* was driven sideways. In that moment, Ethan's hopes that the Bullocks and the whaleship crew could get away died.

Knowing the whaleship was done for and that the British ship was about to brush her by and leave her stranded in the ocean for all the crew to drown, Ethan sprang forward.

"Holy!" Ethan yelled. "Lash on! Lash on! The hull is holed!" He caught up a coil of rope and wrapped it around the rails. "Bill, get everyone over here! Stroud, get your men reloaded! We need this ship!"

Holy lashed rope to the rails as well, but knew from the way that the rails creaked and popped that they wouldn't hold long.

"Ethan!" Bill bellowed. "Behind you!"

Ethan turned at once. Captain Harrington stood like some vengeful spirit with a sword in his hand. He brought the blade whistling down for Ethan's head, screaming obscenities. Reacting by instinct, Ethan batted the sword aside, then put his own weapon through the British captain's heart. The blade got caught between the captain's ribs as he fell.

At the same time, a group of British Marines and sailors rushed up from amidships, pursued by McAfee's pirates.

"Down, Cap'n!" Stroud ordered. "Muskets to arms!"

Ethan dropped to the stern deck and threw himself sideways. He put one bare foot against the dead captain's chest and yanked the sword free just as Stroud's musketmen fired at Stroud's shouted command.

The musket balls caught the lead attackers and took them down. The rush broke as the dead and wounded men impeded the others, allowing Ethan to get to his feet with the bloody sword in his fist.

"To me!" Ethan yelled, stepping forward. "Form a line!" He met the lead man with no finesse, slipping the rapier past the man's sword and plunging it through the man's throat. Continuing forward, Ethan plunged the rapier to the hilt and shoved the dying man into the man behind him. He shoved the rapier, cutting through the man's throat, cutting the blade free and nearly slicing his opponent's head from his shoulders. He threw a shoulder against the next man to knock him from his feet.

Holy, Bill, and Merl Porter met the advancing line of Britishers, followed by Stroud and his men, who fought with empty muskets, bayonets, swords, and knives.

Ethan whirled, whipping the rapier around and catching a British sailor from the back. There was no fairness, no honor, to a man who fought for survival. In seconds, the deck turned slippery with blood, but most of the crew from *Reliant* came to *Formidable*. Even Kirkland staggered across after being battered by the slow-moving cannonball, putting arrow after arrow to string and firing into the attacking horde. Only Folger and Larson, who were still too drunk, failed to make the jump.

The three ships bunched together like three nervous horses in a stable that was too small. Ethan felt the shivers of contact as they battered against each other. *Reliant* was going down quickly, as was *Sunfisher,* who had suffered further damage at the desperate measures McAfee had commanded her into.

In a moment, the stern deck was free of attackers. Sword in hand, breathing raggedly, Ethan whirled to his crew. "Cut *Reliant* free! Cut her free before she takes us down!"

Holy called out names, and the men ran to the railing.

"Mr. Stroud," Ethan said, staying low and still hearing musket balls split the air over his head.

"Aye," Stroud replied. He was bleeding from a half dozen cuts, but none of them looked like they were going to take more than blood.

"Load up and look sharp, Mr. Stroud. We're going to hold the line here. There is nothing but enemies out there amidships."

"Aye, Cap'n." Stroud shouted commands to his crew as he knelt close to the stern deck's edge and took cover behind the railing. They rose at his order, took aim, and fired a devastating volley into the struggling mass of British seamen and pirates and dead bodies of both that lay strewn across the deck.

Cut free of *Formidable*, *Reliant* slid away, drifting slowly but drifting away all the same.

Ethan looked at *Sunfisher*, felt the drag the ship was putting on *Formidable*, and knew the dying pirate vessel had to be cut away as well or risk taking the British ship down.

"Mr. Stroud," Ethan said as the musketmen reloaded.

"Aye, Cap'n."

"I've got to cut *Sunfisher* free before she causes damage to this ship."

"Ye'll be takin' yer life in yer hands if'n ye go down there."

"We don't have a choice." Ethan wiped the rapier clean on the shirt of a dead British seaman. "Keep them off of me, Mr. Stroud. I'll be quick as I can." He swallowed and took a breath, watching the men hiding on the deck. Stroud's muskets had made believers and dead men of the ship's original crew and the pirates. "As soon as you're ready, Mr. Stroud."

Stroud settled in behind his weapon. "We're ready enough, Cap'n. God keep you."

Ethan rose and in one motion threw himself over the stern quarterdeck railing. He landed on his bare feet, slipped in a pool of blood, then was running for all he was worth. Stroud's muskets cracked and men spun away as they rose from their hiding places to come at Ethan.

Then McAfee was there, a pistol in one hand and his sword in the other. The pirate captain lifted the pistol in line with Ethan's head. Blood leaked from scratches across his forehead and cheek.

Ethan didn't stop, knowing that Stroud and his men were reloading.

McAfee fired.

The hot kiss of the pistol ball struck Ethan in the side of the chest and skated across his ribs, coming through on the other side. Ethan swung his blade at McAfee's head, feeling the shock as the pirate captain blocked the blow with his spent pistol. McAfee thrust at Ethan's stomach, but Ethan swept his left arm out. The sword's edge sliced through Ethan's forearm and across the bone, but he deflected the blade enough that it missed him.

Ethan stepped back to give himself room. McAfee pressed him, moving his rapier with blinding speed, guiding him into a death dance that created two whirling figures. Ethan defended himself, knowing Stroud would have no shot at McAfee as long as they fought so closely and moved so quickly.

There was no feinting. The battle was pitched and fierce, every blow designed to be one that would kill the other. Ethan felt the hot streams of blood cascading down his side and arm, felt the blood pooling in his half-closed left hand. He fought, seeking a weakness, playing to his strength, everything that Teresa had spent so many months teaching him.

He forced himself not to think of her. She had forever changed him, made him more than he was and taken away every chance he had at a future, at becoming the man he wanted to be. He felt *Formidable* rise and fall underfoot, fighting against the drag and pull of the sinking ship tied to her.

Then tentacles appeared over the British ship's bow. They shot out with unerring precision, piercing British seamen and pirates alike, carrying their bodies from the deck as if they were child's toys. Ethan felt the weight of the creature clinging to the ship.

McAfee slipped in blood, his attention torn between Ethan and the monster. Ethan remained relentless, remembering all the times that the pirate captain had shown no mercy to helpless victims. He raked the sword at McAfee's neck, felt the bite of steel into flesh.

Wounded, McAfee stepped back, not seeing the railing between *Formidable* and *Sunfisher* until it was too late, and he was over it. He disappeared at once, with no scream. Ethan didn't know if the pirate captain refused to scream or if his sword blow had cut McAfee's throat.

The remainder of the pirates and British seaman charged toward the ship's stern in an effort to get away from the advancing creature. Stroud's muskets met them before they'd gone more than two paces. Men dropped. The dozen or so survivors threw down their arms and shouted for mercy, surrendering in a half dozen languages.

Breathing hard, Ethan gazed at the tentacles that still hung over the bow railing. As he watched, the creature heaved itself up from the sea.

Patchy sunlight glinted on the iridescent blue-green skin. The creature kept rising till it towered twenty feet above *Formidable*'s deck. At first, the creature looked like nothing more than a mushroom-shaped mass that possessed dozens of tentacles. Several pirates and British sailors squirmed at the ends of the tentacles. As Ethan watched, many of the creature's captured prey jerked into convulsions that left them flopping across the ship's deck. Their skins turned dark, then split open and released torrents of blood.

It's not feeding on them now, Ethan realized. *It's killing those men just to show us that it can.*

Slowly, the creature's upper body shifted and reshaped itself. Obviously taking pains and using great effort, the creature formed a rough head and shoulders. The head looked like a blacksmith's anvil slammed on top of a rounded tombstone that poured down in an avalanche of loose, muscular flesh that flexed restlessly before splitting out into the tentacles. More of the body draped into the sea like a cloak. The fit inside the whale had to have been impossibly tight.

It had been growing. Ethan realized that in that instant. The creature had been growing too large for the whale. That must have been why it had allowed the whale to be killed by Larson and his crew.

The creature leaned forward over the ship's railing. Sunlight glimmered over the skin, catching and reflecting the brightness like polished metal. There were no traces of the wounds it had suffered earlier.

The head shifted again, and the surface changed. A nose appeared, followed almost immediately by a chin and cheekbones, then dimples that might have been eye sockets on a human. But it was anything but human.

"It's mimicking human features, Mr. Swain," Bullock called out from the stern.

"Why?"

"To communicate."

Ethan didn't believe that. The creature hadn't shown a real interest in communication. It was a hunter, and Ethan knew from his own experience that hunters often tried to blend in with an environment to better hunt their prey.

The ill-formed head shifted and twisted atop the creature's great mass as if trying to listen. The misshapen face twisted like a sail tacking into the wind, as if the creature experimented with the best way to present itself.

"Bill," Ethan called.

"Aye, Ethan."

"You've got those stern guns back there. Get them ready."

"They're already loaded."

Fear slid along Ethan's nerves like a barber's razor. "Get them pointed in this direction. When you're ready, tell me."

The creature shifted. A tentacle shot out at Ethan's face. He moved, avoiding the thrust but feeling the weight of the tentacle against his shoulder. Primitive fear exploded through Ethan's body as he moved to—

Images burst inside Ethan's brain. The images showed places the like of which Ethan had never seen, in watery deeps, on the land, in caverns. All of the images showed the creature or others like it in battle with other strange beings or impossible mechanical devices. There was even an image of stars, a golden green sun, and a plummet through clouds, a blue sky, and a sea draped in night.

Hunter.

The word formed in Ethan's mind as slow as the last bubble that surfaced from a drowning man's lips. Ethan felt the energy of the word being pulled back toward the creature as surely as a compass needle pulled to magnetic north.

Prey.

That word pushed at Ethan, and he knew it was meant to describe him. He felt the thing in his mind, spinning through his memories, tapping into his emotions, searching through the essence of him.

A pull of recognition. *Hunter.*

A push of acknowledgment. *Prey. Ethan. Prey, Ethan. PreyEthan.*

Dizziness swam through Ethan's mind. He pulled back from the creature's presence inside his skull, trying desperately to break contact.

—duck and throw himself to the deck as the tentacle wrapped around his neck and came hurtling back at him. Ethan skidded across the bloody deck, feeling the shiver of impact as the tentacle buried in the plank only inches from his face. He pushed himself up, caught a flash of movement on his right, and swung the rapier, cutting through another tentacle that streaked for him. He ran, dodging behind the mainmast, unable to keep himself from glancing back at the impossible creature that hung on to the ship's bow.

One of the tentacles brought Creel's body out again. *"Eee-than. Eee-than,"* the monster taunted. The feature melted away, and the head and shoulders collapsed back into the mushroom shape. *"Die. Die."*

The creature hovered near the anchor windlass that kept *Formidable*. If it stayed there, which it gave every indication of doing, they wouldn't be able to lift the anchor from the ocean floor and get away.

More tentacles zipped toward Ethan.

"Bill, fire!"

The cannon went off and Bill's marksmanship punched a cannonball through the sails and 'yards and hit the creature dead center, rocking it backward and stunning all the tentacles. They dropped like ropes to the deck.

Ethan turned and ran, his mind seeking possibilities and weaknesses. He ran up the companionway to the stern quarterdeck, gazing past his bedraggled crew and seeing *Reliant* listing badly behind the British ship. A desperate idea formed in his mind.

Stroud's men fired at Creel's corpse and the tentacles surrounding the dead man as the creature recovered. So far, the creature didn't seem inclined to come any farther forward.

"Holy," Ethan called, shoving his bloody sword through his waist sash. "Give me a hand." He grabbed a grappling hook and a line from a chest nailed to the quarterdeck, part of the boarding supplies the British had gotten ready, and climbed up into the mizzen shroud lines.

"Ethan." Holy followed at once. "What are you doing?"

"Probably getting myself killed," Ethan admitted. "But it's the only chance we have. We need a bomb. A really big bomb." He leaned on the shrouds, upper body above the mizzen masthead. He swung the grappling hook over his head, then let fly.

The grappling hook sailed true, falling far lower than he'd hoped, though. Instead of catching in *Reliant*'s rigging, the hook caught on the whaleship's fore-sail 'yard and rigging.

Ethan looped the end of the grappling rope over *Formidable*'s mizzen topgallant 'yard. "I need you to keep this line tight, Holy. Damned tight."

Holy took the line that Ethan pressed into his hands and pulled the slack out of it. "What are you going to do?"

"Get back to *Reliant*," Ethan answered. "See if she's going to own up to her name one last time."

"That's insane, Ethan."

"Maybe," Ethan admitted. "But we don't have a choice. *Reliant*'s got whale oil aboard her. And powder. If I can trap that damned thing inside her and set that off, maybe we have a chance."

"That's no chance at all."

Ethan nodded toward the creature clinging to *Formidable*'s bow. "That's no chance at all. That thing's a hunter. It won't rest until we're all dead. It was made to learn things about its prey, to become smarter so that it can kill them all."

Disbelief clouded Holy's face. "How do you know that?"

"Because I heard it. The damned thing talked to me, or maybe it only learned from me. All I know it that it wants me."

On the ship's deck, Creel's corpse danced insanely while Stroud's men fired into the mass again and again, and Bill reloaded the stern cannon. *"Eee-than! Eee-than!"*

"It wants to kill us all, Holy. That's all it knows to do." Ethan cut a piece of rope from the end of the line. "Now hold on tight to that line."

Holy nodded. "Godspeed, Cap'n."

Without another word, Ethan looped the rope over the line, grabbed the rope in both hands, and pushed off from the mizzen rigging. The line bowed for just a moment, not enough to stop him, but quickly remained taut.

Ethan slid across the open ocean between the two ships and dropped to the whaleship's deck. He rolled, coming to his feet at once, his legs getting tangled up in his sword for a moment. He ran for *Reliant's* hatch and scrambled through. He took up an axe from the belowdecks kit and continued down into the hold.

The stink of blubber mired every breath. Water was already waist deep and rising in the hold, flooding in through the hole *Formidable* had stove in her hull.

Working quickly, Ethan smashed a dozen whale oil barrels open and kicked them onto the piles of other barrels. The whale oil ran into the water. Lighter than the seawater, the oil quickly rose to the top, then began running together to form one large pool. In seconds, the growing pool of oil began to spread throughout *Reliant's* hold.

On the run, listening for the creature, not knowing if he would hear it, Ethan went to the whaleship's powder magazine just aft of the main hold on a raised section under the stern that kept the area dry. He sorted through the debris for powder kegs. He grabbed two kegs and cracked them open with care. He used one of them to pour a line of powder leading to both kegs, trusting that when the two were set off the others in the magazine would go as well.

Gazing at the water, he knew that he didn't have much time. The water level in the hold was rising and would be at the same height as the stern area in minutes.

He returned to the main deck and peered at *Formidable*. The creature still clung to the ship's prow but hadn't yet started to hunt the people aboard her. Creel's corpse spun and twirled like a marionette.

Gazing at the thing, not knowing if it was simply an animal crouching to watch its helpless prey or an intelligent entity as sadistic as McAfee was capable of being, Ethan hated it. The creature was toying with the people left aboard ship, letting them know it could come for them at any time. Ethan focused on his hatred, letting that emotion burn away the fear he felt.

Ethan grabbed the block-and-tackle rig and swung it around. He climbed down the rope, feeling the boom arm give as the bolts pulled free of the deck. Evidently the blast that had shorn the mizzen had weakened the boom arm. Ethan prayed that it would hold long enough.

He dropped into the water, kicking his feet and swinging his arms. The wound in his side and forearm stung with the salt.

"Over here, you damned beast!" Ethan yelled. "You've got fresh meat in the water." He kept kicking, knowing part of the creature's senses would pick up on the motion.

Aboard *Formidable*, the creature's tentacles tightened on the bow, and it pulled itself up, exposing the great center mass of blue-green iridescence again. Ethan thought the creature was making itself look huge, the way a bear stood up to become more frightening or a cobra stood with its hood flared—or like a huge bully in a barroom brawl.

The tentacle bearing Creel's body glided across the deck and hung out over the water as if coming to look at him. *"Eee-than. Eee-than,"* it called.

Then, in a liquid rush that acted like there wasn't a bone in the creature's body, the thing dropped into the water and dragged all its tentacles after it, pulling the dead bodies of its prey in as well.

Ethan climbed the rope attached to the boom arm. As he drew level with the railing, he felt the arm wrench free, all the bolts pulling loose or shearing. He grabbed for the railing as he dropped, managing to catch hold of the deck. His side flared with renewed agony, but he managed to leverage himself aboard the whaleship.

By the time he reached the hold, the creature—*God, it is fast!*—was already shooting tentacles over *Reliant's* side.

Ethan dropped through the hatch, catching the edge, and swinging himself clear of the belowdecks hatch. He dropped again as he felt the whaleship tilt under the creature's weight.

In the hold, Ethan raced for the lantern he'd left hanging on the wall.

A shadow stepped from hiding, naked sword in his fist. When Ethan first recognized McAfee standing there, he thought that the creature had somehow found the pirate captain and taken over his body as it had Creel's, moving him like a mannequin.

"Ethan," McAfee said. A flap of skin hanging loose at his jaw showed where

Ethan's blow had missed his neck. He touched the wound with his fingertips, which instantly turned crimson. "You missed." The wound caused him to slur his words. "I watched you as you cut *Sunfisher* free, saw you come over here." He gazed at the powder line and the kegs only inches above the waterline. "Another one of your little surprises?"

"Aye," Ethan said. "The creature's coming, Jonah. That thing is aboard this ship. It will kill us if it finds us." He backed away, coming up against the stern hold wall behind him.

"I don't care. I'll have my vengeance, Ethan." McAfee raised his sword, giving Ethan no chance to raise his own.

"You'll die, Jonah." Behind the pirate captain, Ethan could already see tentacles flowing through the hatch above the cargo hold. He didn't know how long the creature would stay aboard once it detected the whale oil, didn't know if it felt the whale oil, smelled it, or sensed it in some other fashion.

All he knew was that he was out of time.

"Why did Teresa prefer you?" McAfee challenged. His face was pasty, drained of blood, and his eyes appeared deep-set in the shadows that filled the cargo hold despite the light that came in through the hatches from above.

"I don't know," Ethan said. "I never thought to ask. Maybe she only liked me because it tormented you. That was what she was really like, Jonah. You just never saw that about her. She killed those innocent people that day, killed Cat's-Eyes John, because she knew it would hurt me. I think she enjoyed hurting you, and I don't think she ever learned to like anyone. Not even herself."

"Liar! You were no better than me!" McAfee thrust the sword toward Ethan's neck.

Ethan moved, shifting to one side, and heard the dulled *thunk* of the sword point digging into the wooden wall behind him. For a moment, McAfee fought to free his blade. Ethan slammed his head forward, catching the pirate captain in the face, breaking his nose and splitting his lips. Before McAfee could recover, Ethan grabbed the man's sword arm, then drew the rapier he carried from the sash at his waist and dragged the blade against McAfee's throat, cutting his neck all the way to the spine.

McAfee's eyes widened in surprise as his life pumped from him. Then he shivered, and one of the creature's tentacles burst through his chest. In the next instant, the creature yanked McAfee back.

"*Eee-than! Eee-than!*" McAfee's corpse roared.

Ducking the tentacle that shot toward him, Ethan dropped his sword and scooped up the lantern as he ran for the stern area where he'd set up the powder. He smashed the lantern at the end of the powder trail and watched it catch fire, spewing gray smoke into the hold.

Running flat out, Ethan hurled himself toward the hole in *Reliant*'s side. He hit the water in a shallow dive and kicked out at once, eyes open against the stinging brine and focusing on the breach in the hull.

He passed through the opening and swam straight out, trying to put as much distance between himself and the ship as he could.

A shadow hung over him.

Glancing up, Ethan saw the true horror of the creature. The center mass was at least forty feet across and leaned heavily on *Reliant*'s top structure, like a cat poised expectantly over a mousehole. The tentacles were seventy or eighty feet in length. There were dozens, maybe even a hundred of them.

And from many of them, corpses hung like fat fruit from a tree. Several of the dead men were in various stages of decomposition, and several more were fresh from the decks of *Formidable*. Their faces, when they had them, held pain and fear and disbelief. Robert hung limp, his arms and legs splayed in the water. Folger and Larson still fought feebly, but Ethan knew both men were done for. Evidently the monster had gotten them when it had climbed aboard.

Ethan swam among them because he had no choice, pulling himself as hard as he could and hoping that in the confusion the creature might not notice him or, if it did, might not be able to catch him with one of the tentacles. If the explosion aboard the whaleship didn't kill him, the creature would if it survived.

PREY.

The word slammed into Ethan's mind like a spike driven by a sledge. He knew immediately that the word hadn't come from his thoughts. The term had come from outside him.

The realization threw his timing off. Where he had once had a clean stroke that took him quickly away from *Reliant* and angled him gently toward *Formidable*, his arms and legs refused to work together anymore.

HERE PREY.

Unable to help himself, Ethan looked up. A parade of bodies whirled in front of him. Robert was there, as were Parsons and Arnett and men dressed in British uniforms and pirates.

No

Escape

You

Die

Eee-than.

Ethan tried to swim again, but he couldn't. The great mass of the creature hung over him like a cloud of shimmering blue-green egg whites. He felt the creature, felt its attention, and felt its anger and confidence and exultation.

A siren song spun in Ethan's head. The song felt as soft as the gossamer strands of a spider's web, but its touch cut like a dairyman's cheese wire. He stared up into the great bulk of the creature as it clung to *Reliant* like some monstrous barnacle. He saw the great center of it more clearly as he hung suspended under it.

There, at the very heart of the creature was a great, pulsating maw. The opening dilated and closed with slow, deliberate rhythm. Ethan felt the hunger calling to him from the orifice. It . . . *wanted* . . . *needed*.

Panic flooded through him like a dam gate opening. He kicked with his feet, intending to swim again. The powder had to nearly be burned to the kegs and the magazine. Death waited in the water, one way or another.

NO!

A tentacle cut through the water like an arrow, coming straight for Ethan. Before he could dodge, the tentacle pierced his chest, passing through under his shoulder and out his back in an explosion of misty scarlet that flooded the water.

His breath froze in his lungs at the impact, and for a moment he thought the thing had pierced his heart. Then he realized that if it had pierced his heart, he would be dead and wouldn't feel pain, and his lungs wouldn't be aching for air.

Eee-than.

Come.

Still paralyzed by the pain and shock that filled him, Ethan didn't fight as the tentacle dragged him to the heart of the creature. He floated among the dead men, seeing how their bodies had caved in as the creature had fed on them, sucking their insides out. Up close, the tentacles offered limited visibility, like warm breath on a cold glass on a winter morning. Hypnotized, Ethan watched as the closer tentacles alternately pumped clear fluids into the corpses, then sucked brown-and-pink masses out in clots and chunks and liquid the consistency of heavy cream.

The creature seemed to feed all the time. Already a dozen corpses lay nearly consumed. Tentacles released two husks that were little more than bags of skin over bones.

Looking at the creature, Ethan knew that the thing he was looking at could never have entirely fit inside the whale. The thing had grown even since the night before, when it had escaped from its chosen host.

And what would it do now, he wondered, when it realized it had no place it could hide? At least, not inside another creature.

No

Hide

No

Hide

Eee-than.

Kill

Kill

Kill . . . ALL.

The tentacle continued dragging Ethan toward the pulsating orifice. He felt the creature darting around inside his mind. Emotions overwhelmed him, sadness, laughter, love—

He saw his family flash through his mind, saw Nantucket speed by from spring to summer to fall to winter to spring again. He saw ships he had been on, people he had met, foreign ports he had been to.

His vision cleared again, and he realized he was almost inside the great pulsating chamber. The creature was dragging him inside itself.

And he wouldn't be alone.

Ethan saw other bodies inside the creature. They lay on their sides or floated, buoyant in the water. All of them had tentacles driven up into their heads from the base of their skulls in through an ear or an eye socket. Some of them still twitched and moved.

Fear broke the spell Ethan had been under. He didn't understand why he wasn't dead already. The professor had stated that the venom worked fast. Dread hammered him as he gazed down at his wounded chest, expecting to see the flesh already pulling away from his breastbone, maybe even see his heart slamming against his rib cage. He'd lost all sense of time, but he knew that while the creature held him in thrall, time was elastic. He had not drowned yet, so not nearly as much time as he had thought could have passed.

The creature invaded his mind again, ripping through the strongest emotions he had. He saw his family again, saw McAfee as he'd first met him, and he saw Teresa Santiago. He remembered Teresa fighting with him, remembered how she was in bed, and he remembered how she had looked while holding Cat's-Eyes John's severed head, laughing maniacally at Ethan begging her not to kill the innocents. Memory returned in a heated rush, bringing with it the feel of Ethan's blade cutting through Teresa's throat, then slamming through her spine just beneath her skull. He saw her head bounce from the bloodstained deck, her body standing grotesquely still for a moment, like a praying mantis with its head snipped. Then she fell. When he'd killed Teresa, Ethan had stood there in stunned surprise, as if he hadn't been able to believe what he had done. But he hadn't gotten to stand long. In the next heartbeat McAfee had drawn a blade and been at him. When Ethan had been knocked down, McAfee had and put a ball dead center in Ethan's chest, then watched him tumble over the ship's side.

Eee-than. Killer.

Learn kill all.

The other end of the tentacle swept toward Ethan's face. With the creature still fumbling through his mind, he thought of Katharine. At least she was safe on *Formidable*.

Eee-than. Kath . . . rine. Die.

An image formed in Ethan's head of Katharine floating into the creature's pulsating maw with a tentacle stabbed through one of her eyes.

Ethan rebelled, breaking free of the spell the creature had him under just as the tentacle streaked toward his face. He grabbed the tentacle, felt it swell in his hand, saw the end start to dilate and the barb enclosed within it jetting forward. He grabbed the tentacle, moving quickly even against the water, driven by the fear and hate and survival instinct that careened within him. He felt the tentacle swell to bursting but before it could release the barb, he slashed the tentacle from the creature with his knife.

"No!" The denial exploded from Ethan's lips, gusting out in a large air bubble. He would not give in to the creature. *Go back to whatever Hell you crawled out of,* he thought in his mind, hoping the creature understood. *You're going to burn.*

BURN! BURNBURNBURNBURN!

The image of *Reliant's* hold filled with whale oil and spiked with gunpowder filled Ethan's head. He felt the creature's attention leave him. The great bulk of the creature shifted on the whaleship.

It understands, Ethan realized. *Maybe not the trap itself, but it understands that there is a trap.*

NO BURN!

Ethan hacked at the tentacle again, slicing himself free of it, then swam away with a piece of the creature still embedded within him. His lungs screamed for air. He swam between the tentacles and dead bodies, bursting free of the outer fringes of the creature's reach.

The sun framed the water between the two ships and above the creature. He swam for it, feeling the creature moving in the water behind him, disentangling itself from *Reliant* and starting to give pursuit.

Eee-than. No burn. Kill Katharine.

Then a great fist slammed into Ethan and drove the breath from his lungs. He almost blacked out, spinning in the water as the concussive wave took him. Fragmented images of orange-and-yellow flames jetting out into the sea ran through his mind, followed by other images of the dead men being torn from the creature's tentacles, and of the creature being ripped apart by debris from the ship and coated in flaming whale oil.

Ethan was numb, unable to move, overwhelmed by the explosion. He had no strength left. The creature's tentacle writhed in his chest. He knew he was going to die. None of the whaling crew could swim well enough to save him, and he wasn't strong enough to hold on to a line even if he somehow managed to see it.

He heard Professor Bullock's shout above him, muted by the water. "Katharine, no!"

"I see him! Ethan is down there! He's escaped!"

Then Ethan felt someone in the water with him, diving down and taking him by the hand.

Katharine looked at him, then got behind him and hooked her arm under his chin. Before he reached the surface, being pulled through the cool green water of the ocean's shallows, he passed out.

EPILOGUE

Pacific Ocean 12° 31' S. Lat—98° 42' W. Long.

ETHAN STOOD ON *Formidable*'s stern deck and watched *Reliant* burn down to her waterline. The process had taken a long time.

Hours had passed while he'd remained unconscious. During that time, Stroud and Holy and Bill had gotten the captured ship squared away and locked away the surviving pirates and British seamen in the ship's brig. As a military vessel, *Formidable* had quite a lot of room for prisoners.

"How are you feeling?"

Ethan turned and found Katharine crossing the deck toward him. "Better," he answered. There was still a ringing in his ears and some deafness from the explosion, but he thought that would clear in a few days. In the meantime, he hurt all over. Bullock and Katharine had tended his wounds, stitching his arm and his side where McAfee had put the ball through, and removing the piece of tentacle from his chest. Luckily, none of the venom had entered his body.

"Do you feel well enough to eat?"

"Maybe later."

"Good. By that time we'll be done with *Sunfisher,* and I can eat with you. Cook says the British have quite a larder. You need to get your strength back."

Ethan gazed across the water, where Stroud was helping Professor Bullock pack salvaged journals and documentation from the pirate vessel before it sank. He nodded at the ship. "Was it all there?"

"Very probably," she replied. "Captain McAfee kept everything he took from us. He was serious about trying to catch the creature."

Ethan stared at the waters behind the stern and saw the burned and ripped mass of the creature floating limply in the sea. There was no doubt that it was dead.

"Mr. Fedderson is planning on using the ship's nets to gather the body," Katharine said. "At Father's request, of course. Mr. Fedderson was quite accommodating, but you could tell his heart wasn't in the work."

"Mine wouldn't be either," Ethan admitted. The incessant headache slammed within him, dizzying in its intensity.

"Of course," Katharine said, "Father still feels he must ask your permission for that."

Ethan was puzzled. "My permission?"

"As captain of this vessel," Katharine told him, "it's my understanding that you have final say over the cargo you carry."

"Captain?"

Katharine nodded. "While you were recovering, Holy and Bill gathered the men and put the matter to a vote. They made you captain, and the rest of the crew will be placed at your discretion."

"Captain?" Ethan asked again.

"*Formidable* is your ship, Captain Swain. By the very spoils of war that Captain Harrington was going to enforce against you."

Ethan looked at the vessel. "My ship?" The concept staggered him. His knees buckled, and he sat on the—*My ship's*—deck with his back to the railing.

Katharine gazed at him with concern. "Are you all right?"

"Aye," Ethan replied. "It's just all . . . a little much. At one time, I mean."

"While you slept," she said, "I told Mr. Jordan, Mr. Fedderson, and Mr. Stroud of your hopes to one day own a ship of your own. A ship with which you could earn a living—an honest living—for yourself and your crew. They agreed to throw their lot in with you."

Ethan looked at her. "You did that?"

"Yes." Katharine knelt beside him, still trim and proper somehow in her breeches. "You faced the monsters, Mr. Swain. Your own monsters from your past and that creature out there in the sea. A man—a hero—who slays monsters, why he's entitled to rewards. This ship is one of them. The loyalty of the crew that surrounds you, that's another."

Ethan felt her hand warm in his. "And what about love? Isn't there something in those stories about a hero winning the heart of a fair maiden?"

Katharine colored. "Those are just stories, Mr. Swain," she answered. But she didn't move away from him as he leaned in to kiss her.